G000244133

BLACKSTONE COTTAGE

BLACKSTONE COTTAGE

ALIX ROBINSON

Riverside Publishing Solutions

Alix Robinson asserts her moral right to be identified as the author of this book.

Published by Alix Robinson
in partnership with Riverside Publishing Solutions
www.riversidepublishingsolutions.com
Copyright © 2021 Alix Robinson

Cover illustration by Caitlin Angell

Blackstone Cottage paperback edition
ISBN: 978-1-913012-54-0

This is a work of fiction. Names, characters, businesses, places, events
and incidents are either the products of the author's imagination
or used in a fictitious manner. Any resemblance to actual persons,
living or dead, or actual events is purely coincidental.

All rights reserved. No part of this publication may be reproduced, distributed,
or transmitted in any form or by any means, including photocopying, recording,
or other electronic or mechanical methods, without the prior written permission
of the publisher, except in the case of brief quotations embodied in critical
reviews and certain other non commercial uses permitted by copyright law.

For permission requests, write to the publisher, addressed
"Attention: Permissions Coordinator," at
contact@riversidepublishingsolutions.com

Printed and bound in the UK.

I dedicate this book to my husband John
with thanks for his love and support
over the many years of our marriage.

Acknowledgements

This story was written during the first Covid Lockdown and while I was recovering from a major operation. It kept me well occupied during that difficult time.

I would like to thank my family and friends for all their encouragement and support, and specially Julia Brigdale and Ally Bowen for their time and very helpful editing and suggestions upon reading the draft copy.

Duncan and Paul of Riverside Publishing Solutions also deserve many thanks for their expertise and help.

Last but not least I would like to thank Caitlin Angell for her beautiful and atmospheric cover design.

Chapter 1

If you had asked me six months ago what I would be doing on this day six months later, I would never have guessed that I would be travelling on a train to see my cottage. Yes, *my* cottage – a cottage that has been left to me in my Aunt May's will. She has also left me a "tidy sum of money", as described by Mr Floyd the solicitor – and – a car! This will probably be a rather old car, as Aunt May was not renowned for spending her money unnecessarily, but any car will be more than welcome. The past three and a half years have been the worst years of my life and I can't bear to think about them, so this is literally a gift from heaven and I am hoping will give me a fresh start, so I can put the past behind me.

At least during recent years, whilst living near London, I have managed to begin to be familiar with modern technology and hope to be able to get a job eventually. I certainly don't intend to be a lady of leisure. I have also passed my driving test first time, so I have something to be proud of. It will be lovely to be able to do a bit of travelling. Well, that's my plan. Mr Floyd seemed to think it rather irresponsible of Aunt May to leave all her worldly goods to a young girl of nineteen, or that's the impression he seemed to be giving me, but I think I reassured him that I wouldn't squander it all away on drink or drugs.

So here I am, sitting in this train, on a cold, dark, November evening, on a journey that is taking much longer than it should to reach my destination. It seems there is trouble on the line ahead, but no one in the carriage can make head nor tail of the recorded announcement and at the moment the train is at a complete standstill and it is getting darker and darker outside. I had planned my journey to reach the cottage in daylight and this is obviously not going to happen now, as I think we are only about halfway down the line. On my lap I have a paperback novel, which I bought at a charity shop, and I am finding it difficult to concentrate on reading it and haven't got further than page nine.

While I sit there, I think of the mysterious letter I had received from Aunt May and take, what remains of it, out of an envelope and put it on the table in front of me. The person opposite is dozing, so I can look at it once again and try to make sense of it. I must explain, the strangeness of the letter is that it was eaten by snails. I didn't realise that snails ate paper but understand now that it is not that uncommon. It seems that Aunt May wrote me this letter shortly before she died and posted it in the letterbox in the lane near her cottage. Apparently, it was a post box, set into an old stone wall and it was not unheard of for snails to get in. The regular postman was on holiday and the relief postman forgot to empty the box for two weeks and Aunt May was the only one to use the box apart from the snails, who had a feast.

Aunt May had addressed the letter to me care of Mr Floyd, as she wasn't sure where I was living and luckily there was enough of the address remaining legible to reach his office in London. It had been handwritten on very flimsy airmail paper and enclosed in a lightweight envelope. The snails chewed all of the right-hand side of the envelope and contents, so it is frustratingly difficult to make any sense of the meaning.

This is what remains of the left-hand side of her letter:

Blackstone Cottage
12th...

My dearest Lora,
You may not know this, but I've bee...

Three years and I've not...
Therefore, I'm hopin...
Around during the rec...
Any support. I am trust...
Cottage and the fin...
You will find a more detai...
Cottage. I didn't want anyone else t...
Personal, so I have put it...
You have alwa...
Do what is be...

Your ever lov...
Aunt May

As you can see, it doesn't make sense and I find it so frustrating that the meaning may probably never be known, unless, of course, she has taken a copy and that I might find it in the cottage amongst her things. The feeling I get from it though, is that she is trying to tell me something important. Perhaps she is feeling guilty at neglecting me during recent years, when I was in trouble, or for not always being there for me when I was a child living on the island. I can't think of any other reason for her leaving nearly all her worldly goods to me and only a very small amount to the group of people she lived with for much of her adult life and whose way of life she had followed for several years.

. . .

"The Ray of Hope" commune was based on a remote Scottish island called Morg. Aunt May told me she was forty when she moved to the island with her sister, my mother, Rose. May was ten years older than Rose and I understand she persuaded my mother to move there with her, as they both needed to make changes in their lives. I was just a tiny baby and I'm not sure whether I was born on the island, or before they moved to it.

Their younger sister Isobel, who was then in her late twenties, had formed the group and moved to the island with her partner Pete. Isobel became the manager and inspiration for the commune. Although the youngest, she has a very strong personality and she really ruled the place. I was told she had previously been living with a much older man in a commune in America since her teenage years, so I presume this is where her ideas came from.

The community on Morg consisted of about ten to fifteen people of both sexes – or perhaps I should say 'various sexes', with a few children of mixed ages. People came and went a lot and sometimes there was just our close family. To begin with all went well, but soon there were personality difficulties as, living in those meagre conditions, not many people found they could cope for long, especially during the winter and bad weather. We were supposed to be self-sufficient, but the climate and poor soil meant that we relied a lot on inherited family money and money received from visitors who came (mostly in the summer) for "peace and quiet and restoration of souls" as the leaflet stated.

Eventually the group split up and left just us, the close family, living on the island, with paying summer visitors and the occasional birdwatchers who braved it in the winter. About three years ago, after I had left the island, Isobel and her daughter, Maisie, moved to Red House near Wasbury and Pete, Isobel's partner, went to New York.

Aunt May bought her cottage just down the lane from Red House. I don't know why she decided to move in on her own, but I have not been in touch with them for a while, so maybe she fell out with them. They have always called themselves a kind and loving community, based on the teachings of Jesus and the Buddha and other peace-loving souls, but I think these examples got well-lost along the way and now, having lived away from it myself for over three years, I realise that behind all the prayer and meditation and hard physical labour of existing in that remote cold place, there was something far more selfish going on underneath the surface of their perfect lives.

Maybe Aunt May felt guilty about my mother, who, I was told, was not well and didn't really want to live on the island but had nowhere else to go… No, I must not think of that now, or I will be in no mood to find my way to this strange cottage in the dark.

. . .

I gather up the letter carefully and return it to the envelope, as the train lurches forward once more and we all look hopefully at each other, only to be disappointed when it stops once again. The only thing to do is to try to get some sleep, but I daren't sleep in case I miss the station. I haven't been sleeping well since getting the news of the cottage. There has been so much to think about and I feel so ill-equipped to cope with this potentially new way of life.

I have been sitting on the train for over four hours and am becoming very anxious. The journey was meant to take about two hours, but with two changes and now this, what seems like a permanent stoppage, I wonder if I will ever get there.

I don't usually worry about time. Time is something I have had plenty of recently, but tonight it was important to arrive in daylight, as I have never been to the cottage before and there is no one to meet me at the station. I understand from Mr Floyd from Becker and Floyd, that the cottage is about a mile from Wasbury station and to find it in the dark, with no torch and no streetlights, could be tricky. Of course, I had intended to arrive in daylight, but had misread the timetable and forgetting it was a Sunday, had found that the trains from Waterloo were far less frequent than on a weekday. I had just missed the one that would certainly have got me there on time and had to wait an hour for the next one.

It is no use worrying, so I will sit back and try to concentrate on my book – but no such luck. There is a young man going on about problems with this railway line. He is sitting diagonally opposite me across the aisle and when he is not talking to his neighbours, he stares at me. I try not to look back but can't help noticing how he keeps staring. He doesn't look much older than me, but it is difficult to see in this light and he has what looks like about two-days growth of dark stubble on his face and shoulder length greasy hair. He is wearing a dirty anorak and filthy jeans. However, he has a pair of very smart, clean trainers, inside which I notice he is wearing one bright red sock and one pale green one. He keeps making odd remarks to the people around him, who all seem to be agreeing with his comments about the train.

'This happens all the time on this line', he says. 'The line to nowhere we call it'. A voice then comes over the intercom for about the sixth time, apologising and telling us 'There has been an incident on the line'.

'An incident!' exclaims Odd-socks, as I have decided to call him. 'That's what they are blaming it on today. Perhaps that means there's a cow on the line – that's happened before now.' The woman sitting opposite him peers out of the window, but it is now so dark outside that only a vague outline of bushes can be seen. All the passengers are getting more and more impatient and rather fed up with Odd-socks who won't shut up.

He seems to be drunk or on something and prattles on for a bit. I manage to ignore him but when I look up from my book, I see he is staring at me again. He notices me glance in his direction and says, 'So where are you going then?'

I am taken by surprise by his sudden question and reply 'Wasbury, if I ever get there', but then hurriedly look away from him. Why did I reply to him? I am annoyed with myself. Perhaps he is going there too. But he doesn't respond.

Suddenly the train starts and progresses a few feet and then stops again. The passengers cheer and then sigh. Then it starts to slowly creep forward. I look out of the dark window and gradually I can see people with lights, standing at the side of the track. 'I expect it was a suicide' says one of the passengers 'and they had to wait for the forensics.' He talks as if this is a regular occurrence.

The train gathers speed and the atmosphere in the carriage is one of relief and optimism and a few moments later we arrive at a station. I can just see the name 'FORD' on the sign on the platform. So, the next stop should be Wasbury. To my dismay all the other passengers get up from their seats except Odd-socks and soon we are left, just the two of us, alone in the carriage as the train starts up again. I am just thinking of gathering up my rucksack and moving to another carriage, when he says,

'I'm going to Wasbury too. Can I come and sit with you then?'

'No', I reply hastily and firmly. 'I want to read my book'.

'Well, why haven't you turned a page in the last half hour? You must be a very slow reader.'

'How can I fucking well read with you waffling on?' I reply angrily.

He shuffles in his seat and for a moment I think he is going to come over, but he just looks furtively at me again and then…

'Why are you travelling all on your own at this time of night, to such a dead-end place as Wasbury? Got someone meeting you at the station?'

'Yes'.

'Won't they wonder why you're so late – you could phone them on your mobile – or perhaps you haven't got one?'

'Just leave me alone and mind your own business', I reply and grabbing my book and rucksack I hastily get up to move to another carriage. He just stays in his seat, but I don't want to walk past him, so I turn around and hurry back the other way and into the carriage behind.

To my horror this carriage is empty and I know if I go too far back, I won't be able to get off at Wasbury, as only the front few carriages fit alongside the platform.

He doesn't seem to be following me, but just to be safe I go through to one more carriage. I walk right to the end but there is no one there either and just as I reach the end, the train starts to slow down and I can see the sign WASBURY on the platform.

I hurry forward to the part of the train that just reaches the end of the platform and I climb down with trepidation. There are one or two lights further down and I wait a moment or two, hoping that if Odd-socks has left the train, he will be well ahead of me. I can see no-one else on the platform as I make my way to the station buildings, with the cold night air stinging my face, and when I get there, there is no one to take my ticket. I look for a telephone number for a taxi, as it seems the station is absolutely deserted now that the train has moved off, and I hope and pray that Odd-socks has left the station. On a wall I find a scruffy notice with two faded telephone numbers for taxis. I am taking out my mobile from my rucksack, when suddenly behind me a voice says,

'D'ya wanna lift?'

I nearly leap out of my skin and a feeling of panic overwhelms me, as I see Odd-socks's face peering at me.

'No thanks!' I say, as firmly as my shaky voice will allow. 'I am phoning my friend.'

'So why ya looking for a taxi number then?'

By now I am feeling *really* scared. I have had enough experience of weirdoes in the past couple of years, and Odd-socks is apparently quite drunk and he smells strongly of alcohol. In desperation I pick up my rucksack and make my way through to the car park, not knowing where I am heading for. There are only two cars in the car park, a small one in the far corner and a large four-by-four car much nearer to us.

'That's my car over there', says Odd-socks, pointing to the small car, but to my huge relief, I see there is someone sitting in the other vehicle, with the inside light on. I make my way to the big car, praying that the person inside will be able to help.

Odd-socks does nothing to stop me and just shouts 'Bye – see you another time', as I rush to the driver's window. Inside is a middle-aged woman talking into her mobile and she looks startled as she sees my anguished face pressed against the glass. She winds the window down a fraction.

'Just a moment', she says to the phone 'there's someone by the car who looks as though she needs help… yes of course I'll be careful'. She winds the window down a bit further.

'What's the problem – are you needing a lift?'

'Yes please,' I beg. 'I've been having a bit of trouble with a strange man.'

By now I can see that Odd-socks has reached his car and has put its lights on.

'Come round', she says and opens the front passenger door. 'You can chuck your rucksack into the back. I'm Angela, by the way,' she says 'and who are you?'

'I'm Lora,' I reply, as I climb in hastily and flop down into the seat. I can feel my heart thumping in my chest and for a moment or two have difficulty getting my breath.

Immediately I'm in, the woman locks all the doors and says to her phone 'I'll phone you later… yes, it's a young girl who's just got off the train, with no one to meet her… yes I think there was something on the line… yes, we are very, very late. I'll phone you when I get back to the house… yes, …love you too.'

'Thank you, thank you,' I say, as she puts away her phone. 'I can't tell you how relieved I was to see you. I didn't see you on the train and thought I was the only one left with the strange man.'

'Can you see if the man is still around?'

'Yes, I can see he has just put the lights on in his car,' I say, but he hasn't moved off yet.

'I'll drive round and see if we can get his number.' She chucks an old envelope and pen in my lap and then starts the engine and turns, so her car lights are shining on the back of his car. I quickly jot down the number.

As we drive out of the car park she asks, 'What actually happened? Do you think we should call the police?'

'Well… he didn't actually do anything… he was just annoying and kept looking at me… and he kept trying to talk to me, and asked me where I was going, so when he offered me a lift, I felt scared.'

'I should think so. Any girl on her own in that situation would feel threatened on a dark night and very late too. So, would you like me to call the police?'

'No, I don't think so. I just think he was probably trying to be helpful.' I don't tell her he smelt of alcohol and how really threatened I felt. I do not want the police to be involved. Past experience tells me to leave well alone.

'Where do you want me to drop you off?' she asks, as we drive through some dark lanes.

'Well, I am going to Blackstone Cottage in Red House Lane.'

She looks puzzled. 'But there's no one living there and the cottage is completely empty – has been for months.' 'Yes, I know,' I reply. 'My Aunt has left it to me in her will and I am coming down to stay a night or two to find out what it is like. I meant to arrive earlier, but what with getting in a muddle with the timetable and train delays…'

'You'd better come and spend the night with me,' she says hurriedly. 'I don't think you can have any idea what a state that cottage is in and anyway, I believe that car is following us and he would see me drop you off. I can take you over to the cottage in the morning.'

A few moments later she turns to the right up a bumpy, rather muddy track with a sign to Ridge Farm and the car that has been following drives on down the road.

Chapter 2

As we arrive at the house, the security lights come on and I can see a vague outline of the shape of a large square house. The garage doors open automatically and the woman, who calls herself Angela, suggests I get out of the car with my rucksack before she drives in, as there is not much room to manoeuvre inside.

We are soon walking towards the back of the house and entering a scruffy porch full of Wellington boots and waterproof coats. There is a strong smell of dog and as she opens the back door a huge dog rushes out. Luckily, I like dogs and it looks friendly enough, which it proves to be and after a quick welcome to both of us, wanders off outside.

'Irish Wolfhound', she says. 'She's called Bess. A rather ordinary name, but that's what she came with – and I told you my name's Angela and – remind me. You are…?'

'I'm Leonora Kaslo, but I'm always known as Lora.' I reply, and I explain how I spell Lora, as it is slightly different from the usual spelling.

'Good to meet you, Lora. Let's go in and get warm and have something to eat.'

We enter a lovely big cosy kitchen with a large cooking range and I can see how different it is from the scruffy and cluttered kitchen of my childhood home. This kitchen is gleamingly clean with modern, cream-coloured cabinets and shiny work surfaces, with nothing lying around that doesn't need to be there. We are soon eating delicious thick vegetable soup with crusty bread.

'Right – now we'd better get to know each other, don't you think?' Angela says in a matter-of-fact way. 'It's not every day I pick up a stranger at the station and shouldn't think you often go off into the night in a strange car.'

'No – it's never happened to me before,' I say with a laugh.

'So – perhaps you would like to know a bit about me and where you have landed up here tonight and then you can tell me a bit about yourself. I'll be brief, as it is very late and I certainly need to get some sleep and I'm sure you do too.' I nod in agreement and she continues – 'I'm Angela West and I live here with my husband Geoff. Geoff works in London at an American bank and comes home at weekends. I work part-time, just one or two days a week, as a Financial Consultant in London and we have a tiny flat up there. Here, we have a small farm with a herd of Hereford cattle, a few sheep and plenty of chickens and ducks. It is more of a hobby farm really, because we both love the country. It doesn't really make money, but it is nice to have one's own produce and we certainly enjoy the fresh air after London.'

While she's talking, I think I am beginning to trust her. Nowadays I'm becoming more skilled at judging who I can trust. She has a very warm friendly face, framed by shoulder length wavy dark hair. She is slightly plump, smartly dressed in a dark trouser suit, smart black shoes and has clear polished fingernails, but it seems to me that she will be more comfortable when she is dressed for the country.

'How do you manage to look after the animals when you are both in London?' I ask.

'We have a couple who live in a cottage in the grounds and they take care of everything when we are not here, and a lad who comes in part time to help.' She replies. 'Now tell me a bit about yourself and then we'll go and find you a bed for the night.'

'First I must thank you again for being so kind. I don't know what I'd have done, if you hadn't come to my rescue.'

'That's fine. I'm glad I could help – so where are you from and what are your plans?'

'Well, I'm here to look at the cottage. I mentioned my Aunt May left it to me and I've got to decide whether I want to live in it or sell it or what. I have been living near London for a couple of years, but before that I lived on an Island called Morg with a family group and we were basically self-sufficient.'

'So, you must be related to Isobel at Red House?'

'Yes, she's my Aunt.'

'So – I don't understand – why didn't you contact her to meet you? She only lives round the corner and a few steps up the hill from the cottage?'

I hesitate before saying, 'She doesn't approve of my having the cottage and has told me that she thinks I should sell it straight away. So, do you know Isobel?'

'Yes, I have yoga lessons with her up at Red House, but she's not a close friend. But surely she would have met you at the station if she'd known you were on your own?'

'Well, she might have if I'd asked, but… um… she likes to tell me what I *should* do and I wanted to just turn up on my own and see for myself, without any input from her. You see, I'm an only child. My Mother died when I was a baby and Isobel has always thought of herself as a substitute mother, although Aunt May was much more like a mother to me. I don't get on with Isobel very well. She always wanted a child of her own and eventually had a daughter, but not till I was in my mid-teens, so during my childhood she took out her frustrations on me and her poor husband, Pete.'

'It's funny' said Angela. 'She comes over as very reasonable and friendly to us at the yoga class. She always seems so relaxed and really kind of serene, as if she hasn't a care in the world, but she is fairly firm with us in the yoga class. Gently persuasive we call it.'

'Well she was certainly firm with me', I reply, 'But I haven't seen her for a while, so maybe she has changed since having her own child' – and I think to myself, I hope she treats her own child better than the way she treated me, remembering all the times in the past when she hit me and the scars from cigarette burns, and I wonder if anyone can change that much – but I don't mention this to Angela.

'So – I'm glad you are doing what you feel is right for you. We should all be in charge of our own lives,' says Angela firmly, 'but, I do think it was lucky I was around this evening. Now, let's get you to bed, so you can be fresh for tomorrow to visit the cottage.'

I realise I do like and trust Angela. She seems a warm and practical person and is soon showing me upstairs to a cosy bedroom on the first floor.

'This is a spare room which we always leave ready for unexpected visitors. The bed is made up and has a duvet, with extra blankets in the cupboard if you are cold. The nights are at their darkest and can be quite chilly, as the heating goes off at night. Will this be all right for you?' she asks.

'Perfect,' I say and mean it. 'But I can use my sleeping bag.'

'Oh, no, no – be comfortable while you can. You don't know what you've let yourself in for, if you are thinking of sleeping in that cottage.' Then she points to a door in the corner of the room. 'You have your own en-suite shower room and loo and there's a towel in there. If you need anything else, I'm just across the landing. Just give me a shout.'

'This is wonderful,' I say and we wish each other goodnight.

This is luxury I have never known. There are big thick, full-length curtains at the window and as I go to close them, I notice that the moon is almost full and I can vaguely see a lawn and flowerbeds. I can also see the drive we came up earlier and the lane at the end – and then my heart sinks. I believe I can see a car parked down there. I close the curtains quickly. It's nearly 1 a.m. Perhaps I was mistaken. Should I mention it to Angela? Perhaps I'll have another look. I peep through the curtains, but there is a cloud over the moon. I decide to undress and get ready for bed and then have another look. When I'm ready I take another peep. The moon is shining brightly again and there is no sign of a car.

. . .

I don't know when I have slept so well, in spite of all the anxiety of the night before. I wake up with a start, wondering what time it is, as I can hear voices outside and a car engine. It still seems very dark, but I soon discover it is the thick curtains keeping the light out and that it is ten past nine on a sunny morning, with heavy clouds in the distance. There is a lovely view from the window of flowerbeds, which I imagine would be full of flowers in the summer. There are only one or two colourful blooms left in this cold November weather, but I don't know the names, as the small wildflowers growing on Morg look nothing like these. I can see the postman driving away in his red van, bumping over the ruts on the drive.

Angela has told me there would be no hurry in the morning, but I get washed and dressed quickly, as I am excited and also rather apprehensive about the day ahead. There is a note on the kitchen table telling me that Angela is taking Bess for a walk and inviting me to help myself to breakfast – cereals and/or toast, fruit juice, coffee, tea etc. I find I am very hungry and tuck into cereals first and then three thick slices of toast and cherry jam (the expensive French sort).

As I eat this lovely breakfast I think to myself how very lucky I am to be so slim – some people call me too thin – and I can eat as much and as often as I like, without getting fat. When I was living on Morg, Isobel used to call me "Spider", on account of my spindly arms and legs and long, dark, almost black hair and the fact that I was always hiding in corners and creeping about, to try and avoid being noticed by her. She also said my blue eyes freaked her out, as they made me look so innocent, but she said she knew otherwise. At least I have reached her height now, except when she is wearing those ridiculously high-heeled boots, and she seems to tower over everyone.

I sit wondering now why Isobel had so much power in that household, even though she was the founder of the group, she was the youngest of the grown-ups, but seemed to be in charge of all the daily happenings. She had an aura about her that seemed to say, 'I am the expert. I have the knowledge. I have experience that none of you have had.' This of course was true, up to a point, as neither of her sisters or Pete had ever lived in a commune before.

I never called her "Aunt" Isobel, as she said it made her feel too old, but in most ways she acted with the authority of someone older than her sister, May, who was actually about twelve years older than her. May did like me to call her "Aunt" May, which felt cosy and comforting. Isobel was tall and beautiful, charming and charismatic to those she wanted to impress. Only those like me who lived with her from day to day, could see her switch from calm and charm to being hard and quite ruthless at times. Sometimes Pete would warn me, 'Don't get on the wrong side of Isobel today. She is in one of her blitzing moods.'

Aunt May was motherly with a round and comfortable figure and a gentle, pleasant nature. They are… were so different in every way, it is hard to believe they were sisters. I could always go to Aunt May for love and support, but she didn't seem able to protect me from Isobel as Isobel was clever at making sure her sister never witnessed her negative behaviour towards me. Anyway, Aunt May wasn't always around when I really needed her support, and the cigarette burns were inflicted when Aunt May was away from Morg.

My Mother?… I was a baby when she died… and only have a couple of photos. Aunt May always mentioned her with huge affection and told me I am very like her. I do so wish I could remember her.

And what about Pete? I think of him a lot. He is a complete mystery to me. He was always kind to me, but completely under

Isobel's thumb. She seemed to have a strange hold over him. He seemed rather a secretive person – very good at mending the generator and the boat and other practical jobs, but didn't say very much. I was told he was a qualified doctor, so he coped with our minor ailments, but we were hardly ever ill.

And – Ade – he is always in my heart, but I will try not to think about him for the moment. It is too upsetting and I will try and switch my mind to the future, which is what everyone has been telling me to do.

For the past two years I have seen or heard very little from Isobel. I have had one or two brief letters telling me about her move to Red House and Aunt May's move to Blackstone Cottage. That is why it was such a shock to receive the Solicitor's letter telling me of Aunt May's death from cancer and her legacy to me. I did not go to her funeral, as I did not know about it. The first I heard was in a brief note from Isobel to tell me she had died... but then recently I have been unwell and perhaps the excuse was not to upset me. Who knows – and I hope to be finding out more about everything once I have seen the cottage and decide what to do next.

. . .

It is now eleven o'clock and since I have been mulling things over in my mind Angela has just come back from her walk with Bess. She takes off her muddy wellies and comes into the kitchen, where I have cleared up the breakfast things.

'Good morning Lora.' she says, flopping down onto a chair. 'A bit chilly out there,' she says as she stands with her back to the range, which is giving off a good heat. 'We've had a very good walk and Bess can wait indoors now till later in the day. Mrs Graham isn't coming in today, so she will have to stay on her own when we go out and she doesn't mind being left for a while... Did you sleep well?'

'Brilliantly. Such a comfy bed and beautifully warm. I didn't wake up till I heard the post van.'

'Good and I hope you've had enough to eat.'

I apologise for having scoffed so much of her cherry jam and she tells me there is plenty more in the larder.

'If it's OK with you, I thought we could drive around a bit and I can show you where the shops are etc. You may want to buy some food and things and then I'll take you up to the cottage. Or…' and she looked thoughtful for a moment – 'Perhaps we'll do it the other way round. Have a look at the cottage first and then you'll know what you need to get. I'll warn you again. The cottage is not in a good state and you would be *very* welcome to stay here, while you get things sorted.'

'That's so kind,' I say, 'but I am sure I'll manage.'

'Well, let's wait and see. I don't have to go to London this week and would be glad of the company.'

Chapter 3

Within ten minutes we are in the car and heading off down the drive and I have brought my rucksack with my few possessions, just in case things at the cottage are not as bad as Angela says. After all, her home, except for the drive, is immaculate and warm and she is probably not used to roughing it like I am. It is only a very short journey along twisty lanes, then we turn left up a fairly steep hill with trees on either side of a very narrow lane. The sign at the bottom says "Red House Lane" and there is also a no-through-road sign. We have passed very few houses on the way and Angela explains that the village of Wasbury with its station is about two miles away, further than I had been told previously. The cottage, certainly, would have been impossible to find in the dark – without a torch or a map – stupid me!! We drive very slowly up the narrow twisty lane, as there is only room for one vehicle at a time. It is quite dark with the trees on either side and the clouds which I had noticed earlier in the morning are now well overhead, looking ominously as if they are about to tip a bucket of water over us.

Suddenly, around the corner, we come across the cottage on the right. It looks dark and foreboding, made worse by the tall trees and the over-abundance of vegetation around it and the dark clouds above. It is obvious nothing has been cut back for months, even maybe years. There is ivy creeping all over it, even extending over some of the windows. The cottage seems to be unfenced from the lane and there are brambles and shrivelled, dying, nettles covering what should be the small front garden and the flagstone path to the front door is only just visible through the weeds. I am shocked to think Aunt May was living here only a few months ago, but Angela says that nature can take over in just a few weeks in this part of the country, given favourable weather conditions.

Further up the lane, to the left of the cottage, as I face its front door, I can just get a glimpse of a big red house behind a group of tall trees. It is on slightly higher ground, which gives it a rather oppressive feel and although it is the beginning of November, there are still quite a lot of leaves on the trees, so it is difficult to see quite how big Red House is. Angela points out that the front of the cottage faces east and there are no big trees this side, so this side of the cottage should be lighter when the sun rises in the morning. Just as the back, facing west, should get good light late afternoon and evening. Unfortunately, the big, tall trees, to the south, between Blackstone Cottage and Red House, could block most of the light throughout the middle of the day. There are some smaller trees and bushes on the northern side, to the right of the cottage, but these probably won't affect the light, and there is just a garage and a couple of sheds on this side.

'What about a key?' says Angela.

'My solicitor gave me the key.' I reply, while rummaging about in the bottom of my rucksack. 'Here it is.' In fact, there are two keys – one small Yale one and a larger silver coloured Mortise type. The Yale key proves to be useless, as the lock itself has been forced at some time and is doing nothing useful in the way of security. The big one is stiff, but it works and the door reluctantly opens when I give it a strong push.

'Would you like me to come in too?' asks Angela, sounding apprehensive.

'Well, if you'd like to have a look,' I reply, not really knowing whether I want anyone else in there with me. I tell her that I'm not one to scare easily over creepy crawlies or rats or mice.

She doesn't seem too keen to come in, or maybe she doesn't like the idea of creepy crawlies – or perhaps she senses I would rather do this alone, and says, 'I tell you what. I am sure you'd like to have a good look round on your own. I have a few things I need to do in the village and I'll come back in about an hour and see how you're getting on.'

Feeling like an intruder, I go through the front door into a tiny little hallway with a flight of bare wooden stairs almost straight ahead of me and doors to the left and right. It feels cold and unlived in – almost colder than outside and I find myself shivering in spite of the warm coat that Angela has lent me. There is a small passageway just to the left of the stairs, leading to a little window looking over the back garden and there is a cupboard under the stairs. As I stand there in the tiny hallway, I suddenly find my old anxieties creeping over me. Am I going to be able to cope with this? For a few moments I feel my feet stuck to the floor and I have to take some low slow breaths and give myself reassuring messages to avoid a panic attack. After a few moments I gather myself together, relieved that I have managed to use my coping strategies, which my counsellor taught me previously, and with a few more gentle breaths and self-affirming messages, I decide to go through the door on my right first. Of course, it feels cold after Ridge Farm, as there can't have been any heating here for a long time.

Although the cottage looks overgrown and deserted on the outside, inside this room at least, it is surprisingly clean. It smells musty from having been shut up for a while, but it doesn't seem damp and there is little dust on any of the furniture. I discover this to be the sitting room. It has fairly large windows looking to the back and front of the house, which I imagine in the summer would make it light and airy, but possibly rather cold in the winter. There are two, comfortable-looking armchairs on either side of an inglenook fireplace, which is on the north wall and contains a wood-burning stove, and facing the fireplace is a small, battered sofa. I sit on the sofa for a minute or two and run my fingers over the soft, but warn, upholstery and, for the moment, I feel surprisingly calm.

On the left of the fireplace there is a desk, with some drawers underneath and some old, rather faded Victorian prints on the wall. On the other side of the fireplace are floor-to -ceiling bookshelves, packed with books, stuffed in at all angles. The stove has ash in it and there are still a few logs stacked up in the inglenook. I get up from the sofa and tentatively open the drawers in the desk and find they are still full of papers, old photos, odd bits of string, paperclips etc. I will have to sort through those sometime and as I think of this, although I am feeling sad, Aunt May seems to be giving me permission to pry. It really is as if she is still around and everything looks as I would imagine she would have left it if she had only gone out for the day somewhere. The cushions on the chairs look squashed, as if someone has recently sat down and there are what I presume are cat's hairs on one of the cushions which has a little blanket covering it. 'Oh, Aunt May,' I say out loud. 'I miss you so much, but I still feel you are here with me – and please help me cope with all this responsibility.'

The view from the back window looks out onto a large lawn, where the grass and weeds are not as long as on the other side of the house and it looks as if someone may have cut it sometime at the end of the summer. There is a wooden bench to the right, looking out across the lawn. Straight ahead there is a tall hedge at the end of the garden, which is very wild and overgrown and I cannot see what is on the other side.

I go through the little hallway and into the other room. This is the kitchen and is big enough to contain a small, square table and a couple of chairs. There is a door with glass above, which leads to the back garden and a small window overlooking the front garden. The kitchen sink looks reasonably clean and there is some crockery on the draining board, which is clean and appears to have been left to drain. The cupboards contain all sorts of jars and packets – again it looks as if she has only just left. The fridge has been switched off and the door left slightly open and is empty, so somebody must have been into tidy and wash up. Perhaps it was Isobel?

By now the black clouds in the sky have turned to heavy rain and it is getting rather dark and even colder indoors, so I try the lights. The electricity is not switched on, but having read Mr Floyd's letter previously, I discover the switchboard in a cupboard under the stairs and I am glad to find that he had arranged for the power to be connected before I came. I test the landline telephone, but it's dead, so I must get it fixed, as Angela has warned me that reception for mobiles is very patchy in this area.

The stairs are steep and would be very dark at night without the electric light at the top. I reach the top and again there are doors to the left and right. I brace myself to go through to the right and find a good size double room, with two windows looking to the back and front of the house. There is a large double bed and I gingerly pull back the corner of a flowery bedcover and find the bed is made up with sheets, two pillows, two blankets and an old-fashioned eiderdown quilt. This must have been Aunt May's bedroom I guess, as the cupboards are still jam packed with clothes. It all smells very musty, like the storeroom in a charity shop. There is a little dressing table, still with her hairbrush and comb and pots of face cream on the top. The top drawer has further jars of cosmetics, a hairdryer etc., and the other drawers have undies and jumpers and things which would not have been hung in a wardrobe.

I suddenly feel rather sick and faint and like an intruder again after looking through all her personal belongings and I hurry through to the other door across the landing. This leads to a little bathroom at the back, with a tiny bath and a shower over it, and there is also a loo and a hand basin. I need a wee, so I sit on the loo for a few moments – then get up and splash my face with very cold water from the taps in the hand basin. There is no hand towel, but the water has revived me enough to leave the bathroom.

Just to the left of the bathroom is another door and this leads to a small bedroom, which faces the front of the house. It has a padded bench under the window and this is obviously the room where Aunt May does (or I should say *did*) her ironing and sewing. I remember she used to make her own clothes and there is a tailor's dummy in one corner and an ironing board and lots of bits of material lying about. Looking at all this, once again, I can't believe she's not still alive.

Before going downstairs, I look out of the little landing window by the bathroom, which, like the main bedroom, overlooks the back garden and I catch a glimpse of a black cat on the lawn. It quickly disappears into the bushes, as it must be getting very wet in this heavy rain. I wonder who it belongs to? I know Isobel does not like cats, so it is unlikely to be from Red House.

After exploring the house, I realise I haven't found the car yet and search my rucksack for the garage and car keys which are linked together. Although it is still raining, it is a relief to get outside. The garage is wooden and looks rather rickety. The door is secured by a large stiff padlock and I get rather wet while trying to open it. Inside I find a dark blue Ford Fiesta and the body work looks in good condition, as far as I can see, as I wipe away the dust. I find a handbook and servicing book in the front pocket and see the MOT is out of date, which will mean the tax is as well. I only passed my driving test fairly recently, and at this very moment I'm not feeling as if I will ever have the courage to drive.

. . .

After a while, the rain slows down and Angela arrives back, as promised, and I show her around and I feel more at ease with her there with me. She doesn't say much to start with, just things like, 'Yes, I see… This could be nice… there's a lot to do isn't there?' I can sense that, like me, she feels awkward being amongst Aunt May's personal belongings.

'I feel like an intruder', she says at last.

'So do I.'

'Yea, but you're family and what's more, she means you to be here… What heating has it got?' she asks suddenly. 'It certainly needs warming up and drying out a bit and if the rain would stop we could open the windows and let some fresh air in.'

'As far as I can see, there is just the wood-burning stove and an electric fan heater in the kitchen,' I say. 'I haven't tried the fan heater, so I don't know whether it works.'

'Are there any logs?'

'Yes I've found some in a lean-to on the side of the house. They are well covered, so should be dry.'

'Well, that's a good start, because if you light that stove it will soon warm the house through and begin to feel more like home.'

Angela comes up with various practical suggestions and then asks…

'So – are you wanting to stay overnight, or would you rather come back with me?' She sees me hesitate and comes to my rescue. 'Come on,' she says. 'I think one more night at least, will give you time to think things over. There are a lot of things to consider and much easier to do with a good meal inside you – and you certainly need to warm this place up.'

I am so relieved at the idea of spending another night in the warmth and comfort of Ridge Farm, so I say, 'This is really, really kind of you. You are right, there's lots to think about and I must admit it does feel a bit daunting and I think another night would give me much more idea of what I need to do first.'

'Such as – getting the place warmed up,' says Angela. 'There's a good little pub in the village – let's go and get some lunch,' she says, as if reading my thoughts.

I am now beginning to feel slightly more relaxed and even a bit hungry. 'Yes, that's a lovely idea,' I say, 'but I insist you let me pay. I have plenty of money' and I tell her about my "tidy sum" and 'I insist on paying my way, if I'm staying with you another night.'

'Well, that's good of you my dear, but there is really no need. I said I would be glad of the company.'

. . .

The village of Wasbury is larger than I imagined. Apart from the station, it has a church, two pubs, a village shop/post office and several other small shops in the High Street, which include an Estate Agent, Ironmonger, Greengrocer and Butcher.

'It's quite a busy little place for the area,' says Angela, as she drives into the car park of the "Black Swan". 'Having a station, makes it very convenient for commuters… For people working in towns further down or up the line… or part-timers like Geoff and me. So, it has grown a lot in the past few years. Luckily for us it's a Conservation Area, so it's unlikely any more development will come in our direction… and that applies to Red House Lane as well. If you decide to sell your cottage, you would probably get a good price.'

'Another "tidy sum"?' I suggest.

She laughs. 'Yes, I would think it would be very tidy.'

We sit down to a simple ploughman's lunch and Angela insists on buying the drinks, as she has finally agreed to me paying for the food. We both have a glass of wine and I begin to feel much more relaxed after my intrusion on Aunt May's home. Angela tells me a bit about her job, which sounds way above my head, but she obviously finds it very interesting – and lucrative. After a while she sits back in her chair and says…

'I find you a bit puzzling. How old are you again – I think you told me – nineteen is it?'

'Yes – why's that puzzling?'

'Well, most nineteen-year-olds I know are… I can't really explain what I mean. For a start they wouldn't even consider spending time in a creepy cottage like that on their own. I know you haven't got parents or close family… except Isobel of course, but in some ways you come across as very much older than you are, and then suddenly you look very young and vulnerable. I'm sorry… I don't know what I am talking about really. You are very pretty… in fact, beautiful, with your long dark hair and really deep blue eyes, but your clothes don't somehow go with your age.'

'What you mean to say is that my clothes look as if they come from a charity shop?' I suggest with a smile.

'Well yes… Oh dear, that sounds so rude,' she says, sounding more and more embarrassed.

I come to her rescue 'Well yes they do actually. I haven't had the opportunity or money up to now, to go shopping or do any of the things that teenagers would normally do. In fact, I've never really been a teenager. I have discovered I rather like buying clothes from charity shops, as they seem to have more character than new stuff – and are much cheaper.'

'I'm so sorry to be so nosey, but Geoff was asking me about you on the phone this morning and he thinks me rather odd to take in a complete stranger without knowing very much about you. So, what have you been doing the past two years in London then?'

I wonder how I can answer this, as I don't want to tell her the truth – not yet anyway, and I don't know if I can trust her that much. 'I was sharing a flat with four others in South London. Um, my mother left me a small amount of money and Isobel and the Morg lot helped me out. You see, at Morg we all lived as a small community. I never mixed much outside the group. I had only been to the mainland a few times in my life and when I eventually went to live on the mainland, the girls I lived with in a flat all had different interests, and so we went our separate ways.'

'You said "lived" with… as if in the past? Where are you based now?'

'Nowhere… except of course, Blackstone Cottage.'

'What?' she exclaimed. 'Do you mean to say, you have nowhere else to live except the cottage?'

'Well – I'm very lucky to have that aren't I?

'Yes, yes, but a bit of a risk giving up the flat wasn't it? And where are all your belongings?'

'In my rucksack,' I say, enjoying the surprised look on her face. 'I think Isobel would take me in if I was desperate,' I add. (But I would have to be desperate, I think to myself).

'Yes, of course, I keep forgetting you have Isobel close by.'

'I haven't seen her for a while,' I say, 'but I imagine she is running Red House on the same lines as on the island. Morg consisted of several small cottages and was not a large area, and I was told that Isobel moved to Red House to be able to have more space to expand her business – of running courses – yoga etc.' Angela is looking very thoughtful. I expect she's wondering why I left the island – but I expect she'll ask me that and I'll have to invent a good answer. But, then I think to myself, surely nineteen-year-olds do leave home – go to college, get a job, so what's strange in that?

Chapter 4

After accepting Angela's offer of another night at Ridge Farm, it seems essential to do a few basic preparations to Blackstone Cottage, before moving in. As I mentioned before, I am used to roughing it, and could perfectly well sleep on the sofa, but, as Angela suggests, it is a pity to rough it when I don't need to and the first thing to do would be to sort out the bed. I certainly don't want to use Aunt May's bed until I have got a new mattress and new bedding, and then it will really be my bed. Angela takes me down to Ford, which is a bigger town and I choose all my stuff from the bedding shop, "Softly Sleep." They assure me they can deliver the mattress early tomorrow afternoon and take away the old one. It is about 5pm by the time we get back to Angela's home, after having bought essential provisions for tomorrow, so we have a lovely relaxing evening chatting, watching the television and, I am glad to say, no more prying from Angela.

We go to bed about ten thirty, but I have huge difficulty getting to sleep and in spite of doing some relaxation exercises and trying to think of positive, unrelated things, find my mind inevitably going over the events of the day and thoughts of all the mammoth tasks ahead. Of course, everything always seems more worrying in the depths of a dark night, even in a cosy warm bed and after lots of tossing and turning, I eventually fall asleep well after two thirty.

Angela doesn't wake me in the morning, but I awake about nine and after a hurried shower I go down for more toast and cherry jam for breakfast. Angela offers me a cooked breakfast, but after my disturbed night I don't feel I could face it.

. . .

My stomach is going round and round in anticipation as Angela drives me to Blackstone Cottage. It is a grey morning, but not raining and not too cold and there is a damp autumnal mist amongst the trees.

'Don't forget,' she says emphatically, 'I am more than pleased to help you in any way. You've got my landline number and my mobile number and please, please, don't hesitate to phone if you need to… And if that mattress doesn't arrive…'

I assure her I will keep in touch and thank her profusely once again. She kisses me on both cheeks and then drives off, waving as she leaves. I know she has various business emails she needs to do this morning, so she seems to have forgotten that I haven't tried to get a signal on my mobile from the cottage. I try it from various places inside the house, without any success and begin to feel panicky, but then, thank goodness, I find if I go out to the back garden, I can get a faint signal. That's another thing to do urgently – contact BT and get the landline connected!

It suddenly seems really lonely being all alone in the cottage, with my few meagre possessions, but I want to be able to get moving as quickly as possible and to make the place feel like home, and I tell myself loneliness is something I'm quite used to. The cottage has such a sad atmosphere, with all the overgrown plants surrounding it and the ivy creeping across the windows and the damp autumn mist, all giving a rather sinister feel about the place. I have to keep reassuring myself that, if I can't settle here and find a job locally, I am so lucky to have the option of selling up, but for the moment it has to be my home. The money Aunt May has left me has been safe in shares and a savings account, during the few months when probate was being sorted, so I should be able to do essential repairs and if I really can't cope, I could get a bed sitter somewhere temporarily.

I firmly pull myself back into the here and now. Angela has told me it would be about a forty-five minutes brisk walk to Wasbury, so I realise it is essential that I get the car on the road. Angela has given me a good list of useful local numbers, so I make my way to the back garden and after putting a plastic bag on the damp bench, I sit down to make a few phone calls. I have difficulty getting through to the right people to find out what I need to do about things like the car and contacting BT about the phone. It all takes a long time and as I don't have much success, I am so glad it is not raining.

Feeling really tearful, very frustrated and fed up with difficult phone calls, I then decide to let off steam and start tackling the ivy. This is extremely therapeutic and it takes me the rest of the morning, with the help of an old broken knife, to peel its stubborn tendrils off the windows. I have found quite a substantial ladder in a shed, so I can clear the upper windows as well. There are great thick stalks growing up the walls which will have to wait till I find a saw, but just clearing the windows and the smaller pieces from the walls, makes the house look a little more welcoming.

After a while, as I am looking at my handiwork and my torn fingernails, a car goes past down the lane, presumably from Red House. I don't get a chance to see who is in it but hope no one has seen me. I really want much more time to myself, before interruptions from Isobel. Having got a bit more light into the house and with the morning mist having lifted, I am feeling very much more optimistic and make myself a sandwich. I am about to clean out the fridge when there is loud hammering on the door and my heart seems to beat as loudly. To my relief it is not Isobel but the man from "Softly Sleep", bringing the mattress. He takes it upstairs for me and takes the old one away and soon I am putting on a new sheet, a lovely, bright-coloured duvet and a couple of fluffy pillows. I flop down on the bed and think to myself that this is probably going to be OK, once I've cleaned and moved the furniture around a bit and put a few more personal bits and pieces on the shelves. My rucksack doesn't contain more than the bare essentials, but I have two books to add to the shelves, my mother's silver-backed hairbrush and hand mirror and a few of her little trinkets, which I keep for sentimental reasons.

By the evening I am feeling quite optimistic. I don't dare light the stove till the chimney has been swept, but Angela has lent me a fan heater which I have switched on upstairs and the one from the kitchen seems to work fine and is warming the sitting room. If the cottage wasn't so close to Isobel, I would be feeling even better, but I hope I am now strong enough to cope with her. I have emptied my rucksack completely, and although there is a washing machine in the kitchen, I am not sure how it works yet and need to find the instructions, so I wash through some of my clothes by hand and hang them to dry on a wooden fold-up drier in front of the blower. By now it is time for bed, having been a very busy day, getting things to feel more like my own home. I am feeling far less intrusive on Aunt May's space, and I can imagine her welcoming me into her home. She wouldn't have left it to me if she didn't want me to be here, would she? I still feel a bit uncomfortable about sleeping in her bed, as I don't know the exact details of her death. I heard she had had cancer – but did she die in this bed? I have always presumed she was in hospital, as I can't imagine Isobel nursing her at home. This is something that no doubt I will find out from Isobel, when we inevitably meet up.

. . .

By eleven thirty I am snuggled down in my new bed and the bed linen smells all fresh and new and feels slightly crisp. I was told I should wash it first, but I don't think it will do me any harm. The room feels warm, although I have now switched off both heaters for the night. I must admit, that although I feel very tired, it is still difficult to get to sleep with all the thoughts going around in my head and I now I realise I haven't taken my meds today. I am trying to cut down slowly, to one tablet a day instead of two, but missing them altogether is probably not a good idea. My doctor doesn't know I'm cutting down, but I'm sick of feeling like a zombie. However, with all this new stress it is probably not a good time to cut down, so I fetch a glass of water and swallow one down. This seems to do the trick and I don't wake up till 8 o'clock next morning, feeling cautiously optimistic. The bed has been very comfortable and as good as the one at Ridge Farm, without the plush surroundings.

The window curtains are a rather faded chintz and certainly not very thick, and have started to wear thin in places, where they have been folded in the same position for a long time, but still, they have kept the night out and are now welcoming the morning, as I open them. Looking out to the front of the house, I can see a rather pale sun peeping over the horizon, so maybe the weather is improving. The view out of the back window, which is near my bed is beautiful. The light is just beginning to reach the distant hills, which I can now get a glimpse of as the air is a bit clearer – and I long to trim the hedge.

The electric shower is very efficient and I wash and get dressed as quickly as I can and have a hurried breakfast. I don't trust the weather to stay fine. I put on a good warm fleece jacket which Angela gave me yesterday, which she said was too small for her, but I don't know if she was just being kind. I find some good strong loppers in the shed and the hedge proves quite easy to cut, as it consists of tall spindly growth at the top. I soon find I can get a lot of it down to a level at which I can see over the hedge from downstairs and view the distant hills more clearly. When all the autumn leaves have fallen, it should lighten up the whole place. I have managed to clear quite a large area and I am feeling quite pleased with myself and very glad that I have learnt self-sufficiency skills from childhood at Morg. Suddenly there is a loud knocking on the door, which breaks my mood and, as I suspect, it turns out to be Isobel.

Isobel has large, pale grey eyes which seem to look straight round each side of you, so when she is facing you, your eyes never meet hers. It is a very strange feeling and it is as if she is not actually with you, but she is absorbing you in some way, with her mind focussing elsewhere. She is tall and willowy, with long light brown hair, which she is wearing in a bun (I think that's what it's called) at the back of her head. Her hair is held together with elegant clips and there are a few obviously intentional wisps hanging down each side of her face. She is wearing a long, grey/green coat, which swirls around as she stands in the doorway.

I can't help feeling the power of her presence as she stands there looking around me and I feel the usual cold tingly sensation that invades my body in her presence. There is a pause, as neither of us seems to know what to say, and then she starts questioning me, in her abrupt, cold manner, which she reserves for me and with none of the charm with which she approaches other people, she says...

'So... how long have you been here then?

'Just a couple of days,' I reply.

'And how long are you planning to stay?'

'As long as it takes.'

'As long as what takes?'

'As long as it takes me to find out whether I want to stay permanently or not.'

'You can't honestly be thinking of staying here full time, surely?'

'Why not?... Anyway, that's not much of a welcome is it? I thought you'd be pleased to see me hale and hearty and back in the land of the living, without you having to cough up money for me all the time.'

'Don't be facetious,' she says, and then continues, 'Well – it's a spooky house to start with. I never knew how May could live here, but then she always was a bit of a psychic freak. You know it is said to be haunted don't you?… And May died in strange circumstances.'

'No, I didn't know it is haunted and how did Aunt May die – I thought it was cancer?' It is typical of Isobel to start off on a negative note and make me feel off-guard and threatened.

'Well let me in and I'll explain,' she says, peering round the door, so reluctantly I invite her into the kitchen and offer her coffee.

We take our coffee into the sitting room and as she glances round the room, she seems surprised that I have made it so homely in such a short time.

'We had the chimney swept.' She says, 'just after May died and the fire hasn't been lit since. There's a cowl on the chimney, so there can't be birds' nests in it, so you can light it and warm the place up a bit.' She pretends to shiver, but I don't think she is really cold. She appears so warmly clothed, with her customary long leather boots, as well as her coat.

'Thanks,' I say abruptly.

'And what are you doing about other things, like food?'

'I've got enough for another few days and then I can go to the village. I am planning to get a bike and use Aunt May's car when all the paperwork is organised.'

'But you can't drive.'

'Yes I can. I passed my driving test last month.'

'You are a dark horse. What else have you been up to then? I do hope Doctor Fanshaw approves of what you are doing.'

'Yes. He seems to think this is a good idea. After all, I am much luckier than most of the others who were there with me. I shouldn't have any money worries.'

'Have you got yourself a doctor down here yet?'

'No, I've only been here a couple of days.'

'Got enough medication? I suppose you are still meant to be on it?'

'The answer to both questions is yes,' I lie. In fact, I haven't got many pills left and I must get around to signing on at the local

Practice, so I change the subject quickly.' What were you going to tell me about Aunt May?'

Isobel then sits down in one of the chairs. (The one without the cat hairs). 'Firstly,' she says, 'yes, May did have cancer. It started as breast cancer and eventually spread right through her body. She wouldn't have anything to do with orthodox medicine, which is typical of her. But she was found dead at ten o'clock in the morning. We had had a short spell of really cold nights and she was found sitting outside on her garden bench, wearing only her nightdress, with her cat on her lap. The cat was fine, but she was frozen solid.'

'Oh my God!' I gasp... 'What, how, why...?'

'There was no sign of foul play and the post-mortem revealed absolutely nothing, except that she had died of hypothermia. The conclusion everyone came to was that she had deliberately gone out there to die, to avoid further suffering. She had said she wanted to die in her own home, although we were all trying to persuade her to go to the local hospice. Strangely, though, she didn't leave a note, or any explanation.'

'Who found her?' I ask, after a few moments of stunned silence.

'The district nurse, who had been coming in every morning.' Isobel tells me all of this in a matter- of- fact way and no one would guess she was talking about her own sister.

We sit in silence again. I must admit I am lost for words and try to fight back the tears. Aunt May was so dear to me, but I didn't want Isobel to see my reaction. It sounds bizarre, but then perhaps it was preferable to die in this way, rather than have weeks more of pain and distress.

After a while I pull myself together and say, '...and what about the haunting?'

'That's another matter altogether,' says Isobel. It seems that sometime in the nineteenth century there was a farming family living in the cottage and one day one of their children, a little girl of about three or four, ran out into the lane in front of a coach and horses. She was trying to grab her cat, but she was trampled to death. Her parents were so overcome with grief that they put up that large black granite stone.' She points outside towards the lane, to a large stone, almost completely covered in ivy. 'The cottage has been known as "Blackstone Cottage" ever since. The name of the cottage, painted on the side facing the lane in white lettering, has probably worn off by now.' Isobel pauses – probably to test my reaction, so I try not to show any emotion and offer her more coffee.

'Thanks, another cup would be nice,' she says and continues, 'Every now and again someone sees a pale figure of a little girl carrying a cat and sometimes the cat is seen on its own.'

I go to fetch her another cup of coffee, but don't want one myself. I feel glad of the chance to try and calmly absorb what she has said and wait a moment in the kitchen to stop my hand shaking, before I carry the mug of coffee back to her.

'Where are they seen?' I ask, trying to sound nonchalant, but feeling very nervous, as I sit down on the sofa.

'Usually in the back garden, or sometimes in the lane. May said she used to see them quite frequently.'

'Not inside the cottage?' I ask as casually as I can.

'I don't know – May never mentioned seeing them inside – but then she probably wouldn't think to say anything, as she was so matter of fact about anything like that. It certainly wouldn't have phased her.'

I am just trying to get my head round what she had just said, when she suddenly says, 'By the way, rumour has it, that one should never try keeping a black cat at the cottage. They always seem to bring bad luck or have a nasty accident themselves. Other colours are all right, but black ones are not a good idea.'

'But I saw a black cat in the garden, yesterday I think it was.'

'Well, that would have been the ghost I expect,' she says with a laugh. With this she looks rather pleased with herself, as she must have seen my startled look and says, 'I can't imagine you'll want to stay in this place for long. I mean, apart from its sad history, it's so dark and depressing amongst all these trees and I wouldn't think it is in any way a suitable home for a young girl, being way out in the country like this, especially someone like you.'

'What do you mean, someone like me?' I ask. 'I've lived in a wilderness almost all of my life,' I say, knowing perfectly well what she will reply.

'Well, you've been ill for a while and you should now be with other people of your own age and having a social life. You shouldn't be on your own too much, it will give you too much time to think and surely you don't want to end up in the state you were in after your... er,... sad event, do you?'

'No,' I say. 'But I don't think that'll happen. I've put all that behind me and can see things rationally now and realise that it was the shock of it all, my hormones, etc. that made me lose my sense of reality. No – things are quite different now.' I say all this quite firmly as I am feeling angry at her assumptions.

'You can't be too careful though. You should give yourself as little stress as possible.'

'Yes – I know all that, so I'll see how it goes. Anyway, I've nowhere else to live at the moment, so I might as well stay here and look after the ghosts, until I find somewhere more suitable.' I say all this to try to reassure her that I'm not going to give her trouble, and I notice there is no sign of her offering to let me stay with her at Red House. The last thing Isobel ever wants is trouble in her life, which is organised totally around her and the way she chooses to live. No, I see I have to convince her that I am normal in every way and am not going to be any kind of nuisance to her or others at Red House. Isobel is single-minded and woe-betide anyone or anything that gets in her way. However, what I am saying is true, as I do believe I'm on the mend and the past three and a half years since I left Morg, seem like a bad dream.

'And how are you getting on at Red House?' I ask (with half my mind still on what she has just told me).

'Yes – fine. We've been here well over two years now and have got a lot of things going on during the summer. We have several life-changing courses running, mostly in alternative therapies. We also have people coming for short-stays, mostly at weekends, to get away from pressures of life. We are planning two restful weekly retreats running each summer and part of the house is going to be made over for this.'

'Sounds like Morg?' I suggest.

'Yes – but I am living here alone now with Maisie. I have occasional outside staff coming in for various jobs, such as running the market garden, as we have a very big walled vegetable garden. It is a very large house and we are lucky that it was in such good condition when we bought it. Even so, there is a lot of work involved in running a place this size, so you can imagine I am very busy during the summer season. There is not so much going on at this time of the year, but I have yoga classes now and again – and all the planning for the summer.'

'So where is Pete?' I ask. I cannot imagine Isobel without Pete, her long-term partner.

"Oh, we're not together anymore, but he is still my business partner and comes to stay occasionally. He's living and working in New York now.'

'I still don't know why you left Morg.' I continue.

'Well, Pete landed this very good job in New York and I felt I needed more space for my work. Without Pete there for the practical things, like the generator which always seemed to be playing up, the boat needing attention, the weather – it just seemed a sensible move. Aunt May had bought this cottage and when Red House came up for sale, it seemed the perfect solution.

'So, what happened to Morg?' I ask.

We sold the island to a businessman, who is converting the site to holiday cottages. How he got planning permission I don't know. Anyway', she said as an afterthought, 'here people can come to visit by car or on the train, if they wish, and we can always arrange to meet them at the station. By the way, how did you get here?'

It is obvious Angela has not said anything to her yet, so I tell her I came by train and omit to tell her anything further.

Isobel gets up as if to leave, but first walks over to the window and looks out at my hedge cutting effort. 'That's an improvement. The hedge, I mean. You know you are going to have to do a hell of a lot here to maintain this place. It'll be very hard work. If you want a paid job there's not much opportunity in Wasbury you know.'

'You sound as if you mind if I stay,' I say, knowing perfectly well that she does.

'No, of course I don't mind if you stay, but I don't think it is suitable for you and I'm afraid I am much too busy to be able to give you any help.'

'I know – and I don't want any help thank you. You've already done your bit with financial support recently and I'm very grateful. In fact, when I'm settled and sorted, I hope I'll be able to start paying you back.'

Isobel doesn't reply to this and makes her way towards the door. 'Well, thanks for the coffee. I'll leave you to get on with it. Let me know if you need anything *urgently*, won't you?' And with that she leaves and surprise, surprise, doesn't invite me to visit Red House!

As Isobel leaves, I suddenly think of Aunt May's cat and ask her what happened to it.

'It went to a good home and I gather is very happy', she says.

'Is it black?' I ask.

'No – it is a big grey fluffy, scratchy, thing. I didn't like it very much, so I didn't want to take in on myself. Luckily someone else did.'

. . .

After Isobel leaves, you can imagine, I feel quite stunned by all that she said. It seems to me that maybe Aunt May's snail-chewed letter was actually trying to explain things to me, so I realise that one of the first jobs should be to sort through her things to see what I can find in the way of important or interesting papers in the spare room, but at the moment I don't feel up to it. Unsurprisingly, Isobel's visit has unsettled me.

How am I going to manage living in the cottage, I wonder, knowing about the girl and the cat, let alone Aunt May's death? Every time I look out of the window, will I imagine her sitting on that garden seat? I catch my breath at the thought. Then I decide I have got to be strong and I will certainly take my meds twice a day. After all, I'm asking a lot of myself to cope with everything I've been told. On the other hand, I tell myself, I have never really believed in ghosts and have coped with a lot of adversity in my life and have survived so far. Also, I know how Isobel does her best to make me feel uneasy and I have got to stop letting her get to me in such a negative way. I have to remember what my counsellor, Maggie, used to say to me about being confident in my own judgements and believing in myself; putting the past behind me and making my own future. Most of all – I know Ade would be determined for me to stand up to Isobel. He did not respect her at all and could see through her phoney messages of love and caring. He couldn't understand, either, how she had such an influence over his father, Pete. I imagine myself telling Ade about Isobel's story of the ghosts.

'Isobel's hocus pocus,' he would have said, and we would both have done a mocking dance.

I will not let Isobel tarnish my future life, especially as Aunt May has been so loving and generous.

Chapter 5

It has now been a couple of days since Isobel came to see me. Angela has been over and lent me a bike and I've cycled to Wasbury and seen a very busy Doctor at the surgery there. As I hadn't an appointment, I had to wait two hours before seeing anyone and then of course there was time taken finding my records online – lots of questions – but eventually I was given more pills to tide me over and told to make a further appointment for an up-to-date assessment. I had felt this was the most urgent thing I had to do and couldn't risk going without my meds, after having heard about Aunt May's death and alleged hauntings. In spite of my resolution to be strong, I had been feeling really edgy and nervous since Isobel's visit and had to keep reminding myself that this was just typical of her behaviour towards me; always seeming to delight in making me feel scared and unsure of myself. She is certainly doing all she can to make me want to leave the cottage and surely there must be a very strong reason for her not to want me there? I know it is not my welfare she is thinking about.

Angela thinks I have been extremely efficient and grown up about everything and she certainly seems impressed at how I am coping, especially when I tell her about Aunt May and the ghosts. I have been gradually feeling more relaxed and confident, now I have my medication as back-up and being able to talk to Angela, who is so sensible and down to earth. Neither of us has seen or heard anything of Odd-socks or his car, so I have almost forgotten about that experience.

I have managed to do quite a bit of general tidying and cleaning of the cottage and it is beginning to feel like my own home. Angela has been over with Bess a couple of times to see how I'm getting on and I am feeling so much better. The stove was quite easy to light, once Angela had found me some dry kindling, and the logs are well-seasoned and burn well. It is so cosy and it warms up the whole place, which is beginning to dry out and smell less musty.

. . .

It is Saturday today and there was a slight frost this morning and now the sun has come out and it looks as if it will be a fine day. I cycle to Wasbury, where I had noticed a small clothes shop and after a lot of trying on and discarding and then asking the assistant for help, I come away with a new pair of jeans and a red top. I cycle back home with the smart bag hanging from my handlebars and feeling rather pleased with myself and my purchases – though, is the top a bit bright? I can take it back if I change my mind.

Angela has invited me over to Ridge Farm for supper and she picks me up at six p.m. She is on her own, as Geoff is away somewhere.

'You look very smart,' she says, admiring my new jeans and red top.

'Thanks, I got them in Wasbury this morning. Do you think the colour of the top is too bright?'

'No, I think it suits you, with your dark hair.'

'That's a relief,' I say. 'I'm not used to bright colours but the shop assistant persuaded me to be brave.'

We are soon at Ridge Farm and I am getting an exuberant welcome from Bess, who nearly knocks me over in her excitement.

'I have been wondering,' says Angela, 'have you thought of getting a dog? It would be good company and might make you feel a bit more secure on your own?'

'It might – but if I get a job it could be awkward and it could limit me to the kind of job I get.'

'That's true. But it's something to consider.'

'Also, if I decide not to keep the cottage, it could limit me to where I move to. I have thought I might like to do a bit of travelling, as I have some money and I wouldn't want to have to leave a dog in kennels.'

'Well, a cat could be company,' she suggested, 'and cats are much more independent and can be easier to look after.'

'As long as it's not a black one,' I reply, having told Angela about the fate of black cats at the cottage.

Angela laughs and says, 'no there are plenty of other colours and anyway some people think black cats are lucky.'

Angela has produced a lovely supper of roast vegetables – broccoli, carrots, parsnips, butternut squash and potatoes, which she says are so easy to cook on her range. This is followed by a delicious chocolate mousse, not from the range, but the local supermarket. I have one glass of wine with the meal, as more than that can seem to affect my pills and Angela only has a small glass, as she is going to have to drive me home. After supper, while Angela takes a phone call from Geoff, I clear up in the kitchen and then we sit down by a lovely log fire in her smart drawing room and she tells me more about herself.

I gather she and Geoff have been married for twenty years and both very much enjoy their work and their free time in the country.

'You may be wondering if we have children,' she says quietly and then, 'the answer is no. We were never lucky enough, but now we enjoy our lives and see the benefits of the freedom without that responsibility.' She adds this rather hastily as if she can tell that this a touchy subject for me... but how would she know that? Has Isobel been talking to her, I wonder?

There is a bit of a silence before she changes the subject and asks me where I went to school and did I enjoy it? I tell her that I didn't go to school, but was educated on the island by the family, mostly Aunt May, who was a qualified teacher; and sometimes other adults visiting the island. I tell her I wasn't considered to be academic, but my friend Adrian, Pete's son went to boarding school from the age of twelve, as he always wanted to do medical research, from as early as any of us can remember'. But then, I regret mentioning Ade and hope she won't ask me about him.

Then, luckily, she changes the subject again and says, 'I saw Isobel this morning at my yoga class. She mentioned that you had come to live at Blackstone Cottage.'

'Did she know you had met me?'

'No, she didn't. The subject of you came up in a general conversation, as someone else mentioned the fact that the ivy had been cleared. I said I'd met you and given you a lift from the station, but I didn't mention about you staying here, as I didn't think you wanted her to know that.'

'Did she make any comment about me and the cottage?' I ask tentatively.

Angela hesitates – then she says, 'She didn't say anything in front of the others, but at the end of the class and when the others were getting ready to leave, she asked me to stay behind, as she wanted to tell me something.'

'And?' – I am beginning to feel anxious.

'Yes... she told me you had not been well for a couple of years and about the tragedy that had caused your illness.'

'Yes... my baby died.' I try to sound matter of fact.

'That must have been *terrible* for you.' She says. 'Did you get much support? I don't expect you want to talk about it to me, but I am a good listener if you feel you would like to.'

'I haven't talked to many people about it since it happened,' I say. 'I did try to talk briefly to my psychiatrist. – I expect Isobel told you I had been in a clinic,' I add, 'but he was always so busy and he said I should open up more to the psychiatric nurses, but they were always so busy too and I never felt I could trust them to know how to cope with my feelings.' After I left the clinic, I did eventually get allotted a really nice and understanding counsellor, on the National Health. She was called Maggie and she was really helpful in explaining my feelings and how to cope. I really felt I could let off steam to her, but our sessions were limited to once a week for six weeks.'

'Was that all the help you had?' asks Angela.

'Well – they were very kind at the clinic, but I think I was rather un-co-operative.' I had plenty of medication, though.'

'Yes, Isobel did mention it briefly, but told me nothing more than the reason for you being there.' She hesitates, and then continues, 'so, just remember, if you ever need to talk, I will be very happy to listen – and this evening if you feel like it?'

I feel that Angela means what she says and she is the first person I have felt a rapport with for a long time. Anyway, the chances that Isobel has conveyed anything to her that is remotely like the real events, is highly unlikely, as she has never seemed to accept the impact that all of it had on me at the time.

'How long have you got?' I say with a wry smile.

'As long as it takes,' she says.

'I do think I am getting over it now.' I say.

'Yes, but that is probably something that few people ever *really* get over.'

'Well, that's not what Isobel thinks. As the whole situation of the pregnancy was a disaster, as far as everyone was concerned. She has always said my baby's death was a blessing in disguise – so I can get on with my life, without a child to tie me down. She certainly wasn't ready for me to fall to pieces for so long.'

Angela noticing my distress, as I tell her this, comes to sit beside me and holds my hand. She gives me a few moments silence and then says, gently, 'Having a child of her own, you'd think she'd understand, wouldn't you?'

'You'd think so, but under all that charm, Isobel is a tough nut.' I say bitterly. 'I cannot imagine what it would be like to be that child of hers, but maybe she is different with her own. I sincerely hope so anyway. Have you seen her daughter, Maisie, at Red House?'

'No, I can't say I have. Some people come with small children, but they are kept well out of the way during the yoga class. I think they run a play group up there, but the children are in another part of the house or in the back garden.'

Angela gets up and stokes the fire and then as she comes to sit down beside me again, she says, 'Do you want to tell me more? Sometimes it is good to talk and sometimes better just to be quiet. I will quite understand if you don't feel comfortable to talk, but I am really interested to know more about you, as I admire how you seem to be coping.'

I am silent for a minute or two and then I say shakily, "Yes, I would like to tell you a bit more if you really don't mind, as it is not often I have had the chance to talk to someone I like – and feel I can trust and you have been so kind and understanding."

Angela sits back in her chair and says 'No of course I don't mind, so do please continue."

Just as I am about to begin, we hear an explosion of fireworks coming from the direction of Red House and we both realise that it was Guy Fawkes night during the week and being a fine evening, it is probably Isobel enjoying herself. I remember she has always loved fireworks.

. . .

Angela and I sit by her fire, with a mug of hot chocolate each and with Bess at our feet. I am feeling a bit nervous about how to begin my story and Angela can see this, so I hesitate and say,' I would like to just tell you things as they come into my head. Some of which I may have told you already, or you may have heard from Isobel. Is that OK?'

'That's fine,' she says. 'just feel free to say what you want – or just stop if you would rather. I think you know me well enough by now, not to need formalities.' She sits back in her armchair and strokes Bess, who snuggles up as close to her as she can without actually being in the chair with her.

As the fire is getting a bit low, Angela suggests I sit on the sofa with my feet up and Bess grumbles at being disturbed, as Angela gets up to readjust the logs on the fire.

Feeling relaxed with my cocoa in my hand, I begin. 'I think I've already told you I was brought up on the island of Morg. I am not sure if I was actually born there.'

'So, who did the island belong to and how did your family come to live there?'

'I believe the island originally belonged to a distant relative, but I am not sure who. Isobel and her two sisters and Isobel's partner, Doctor Peter Wesley, known to us all as Pete, had decided they wanted to live an alternative kind of lifestyle, with very few mod-cons and on the lines of a sort of commune, where whoever was living there would share all the jobs.'

'Yes,' says Angela, 'I had heard that Isobel had previously lived that sort of life in The States. Am I right?'

'I think so. All the ideas seemed to come from her. Isobel was always very much in charge, in spite of being quite a bit younger than her two sisters. She introduced them to what she called a spiritual life and ran courses and retreats for people to come and relax and get away from the rat- race and enjoy the solitude and peace of the island. She taught meditation and yoga and what she called life skills. I expect Isobel has explained this to you.'

'Well, yes – it sounds very much what she is doing now at Red House,' says Angela and then adds, 'And what about Pete? Did he play a part in teaching the courses?'

'No, he kept out of all that and did all sorts of practical jobs, like maintenance of the generator – general handyman really. I am not sure if Isobel and Pete ever got married, but they were certainly "an item" and Isobel always kept her maiden name and is known as Isobel Gray. I was told that Pete had been a GP in England but had found the stress too great.'

'So, how old is Isobel. I find her quite impossible to guess her age.'

'She must be about forty-five now, as I know she was over forty when Maisie was born.'

'She must have been quite young when they first went to the island, as you are nineteen now and only a tiny baby then. Quite a responsibility to be in charge of the place.'

'Well, she was definitely the boss, 'I say firmly.

'How did they manage for money?' asks Angela.

'I was told, they had inherited a lot of money from some rich relatives and were able to restore some ancient cottages and make them just comfortable and warm enough, with no luxury trimmings. They had a steady flow of visitors through the summer months, when the sea was calm enough for boats to cross to the island. Pete had a boat with a motor that he efficiently maintained and I don't actually remember it ever breaking down – thank goodness. The boat was big enough to carry several people and provisions when needed. The weather was very often much too wild and rough to use the boat, but this made the island more attractive to some people, who really wanted to get right away from civilisation.'

'So, what about your father?' asks Angela.

'I have never known him, and know nothing about him except his surname was Kaslo. I gather my parents were married, but he was not on the island with us and no one would ever talk about him. Unfortunately, my mother was not very happy on the island and she drowned while swimming in the sea, when I was a tiny baby, so I don't remember her at all. Isobel, reluctantly, took on the job of bringing me up. No one ever talked about my mother, either, but Aunt May once told me she was a good person and a lovely sister. I gathered Isobel did not like her and sometimes when I annoyed her she would say, with venom, 'Just like your mother.'

I believe there were more people in the group originally, but that was when I was still a small baby and I don't remember them. When I was a child and growing up, Isobel was the undisputed boss and in charge of everything. She had a way of being able to control everyone, either sometimes by charm or sometimes by sheer force of personality. We all did what Isobel said and even when group discussions were attempted, she always managed somehow to get her opinion agreed upon. The running of the Island was very successful and we grew what we could on the sparse thin soil and the rest came over by boat when needed. I remember stores of tins in the cupboards, which went rusty quite quickly in the salty sea air, but the contents were fine. There was a rather unreliable generator for electricity, which was just strong enough to run a fridge, but lighting was candles and oil lamps. Water for washing came from water butts on the cottages, as there was plenty of rain to keep them topped up. Drinking water came over from the mainland by boat, as we couldn't risk poisoning our visitors with water from the butts. We had peat fires for heating in the winter and camping gas stoves for cooking. Oh – and we had composting toilets.

It was really like a permanent camping situation and because I had never known anything else, it seemed quite normal to me. Of course, I grew up knowing how to do all sorts of practical things and became very independent and self-sufficient, as Isobel never gave me any attention except criticism. We all joined in with all the chores and general maintenance, so that is why I am not daunted by taking on Blackstone Cottage. I must say Aunt May and Pete were always very kind to me, which made up to some extent for Isobel's coldness.'

'Were there any other children on the island when you were a child?' asks Angela.

'There weren't any other children there permanently, but several came and went with parents, who stayed sometimes for a few days and sometimes several weeks.'

'Did you ever feel lonely and needing others of your own age?' asks Angela…

'Not really. I loved the sea and the birds; and the wildness of it all but…' and I am about to tell her about Ade, when her phone rings.

'Oh – damn' she says, 'I'd better take this. I won't be long, and she takes her phone out to the kitchen. For a few moments I transport myself back to Morg; the feel of the fresh sea air; the cry of the sea birds; and the wonderful feeling of swimming in the cold, bracing water. Then I feel an ache; a yearning, as I remember Ade swimming with me and the huge waves crashing over us, as we dared each other to swim in rough weather. Sometimes we would cycle over rough, bumpy tracks and Pete would treat our grazed limbs, after many a fall. The quiet times we had also; bird watching and paddling in rock pools; the sharing of books and ideas.

As Angela comes back into the room I realise that I do want to tell her about Ade, as I feel she would understand, so I brace myself.

Angela sits down and says 'I'm so sorry about that and you were saying?'

I take a deep breath and say, in a matter-of-fact way, 'Adrian came to live with us when I was twelve and he was a couple of years older. He was Pete's son and went to boarding school and so was only with us for holidays. He and I became very close friends from the moment we met and spent all our time together on the Island in the school holidays. In those days there was no internet connection with the mainland and no telephone, so all communication with the outside world, apart from a crackling radio, came by letters or messages via a boat which came when the weather was OK. As we became older, Adrian's contact with the mainland gave me such an interest in the outside world and he lent me all sorts of books to read and we had such long interesting discussions. I was determined to get as much education as I could and was tutored in general subjects by Aunt May, who was a qualified English teacher. Adrian, or Ade, as he was known, was very keen on all science subjects and was determined to eventually qualify in medical research' – I am feeling very emotional when talking about this and Angela senses this and asks me if I want to go on or have a break. I tell her I would really like a glass of water, but feel a need to continue, if she is still willing to listen. She says of course she is willing to listen and gets me a drink and stokes up the fire with more logs, so we can sit uninterrupted for a while.

It feels so good for me to be able to pour all this out, so I continue:

'Ade was a wonderful part of my life and the fun we had as teenagers was enormous. We used to swim together, even when the sea was quite rough. We were both very strong swimmers. He used to tease me because all the toes on my left foot are webbed and he said that I was amphibian and that was why I could swim so well. I have always felt completely at home in the water and can hold my breath for ages under water. Sometimes I would frighten him when I did not appear from under the waves for quite a long time. I still think about that wonderful feeling of freedom, with the waves rushing over me and carrying me along. I never felt any fear. Sometimes since then, when things have been so difficult in my life, I have wondered what it would be like just to surrender myself to the sea – like I believe my mother did.'

Angela looks concerned as I say this, but I reassure her that I am not feeling that way at the moment and that I would really like to tell her more, if she is still willing to listen. She assures me that she is really interested, so I continue;

'As I said, Ade and I were very close friends and when I was about fifteen and he was seventeen, we gradually fell in love in a big way. He found it difficult going off to boarding school and leaving me, but we pledged our lives together and both agreed to be 'grown up' about things and continue to study in our different academic ways, so that eventually we could go away and live together. But then the inevitable happened.' I pause a moment – then.

'We hadn't been as 'grown up' and sensible as we should have been and I became pregnant.'

Although I try my hardest not to, I start to cry and Angela comes over and puts her arm round my shoulders. 'That's all right,' she says soothingly, 'just let it all out.' She holds me while I cry great tears of grief, then, as I calm down, asks, 'do you want to continue, or have you had enough?'

I pull myself together, and between sobs, I say, 'No I would like to tell you a bit more, if you can bear with me.'

'That's fine.' she says.

'I discovered I was pregnant a couple of months after Ade had gone back to the mainland. I had been feeling very sick in the mornings and thought it was just because I was missing Ade so much. Aunt May had left for America, so there were only the three of us on the island. Soon I realised what was happening, as I missed a couple of periods and could not deny this to myself anymore. On a dreary Christmas day, when I couldn't face my lunch, Isobel shouted at me "What on earth's the matter with you. You have been like a bear with a sore head ever since Ade left. We've got some visitors coming in a few days to celebrate the New Year and there's loads to be done to get ready, so pull yourself together".

'I'm pregnant,' I announced. Pete stared at me, lost for words. Even Isobel was speechless and she just stalked out of the room, slamming the door after her.

A few days passed when there was general mayhem around me. They were discussing what to do about me, with very little consulting with me. At first Isobel insisted I should have an abortion, but then kept changing her mind – "sanctity of life" etc. Pete just agreed with Isobel in his usual way but was mostly concerned about Ade and the fact that I was underage, only fifteen and a half, and that Ade might be accused of illegal sex with a juvenile. There was a lot of slamming of doors and then whispering in corners, with me being left out of the question.

They were just worried about themselves, if they kept the baby – not if I kept the baby – please note – and how this was going to affect their lives and how would they answer the fact that they should have been responsible in looking after me? One thing they were definite about was that Ade should not know. Soon after going back to the mainland, he had been offered an opportunity to go to Africa to help in a charity. This was considered to be a great experience for him and he had left just before Christmas, without coming back to Morg. I didn't even get a Christmas card.

I just felt so bewildered, sick most of the day, and bereft at the thought of not being able to see or talk to Ade, and just generally in despair. Nobody seemed to be wanting to make any decision, or ask me what I wanted, so I just retired into myself and kept out of the way as much as possible. I heard mutterings every now and again from Pete saying that if an abortion was the answer, they had better get it organised before it was too late, but still I think they were both in shock like me.

Then a strange thing happened. Isobel seemed in a funny mood for a few days. She was very quiet and a bit absent-minded and kept forgetting to do little things, which were in her usual routine. Pete was particularly attentive to her and they kept making comments to each other in quiet places where they could not be overheard. The New Year visitors were cancelled and Isobel went over to the mainland for a couple of days, leaving me on Morg with Pete. Pete was very kind and considerate with me while she was away and I can remember wishing she would not come back.

Then a big shock. On her arrival back home, Isobel announced she was expecting a baby too. We all knew that she and Pete had been hoping for this for a long time and had concluded that this would never happen. So, there was joy all round and she even welcomed my pregnancy as being a very positive thing, saying how wonderful it would be for the two babies to be brought up together. Obviously no more mention of an abortion for me, or even consulting me on the matter. My opinion or feelings were irrelevant.'

I am beginning to feel very unsettled again and am not sure if I can go on. Angela senses this and says, 'Do you feel you need a break now? It must be very difficult for you going through all this and I think you are being very brave.'

'No,' I say, trying to stay strong. 'I just need to tell you one more thing and then I don't think I can continue as it is all too painful.' I feel my voice breaking up and it is difficult to catch my breath.

'OK, Take your time,' says Angela, sounding very concerned and sympathetic.

I take a deep breath and then the words tumble out... 'Ade was killed in a car crash in Africa.'

I burst into tears again and Angela holds me close to her, as I cry and sob in a way that I have not allowed myself to do since this all happened.

'You are going to stay here tonight,' she says, as she takes me upstairs. She puts me to bed in her lovely comfy spare bedroom, and after calming me down and reassuring me that she will take care of me, she stays with me till I eventually stop crying and fall into a deep sleep.

Chapter 6

In the morning I wake suddenly at 9 a.m. and for a moment wonder where I am, as I realise I'm wearing a strange cotton nightdress. Although I remember having had many muddled dreams, I have slept very well. Angela is downstairs when I rush down, having showered and dressed quickly in yesterday's clothes. I feel very embarrassed as I enter the kitchen and start to apologise for the night before. Angela very quickly reassures me that everything is OK and that she felt honoured to have listened to my sad tale and understands how difficult life has been for me.

Angela is at the range cooking a breakfast that smells delicious and I surprise myself at feeling quite hungry. 'I do hope you feel you can talk to me at any time,' she says.'

'Thanks,' I say 'but there is not much more I can tell you, as I don't remember much, anyway. I don't remember the birth, except being told that my baby died soon after and I didn't even see him.' As I see Angela's shocked look, I continue. 'You see, I was ill in hospital for several months, with all sorts of fantasies and hallucinations. The doctors kept trying to reassure me and telling me that I was sick and my imagination had sort of gone into overdrive. I was making all kinds of accusations about Isobel and Pete having stolen my baby, and none of it made sense to anyone, even me. I can see now that I was not at all well. They put me on strong medication and gradually I began to recover and to understand the reality of things that had happened.

As I recovered, I managed to apologise to Isobel for all the trouble and expense I'd caused. She was surprisingly understanding and assured me that the doctors had explained that my behaviour was due to post-natal depression, the hormone disturbance and the grieving process I had been going through. So, Isobel was very keen for me to start a new life away from all the past associations and that is probably one of the reasons why she is not happy for me to have moved into the cottage.'

'Yes, I can see. She probably would not think moving to the cottage was a good idea, with her and Maisie so close. She might be worried that it would stir things up for you again.'

'Yea – I'm sure that's the main reason.'

'What other reasons could she have?' asks Angela.

'Well, she never has liked me. I've never liked her either and used to call her a witch when she punished me for trivial things as a child. I still think of her as a witch. She has such a control over those around her and I don't understand why no one else seems to see how phoney she is. All the love and compassion she preaches is complete shit. Please don't mention any of this to her or anyone else will you.' I say in great agitation.

'No, of course I won't,' says Angela. 'But, I can understand, that if you and she dislike each other so much, perhaps she is right in wishing you were not living so close. Isobel had mentioned to me about your troubled past and about the tragedy of your baby. She did seem to be sympathetic and said she would like to be able to keep an eye on you if you would let her and she wished she had a key to the cottage, just for safety and in case you become ill again.'

'Bullshit', I say loudly and then 'Sorry, she will always appear so sincere – and her yoga and meditation classes are very convincing – and I certainly won't give her a key to my cottage.'

'Well, that says it all,' says Angela, giving me a knowing look,' but I must admit,' she adds – 'in the yoga group, we all find her very helpful and kind – but I do understand your experiences of her are yours alone, and people can be very different to different people, in other circumstances. We can't like or get on with everyone.'

I know I haven't convinced Angela about the real Isobel, but still, it doesn't matter and I know my memories are very muddled and prejudiced, so I don't comment any further, as Angela serves up a delicious breakfast of fried mushrooms and tomatoes on toast and after we finish clearing the breakfast things, Angela asks me whether I would like to stay with her a bit longer.

'It was a very stressful evening for you and obviously stirred up very painful memories. And anyway, Bess and I like your company."

'Oh no – I'm absolutely fine, after your wonderful care and I need to get back to the cottage, as I have loads to do, and I've taken up too much of your time already.'

'Are you sure you will be OK? You were so upset last night and I do hope you'll be all right on your own. I shall be around the rest of the day, apart from walking Bess, so you can phone me.' Then she adds, looking worried,' unfortunately, I have just heard that I need to go to London tomorrow for a couple of days, so you must promise me that you will contact Isobel if there is a real emergency.'

I reassure her, 'I am fine and feeling much better for letting off steam last night. You have been so very helpful and I really feel fighting fit again to face the world'.

As I say this, I don't think this is the moment to mention the difficulty with the phone and having to go into the garden to make calls, especially when it is raining and I need bits of paper to refer to. She has been so helpful and kind and I don't want to impose on her too much, but maybe sometime soon I could ask her to help me contact people like BT and the garage about the car and getting it registered etc. There are so many things I have never had to do in the past and although I am very good at practical things like hedge cutting, cooking and general domestic things, I have a hazy knowledge of how to cope with all the other technical matters that people owning a house and living in 'the real world' have to do.

. . .

As we arrive at the cottage and I get out of the car I notice how dark the cottage looks, with the big oppressive trees towering above it. They are on slightly higher ground than the cottage. Red House, also on higher ground, is just beginning to become more visible through the trees as winter advances. The leaves are starting to drift down, some of them landing on the roof of the cottage, where they sit for a moment and then gently waft away in the wind. The sky is dark and cloudy at the moment; there is a very chilly breeze and Red House seems to look rather menacing, as I get glimpses of it looming through the spaces between the trees, like some large monster waiting to break through.

I brace myself before getting out my key and entering the cottage. Part of me simply cannot believe that the cottage could be haunted, by a black cat, or small child. Aunt May was such a lovely warm-hearted person and would have made the house and surroundings feel loved and cared for. On the other hand, Red House and Isobel do seem to overshadow it and give an unsettling atmosphere, which makes me wonder whether perhaps I should be doubtful about staying here.

Then I decide – no – I am not going to be beaten by my past life and I decide I must get rid of the dull chipped grey paint on the door and paint it a cheerful colour. Although the cottage can be shaded from light for some of the day, in good weather it gets the sun in the early morning and the late afternoon and evening.

I go inside and make myself a nice hot cup of coffee. I get the fire going and try to think what is the next important job to do. I decide I ought to take the fan heater upstairs into the spare bedroom and sort out some of Aunt May' s things, especially some clothes and various dressmaking materials in a cupboard and some drawers. I am wondering whether I might find some more clues about the snail-chewed letter that she had written to me and maybe even find a copy of it somewhere tucked away. I had looked through the papers in her desk the other day and could find no trace of it. This is the only room that I haven't really tackled yet, having felt intrusive on her past life and then I tell myself, no this is ridiculous, as she wanted me to have the cottage and would want me to make it my own, and I'm sure she would not expect me to keep all her stuff.

As I go through the bedroom door, I suddenly stop and gasp. I feel my heart starting to beat faster, because there in front of me is her dressmaker's dummy, which I am positive was naked when I last looked in, and it is wearing a pale blue blouse. I stand for a moment with my eyes closed and my hands clutching my head. I am absolutely sure I didn't put a blouse on the dummy – but can I really be sure? Who else could have done it, and why? I begin to doubt my sanity again and I creep in a little closer and notice only the top button is done up. I don't remember having seen the blouse since being in the cottage, but I do remember it is one that Aunt May used to be fond of and wear quite often. It is pale blue silk and slightly creased, as if it has been hanging close to other clothes in a cupboard for some time. I find myself shaking, but then talk to myself firmly. I tell myself that it is easy to remember things slightly differently, especially as I had only glanced into that room before and had decided to tackle the contents at a later date.

I decide to go downstairs for a bit and try to clear my head, but doubts keep creeping into my mind. Do I believe in ghosts? We were brought up to be more than open-minded about the possibilities and were always being told the importance of a spiritual life and beliefs. We were told about the love of God and how we must always trust him to take care of us, but there was always a feeling of the threat that if we didn't please God we would be punished.

After a few minutes of washing up and clearing away things downstairs, I begin to feel more at ease and start trying to question things logically. The possibilities are (1) I did not notice the blouse in the first place; (2) Someone else has a key to the house and could let themselves in when I was out, but who would do this and to what purpose? Isobel has already told Angela that she hasn't a key and she is the only person I can think of who would want to alarm me in this way; (3) Perhaps the place is haunted and Aunt May is trying to send a message to me. I decide the most likely answer is the first one, but still find I am feeling shaken and uneasy and don't feel like going back into that room just yet.

After a couple of hours of finding it difficult to settle to doing anything useful, I decide to phone Angela and ask her advice. It is cold outside and I am shivering as I tap in her number.

Angela takes a while to answer the phone and when I am just about to ring off, having left a message for her to ring me, she picks up the call. She sounds breathless and apologises for the delay. She sounds harassed and says she had been washing Bess, who doesn't usually like water, but she had decided to chase a rabbit and fallen into a green, muddy pond on a walk. I start to explain myself, then hesitate and offer to phone back later.

'Just give me a few minutes to finish this filthy job and I'll ring you back,' she says, sounding a bit impatient.

I stay out in the garden and wait for her call and after a few minutes she rings back but it is obvious she thinks I am making a fuss about nothing. 'It sounds very unlikely to me that anyone has come into your house and put a blouse on a dummy. Come on Lora – you must have just not noticed it before. Have you checked the rest of the house to see if anything else is different, or is anything missing?'

'No, I can't see anything else suspicious,' I reply.

'Well, I can only suggest that you try and put it out of your mind. Do phone again if you are really worried, but I can't believe there is anything strange going on.'

'No, I'm so sorry to bother you yet again,' I say. 'I am sure you are right and I just didn't notice it before.'

'So, are you all right now?' she asks sounding in rather a hurry.

Yes, yes, I'm absolutely fine,' I reply and we finish the call.

Angela phones me back before I have had time to get back into the house. 'No, you are not all right. I can tell something else is bothering you and I didn't mean to sound impatient.'

So, I confess. 'The trouble is,' I say, 'my phone reception is so bad here, I have to go into the garden to make calls. Sometimes I can pick up ones from you when I am indoors, but they break up so much, I have to go outside to listen... 'I pause a bit and I wonder if she notices my shaky voice. 'you see I have so many things I need to arrange, like the car, and talking to BT about the landline phone, wi-fi etc. I can't look information up online and trying to handle bits of paper when I'm on the phone in the garden is really diffi...'

'Oh you poor love. I am so sorry. I have been completely stupid about all this. Of course you can't manage to do all those things when you can't contact anybody. Look – when I get back from London, if you like, I could spend some time with you, up here sorting out things like BT. We could arrange to have your locks changed as well to give you more peace of mind. I really should have thought of all this before.'

'But why should you have to bother to do all that for me? I feel very guilty when you aren't even my family.' I protest.

'Well, I would like you to think of me as your family. I've got very fond of you since you arrived here and I really would like to help you. Anyway, organising things is what I am good at and really enjoy, so shall we make that a date – Wednesday morning then, half past ten? I'll pick you up – OK?'

'Oh, that's so kind of you,' I reply. 'That would be such a weight off my mind.'

'Remember' she says, 'if you have a real emergency you can dial 999 and this should connect you automatically to the emergency services – or you could even call Isobel.'

After finishing the call, I feel a little more confident and very relieved at the thought of help. However, after a while I begin to feel edgy again and have to talk to myself quite firmly. A couple of days seems a long time to wait and I am realising how much I am starting to rely on Angela's support, having only known her a few days, so I must pull myself together. After all I have chosen to pursue this course of action and I really can't expect to be able to run to someone else for help, when I begin to feel a bit wobbly.

. . .

The days are getting shorter now. It is only 4 p.m., it's beginning to get dark already and I can hear a few spots of rain tapping on the window. It soon starts to rain quite heavily and the wind makes a low droning sound in the chimney. I draw the curtains, put the lights on and open up the vent on the stove to boost up the heat. When the stove is working well, it keeps the small cottage quite warm and cosy and I haven't had any really cold weather yet to test it to extreme. Then I realise I haven't got enough logs in to last the evening and will have to venture out in the rain and wind to get some more from the garage. I grab, my coat and the garage key and rush out, splashing through puddles that are filling up fast. I pick up as many logs as I can carry and hope they will last me till the morning. I splash my way back to the door and find the wind has blown it open and flung a whole lot of dead leaves through the doorway. As I get in I slam the door shut with difficulty and the wind sounds angry at me for having spoilt Its fun. I go into the sitting room with the logs without bothering to pick up the leaves. They can wait there till morning.

I sit down in the comfy armchair by the fire and think about May, who would have sat in this chair many times. It is a well-worn chair, with a slightly droopy seat and the padded arms are showing signs of wear. It gives me comfort to think that Aunt May must have felt at ease and happy in this cottage where she lived for a while. I say 'thank you – Aunt May' and suddenly feel a warm glow, as if she is there with me. But although I know this is partly due to the fire, which is flickering in a quiet, gentle, confident way, I am feeling much more optimistic.

After writing notes about my feelings in my notebook for a while, which Maggie my counsellor had suggested could be very helpful and then browsing through some of Aunt May's books on the shelves and putting aside one or two which I think I would like to read eventually, time seems to have passed quite quickly. I decide it is time to find something to eat. There is not much in the fridge, but I find enough to make scrambled eggs on toast, with extra toast as I'm hungry, and there is also come chocolate cake in a tin. I realise I will have to take the bicycle tomorrow to top up with essential things like fresh veg and milk. After my shopping trip with Angela, we put quite a lot of food in the freezer in the garage and I know there are some lovely tasty ready meals in there, but I am certainly not going to brave the weather now, so eggs and toast are fine…and chocolate cake of course!

Having eaten and enjoyed my supper and snuggled down by the fire with "Wuthering Heights", which I found in the bookshelf, I realise that this is probably not the best sort of book to read in my present state of mind, with the wind howling outside. I am just getting up to replace it with something a bit less spooky, when I suddenly hear a scratching noise coming from somewhere. My heart starts to thump. Perhaps it is a rat, I think. If so, I can cope with that. Wildlife has never been a problem for me and then the scratching becomes louder and seems to be coming from the direction of the kitchen. I haven't got any shoes on, so I creep out and go stealthily into the kitchen. As I get near to the fridge, suddenly there is a loud hiss. Oh my God, is that a snake? I rush back to the door and then the scratching starts again and it is definitely coming from a gap between the fridge and a storage cupboard next to it. I feel very vulnerable without my shoes, so I go and put on Aunt May's wellies which are by the front door and feel safer in these whatever the creature is.

I creep stealthily back again until I can just see into the gap. To my huge surprise two large round green eyes are staring at me. They gradually come towards me and a black creature meows at me. My God – it's a black cat I realise and funnily enough I don't feel frightened. I think it is a relief to realise it is a real, live cat and not a ghost. It must have come in when I was in the garden on the phone earlier, or more likely when I had gone out for the logs and it probably came in out of the rain. What do I do now, I wonder? It has slunk back into its little hidey-hole. I haven't got any food for it and I know you are not meant to give cats milk and anyway, I only have a tiny bit left in the fridge for my breakfast. I remember I had noticed some tins of cat food in the garage, which presumably have been there since Aunt May's cat had gone, so if I go out and get those, and leave the front door open while I get them, the cat might take the opportunity to escape and leave me in peace.

I brave the weather again – the wind has settled down a bit – and I find two rather rusty tins on the garage shelf. When I get back to the house, I find the cat is still there, so with difficulty I open one of the tins, as the ring pull snaps when it is half open. Luckily the contents seem to have been well sealed and there is enough of an opening to scoop the meat into a bowl. I talk quietly to the cat to try and reassure it that I am not an enemy and I leave the bowl on the floor along with a bowl of water nearby. Then I go back to sit by the fire in the sitting room, leaving the door from the kitchen open.

When it is time to go to bed I haven't heard or seen any more movement from the cat and when I go into the kitchen to put my empty things into the sink, I can see the eyes still staring out at me when I peep round, and the food and water are untouched. I bring down Aunt May's cat basket from her work room and I shut the kitchen door firmly before I go up to bed, as I don't want to go to bed thinking of the cat wandering about the house. I just hope it doesn't make a nasty smelly mess behind the cupboard, that would be a real problem. As I lie in my bed, I wonder where it has come from. The only house near is Red House and I am sure Isobel wouldn't keep a cat, as she has never liked cats. I think this must be the one I saw on the lawn and is surely a stray. Tomorrow I can take the bike and go and make enquiries to find out if it has been reported missing.

Chapter 7

I have not slept very well, as have been listening for noises of the cat, shut in the kitchen all night. It is just after seven a.m. with a slightly rosy sunrise, so, after having showered and dressed, I decide to go downstairs and see what the situation is in the kitchen. I open the front door first and see that the ground is very wet after yesterday's wind and rain, with soggy brown leaves that have drifted into piles along the front of the cottage, but it is not very cold. I leave the front door open and go into the kitchen, having shut the doors to the rest of the house.

The cat food bowl is empty and the cat is sitting up on the windowsill waving its black tail and looking down at me with a haughty expression, so, I open the kitchen door into the hall to see if it makes its escape. I then go into the sitting room and shut the door and peer through the window, to see what happens. Sure enough, the cat rushes outside and disappears round the side of the house, in a flurry of leaves, and I feel rather relieved that I don't have the responsibility of finding out anything more about it, but also feel a little disappointed that it has gone. Apart from the empty food bowl, everything in the kitchen looks as I left it and I am very relieved to find that there seems to be no sign or smell of cat mess.

It is Monday and I won't be seeing Angela until Wednesday, so I will have to think of practical things to do, which will not need technology. It will be a good chance, to take the bike to Wasbury and buy a few essentials, so I use up my last bit of milk in some coffee and make some toast, spread with some of Angela's delicious jam that she has given me. I am munching my toast by the window in the sitting room when the cat startles me by jumping up onto the sill outside and looking at me and meowing. It is quite a big cat but looks very lean and I expect it is hungry again and I wonder, if I open the door again and put some more cat food in the bowl, whether it would come into eat.

Sure enough, this is what happens and I keep out of the way not to frighten it. After a while I peep into the kitchen and see the food has gone again, and the cat is curled up in Aunt May's cat basket. As I go quietly into the room, the cat jumps up and comes boldly towards me and rubs itself round my legs, snaking back and forth and purring. It is certainly very thin and it is not at all nervous, and I bend down to stroke it. In fact, it seems extremely friendly and I realise I am going to have to try to find out more about it.

When I go downstairs the cat follows me about as if it is asking for more food. 'I'm sorry', I say. 'You are going to have to wait, as I need to go to the village to buy you some more, and also find out who you belong to.' I make sure the cat is outside the house when I lock up and go and fetch the bike from the garage. It looks a bit puzzled as I cycle off, down the lane. It is not a very cold morning and it is still fine, but I am glad of my coat and a scarf and gloves which I had found in one of Aunt May's drawers. I seem to have the same size feet as her and I have found a cosy pair of short fur-lined boots, which are going to be very useful if the weather gets colder.

The bike has a basket in front of the handlebars and a flat rack at the back. I have brought a couple of shopping bags and some string, and hopefully I can bring back a bit of shopping. It is mostly a gentle slope downwards and the bike is a solid old-fashioned one with no gears, so it will be harder work cycling back home afterwards. I enjoy the feel of the cool wind in my hair (please note – no helmet!) and the smooth feel of freewheeling on tarmac.

There are a few potholes here and there, but nothing like the rough terrain I was used to on Morg.

It only takes me a few minutes to reach Wasbury, passing a few houses scattered along the roadside as I approach the village. I had been here a few days ago and bought my new jeans and top in a little clothes shop, but now I need to get a few essential food provisions and some cat food, just in case the cat comes back to the cottage again. I go to the post office first to see if anyone has a notice in the window about a lost cat. There is nothing among all the little notices, so I go inside where there's an elderly woman behind the glass counter.

Having introduced myself and told her where I am living, I tell her about the cat and ask her if she would have any idea who owns it. For a few moments she says nothing and looks a bit startled.

'Oh, so you're the young girl what's moved in up there then. I was told you were up there now. Bit spooky ain't it?'

'No, it's fine,' I reply, sounding as positive as I can. 'I'm settling in well and sorting things out and It's beginning to feel quite homely. It belonged to my Aunt…'

'Oh yes, I remember her. She was a dear person, Miss May, as we knew her. Kept herself to herself, but was always friendly. So sad the way she went. That sister of hers, up at Red House didn't seem to care about her as she got ill. Sorry – I shouldn't have said any of that. It's none of my business, but you can't help caring, can you?'

I feel a bit embarrassed and don't quite know how to respond, so I just say, 'Well I am not really sure of the circumstances, but anyway Mrs…'

'Oh, I'm Janet Long and if you need any help let me know and I can probably point you in the right direction.'

'Well, I do want to find out about the cat,' I remind her.

'Well, no, I can't recall anyone missing a cat recently. You'd better take it to the vet. There's one in Ford. They can see if it's got a micro…'

'Yes, a microchip,' I say,' but in the meantime, if you can give me the phone number of the vet, then I could find out if a cat has been reported missing.'

Janet seems to have a huge list of numbers on the wall behind her and searches through until she finds the vet. She hands me a bit of paper with the name "Jackson and Hobbs" scribbled on it. I thank her and am not sorry to leave the shop. I don't think I like Janet very much. She seems the gossipy type.

Having bought a few necessities, including some cat food, I load up my basket on the front and tie some bags onto the rack at the back. The journey back to the cottage is hard work and although I haven't a huge amount of shopping, it feels as if I am carrying lumps of lead. Also, my clothing is rather warm for struggling uphill. It was just right for the freewheeling journey down.

As I go, puffing and panting, round a slight bend at the top of the road, just before the cottage, I see a car parked by the side of the road. There is no one sitting in the driver's seat, but I can see a small girl in a child seat in the back. I take another look at the front of the car and am shocked to see it is a number I recognise and I am struck motionless for a moment, as I realise it is Odd-socks's car. What shall I do next? I am standing there like an out- of- breath dumb idiot, when I see a man coming back to the car from the direction of my cottage.

'What do you want?' I hear myself ask rather rudely and I start backing away slightly. Is it Odd-socks? I am not sure. He certainly looks less of a mess than on the train and although he has overalls on stained with paint, he does at least look as if he has washed fairly recently and his hair looks clean and shiny. Yes I'm pretty sure it's him.

'I'm Dan – and I've come to apologise,' he says, while looking at the ground and moving from one foot to the other, 'and please hear me out and don't be scared.' He must be noticing me backing away. 'I realise I must have scared you the other night.'

'Yes, you certainly did' I reply, while trying to sound strong and rather indignant.

'Would you have a minute to let me explain?' he says pleadingly.

'OK' I say, 'Just a minute though, as I've lots to do.'

Just as he is about to start, the child in the back of the car begins to look restless and calls 'Dan – hurry up?', in a whiney impatient voice.

'Yes, Maisie, I won't be long'.

'Is that Isobel's daughter?' I feel very confused. What on earth is she doing in Odd-socks's car I wonder?

'Yes, my sister Emma takes her swimming every week and I'm on the way to the pool in Ford. Anyway, I just want to explain what happened the other night on the train.'...

'And at the station after the train' I interrupt.

'Yes', he says hastily. 'It's been on my mind ever since, as I realise what an absolute moron I must have appeared.'

'Yes a drunk moron,' I say.

'Yes I was worried you'd call the police and I don't know why you didn't, as I certainly shouldn't have been driving'. Then he went on to say with a rush of words, 'You see I don't usually get like that and I don't usually drink and drive, but I'd been to a gig and was trying to drown my sorrows, as my girlfriend had dumped me the day before.' He pauses and I look at him expecting more and he says, 'Yea... I know that's no excuse, but I thought perhaps you might understand.'

'Well, perhaps – maybe', I say, 'but I am very curious to know how you have Maisie with you. You must know Isobel Gray quite well.'

'Yea, I'm a carpenter and I have been doing up her kitchen for the past few weeks. Haven't you seen my car going past?'

I admit that I have seen the odd car going to and from Red House, but haven't noticed his and it would probably have freaked me out if I had.

'You really were quite scary.' I tell him.

'Oh God, I'm so sorry' he says, looking very remorseful and then,'
Anyway, I am so glad I've seen you. I'm Dan and I know you are
Leonora, because Isobel told me you are living down here. I better
get on now. Emma will be waiting at the pool, and as I expect you
have discovered, mobiles don't work up here.' He goes hastily to the
car and as he goes he says, 'I'll drop in my card sometime, in case
there is any work you need done on the cottage.' With a quick wave,
he gets in the car and zooms off down the lane.

So, Odd-socks is really called Dan and he certainly didn't seem
scary today and in fact, he was very OK – not bad looking either –
so I rather hope he will drop in his card, as I am sure I could find
some jobs that need doing! I didn't get a chance to really get a look
at Maisie except she seems very small, but of course she is only
three and a half. I could just glimpse a pale face, surrounded by
straight dark hair, like mine, and I find this interesting, as Isobel
has always had light golden brown, slightly wavy, hair, so the colour
genes for our family must be quite mixed.

Feeling much happier for having seen Odd-s...... sorry, I mean
Dan and finding him not at all scary, I take my shopping indoors
and have almost forgotten all about the cat, I am surprised when it
suddenly comes running round the corner of the house meowing.
It seems very pleased to see me, presumably in the hope of more
food, so having put more food down for it in the kitchen, I go
round to the garden with my phone and dial the vet's number.

A nice-sounding receptionist answers and after having checked
with the vet on duty, she tells me they have no reported black cats
missing at the moment. She suggests I bring it into the surgery
and they can check it for a microchip and give it an all-over
check-up. I tell her it seems very thin and hungry and she says that
cats can stray a very long way and may have been living on prey
that it has caught and that it will almost certainly have worms. I tell
her I don't know what sex it is and say that I will have to wait till
Wednesday to bring it in, as I have no transport and my friend

will probably be able to help then. She makes me a provisional appointment for 3 pm on Wednesday and says to continue feeding, but not too much (and certainly no milk) which I know is bad for cats.

The rest of the day I spend doing odd jobs around the place, with the cat following me around, as if it is making sure I am doing things right. I realise I am enjoying its company and do hope no one is going to claim it, so then I could give it a name. I would have to think of a good name, but also, I need to make sure of its sex first and then I wonder, after Isobel's warning, should I keep it as it is black? There are lots of questions going round in my mind, but I mustn't start thinking too far ahead, as it is probably someone's long lost pet.

. . .

The cat is now asleep in the kitchen, after rather a lot of food and I am raking up some leaves and hacking down some brambles and weeds from in front of the cottage with an old scythe. A robin and a blackbird have been following me, picking up the worms which I have disturbed from under the debris. This is the closest I have been to a robin, apart from on a Christmas card and I presume the other is a blackbird, as it is black. I am just contemplating going into look at Aunt May's bird book, when I hear a car coming up the lane and it turns out to be Dan again, returning Maisie to Red House.

He winds down the window and calls out, 'That's a good job you're doing. The house is looking happier already.'

'So am I', I reply. 'I'm trying to make it look a bit less neglected, and I continue quietly, so Maisie can't hear, 'please don't tell Isobel you've talked to me,'

'Oh,' he says 'why, what's the problem?'

'It's a long story, but we don't get on and she doesn't want me living here, so let's just leave it at that.'

'OK, fair enough,' he says looking puzzled, and still keeping his voice down, 'but I was talking to Emma about you and we were wondering if you would like to come swimming with us sometime, as you are stuck up here on your own?'

'Oh, I love swimming,' I reply. 'I've only swum in the sea – and never been in a swimming pool. Perhaps I'd better not come with you though, as I'm sure Isobel wouldn't allow it.'

Dan looks puzzled again, 'But let's talk about this another time. I must get Maisie back home, as it is a bit late for her tea. See you again.' He smiles and drives off. Maisie gives a little wave and I wave back, hoping she won't tell her mother that Dan and I have been talking.

. . .

It is beginning to get dark and I am still chopping and slashing at brambles when Dan's car appears from Red House direction, having dropped off Maisie. He gets out and comes towards me.

'I felt I had to stop and talk to you,' Dan says, 'Isobel was being so strange, especially when Maisie mentioned seeing a 'lady cutting things' at the cottage. She took me aside into another room, where Maisie couldn't hear and was very mysterious as to why I had to keep Maisie away from you. She wouldn't go into any detail, but just said you had not been well and she didn't want you having much contact with Maisie, as it might upset you. I am sorry… I know this is none of my business. I would really like to know what it's all about – but only if you feel like telling me. Of course, if it's something private between you and her, then – I don't want to interfere.'

'No, I am sick of being treated like an outcast by Isobel, when what happened nearly four years ago is all in the past and I am trying to put certain events behind me now and she doesn't seem to realise that I am not the person I was then.' I see Dan looking uneasy and continue, 'Don't worry, I'm not a murderer, or paedophile, or anything sinister, I just had a breakdown after my baby died.'

Dan starts to say, 'I'm so so...'

'No don't say anything now,' I interrupt, as I notice the feelings of panic creeping up on me. 'I still find it very difficult to talk about and don't usually tell people, especially someone I've only just met.' He looks awkward, so I say, 'would you like to come in and have a cup of tea... or are you needing to get home?'

He hesitates and then says, 'yea, that would be good. I'm in no hurry to get back.'

We go inside and he comments on the cottage and how cosy I have made it. He says he did not know Aunt May, as he has only been working for Isobel for a couple of months on and off, but he has always noticed it as he has driven past and wondered about its history. I tell him about the ghost stories concerning the cottage and how now I have found a black cat, which seems to want to come and live with me and how I am hoping to take it to the vet with Angela to see if we can find out where it has come from. While I am showing him the kitchen, the cat does a big stretch, but doesn't bother to get out of the basket, just curls up again and goes back to sleep.

We chat about general things and I discover that he lives with his twin sister Emma, who is a single mum and has a little boy called Charlie the same age as Maisie and that is how they have come to take the children swimming together. They are living in Wasbury in the house they were born in, which was owned by their mother. Their father left home when they were six and they have never seen him since and their mother died when they were in their late teens, but, he says, at least they are lucky enough to have somewhere to live. Emma has been doing cleaning work in a hotel in Ford and she can take Charlie with her, as the hotel owners are very easy going. Dan did an apprenticeship with a carpentry firm and has been working freelance since then – hence the job at Red House.

'So, what's your story?' he says. I tell him about my life on Morg and my missing father and my mother's death. We realise we are both kind of orphans, but he and Emma have been lucky to have each other, whereas I have had no one really close – until Ade that is.

I tell him very briefly about Ade and the baby. Having off-loaded so much on Angela, I find it much easier to talk about the past. He also, like Angela, seems such an easy person to talk to and he is very sympathetic about my reaction to these events.

'You must have had a terrible time,' he says, 'so I can't understand why Isobel is so hostile.'

'Well, you see, after my baby boy died and I was mourning, both his death and Ade's, I went completely… well… mad really. I was accusing Isobel of taking my baby and I couldn't sleep and I was not eating and threatening to kill myself. I was convinced that Maisie was really my baby, as Isobel had her a few days after my baby boy was born. They couldn't convince me, even though she was the wrong sex and every time I heard her crying I wanted to take her and hold her in my arms. They moved me out to another cottage away from Isobel, but I was getting even more distressed, so Isobel eventually took me to the mainland and I ended up in hospital.'

'Oh God, that must have been terrible for you, so, you think Isobel believes you might try and take Maisie now?'

'Yes, I think she probably does and I suppose it is understandable. It must have been very difficult for her at the time.' Then I continue, 'Apart from all that drama, she and I have never got on. In fact, we really dislike each other.'

Dan is quiet after hearing my story and then says, 'Well, I must admit, I don't really know what to make of Isobel and can't say I feel very at ease with her. She is one of those people full of outward charm – very charismatic, but there is something about her, when you catch her off-guard. When she is with Maisie and others are around, she behaves like the perfect mother, but I have noticed when I have been working on my own in her kitchen and Isobel probably forgets I'm there, and there is no one else in the house, she can seem very cold and impatient with Maisie and occasionally I have heard her shouting at her from somewhere at the top of the house. The other day she came into the kitchen where I was working quite quietly on some tiling and she stopped suddenly in the doorway and said, 'Oh, I forgot you were in here. I was just telling Maisie off, as she was being so difficult.' She then said how she loved babies, but small children were far more of a problem and how she wished Maisie was still a dear little baby who couldn't answer back. Then she had added, 'just joking of course.'

'That sounds typical Isobel,' I say 'and I am so interested to hear that you seem to be able to see another side to her, as most other people seem unable to and it is a relief to me to know I am not the only person who understands that she is not always sweetness and light.'

Just then my phone rings. 'Sorry. Dan. This is a call I am expecting from Angela and I'll have to take this outside.' I say, as I rush to the door into the garden. 'Don't wait, as I may be a while. Thanks so much for your company and listening to my tale of woe and I hope to see you again very soon.' Dan smiles and waves and I smile back, as he leaves the house.

Chapter 8

It is Angela on the phone and she is just checking that I'm OK She tells me she is still planning to come back to Ridge Farm late tomorrow, Tuesday night, and will pick me up on Wednesday morning, so we can tackle the various technical problems. When I tell her about what has been going on, she agrees to take me and the cat to the vet. She asks me how I am reacting to it being a black cat and I say I am just relieved it is real and not a ghost and that it seems very friendly and I am rather hoping that we cannot find its real owner. I tell her I am going to try not to be influenced by one of Isobel's superstitions.

She is also interested to hear about Dan and says how that must be one less thing for me to worry about – providing, that is, he is really a genuine good bloke. I tell her I do think he is and his story makes sense to me and, anyway, Isobel trusts him to look after Maisie. Even so, Angela advises me to be a bit cautious, after his bizarre, drunken behaviour on the train.

. . .

After the hard work I have put in today, with all the chopping and clearing of undergrowth, I am pleased with the way it looks outside my front door. The house seems to have a bit of a smile and it appears lighter, as if it can breathe more easily. I am also pleased to have had a chat with Dan and am feeling very relaxed, although physically tired, as I sit down to have some supper, with the cat beside me eating its own. Maybe things are going to turn out OK I think, as I stroke the cat who has finished eating and is now sitting by my side, purring. I think it would like to have my supper as well as its own.

I am looking forward to visiting the vet with Angela, but a little apprehensive about managing to persuade the cat to get into the carrier/cage which I have brought in from the garage. This must have belonged to Aunt May's cat and still has a soft rug in it, which I am now airing in front of the stove. I have put a few cat treats in the cage, in the hope that the cat will be encouraged to explore it, so by the time we need to leave on Wednesday, it will be used to it. So far, it has just walked up to it and sniffed and looked very suspicious, but maybe if I just leave the carrier around it will get more trusting.

After my supper the cat wants to go outside, so I open the front door and let it out. I realise I am still calling it "It", but I think this is because I am trying to distance myself from it in case we find its real owner.

I am hoping it will want to come back in again before I go to bed, but as the evening goes on, there is no sign of it and eventually, at eleven o'clock I am feeling too tired to stay up anymore and hope that I would hear it meowing to come in, if I leave my bedroom door open. I manage to go to sleep but not very deeply and keep waking and listening. I even go downstairs a couple of times, but there is no sign of the cat. I have to keep reminding myself that it has obviously survived outside for some time previously, but I can't help hoping it is not going to disappear as mysteriously as it arrived. I do manage to fall deeply asleep just before dawn and am woken suddenly at nine o'clock, with someone rapping on the front door.

I grab a coat and rush downstairs to find it is the postman with a parcel of seeds that I had ordered by phone a few days ago and forgotten all about. I thank him and as he drives off I look to see if the cat is around. I call 'puss, puss, puss,' but there is no response.

There is nothing urgent to be done today, but I think it could possibly be a good time to start sorting the spare room, as it is not looking very bright outside… I decide to get dressed and go and have a look for the cat first, before having some breakfast.

A cold wind and slight drizzle greets me as I go out in Aunt May's wellies and I'm glad of a warm coat. As I go round the side of the house and head towards the trees and bushes between Red House and the Cottage, I suddenly stop dead in my tracks. My heart seems to miss a beat and I catch my breath, because up amongst the bushes and trees I see something black hanging from a branch.' Oh my God,' I say out loud. I notice it is a large black plastic bag. I can see something wriggling inside it, and what looks like a leg protruding from the bottom. I go a little closer and can see there is something struggling inside the bag and my immediate thought is that it must be the cat and I realise I must find something quickly to cut the bag open, so I rush indoors to fetch some scissors. Whatever creature it is, it needs to get out, but in my hurry, I slip over as I reach the door. I swear profusely but recover, and covered in mud, I dash to the kitchen to look for the scissors. Of course, they are not where they should be, so I suddenly realise they are upstairs, where I had been using them yesterday.

By the time I get outside again, I see the bottom of the bag is in tatters. What was in it has obviously escaped and the rest of the bag is just swinging ominously in the wind. I scramble through the undergrowth, to get a closer look and see it is a kind of bin liner with handles, which have been knotted together and look as though they have been tied deliberately over a sturdy branch. There is no sign of the cat or whatever other creature could have been in the bag.

It is just out of my reach and I reckon I could get to it by working my way round to the other side where the undergrowth looks clearer. I decide to leave it for the moment, as I feel in dire need of a cup of coffee and am shivering with the shock at the thought of what I could have found. Any animal left in that bag, unable to escape would surely have suffocated over time. I go towards the cottage, feeling very shaken and am still puzzling over what horrible person would hang a live animal in a tree, when the cat appears from somewhere and weaves itself around my legs and starts meowing and looking up at me as if to say 'where's my breakfast'? It looks very dishevelled and wet and is certainly limping slightly, but it looks far less distraught than I feel.

I don't feel like eating my breakfast, but the cat seems hungry enough and only after it has eaten, will it let me rub it with a towel. It seems to enjoy this, until I try to dry its feet and then I notice several of its claws are bent or broken and one foot is bleeding slightly. After a bit of persuasion, it allows me to dab on some antiseptic cream, which I find in the bathroom cupboard, although washing it is not popular and certainly not an option. It then takes itself off and settles down in the wicker basket.

The cat and I decide it is definitely a day for staying indoors and I am still feeling very shaky, so I make sure the stove is burning well, as this keeps the whole cottage warm and dry. I take the cat basket up to the spare room and the cat follows me, looking annoyed at having been disturbed. Where do I start? It will be good to concentrate on something other than the blue blouse on the dummy, so I take it off and hang it up in the cupboard. There are all sorts of clothes hanging there, so I look through in case there is something I could wear myself. Most of them are not my size or my taste, but I know a charity shop would be glad of them, so I bundle some of them up in a box, but I do decide to keep a few items for the time being, including the blue blouse. I go through shelves and drawers and find all sorts of bits and pieces, some of which I put in a bin liner to throw away and some which remind me of Aunt May I haven't the heart to chuck out – and anyway they might come in useful – reels of cotton, bits of fabric, zips, pins and needles and all sorts of things which, I know in my heart of hearts I am unlikely ever to use, but anyway they can stay in the drawers just in case. After all I am not planning to sell the cottage yet – if at all. Of course, the main reason for this exercise is to try to find a copy of "the letter", so I am looking for little hidden compartments or hidey holes in the drawers and shelves. But after a whole morning of careful searching, I find nothing. All the while the cat sleeps on, and as it seems so relaxed, I feel calmer myself and even a little hungry, so I go down and raid the fridge for something to eat for lunch.

I find some salad and bread and make some chunky sandwiches and sit down to eat them by the sitting room window. I am rather hoping that Dan will drive past and I can tell him about the black bag, but I imagine he is probably working up at Red House all day, and anyway, I don't know what time he would finish work, or even if he is working up there today. I am feeling restless after lunch and it still looks cold, damp and dreary outside, so I spend time writing up my notebook for a while. The cat sleeps on and I realise that it will probably want to go out again later, having eaten quite a lot today, but I would certainly like to keep it in until I take it to the vet, just in case something awful happens to it. I am wondering whether there is a litter tray in the garage by any chance. It is a long shot, but I go and have a look. The garage is so full of junk, but sure enough, after a bit of rummaging, I see what looks like a litter tray underneath a pile of pieces of wood and other scraps. I manage to extricate it with difficulty, after nearly bringing a whole lot of junk down on my head.

I seem to remember somewhere noticing a paper sack, which might have had litter in it, and then I find it on the shelf where I had originally found the cat food. The mice had obviously been using some of the litter for nests, as the bag has holes in it, but after finding a plastic bag from indoors, I transfer the remains of the litter into it. It smells very musty and damp, but I hope it will serve its purpose.

After choosing a corner of the kitchen for the litter tray the cat makes an appearance in the kitchen doorway. It looks around and sniffs and wanders over to have a look. It sniffs at it and then looks up at me with a very snooty expression on its face, as if to say, 'You can't expect me to use that.' 'Sorry, mate,' I say. 'No choice,' but I realise I will have to shut it in the kitchen over- night, in case it does decide to choose another part of the house. It is going to be difficult to keep the cat in until tomorrow afternoon.

Later that afternoon, I see Dan's car has stopped outside and he is walking towards the door. Making sure the cat is not around, I let him in. I tell him how I am trying to keep the cat in before going to the vet tomorrow, so I must make sure it does not slip out before he has a chance to say anything, I hurriedly tell him about this morning's event and he can see how uneasy I am feeling.

'I can't be positive it was the cat,' I say, 'but its claws are torn, a foot has been bleeding – and it has been limping.'

'Sounds as if it almost certainly was the cat,' says Dan, 'but anyway whatever animal it was, it would take a very ghoulish, cruel person to do something like that.' He gives me a brief smile and then bends down to stroke the cat. 'You realise it's a "she", don't you?' he questions.

'Well, I was pretty sure, but I am still trying to keep my emotional distance by calling it "it".'

Dan seems to understand the logic of this and continues, 'I just called by to see if everything's OK but it obviously hasn't been. You must be feeling a bit upset. I haven't been up at Red House since I saw you, as Isobel has guests staying, who are arriving today. I've still got a bit more tiling to do in the kitchen, but she said that could wait till tomorrow, so I could spend the afternoon with you if you like?'

'That would be great,' I say, feeling relieved, 'and perhaps you could have a look at the bag in the tree.'

'Yea, I think that would be a good idea, as we should probably tell the police and the bag could be evidence.'

As we go round the house, I look up at the trees and bushes and cannot see the bag anywhere. I am absolutely sure I can remember where it was and am very puzzled to think it could have blown away, as it seemed so firmly fixed. I am worried that Dan is going to doubt my sanity, as this is something I doubt myself. I know it was there.

'Let's go and have a closer look,' says Dan, as we scramble through the undergrowth. We reach the spot and the ground underneath has definitely been trampled on and there are shreds of black plastic lodged in some of the brambles. Dan turns over some of the larger shreds of plastic,' I can't see any signs of blood, but I expect the rain would have washed them off.' As I look closely I can see nothing but rather clean rain-washed bits of bag and then we look at the branch where it had hung and see that the bark and various buds have been rubbed off.

'Well,' says Dan, quietly and looking thoughtful. 'I think this is very strange. What a gross thing to do. Obviously, whoever did it has tried to remove the evidence, so I suggest you keep these bits of plastic, although there is not much to show on them.'

We go back to the house, discussing what sort of person could have the mind to behave like that. Of course, I have my own idea who could have done it, but don't think I know Dan well enough yet to suggest it. Anyway, it is difficult to believe even Isobel would be so cruel and to what purpose? Surely there are other ways to freak me out than to hang a cat in a tree. It does make me wonder, though, whether I should keep the cat, if there is someone out there who is prepared to do such a thing. When we get back inside the house, I tell Dan about my doubts about keeping the cat and Dan suggests we wait until the vet has seen her and checked if there is a microchip, as it is most likely that some person is missing a lovely cat like that and would be very grateful to get it back.

'I think the first thing we must do, is phone the police,' suggests Dan. I don't expect they will be able, or have time, to do anything, as we haven't much evidence, but at least they ought to know someone is out there doing horrible things. Would you like me to phone them?'

'No thanks, I'll do it myself. I'll go out into the garden and phone them now.'

Luckily the rain has stopped and I eventually manage to get through to the local police, who are very sympathetic and say they will try to get to see me within the next few days, but there is not much they can do without evidence and the fact I did not see anyone suspicious around the place. They advise me to keep the cat indoors meanwhile, so I tell them my plans for the cat and that I expect the real owners will probably be found when I take it to the vet tomorrow.

Dan and I then sit by the fire, drinking tea and eating toast and jam, as I forgot to get any biscuits. Dan looks very thoughtful and I watch him as he sits there quietly looking at the flames as they flicker gently in the fire. I think I am going to like him; I've decided. He seems very kind and not a bit "blokeish" and he's good looking in a way that doesn't seem as though he thinks he is. In fact, he is a bit scruffy – but looks just right for the sort of job he does. A comfortable sort of person, with no pretensions.

After a while he looks up and says, 'Are you OK staying here on your own? It must be a bit weird? I mean not knowing who is out there doing odd things. Emma has been quite concerned for you and she seems to find it difficult to understand how you can want to stay up here on your own. You see, we have always lived in the village, with other people all around us, so she says you are very brave to take on this lonely place, with its haunted reputation.'

I had told him about the blouse mystery previously, but I don't want to sound too wimpish, so I say. 'Well, I am used to a lonely sort of life and I don't believe Aunt May would have wanted me to live here if she had felt any unpleasant atmosphere. Yes, there are rumours of ghosts, but I am prepared to stick it out for a while at least. As for the black bag, we will have to wait and see what the police have to suggest. That certainly wasn't done by any ghost.'

'No' says Dan thoughtfully,' but I do remember there were some lads in the village a while ago, who were chasing cats with air guns and catapults. The police found who was responsible and there hasn't been any trouble recently. They all got away with a warning but could be up to old tricks. I could phone Emma and stay here the night, if you like… I mean in the spare room or down here,' he adds hastily.

'No, I'll be fine,' I say. 'If I'm careful to keep the cat in, at least I will know that it is safe.'

Then I think to myself, I am determined not to be frightened. I am very suspicious of Isobel, as I have an instinct about her devious mind. I believe she might do anything she could think of to frighten me away, but would she really do me or a cat any serious physical harm? I am more and more curious to find out what is going on in her mind at the moment. Could she be so cruel to mistreat a cat like that? She must surely realise that I am not a threat to her or Maisie in any way nowadays. She has seen doctors' reports saying I am very well and back to normal now. But am I? I ask myself, as somewhere inside me there are memories which only occasionally come briefly to the surface and I know I am still unsure of the reality of events from the past.

Dan gives me his mobile number and his land line, and I thank him for his support He says he will call in again tomorrow on his way up to Red House. Then I remind him that Angela has promised to help me tomorrow so he wishes me good luck with the cat enquiries and looks forward to hearing the outcome.

Chapter 9

I am awake now and it is 7.30 a.m. I have had a disturbed night, with the cat meowing and restless. I go downstairs into the kitchen where I'm met by a rather stroppy looking cat, with litter littering the floor. I can see, however, that it has used a corner of the tray for the right purpose, so at least I don't think I will have anything nasty to clear up. I sweep up the floor and then get our breakfasts. The night's disturbance doesn't seem to have affected the creature's appetite and I decide I must try to keep it in the kitchen till the afternoon. I get the carrier box into the kitchen and put some cat treats in it, to encourage it to get used to it and then I go out, shutting the door firmly behind me. I then spend some time writing a list of things that I need Angela to help me with, realising it was only eleven days ago that I came down on the train and so much has happened in those few days.

It seems as if it might be quite a nice day, weatherwise and the sun is beginning to creep out from under some light clouds, casting a red glow on the walls of Red House, which is now more visible from the Cottage, as most of the leaves have fallen. Apart from hiding the view of Red House, the leaves looked so much prettier with their variety of autumn colours when they were on the trees, than they now appear as a sludgy mess on the ground.

10.30 comes around quite quickly and as I answer Angela's phone call in the garden, she checks all is OK and tells me she will be right over. We are soon on our way up to Ridge Farm, having made sure the cat is all right in the kitchen with the door firmly closed, no windows open anywhere and the front door locked. We exchange news of what we have both been doing and I tell Angela about the black bag and also that I have told the police. She sounds shocked and suggests we should inform Isobel in case she has a cat.

'I'm pretty sure she won't have a cat. I know she didn't like cats and wouldn't allow them on the island, because of the bird life. We had many visiting birdwatchers over the years.'

'Ah, but she has a little dog and if there are local hooligans about, one needs to be careful.'

'Well, perhaps we should,' I say, but I don't tell Angela that I am suspicious that it might be Isobel's doing, as I am sure she would be horrified at the idea and certainly wouldn't believe me.

Bess seems pleased to see me as we arrive at the door and Angela is very firm with her to make sure she does not jump up. She is such a big dog I am sure she would knock me over with sheer exuberance. We are soon settled round the kitchen table enjoying coffee and biscuits as we look through my list of things to do and Angela reads them out.

'Organise telephone and internet connection; car reg. tax, insurance; set up direct debits for council tax, electricity etc.' The list goes on, with all sorts of other minor things to think about.

Angela takes charge of the list and is obviously very efficient and experienced at dealing with all these practicalities. She makes sure I am aware of everything she is doing and explains when I don't understand.

After a very frustrating morning with long waits on phone calls and eventually getting through to the essential people, we have managed to make all the contacts that we need. The phone and internet connection has been promised, but it will take a week or two, in spite of Angela's protests. Papers concerning the car should be in the post soon. Angela is a bit horrified at my vagueness about organising my money and reminds me that my "tidy sum" from

Aunt May won't last for ever, if I don't plan and budget. At the moment I am living off dividends from shares that came from Aunt May's investments and Angela is very pleased to see that I have inherited a very good stockbroker, who she suggests I contact soon to make myself known.

My head is spinning with facts and figures, while we grab a sandwich, as we realise it is getting late and we have to pick up the cat to get it to the vet by three o'clock and I am hoping it won't be too difficult to get the cat into the box.

As we open the front door I suddenly realise that the kitchen door is open.

'Quick', I shout. 'We must shut the front door. How on earth has this happened? I am positive we shut the kitchen door, aren't you?'

'Yes, definitely,' says Angela, 'and let's hope the cat is still in the house. Someone must have been in.' I rush upstairs and look in the spare room, but it is not there, so I go into my bedroom and there to my huge relief I find the cat curled up on my bed, looking very smug and comfortable. I shout down to Angela with the good news and we decide to bring up the carrying box, with some extra tasty cat treats. We eventually manage to capture it and shut the cage door firmly. The cat looks very indignant, but not frightened and we think it must have been quite used to being carried about like this. I have a quick look round in all the rooms and cannot find anything disturbed anywhere and all the windows are firmly closed. I have had my bag, purse and various private papers with me all morning, and I know I have had all my valuables with me, so we decide to have a more thorough search when we get back from the vet.

We arrive at the vet just in time and are ushered into the waiting room, where we sit with three other people, two with dogs on leads and one man with a very noisy meowing cat in a cage. We have a few minutes' wait and have time to think about the mystery kitchen door.

'I have known a dog who could jump up and open a door if it had a flat lever handle, but your kitchen door is a round knob and it seems to close very firmly,' says Angela.

'I know, the cat couldn't possibly have opened it,' I say, 'and this makes more sense of the blue blouse mystery. Someone must have a key.'

'Ah, we forgot to contact the locksmith,' says Angela. 'We must do that immediately we get back. In fact, we could call in there on the way home. Have you got bolts on the inside of the doors?' she asks.

'Yes, I have good, strong bolts,' I reply.

'Good, so at least no one can come in when you are inside.'

I sit waiting anxiously and am not sure what I am most worried about, finding out about the cat, or my cottage being invaded. At last, we are called into the surgery and we are greeted by a tall thin man in white overalls, who towers over us both like a man on stilts. He shakes hands with us both and he seems aware of the reason for our visit.

'I'm John Jackson and am in partnership in this practice with my wife Meryl Hobbs. I'm on duty this afternoon, so tell me a bit more about the situation with the cat. I gather you want to check for a microchip, to try to find out where it has come from, so let's get the cat out and have a look.'

He seems very calm and gentle and the cat responds calmly as well. 'Well, she's a she,' he confirms and runs his hands over her back and she conveniently rolls over to expose her stomach. 'Ah, and she has been spayed, so no risk of kittens. She is very thin so I would think she has worms, which is very likely if she has been on the run and been eating wild prey.' He notices her torn claws and I tell him what has been going on and he confirms this looks the sort of damage that would have occurred in that situation.

'She is certainly very friendly and trusting,' he says, 'so it seems she has been loved and cared for in the past, and if someone put her in that bag, she was probably quite easy to catch.' He goes off to fetch the scanner, which is a small hand-held object, and holds it over the cat. 'Yes, it's responding,' he says 'I'll just go off into the office and check our records.'

Angela and I are left sitting with the cat. We are feeling apprehensive, but the cat seems quite unfazed and relaxes on my lap, as if it/she (must call her she) is confident that all will be well. After what seems like an hour, but is actually fifteen minutes, John Jackson reappears. 'Well, I have some interesting but puzzling news,' he says, 'let's go into the office and I'll explain.' The cat goes back into the box quite willingly and the vet comments on how amenable she is.

The office is crammed with papers but the vet manages to find some chairs and he sits down opposite us.

'The microchip is traced back to an Animal Rescue Centre, called "Animals R us", a silly name I know,' he says with a smile. 'It is about ten miles from Ford, the opposite direction from which you have come and the woman in charge is Maureen O'Flynn, who is a great character and excellent with the work she does. She told me that the cat was a great favourite with the staff at the centre and that she had belonged to a family with a young child who was found to be allergic to cats and they, very reluctantly, had to find it a new home.'

The vet, John then goes on to tell us the following story.

We gather that the cat had been named "Catastrophe" but called "Catty" by the family, as she was always getting into trouble as a kitten and certainly seemed to have used up a fair share of her nine lives.

She had been in the Centre for three months and, although a lovely nature, they had not managed to rehome her. A lot of people think black cats are unlucky, but the occasional person thinks the opposite and a few weeks ago a woman came in particularly looking for a black cat. She said she had phoned the day before to discover that they had a black cat waiting for a home.

Maureen happened to be out that morning and her young assistant, Karen, was holding the fort. As the woman seemed extremely nice and she and Catty appeared to like each other, Karen took down all the woman's details and told her that she would have to check with Maureen, but felt sure she would be able to take the cat away when all the paper-work had been checked. Unfortunately, the woman persuaded Karen that she had to take the cat now, as she was on her way back home a couple of hundred miles further north and could not get back later. She was about to leave without the cat, but looking very disappointed and even Catty looked sad, apparently. Karen had tried to contact Maureen without success and the woman spun a long story about how her daughter was so upset as their black cat had just died. As it seemed an exceptional situation, Karen agreed for her to take Catty there and then. The woman produced a very new and smart cat carrier, into which Catty was installed. The woman left a couple of hundred pounds as a donation to the centre and then, armed with food and instructions and Catty in the box, she drove off in a large four-by-four.

As I listen to the story, so many questions are going through my head and I wonder if "the woman" could have been Isobel, but don't mention this to Angela, as I still don't believe she could imagine Isobel behaving in such an underhand way.

'Don't they usually let people arrive and take a cat away,' I ask?

'No, it is policy for them to check credentials first and for dogs, particularly, they visit a home first to check suitability. They don't always do home visits for cats, as these are usually easier to settle into a new home, but fitting a dog to a new home can be much more problematic. Maureen trusted Karen's judgement on this occasion and now confesses she didn't follow it up.'

'So, what do we do now?' I ask.

'Well Maureen is trying at this moment to contact the woman involved, to find out what happened, so meanwhile, if you wait in the waiting room, I will try and find out what luck she has had.'

We sit and wait while the vet sees another patient and the girl on reception, says she will let him and us know when Maureen phones back. So, we look at magazines, but don't really take any of it in.

'I wonder whether the woman will want the cat back?' I say to Angela.

'Surely she would have contacted the Centre and tried to track it down if it had gone missing? If it was my cat, I would have tried every possible way to find it. Very odd,' says Angela.

After half an hour the vet comes out to see us and invites us into the surgery again.

'Look, this is very strange. Maureen has tried all the contacts the woman gave Karen and has found they are all false.'

'So, wrong name and address?' I exclaim.

'Yes all completely false. The address does not exist anywhere, not even postcode, and neither the land line nor the mobile numbers exist.'

Definitely Isobel, I think to myself, but still don't mention this. 'Can Karen remember what the woman looked like?' I ask.

'Just that she was smartly dressed in a country sort of way – not a town suit, and she thinks she had light brown, fairly long hair, clipped or tied back. She really can't remember. She was fairly posh (Karen's description) and quite tall. Poor Karen is very upset about it all and says she will try to remember more details when she has more time to think about it.'

'So, what will happen to Catty now?' I ask.

'Well, I suggest I keep her in overnight and check her over thoroughly and give her a blood test and antibiotics for her torn claws and Maureen says she will have had inoculations when she was with them, so she shouldn't need those yet.' He pauses and then says, 'Do you think you will want to give her a home yourselves?'

'I will really have to give this some thought,' I say and Angela agrees. 'It is certainly an odd situation.'

We decide we need time to think it all through and we agree to leave Catty with the Vet overnight.

. . .

We call at the locksmith on the way back and Angela has to be very firm and persuasive to get him to agree to come tomorrow morning, as he says he is very busy. Reluctantly he agrees to be with me at about ten thirty.

I am feeling particularly apprehensive as we arrive at the cottage, as it is quite dark and the air is very cold and still, as if it's waiting for something to happen. I can't believe all the weird events of the past few days and would never have guessed that my visit to Blackstone Cottage would have been so eventful. Angela senses my tension and asks whether I would like to go back to Ridge Farm with her for the night, but I feel reluctant to keep relying on her so much and pretend that I am fine and as long as we check the house carefully now, I feel sure I will be safe and will certainly bolt the doors.

We go in and look through every room carefully and I really can't see that anything has been disturbed. We double check the window locks again and when I tell Angela that I am satisfied that it is OK, she insists that I must phone her if I am at all worried. I remind her about the phone difficulty, but she says it seems to ring all right at her house and even if it breaks up too much for a conversation, she would come right over, immediately. Then, she hurriedly leaves, as she needs to get back for Bess, who has been shut in all afternoon.

As Angela is about to get into her car, Dan arrives. 'Hi', he says, as he gets out of his car and I introduce him to Angela.

'Hello Dan,' says Angela. 'It is good to meet you. I have seen you up at Red House and really admire the work you've done on Isobel's kitchen. She is thrilled with it and shows it off to everyone who visits.'

'Glad you like it,' replies Dan, looking a little embarrassed, as if he is not used to compliments. 'I've been up there today finishing off a bit of tiling and I believe she has one or two more small jobs she wants me to do, which I can fit in before my next job starts. I've just come in now to see how Lora is.'

'I'm fine,' I say. 'Angela's been helping me take the cat, which we have discovered is called Catty, to the vet and we have been trying to find out information about her.' Then I tell him the saga of the day. Dan looks concerned and asks if there is anything he can do tomorrow to help. He has to get back home now, as they have Maisie staying for the night and he needs to help Emma. I thank him, and Angela reassures him that she is not busy tomorrow and has promised to help me continue to sort out the Catty business.

After they have both gone I make sure the fire is burning well with a good store of logs and settle down for the evening. I admit to myself that I do feel very tense and also, I miss Catty, who has become even more of a personality now I know her name. I think I have already decided I want to keep her – but should I? Would it be fair to put Catty in danger, as I am worried Isobel might be involved in the situation? I realise I can't actually accuse her of anything, but, just in case, I think I will try to scare her off doing anything more by writing her a note to tell her what has happened and let her know the police have been informed and are taking the incident very seriously. I will say also, that as there seem to be hooligans about prepared to do such a terrible, unspeakable thing to an animal, she should be very careful to keep an eye on her little dog, as it looks as if they would stop at nothing.

After supper with a note written, ready to put through Isobel's door tomorrow, I try to settle down with my notebook and eventually go up to bed about eleven, making doubly sure again, that everything is locked up. As I settle down in my bed, I am unaware that l will not be delivering that note to Isobel, due to the unexpected events of tomorrow.

Chapter 10

I sleep quite well, but conscious of dreaming a lot. I am just dreaming about a strange person trying to tell me something urgently, when I am woken by a loud buzzing. I sit up feeling very confused and can feel my heart thumping, but then realise the noise is coming from Aunt May's alarm clock. I have never used this alarm before, so it is not a noise with which I am familiar and I don't even know how to turn it off. I reach out and feel a knob on the top which I press and it switches it off. I lie back in bed again after noticing that it is 6.30am and wonder what set it off and think I must have knocked it yesterday in some way. I am just beginning to get back to sleep when it rings again and I press the knob on the top and it stops. When it does this for a third time I put on the bedside light, pick up the clock, and examine it and, at the back, I find there is another On/Off switch which is quite stiff and I switch it to the Off position.

I lie back in bed again and switch the light off, but find it impossible to get back to sleep. As far as I am aware, I didn't touch the clock yesterday and anyway it would take more than an accidental knock to move the stiff switch at the back. My bed is fairly near the window and I can just reach the curtain to pull it aside to see what the weather is like. It looks rather misty and it is still quite dark. I sit on the edge of the bed, wondering whether it is worth getting up yet, when I suddenly notice that there seems to be someone sitting on the bench in the garden. It is very indistinct in the gloomy half-light and I cannot be sure what it is, but it looks very like a person in a cloak or blanket. By now my heart is thumping again and I shut the curtain quickly and switch on the light. 'Oh my God, I must have imagined it', I say out loud. It can't be Aunt May's ghost. I wonder what I should do next? I get back into bed and pull the duvet right over me, while I feel myself shaking. I will wait till it is lighter outside and have another look. Was it my imagination or, the ghost of Aunt May? Either way, I feel freaked out. I stay under the covers, peeping out every now and again to look at the time, which drags by interminably. When it is after seven, I decide to be brave and have another look, and gingerly pull back the curtain. Whatever it is, is still there, so I am slightly relieved to know it was not my imagination and it certainly looks too real to be a ghost. I decide to get dressed quickly and go and look through the sitting room window in case I can get a better view from downstairs. If it is a real person, such as a tramp, I can phone the police, as my phone would work for an emergency.

It is still very murky outside and I find there is less of a view from downstairs. I am too scared to go outside while it is still so dark, so I go upstairs to the bedroom again and get into bed with my clothes on and pull the covers over me, shivering from anxiety and decide I will have more courage as it gets lighter outside. Every now and again I peep through the curtain, without looking down at the bench, but just to see how light it is getting. After about an hour, I take another look and yes, the object is still there, but looking much less like a person. It looks more like a roll of carpet or thick material which has been placed upright on the bench and bent to resemble a seated figure and it certainly can't have got there on its own. Someone must have put it there – so who? Yes, you've guessed what I am thinking – Isobel again. Well, she has certainly scared me this time.

I go downstairs, taking my mobile phone, and put on my coat and wellies and decide I will take a photo, in case it mysteriously disappears like the black bag. I creep round the side of the house, feeling a little less scared and as I get closer, I can see it is not a real person and my fear begins to turn to anger. It is one of Aunt May's long spare curtains, which was amongst the items I had folded carefully and had planned to take to a charity shop, as it was much too long for the cottage windows. It has been rolled lengthways, placed upright on the seat, and draped over, with the bottom edge touching the ground. The top has some dark material, folded over to look like a hood and is bent forwards to resemble a hunched-up figure. It is anchored with a few bits of string here and there. I take a couple of photos and then I tentatively approach it, expecting it to suddenly transform into some ghostly figure, but it does not move. I am rooted to the ground and then suddenly am compelled to find out what it is and I rush to grab at the top of the hood and pull it back.

I jump back in horror and feel I could scream, but nothing comes out of my mouth. There is an image of a black skull, painted on a white beach ball, and tied into the fabric. It stares at me ominously, with its hollow eyes and cavernous mouth and I eventually manage to scream and run back into the cottage, slamming the door behind me and bolting it with shaky hands.

Now safely inside the cottage and having taken several deep breaths, a feeling of fury is overcoming my fear. How can anybody be so unkind and devious? I go to the sitting room window and look out to the right. There is a stillness all around me; The trees are towering over me; there is no wind and, in the dim, sunless early morning, I can see the side of Red House through the trees. I cannot see any light from the windows which seem to stare blindly back at me. I now feel a grim determination. Isobel, or whoever has done this, is not going to get away with it and I must take a photo of the skull.

With anger still burning inside me, I gather the courage to go outside again with my phone, to take a photo of the skull.

This is difficult to do without upsetting the figure, but with a bit of care and in spite of my shaky hands, I manage to get a couple of pictures. I rush back to the cottage and don't check the images till I am safely inside again. They are not very clear, but clear enough for my needs.

Surely now everyone is going to have to take this seriously. The fact is that someone has obviously been into the cottage, when we were out yesterday. The alarm was set to wake me up and frighten me and this monstrosity was enough to scare anyone. I go into the spare bedroom and find the pile of charity shop things and, as expected, the other curtain to match, is still neatly folded amongst other stuff. I wouldn't have noticed yesterday, when Angela and I were checking the house, that one of the curtains was missing, as there was a big pile, all looking undisturbed.

It is now 8 a.m. and I decide to ring the police immediately and dial 999. When I am put through to the appropriate section, I hurriedly tell them what has happened and how frightened I am. They tell me someone will be with me as soon as possible and advise me to contact a friend to come and keep me company, as I am on my own. I phone Angela who says she will be with me within an hour and sounds very worried for me. She turns up as promised and I take her straight round to show her the effigy and, she is horrified when I lift up the hood and show her the face. She rushes towards me and gives me a big hug as I feel lost for words.

'Oh, you poor love,' she says. It is so wonderful to have her here to comfort me. She holds me for a while till I've stopped shaking.

'I can't tell you how glad I am to see you,' I say. 'This is certainly getting beyond a joke.'

'Well, this is certainly no joke,' she says, taking me firmly by the hand and guiding me indoors. 'I have brought some croissants and jam, which we can eat together in front of your stove.' She puts the croissants in the oven to warm them up, and then tackles the stove, which has gone out overnight but she gets it started with kindling and logs. I don't feel hungry, but the croissants and a hot cup of coffee, soon revive me a little, as we sit by the fire, with rugs over our knees. While the fire gradually gets going, we discuss what has happened.

'You see, someone must have come into the house while we were out, as that curtain was one I had put in the pile with its pair to take to Ford sometime.'

'I agree,' she says, 'and remember, we both checked the cat was in the kitchen with the door firmly shut, before we went out in the morning. I am so glad you have phoned the police, because they certainly need to see what's going on.' After a short pause, she continues, 'and I don't think you are going to like what I am going to say.' She looks a bit embarrassed. 'I felt I had to tell Isobel about what's going on.' She pauses and looks at me to await my reaction and I am just about to protest, when she says, 'Look, she is your Aunt, and it is not really my business to be looking out for you... although I assure you I am not complaining and will continue to be here for you as long as you wish, but you must see that it would be very strange of me not to keep her in the picture, don't you think? And, anyway, with something so peculiar going on right next door to her, she deserves to know about it as well.'

'Yea, I suppose so,' I say reluctantly. I am still not going to tell her of my suspicions about Isobel.

'Anyway,' she continues, 'I couldn't get her on the land-line and tried her mobile. She didn't reply immediately, but phoned me back because she said she was in her car and had had to find somewhere to pull over to answer the phone. It seems she has been staying with her friend Rosemary somewhere near Bracknell for the night and was on her way back to pick up Maisie from Emma and Dan's house, where she had left her for the night. I couldn't tell her the details on the phone, but she said she would call into see you immediately she gets back.'

My heart sinks. So, it couldn't have been Isobel's doing. I don't say anything as my head is spinning. I long for the police to arrive, so someone else can try to make sense of it all. I sit trying to puzzle it out, while Angela stokes the fire and makes us more coffee. Did Isobel really go to see Rosemary? I don't know Rosemary and am trying to think of a way of finding out. Perhaps Dan and Emma know who she is and maybe even have a land-line number for her, as they have been looking after Maisie overnight. Surely she would want her child's carers to have details of exactly where she was going to be.

. . .

It is now half past nine and a police car draws up outside the cottage, closely followed by Isobel in her large car. I watch them arrive from the sitting room window and notice that Maisie is not with Isobel. Angela and I both go to the door to let them in and Isobel comes in first and greets me effusively, with a very good impression of being caring, and comes to give me a hug, which I pretend to respond to. There are two police people and they introduce themselves, but I don't take in what they are saying. There is a woman and a man and I rather gather that the woman is in charge. We all sit down in what spaces we can find and once again I go through the details of the past few days and they seem to be a bit disappointed that the plastic bag disappeared so quickly, as there is now no evidence regarding the cat's misfortune. Then we all go out to see the effigy.

The police look rather shocked at the skull face. 'Have you touched anything? The policewoman asks me and I admit that I had moved the cloth to see the face. 'Did you touch the actual head?' 'No, I didn't. I just pulled up the hood and was too horrified to touch it.' She seemed pleased. 'So, your fingerprints shouldn't be on it then.'

She and the policeman wander around looking at things and taking notes and then take some photos of the effigy. They then fetch a plastic bag from their car and, wearing gloves, they put the ball/head in the bag and seal it up, put the rest of the object in another bag and put them both straight in the car.

'We might find some prints, if we're lucky,' she says, 'meanwhile I'd like to ask you all a few more questions.' We go inside and I go through the events of this morning, just stating the facts in a monotone voice. After a few more questions from the police, the policewoman suggests we could all have a cup of tea.

I volunteer to make the tea and go into the kitchen. While I am waiting for the kettle to boil I hear mumbling voices from the sitting room, so I sneak out to listen outside the door and can just hear Isobel's voice, sounding so sincere and upset.

'Poor girl,' I hear her say. 'She has had such a rough time and I am so worried that all these events will have a bad effect on her.' She then lowers her voice, so that I can only get a gist of what she is saying, but I can just hear she is relating my story about the baby and how ill I have been. I can hear the odd reply of 'Oh dear… and I'm so sorry.' She tells them how she has been so against the idea of me living up here on my own.

There are more mumblings of sympathy and I move closer with my ear to door, which is slightly open, and then I hear;

'You see, when her baby died, she accused me of taking it and became obsessed with the idea. She believed that my baby was really hers and that I had stolen it from her. One day she even took my baby, who was born a few days after hers had died, and I found her breastfeeding her. It was really distressing and I had to physically take Maisie from her. Even when we got her professional help on the mainland and she ended up in hospital, she was still accusing me of having taken her baby.'

I am beginning to shake and feel so close to tears, but feel I need to know how the police are responding.

'So why did her baby die and what happened to it?' asks the policewoman, and I hear Isobel reply;

'Oh, he was born completely deformed – quite grotesque in fact. Pete, my partner, and I were deeply shocked. Of course, we did not let her see him, as it was all we could do to accept the shock of it ourselves. He died a few hours after the birth and we had to take the body to the mainland to register the death and have him cremated. Lora was too ill to go to the cremation and we sprinkled his ashes on the island, as that is what she wanted.'

'So, have you any idea who you think would be doing something like this then?' the policeman asks this time.

Isobel hesitates, then says, 'Well… I know this sounds terrible to say… But I think she could be doing it all herself. After all, who could have got into the house and done all the things she is claiming. I haven't got a key and I don't know anyone else who would have one. All keys were put in charge of a local solicitor and even when I cleared up a bit after May had died, someone from the Solicitors came with me and let me in. In fact, we cleared out the fridge, switched off electrics etc. together.'

By now I am feeling paralysed and mortified with embarrassment. Of course, it is true… all true – the story about my baby and my behaviour. But I am positive I did not do any of these recent events. Or did I? Could I still be insane, without realising it?

I creep back to the kitchen and slump on a kitchen chair and can still vaguely hear voices continuing their conversation in the sitting room. After a while Angela appears in the kitchen, wondering how I have been getting on making the tea. She finds me sitting with my head in my hands and I'm crying quietly.

She puts an arm round my shoulder and says, 'You've had a terrible shock today, and what with the cat drama as well. Come on, we'll tell them you've had enough for now.

'I heard what Isobel said' I tell her, while trying to hide my smeary face. 'Do you think I could have done all these strange things? Am I still ill?'

Without hesitating she replies, 'No, I don't think you are still ill – but of course we have to find out what has been going on and why. We both know we shut the kitchen door yesterday morning and yet the cat got into the rest of the house. Also, we carefully locked up the house before going out, both times. I told the police all of this and they were aware of the cat in the bag incident, which they said they were looking into.'

'I think you've had enough for the moment', she says and goes back in to see the others and tells them that I am very upset and suffering from shock and it would be better for them to leave me for now and give me time to recover. I can hear them all agreeing and Angela offers to stay with me, much to Isobel's relief, who says she has to get back home, as she is expecting Dan to bring Maisie back.

Just as they are all about to get in their cars, the locksmith arrives and I can see him from the kitchen window, talking to the policewoman. They both look in earnest conversation. Then the police drive off and the locksmith comes to the door and Angela lets him in. He is a short, dumpy, bald man, with rather large hands, which look as though they would not be able to do a fiddly job, like dealing with locks, but he soon sets about taking out the old ones and putting in some shiny new ones. They look quite sturdy and after he has fitted both the back and front doors, he turns to us and says;

'There – no one's going to get in here, unless you let them in. I've given you two sets, so keep them all very safe. They will fit both the back and front doors'. He then explains that each door has two locks and there is a key for each lock, which I have to manually turn. In other words, they are not the type where the door can slam shut and lock me out accidentally.

'This is the same system as I have had already', I say. 'Yes, but', he replies. 'Only one of yours was working and it is much safer for you to have two, especially as you are fairly isolated here and I gather you have been having a bit of trouble.'

'I certainly have', I reply.

'Well, you should always lock your doors, even if you are just going round the garden. There are lots of opportunists around.

And – don't have a secret hiding place in the garden for your keys, as burglars always seem to be able to find these.' He continues, 'I have also put a chain on your front door. Never leave the chain on, in case there is a fire, or someone needs to rescue you for some reason. It is only there for you to put on if a stranger comes to the door and then you can just open the door a crack and they cannot force their way in.'

I listen to all these words of warning, which are making me feel even more nervous. I then thank him and pay him what seems like a huge sum of money, before he hurries off down the lane to go to his next unfortunate customer.

'He's quite right,' says Angela. 'We are all much too casual about security. It has certainly made me think a bit more carefully, especially as I sometimes leave the door unlocked when I take Bess out for a short run.'

We then start discussing our plans for Catty and I say I would like to visit the Animal Centre, to ask Maureen O'Flynn if she thinks it would be a good idea for me to keep Catty. I am having doubts myself, as I am concerned that whoever is doing these strange things, may try to harm her again. Angela thinks that would be a good idea and she says she is quite happy to take me over there this morning.

After contacting Maureen, we are just putting our coats on and getting ready to try out the new locks, when Dan's car comes down from the direction of Red House, where he must have dropped off Maisie. I had noticed the car going up while the locksmith was here. He slows down and I wonder if he is going to stop, as he obviously sees Angela's car. He does stop and gets out of the car and comes over.

'I'm so sorry to hear you have had more trouble,' he says. 'I've heard all about it from Isobel. She sounds quite worried for herself as well as you. She left Maisie and Whisky, the dog, with us last night, as she went to spend the night with a friend in Bracknell. When she had

Angela's phone call this morning, she was wondering what she would find back at Red House this morning, but everything seems fine.'

'Oh good,' says Angela – 'but we must get off now and try and sort out the Catty situation, as Lora is not sure whether she should keep her, bearing in mind what has been happening.'

'OK I'm off to the suppliers now to get some bits for another job for Isobel. I will be at Red House for most of the day and could drop in on my way back this evening if you would like, Lora?'

'Yes, that would be good,' I say. And am relieved to know I have at least two people looking out for me.

Chapter 11

Angela and I drive off to visit the vet and are anxious to know how Catty has been overnight. I am still feeling very shocked and rather numb, after all that's gone on this morning, but Angela is very calming and tells me she is sure we will find out soon who is behind all the odd events. I am pretty sure she is not suspicious of Isobel at all, and I also don't think she would believe that I would do any of it.

As if reading my thoughts, she says, 'There must be someone who still has a key and has had access to the cottage – but why would they want to do all these strange things?' I am silent while she continues, 'And at least we have had the locks changed, which should stop any more unwanted guests, and don't forget, if you are feeling you need to get away or have company, you can always stay with me for a bit, until the police come up with an answer.'

'Thanks, Angela, you're amazing, but what about Geoff? Is he coming down this weekend and surely he won't want me there?'

'I have kept him informed of everything that's going on and he suggested it himself that you might like to stay with us for a while.'

I feel so overwhelmed by this kindness and can't quite stop the tears, as I thank her profusely, and at the nearest safe place, she stops the car and puts her arm round my shoulder and waits till I have calmed down, before driving on.

. . .

John, the vet, shows us into the room which Catty is sharing with four other cats, all in their separate cages. She seems very pleased to see us and we are told that she has been fine and they can't find any problems with her health, apart from being rather thin. This is understandable if she has been on the run for a while, so they have given her worm and flea treatment and results of blood tests should be back in a day or two.

'I don't know whether I should keep her,' I say to John. 'There have been more odd things going on at home and I am a bit worried for her safety.' I tell him briefly about the police coming, but not all the details.

'Well, if you are going to see Maureen at the Centre, you could discuss it with her. Catty is a lovely little animal and Maureen is very experienced and may have something to suggest.' He helps us put Catty into our travelling cage and having paid rather a large bill, we set off for the Animal Centre.

We are welcomed by a chorus of barking dogs, most of which are in large runs. Maureen soon appears and introduces herself. I am bad at judging ages, but I would think she is about forty. She is quite short and plump and wearing dungarees, with a rather dirty green fleece jacket. She has a pleasant face, and short, curly dark hair.

'Yes, I remember Catty well. She was with us for quite a while for some reason. It is just luck sometimes and the right person can take a long time to turn up. Karen was very upset when she heard what had happened to Catty. It is her day off today, so I am sorry she is not here to see her, as she was very fond of Catty.'

'Can Karen remember anything more about what the mystery woman looked like?' I ask.

'No, nothing more than I've told you already. She said she felt a bit flustered by her and she can't think why. It sounds as if she was rather pushy and obviously very persuasive and seemed in a hurry. I don't know if John Jackson the vet told you, but she gave Karen her name as Mrs P. Brown and a completely fictitious address and phone number. Why do you ask? Do you think you might know her, after all Catty has turned up at your home, which could indicate she lives somewhere near you?'

I am still not going to say I am suspicious of Isobel, so I say, 'No, I am thinking the same as you. If Catty turned up near me, then it does seem likely that the woman is actually local and it is still very odd.' I pause for a bit, then I hesitantly say, 'I'm not sure if I ought to keep her after her experience with the black bag. The police are meant to be looking into the situation, but we have had another incident since then and they are even more involved now.' I briefly tell her about the latest happening.

'In my experience, once the police are involved, this seems to frighten off any hooligans or such like. If you want to keep Catty and I have a feeling that you do, I think it would be worth the risk,' she says. 'If you can try to keep her indoors at night, I think she should be safe. She enjoys her food doesn't she?' I agree with this and Maureen continues. 'Well, feed her at a regular time in the evening and then make sure she stays in. It is difficult to keep a cat safe all the time. Not like a dog that you can keep in a well-fenced garden, cats like to lead an independent life and she could just as easily come to harm in another home. So many cats get killed on roads.'

I am still not feeling sure about this and Maureen senses this. 'So, you want to keep her, but are still not sure about her safety?'

'Well, yes,' I reply, looking and feeling uncertain.

'How about if we keep her here for a week or two, or until you feel things have been resolved at your home. We would certainly not let her go to anybody else, unless you decide you don't want her.'

'I would feel happier if you could keep her for a while, but I really would like to have her eventually, as I have become very fond of her, but she would be one more thing to worry about at the moment.'

'Good, and I think that would be the best idea – and anyway, I am sure Karen will be pleased to see her and we'll take good care of her.'

· · ·

We reluctantly leave Catty with Maureen and make our way back home and I have mixed feelings of relief and sadness, but Angela reassures me that I have done the right thing. I am feeling apprehensive about going back to the cottage and am wondering to myself if I can cope with the uncertainty of what is going on. Is Isobel winning? Could Isobel have been responsible for this latest event? How could she be if she was at Bracknell? Do the Police think it's me – mad me? I am hoping Dan will come in this evening and I can find out more details about Isobel's movements last night. What time did she drop Maisie off and did she really go to stay with her friend?

We buy some pasties and biscuits to eat at the cottage and Angela stops off at Ridge Farm to pick up Bess, as she doesn't want to leave her alone at home too long. She decides she can give Bess a walk this afternoon from the cottage and says she is sure Bess would like to explore a new area. It is about one thirty when we get back to the cottage and we are just sitting down to eat our pasties when the police car arrives. Bess goes to the window and barks as if she owns the place.

'I had better put her in the car for now,' says Angela, as we open the door to the same policewoman, but this time she is on her own. Angela takes Bess to her car and the policewoman smiles at me in a more friendly way than this morning.

'I'm Chris,' she says and I just need to have another chat and see if we can begin to make sense of what has been happening here.'

I show her into the sitting room and ask her if it is OK for Angela to be here as well.

'Yes, that's fine,' she says as Angela comes back inside. 'We met this morning, Mrs West, and I understand you have been a good friend to Lora since she moved in here very recently.'

'Yes, she's been wonderfully kind to me and I can't thank her enough.' I say.

'Well, she's been good company for me as well,' says Angela and she explains how she works in London part-time and it can be a little lonely down here during the week, especially when her husband is away abroad on business.

'So, we'd better get down to business,' says Chris. 'I haven't got a lot of time now, so let's get started. Firstly, I need to tell you that there were no fingerprints on the white ball-head. We didn't expect to find any, as most people doing something like that would be very careful not to leave evidence as obvious as that, but sometimes you get an idiot who doesn't think of the obvious.'

Chris then goes through all the questions again. Perhaps she is trying to catch me out, if I say something different from before. She writes careful notes and checks every detail of where I was and when.

'So, have you any idea how anyone could have got into your cottage, as it seems no one else is meant to have had a key?'

'I have no idea,' I reply. 'It is a mystery to me, but Angela and I checked all doors and windows before we went out, so someone must have had access.' I look at Angela as I say this and she agrees. 'I know Isobel – um Mrs Gray – at Red House, next door, thinks I am doing it myself. I overheard the conversation this morning. She is my Aunt and I know she is still worried about my health and I don't think she can trust me yet. I feel very hurt that she could believe I would invent something like this.'

I feel the tears coming and take a hold of myself, while Chris continues her notes, then she looks up and says, 'Well, I am going up to see Mrs Gray when I have finished here. Do you know whether she has any staff at her house? Anyone who could have had a key originally and not returned it?'

'I'm sorry, I don't know what her staff situation is,' and I look at Angela who says,

'I know she has a number of part time staff indoors when she is particularly busy with guests, and she has a head gardener, Jock Jones, and I believe several younger lads working with him part time. Jock Jones is elderly and well known in the village. Lived there all his life. He comes and helps me occasionally with pruning, and the sort of jobs that I am no expert at. Apart from that, I know she has someone from the village to help with cleaning regularly a couple of times a week and if there are visitors staying, I believe she has more help then, but I am sorry I don't know more than that.' Then Angela looks thoughtful and says, 'Oh – there is Dan, who has been doing some kitchen carpentry for her, but we are told that he and his sister Emma looked after Isobel's daughter, Maisie at their house in Wasbury last night. I am sorry, but I don't know his surname. Do you Lora?'

'No, I'm sorry I don't,' I reply and realise I have never asked him.

Chris then decides she has asked enough questions for now and says she will go up to see Isobel.

'There doesn't seem much more that we can do at the moment, so I suggest you let us know if you see or hear anything more suspicious and now you've had the locks changed you should feel much more secure.' With that remark, Chris puts her notebook away and I show her to the door and watch her drive off up to Red House.

Angela then says she will take Bess for a run. 'There are a few footpaths round here and I have my local map in the car, so I will look around me as I go and see if I can see anything suspicious, such as gaps in hedges or trampled grass.' She sets off through my garden and goes through a dilapidated gate at the end of my hedge into the field beyond. While she is gone, I have time to gather my thoughts and suddenly think. The name Mrs P. Brown seems to nudge at my brain and then I realise. Isobel's middle name is Penelope. She has always hated it, as people used to tease her when she was a child and call her "Penny-lope" and she never liked to acknowledge the name to any of us. Then there is another thing I notice. She gave her name as Mrs Brown. This would seem an odd coincidence, as her surname is Gray.

Angela comes back after about half an hour and says how Bess has enjoyed galloping about the fields. There are no cattle or sheep in the fields at the moment, so she could have a good free run and she tells me there is a footpath from my garden gate which goes down to the Church in Wasbury and says that local people probably know this, so someone could have easily come up from the village to access my garden. It seems the footpath also branches up to Red House through the trees, although it does look very overgrown with brambles. I am still reluctant to tell Angela of my suspicions, but hope that Dan will come this evening, as I think he is more likely to believe me. I want to ask Angela if Isobel could have possibly known that I would have been out most of the day with her yesterday, but she would think it odd of me to ask this.

Instead, I say, 'I do hope you are not missing out on your yoga class because of me.'

'No, I don't go every week and as long as I tell Isobel whether I am coming or not, she is OK with that. She has a class every Wednesday, but as I've just said, I don't go every week.'

'Oh, dear, so you could have gone yesterday if you had not been taking me out. I am so sorry. I don't want to disrupt your life. You are being so kind. Did Isobel mind that you had to cancel because you were taking me out?' I realise I am fishing here and Angela goes on.

'No, she knows I've taken you under my wing and she seems quite pleased.'

'Did you tell her about Catty and how we were taking her to the vet?'

'Yes, I had already told her about the black bag and warned her to look out for her little dog, Whisky, and I gather the police had been in touch to warn her as well.'

This tells me that Isobel knows we were out most of the day.

It is beginning to get dark, now, so after a cup of tea and finishing off our pasties, Angela persuades Bess to leave the warm fire by saying 'supper', to which Bess responds immediately and goes impatiently towards the door. Angela asks me if I am going to be

OK on my own again and repeats her invitation for me to go with her to Ridge Farm. I say I feel fine with my extra new locks and also I think Dan might call in on his way home from Red House.

. . .

At half past five, Dan appears at the door. He is looking a bit tired and has a few small wood chips in his hair.

'Phew, what a day,' he says wearily. 'One of those days when nothing goes according to plan. A cupboard I am making for Isobel, was not quite how she wanted it and it took a lot of sawing, adjusting and joining together, before it was just right. She was apologetic, but it means I am behind with another job.' He sighs, 'Oh well it is all work and so far she is paying me regularly, so I shouldn't complain. Anyway, I am very interested to know what has been going on here?'

'It is difficult to know where to begin and I am not sure how much you know already?'

'Isobel told me what she knows and Chris the policewoman has been up at Red House talking to her. I couldn't hear what they were saying, as they went into another room. Chris then came in and questioned me, about my whereabouts over last night. I told her that Emma and I had Maisie and the dog for the night and that we had both been in all the time. As Chris was leaving, she said to Isobel and me that we should just look out for any strange goings on and that they were still making enquiries. There had been some lads from Ford, who had been causing a few problems with burglaries in the Wasbury area, connected to getting money for drugs, but, as they didn't seem to have stolen anything valuable from the cottage, it seemed unlikely to be connected to them.'

I realise that we have been talking in the hallway and suggest we go into the sitting room by the fire.

'Are you in a hurry to get home?' I ask. 'I can offer you a glass of Aunt May's sherry, if you like. There's an unopened bottle in the cupboard and I don't think it would have gone off, would you?'

'I've no idea,' he says, laughing. 'I must admit I've never drunk sherry. Beer's more my thing.'

'I've never tried sherry either,' I admit. 'Shall we open it and see what it's like?

We open the bottle and smell it and it has a very sweet, but alcoholic smell so I get a couple of small glasses which are on the shelf in the cupboard. They look rather dusty, but after a quick wash, we pour the sherry into them. It tastes all right and we both giggle as we sit by the fire like a couple of oldies.

'Emma is expecting me at about seven, as she will have cooked something for us both after Charlie's in bed,' he says. How would you like to come down and have something with us? I can go into the garden and give her a call if you like.'

I hesitate, then say,' That would be great, if you don't think she would mind.'

'No, she's very easy going and we could drop off at the shop if there is anything extra she needs.'

That is soon arranged and we sit down again to finish our sherry. We are not sure whether we should have another glass, as we don't know how old the bottle is, but it does taste fine.

We sit in silence for a moment and then I say, 'I want you to be really honest now and tell me what you think about all that's been going on. I mean, do you think I am making it all up and that I have engineered it all? I know Isobel has been telling the police all about my background and she sounds very convincing, as I could hear what she was saying here this morning. I was listening outside the door, when I was meant to be getting tea for everybody and I was very upset and beginning to doubt myself.'

'Well as you know, I am familiar with the cat bag,' He says, but I would like to hear from you what happened overnight last night. I don't think for a minute that you have been doing this yourself. So, tell me now exactly how you found this strange object on the seat.'

Once again, I go through all the details that I can remember, and exactly what I have told the others. Then I look at Dan to see his reaction.

'So, it seems, someone got into the house when you were out with Angela, dealing with Catty. It is certainly possible that someone has still got a key from after May's death. I know Isobel says they were all given in to the solicitor, but how do we know there wasn't another spare?'

'So, you don't think I'm bonkers then? You haven't known me long, and I can assure you there was a time when I was far from normal in my behaviour.'

'No, I realise I haven't known you very long, but I think you're fine. I don't know why I do, but I just do. And, anyway I feel far more sure of your sanity than Isobel's. I have said to you before, that I think her very strange indeed and the more I see of her at her home, when I catch her off guard – I can't really explain what it is about her, but she is… weird.' He pauses, looking thoughtful and then says, 'In fact, I wouldn't be surprised if it is Isobel doing all this – or someone she knows. It seems pretty obvious to me that she doesn't want you here. She is always going on to me about the unsuitability of the cottage, but she doesn't make it sound as if it is really your welfare she is interested in. She could easily have kept a key to the cottage without anyone else knowing she had still got one.'

I give a huge sigh of relief. 'Oh, I can't tell you how relieved I am to hear you say that, because I have been thinking this all along and haven't dared say it to anyone, as I am sure they would all think I am out of my mind – but how could she have done anything last night, if she was in Bracknell. What time did she leave Maisie with you?'

'She dropped Maisie and Whisky off at about five-thirty and said she was going straight off to Bracknell, but we don't know if she did go straight there.'

'Do we know that she did actually go there?' I ask. 'Did she leave you a contact for Rosemary?'

'Yes, she gave me a landline number and her own mobile, which I already know. She rang me from Rosemary's at about eight thirty, I think, saying she'd had a terrible journey and just remembered that she had promised to contact somebody about an electrical job and hadn't got their number. I said I'd have to look it out for her and would ring her back. She said her mobile was playing up and to ring back on the landline, which I did and Rosemary answered the phone.'

'That proves she was there then,' I say, and I think to myself maybe getting Dan to phone on the landline would show him she was actually there.

'I wonder if she would have had time to put the effigy on the seat before going off to Bracknell. How long would it take to get to Bracknell do you think?' I ask.

'Oh, I should think it could take a couple of hours in bad traffic. It could be heavy traffic that time of day.'

'You and Angela were both with me here just as it was getting dark, so I doubt she would have had time to do it then, so she could have come back before going to Bracknell.'

'Yes, it is only a few minutes from my place and if she had it all prepared, it wouldn't take her long to carry it down on foot. Did you hear a car going past?'

I admit I heard nothing and it all begins to sound even more preposterous, the more we talk about it. I stoke up the stove before we leave, so that the cottage is not too cold for when I get back, and we set off down to Wasbury, having thoroughly checked all locks everywhere and left some lights on to look as if I am there.

Chapter 12

Dan drives us down to his house and although it is dark now, I can see that it is a narrow, three-floor, red brick, terraced house, almost in the centre of Wasbury. It has a small front garden with a little squeaky metal gate and a few shrubs and pots, which are empty of growth at this time of year. Dan opens the front door and calls out to Emma to say we've arrived, and takes me through to the kitchen at the back of the house, where Emma is cooking spaghetti, which smells delicious.

I like Emma immediately. She is very friendly and, although she doesn't really look like Dan, there is a resemblance which is difficult to define, and I can understand that they are twins. Emma has straight, short blonde hair, with darker roots, which indicates she colours it and that it would naturally be darker, more like Dan's, which is a sort of light brown. She is quite a bit shorter than me, but I am quite tall and she is shorter than Dan, who is about the same as me. She is wearing jeans and a large loose knit, cream sweater and on her feet are a pair of fluffy slippers.

'I am so pleased to meet you at last,' she says, as she stirs a pan of mince. 'Dan's told me all about the odd goings on at Blackstone Cottage. You must be feeling really spooked by it all.'

'It is a bit scary, I must admit, but thanks to my friend Angela and Dan here, I am being well supported.'

'Yes, I gather Isobel is your Aunt and that you don't get on?'

'No, it is a difficult situation, because she really doesn't want anything to do with me, but that's a long story.'

'Dan's told me a bit about your story and it sounds as if you've had a pretty rough time. Anyway, let's hope things will get better and that you will start to enjoy Wasbury and the area. It really is a lovely place to live round here, with plenty of friendly locals and we can introduce you to our friends, who I am sure will welcome you.'

'That's really kind,' I say, 'and can I do anything to help here now?'

'Yes, you can stir this mixture, so that it doesn't burn. Dan will lay the table, won't you Dan, while I go and check on Charlie?'

Dan gets a mixture of knives and forks and an odd array of plates. 'Sorry, we don't have sets of anything here,' he says.

'I only have sets of things, because Aunt May left everything so neat. I expect I will break a few plates soon, though.'

Emma comes down again fairly quickly. 'Wow, he's gone to sleep very quickly tonight,' she says. 'He's had quite a busy day and went to a birthday party. I thought he would be overexcited, which usually happens, but no, he's sound asleep, so I can have supper in peace for once. I've put the baby monitor on.'

We sit down to eat big piles of spaghetti, with a salad.

'The salad's an attempt to be healthy,' says Dan. 'I can't say I like it, but Emma is more sensible about what we eat than I am.'

'I like salad,' I say, 'as we couldn't get much on Morg, so it is quite a treat for me.'

After the spaghetti, Emma produces some chocolate ice cream and we take it and sit by a small fire in the front room. I am told they have two bedrooms upstairs and a bath and shower room on the top floor. It is about the same size as Blackstone Cottage, but a different layout and they have a small garden at the back. After supper, Dan goes up to have a shower and Emma and I have a relaxed chat by the fire. I tell her about my life on Morg (but not the sad end to it all) and she tells me about her work at the hotel and how she hopes to progress to something more interesting than clearing up bedrooms after some of the disgusting guests.

'You'd never believe how some of them leave their rooms,' she says.

'Oh yes, I know what you mean. Some of the visitors to Morg were pretty disgusting and it was always the unexpected ones,' I reply.

Dan comes down looking very spruce, in clean jeans and a t-shirt with the logo "Arcade Fire" blazoned across the top. He tells me that this is a band he went to see at a gig recently. In fact, the one he had been to when we first "met" on the train.

'Talking about that,' says Dan. 'You wondered why I was staring at you – well, I think Emma will agree with me – you and Maisie are so alike – not just to look at, but kind of facial expressions sometimes.'

I freeze for a moment, as feelings come flooding back, then I pull myself together and say, 'Well, I am her Aunt.'

'Yes,' says Emma, 'but Dan didn't know this at the time on the train, did you Dan?'

'No, I didn't and if I hadn't been so drunk, I wouldn't have embarrassed you so much.'

'I agree with Dan. You and Maisie are so alike and genetics have a funny way of sort of... moving about in families. I mean, I look like our mother, but Dan doesn't look like anyone in our family.'

'Thanks,' says Dan. 'So, you think I'm an alien?'

'No, of course not,' Emma says laughing. You obviously get your genes from someone in the family and Charlie looks very like you and you are his uncle.'

We talk a bit more about the magic of genetics and I learn a bit more about their background. They are twenty-five and Emma studied English at Exeter University, but has not found a job that really interests her yet and she is hoping that a career in the hotel business would suit her. Charlie was a result of a "careless affair" (her description), while she was in her last year at uni. and she managed to do her finals just before giving birth. She says Dan was a huge help to her at this time, as the guy involved didn't want to know.

'How did you manage financially?' I ask, realising how much I have been helped through all my time of illness, by Isobel and Pete, and now dear Aunt May.

'Dan's helped me enormously. I don't know how I could have managed without him and, of course, we are both really lucky to have this house. Now I am earning a bit and I have managed, with difficulty, to get some maintenance from Greg, the absent father.'

I am just feeling curious to know a bit more about Dan, when Emma says, 'Dan's followed in the family tradition and with a surname like Woodman, what else could he do?'

'I am glad to know your surname at last. Somebody asked me today what is was and I felt rather stupid not knowing the answer.'

'Yes, I'm the third generation of carpenters that we know of and maybe there were more before us. I will have to do some research one day. Our Dad made the furniture in this house,' and he points to a beautifully made, plain, pine table near the fire. 'He had a serious drink problem and various things were unfinished and then he left home and we don't know what happened to him. Our Mum was a schoolteacher, so luckily she had a good job and we went to school with her – which had its good and bad points.'

'So how did you both cope later on then, when your Mum…' I am about to say passed away, when Emma says, 'It was terrible, but we had each other and we do have some lovely relatives, specially Aunt Jane, our mother's sister, so we weren't neglected.'

We chat on for a while and then I suddenly look at my watch and realise it is nearly eleven thirty and although I don't have any reason to get up early tomorrow, as I am a "lady of leisure", Emma and Dan are both leading useful lives and I apologise for keeping them up.

'Don't worry,' says Emma, while I quickly help them to wash up. 'We are terrible about getting early nights and it has been lovely having you here and getting to know you. You must come again soon.'

'I would love to,' I say 'and you must come to see my cottage and have a meal with me – bring Charlie, of course – maybe at a weekend?'

Dan is finding his car keys, which he has left upstairs in his work jacket pocket and while we wait, Emma says, 'How about coming swimming with us tomorrow? Isobel has asked Dan to look after Maisie in the afternoon. Friday is not our usual swimming day, but I am free tomorrow afternoon and said I would take her.'

'I would love that', I say, 'but I am sure Isobel would not like it.'

'Does she have to know?'

'Well, won't Maisie tell her?'

'Perhaps we could tell a white lie,' says Emma with a smile. 'If Maisie mentions it to Isobel, we could say we met you there – purely coincidental of course – what do you think?'

I look doubtful, but Dan comes in the door and says, 'Brilliant Idea. To hell with Isobel. You are entitled to enjoy a swim.'

When we are in the car on the way back to the cottage, I say 'That's all very well, but Maisie will know you have given me a lift. Perhaps it would be a good idea if I can ask Angela to take me to the pool as I think she goes food shopping in Ford on a Friday and I could do with stocking up myself. I needn't tell her I've arranged to meet you and Emma.'

'OK, if you think that would be better.'

'Yes, I think it would and we don't want Isobel to stop Maisie from going swimming if she thinks I am going with you.'

'Fair enough,' he says as we reach the cottage. 'I'll see you safely in and locked and bolted.'

I find my new keys and my hands are a bit shaky, as I fumble with the lock. 'I'll come in with you and we'll search the house for magic intruders,' he says, and I laugh nervously as we go inside. Dan insists on going right through the house and jokingly looking in cupboards on the way. 'Yes, all clear for a quiet night,' he says and although I logically know there will be nothing strange to find, I am glad he took the trouble to give me peace of mind.

'Thank you so much for the evening,' I say. 'I have really enjoyed it and I do hope we can arrange some swimming tomorrow.' We exchange a quick hug and I agree to phone him in the morning, after I have contacted Angela.

. . .

It is Friday morning and having had a rather restless night, with some disturbing dreams, I wake to a cold, frosty morning with a hazy sun. It is eight o'clock and I think it is a bit early to phone Angela and it will be cold outside, so I make some porridge and eat it with milk and honey. The cottage feels very still and quiet and I stoke up the fire, wishing I had central heating. It has been a warm November up till now and, although there's not much wind, the air is cold with a feel of real winter advancing. It doesn't feel very much like weather for swimming, even in an indoor pool, so I am quite relieved when, phoning Angela from the cold garden, she says she is going shopping this morning and needs to be back by twelve, as she is picking up Geoff from the station at two and wants to cook him something for lunch, as he is always hungry after a train journey.

'He doesn't like eating snacks on the train,' she says, 'so I know he will welcome something hot on a cold day like this, but you are welcome to come shopping with me if you don't mind a bit of a rush.'

'That would be great,' I say, 'as I am getting a bit short of essentials.'

Angela agrees to pick me up at about nine thirty and so, still shivering in the garden, I phone Dan and tell him I won't be able to swim today. He says he will drop into see me after he has dropped Maisie back home after swimming and I tell him I am disappointed about the swim, but also a bit relieved at not having to deceive Isobel. I have about half an hour to kill before Angela arrives, so put on my coat and go and collect some logs from the store in the garage. I still have quite a lot left, but realise I will need to order some more as they won't last long if the weather is getting colder.

I get as far as the garage when I hear a child, presumably Maisie, shouting and screaming somewhere outside Red House.

'Isbel, Isbel, open the door,' she screams. Then I hear thumping, as if she is knocking on the door. More screaming, then, 'Isbel I'm cold – can't reach.' Then there is silence and I am about to go up there to see what's going on, when suddenly this little figure comes running down the lane, sobbing. She is just about to run straight past my house, so I run out and catch her by the arm and say, 'Maisie, what's the matter. Come here you're freezing cold.' I pick her up and can feel how cold she is. She is wearing thin pyjamas and a short cotton cardigan and a pair of flip flops on her feet. As I glance at her feet, I feel a huge shock of recognition at what I'm seeing. I try to gather my thoughts and bring myself back to this present moment. I look down again. Yes, she has my feet. Not literally, but all four of the small toes on her left foot are webbed just like mine. After a few seconds I pull myself together and realise I have to concentrate on the job in hand.

'She struggles in my arms and looks frightened and then, between sobs, she says, 'Put me down. Isbel very cross. I want Dan and Emma.'

'It's OK Maisie. You can see Dan and Emma another time. You can't run that far in this cold weather, but I'll have to take you back to Isobel for now. She will wonder where you are.'

'Isbel so cross. I don't want to go back now,' she sobs and struggles again.

'I'm sorry Maisie, but I will have to take you back now. Isobel will be worried about you. I'll take you back and talk to Isobel and try and make her stop being cross, OK?'

Maisie nods her head. I put her down, take my coat off, and wrap her up in it and am about to set off to Red House, when Angela's car appears. I explain to Angela what has happened and she offers to take her up in the car, but I say I will take her up myself, as it is only just round the corner and I add with a laugh, 'I would like Isobel to see I am not trying to kidnap her.' I suggest Angela goes into the house for a minute, as I haven't locked up yet and she could keep warm in there.

I hammer on the door of Red House, and after a short while, Isobel opens it and looks shocked to see me. 'What are you doing with her?' she says accusingly.

'What are you doing – letting her out in this freezing weather – and in her night clothes? I heard her shouting and screaming outside your door and then she came running down the lane. It was just lucky I was outside getting in some logs.'

I look at her angrily and then she says, 'I was cross because she wouldn't get dressed and I'm in a hurry and have some visitors arriving this morning. I didn't know she had gone outside.'

As she looks at me defiantly, I say, 'Anyway, Angela has just turned up to give me a lift to go shopping, so I must rush and please take more care of your daughter – and don't be cross with her – she is only three and half and doesn't deserve your wrath.' Then, I give Maisie a kiss and hand her over and as I take back my coat, I add, 'And Isobel, I remember what you are like when you are angry,' As I say this, I pull up my sleeve and show her a couple of burn marks on my arm.

I don't bother to wait to see her reaction. I hear her door slam as I rush back down to the Cottage, feeling angry and distraught. It takes me a few moments to go back into the house and face Angela. Holding Maisie like that and seeing and feeling her fear and then noticing her foot, so like mine, I am thrown back into my own childhood situations and for a moment I feel terrified for Maisie. I have got to do something to help her.

'What was all that about?' says Angela, as she comes to the door, wondering why I am not coming in. I feel I can't talk to Angela about it at this moment.

'I don't know,' I reply. 'She said Maisie wouldn't get dressed and she was in a hurry with visitors due to arrive and said she didn't realise Maisie was outside.' (Or I think to myself – Isobel deliberately shut her out because she was angry. The sort of thing Isobel would certainly have done in the past).

As we drive off we are both silent for a while and then I say, 'I am very worried about Maisie. I've seen that look on Isobel's face so many times in the past and I can remember how... cruel she can be. I did hope she'd be different with a child of her own.'

'Was she really cruel?' asks Angela, 'I mean, some people are much stricter with children than most modern parents. I remember my parents were very strict with me and my brother and we got smacked regularly if we were naughty or even answered back.'

'Yes, but I don't expect they burnt you with cigarettes.'

'No, they certainly didn't. Why, did she do that to you?'

'Yes, and I have two scars on my arm to show for it. Also, sometimes she would hit me really hard, so that I had bruises all over.'

'Did you ever tell anyone about it?'

'Well, there was no one around when she did it. She was always very careful that no one witnessed anything she did to me. When I was ill in hospital after my baby died, she convinced the Doctors that I had made the burn marks myself, you know, like people cut themselves when they are stressed.'

'Gosh, that's terrible,' says Angela.' Did no one ever notice your bruises?

'No, I kept them hidden, as I knew she would take it out on me later if I told anyone.'

'Do you think she is doing that sort of thing to Maisie?'

'I am sure Dan and Emma would have noticed any physical marks, as they take her swimming frequently. They have asked me to go swimming with them and I must admit I am reluctant in case Isobel stops her going with them. All the time she is with them, I feel she is probably safe.'

We are both silent for a while, as Angela has to negotiate some difficult traffic and when we find a parking spot in the supermarket carpark, she stops the engine and sits quietly for a moment.

'We are going to have to do some serious planning about this,' she says while looking thoughtful. 'I mean, this morning may have been a one-off event. I realise I have never had much to do with small children, but I do see from some of my friends and mothers who take their children up to Red House to play with Maisie, that small children can be very headstrong and difficult. I think we are going to have to play this very carefully.'

'Yes, I agree, but I think Isobel could have deliberately shut Maisie outside, because Maisie was shouting that she couldn't reach the handle and if she could reach it inside and open the door, surely she could reach it from the outside and I didn't notice a big step up to the door.'

'Well, that's certainly something I can check when I next go up there,' says Angela, 'but meanwhile, we must get on with our shopping. I promise you, though, I will take this seriously. But I think we are going to have to be very careful not to alienate Isobel in any way to put her on the defensive more than she is already.'

'Yes, you are right,' I say, but I still don't feel I can tell Angela yet about my fears that Isobel is to blame for the odd goings-on at Blackstone Cottage.

· · ·

We do our shopping and I get myself enough essentials to go on with and a few extra things to store in the freezer. Angela's car is pretty full, especially after we stop off and buy a huge sack of dog food for Bess.

On the way back Angela brings up the subject of Isobel again.

'I think the best thing to do for the moment, is to try to be pleasant and polite to her, so she doesn't become suspicious that we are checking up on her. At the same time, we can try to keep a discreet watch on Maisie. You can make your fears known to Dan and Emma and ask them to look out for physical signs of abuse, or signs of real unhappiness. When I go up there for yoga, I will try to keep an eye out for Maisie. Come to think of it, I could take some leeks up to Isobel at the weekend. We have rather a lot of leeks in the garden that need pulling up before the really cold weather comes. She told me that this year her leeks have not done very well in spite of Jock's nurturing and I know she will offer me some other veggies in return.'

'That sounds a good idea,' I say, 'and I know Dan and Emma are aware already that I don't trust Isobel and I know they are very fond of Maisie, so I am sure, when I tell them about this morning, they will be especially attentive to her. I will ring Dan immediately I get in.'

As Angela drops me off she asks me if I would like to go to lunch with them on Sunday and meet Geoff. I hesitate and say that I am sure she must have had enough of me and my troubles and surely she wants a nice quiet weekend with Geoff. She assures me that Geoff wants to meet me and, unless he has other plans, she knows that would be fine with him. We agree she will let me know either tonight or tomorrow.

As promised, I ring Dan right away and tell him details about this morning's event. He says that he and Emma will check Maisie carefully for any signs of rough treatment and he will be in touch this evening, after they bring her back from swimming.

Chapter 13

This afternoon I am feeling at a bit of a loss as to what to do after unpacking my shopping and having a sandwich. As I sit by the fire warming my toes, I realise I will have to get advice about heating the house, because, although the wood burner has been fine up to now and makes the sitting room very cosy and my bedroom above is warm enough, I remember frozen pipes on Morg when there was really icy weather and I can't bear the idea of having to cope with burst pipes in the kitchen or bathroom. I am feeling lazy and sitting contemplating on how to be "nice" to Isobel and try to get her trust, when there is someone knocking on the front door. I peep through the window and to my huge surprise I see Pete, Isobel's partner, standing and looking around.

'Hi,' he says, smiling, as I open the door.

'Hi,' I say, being a bit lost for words and obviously looking very puzzled.

'I'm staying for the weekend with Isobel and heard you have been having a bit of trouble so thought I would pop in and see you, if you are not too busy. Is that OK?'

'Yes… that's lovely,' I reply, not really knowing whether it is. My immediate thought is what has Isobel been saying and I am bracing myself for an onslaught of questions as I show him into the sitting room, and offer him a seat.

'This is very cosy,' he says, as he sits down on the chair, which I have previously cleared of cat hairs. 'How long have you been here now?'

As I sit down opposite him, I say, 'Oh, a couple of weeks now, but it seems much longer as so much has happened, as I am sure Isobel has told you. Anyway, I feel I am settling in, in spite of some weird goings-on.'

'Yes, she has told me and has been worried about you. Are you OK here all on your own?'

'Yes, I'm fine and I know Isobel thinks this place is completely unsuitable for me, but for the time being I intend staying and see how I get on. I have made some good friends already and they have been very supportive throughout all the strange occurrences. The police have been involved, as I am sure you know, and they don't seem to think there will be any more trouble. I've had all the locks changed, so at least I feel quite safe indoors now.'

'So, how have you been health wise? I gather you weren't too well after I left Morg.'

That's an understatement, I think to myself. I wonder how much he knows about how ill I was. I certainly don't want to go into all that, so I pause and then I say, 'Look Pete, I know Isobel is still worried about me, but I can assure you that I am feeling one hundred percent OK now and nobody need worry about me. Of course, I am sad about the tragic events, but I really am past all that now. In fact, I am so relieved that I haven't got a child to care for at my age. You were all quite right. I can see that now. I have lots of ideas of what I want to do and certainly a small child would make all that impossible. So, I have all of you to thank for all your help and support.' I am hoping what I have said will ring true and put an end to Isobel's suspicions.

'Well, that's a great relief to hear,' he replies, relaxing back into the chair. 'I often think of you and wonder how you are, but Isobel has always assured me that you are fine and want to start afresh, away from all past memories, so perhaps that's why she thinks this cottage is not the best place for you, as you are so close to her. By the way, she doesn't know I've come down to see you. I just wanted to make sure for myself that you are OK.'

'Yes, I can quite understand Isobel might be concerned. I really was quite unwell for a while and the Doctors have all assured me that it was all due to the shock of Ade's death, then the baby, with the added hormonal problems of postnatal depression. Anyway, I'm absolutely fine how.' I pause and take a deep breath and then continue, 'and how are you and where are you living now?'

'I'm in London at the moment at a medical conference, but I am living and working in New York. Ade's death shook me up enormously and I took a long time to get over it. As you know, he was my only child. He had such an interesting and fulfilling life to look forward to. It shook Isobel up as well, although he wasn't her son and she never really got close to him.' Then he adds, 'and we know what a terrible tragedy it was for you.' He sighs, and then continues, 'It was a desperate time for all of us.'

'Yes, it must have been awful for you too. I was so wrapped up in my own grief, I don't think I ever gave you a thought at the time.' Then I feel compelled to ask.' What I don't understand and I'd really like an explanation, is why did you leave Morg so suddenly? You just seemed to vanish, leaving Isobel to cope with a tiny baby and me, not in the best state to cope with myself? It seemed so unlike you.'

'I'm so, very sorry, but I simply can't go into that now. It is extremely complicated and nothing I can be proud of, but one day I would like to explain exactly what happened.' He suddenly looks very anxious and says, 'Look, I can't stay very long as Isobel will wonder where I have got to.'

'So, when did you arrive down here?'

'Isobel picked me up from Wasbury just after lunch.'

'You've come to see Maisie I presume?'

He hesitates and then says, 'Yes, yes, of course. I've come to see Maisie – and see how Isobel is getting on in Red House. They do come and visit me a couple of times a year, which is lovely. Maisie is growing so fast and seems to be quite a strong personality already.'

'Yes, she seems to be thriving,' I say.

I look at Pete and wonder what's going on in his head right now, as he appears unsettled. Physically, he looks much the same as I remember him, a little shorter than Isobel, but he is looking smarter than he used to on Morg, has shaved off his beard and has designer stubble instead, and he has had his hair cut in a shorter, more manageable style. He has a smart pair of jeans and a dark blue corduroy jacket, over a paler blue roll-neck sweater. He is looking a bit older and rather thin and there seems to be less of him altogether. He must be about sixty now, I think, as I remember Isobel teasing him and calling him her 'old man', as he is about fifteen years older than her.

I offer him some coffee, as I know he never drinks tea, or any of the herbal things that Isobel always preferred. He surprises me by saying, 'No thanks, – just a glass of cold water would be fine, but I mustn't be long.' I go to the kitchen and get myself a coffee and glass of water for Pete He follows me in and as he looks out of the window at the back door, he says,

'Aren't you a bit worried by the strange events that have happened to you during the few days you have been here? I don't think I would want to stay another night after those experiences.'

I don't quite know how to answer this. Is he in a scheme with Isobel? Do they both want me to leave here for some reason? Has he been influenced by Isobel to believe I am still unwell and am doing these weird things myself? Maybe he is worried for Isobel being up in that big house alone with Maisie a lot of the time, if there are strange people around.

I have to take my time to respond in the right way, so after a pause I say, 'Yes, it has been pretty scary, but the Police have been very attentive. They say that they are doing all they can to find the culprit, but I know they are particularly busy at the moment with a spate of burglaries locally. They don't seem to think my strange events are anything connected to that. Anyway, I have had new very secure locks put on the doors and the windows are already double-glazed and locked, so things shouldn't disappear from the cottage again.' Then I add, 'I believe Isobel thinks I did it all myself for some reason. I can't see the logic of that. What on earth would be the point? It must be someone with a very warped mind to hang a cat in a tree – she really must think I am still insane to even contemplate doing something like that.'

'Well, she is wondering,' he says, looking worried. 'She is so sure no one else had a key to the cottage. She was there when they were all handed in.'

'Yes – I know about that, but anyone could have had a spare set cut while Aunt May was alive. She had people coming and going to look after her in her last days. Anyway – I promise you, Pete, I DID NOT DO IT MYSELF, and if you really think I would behave in that way, then I really don't want to talk to you anymore and you can leave now.' I get up and walk towards the door.

'No, no, I don't for a moment think it was you,' he says hurriedly, 'but of course we are concerned for your safety and I am a bit worried for Isobel and Maisie too. You are all rather isolated up here.'

'Is she worried about her safety?' I ask. 'And has she had her locks changed? She has just as much reason to be worried as I have – and she's got Maisie to think about.'

'No, you know Isobel. She is never afraid of anything.'

How right you are, I think to myself. 'Actually, Pete, has anybody even considered that it might be Isobel doing it all to frighten me away? It has been absolutely obvious to me from the moment I arrived that she did not want me here. The first day I arrived she warned me about ghosts and a black cat. Do you know, she hasn't even suggested I go and see her at Red House and she has made it absolutely clear that she hasn't the time to help me with anything.'

'Oh, I'm sure Isobel wouldn't do anything like that. That's absurd.'

'It is no more absurd than for me to have done it myself,' I say indignantly. 'She doesn't want me here though, does she?'

'Well, she hasn't said so to me, but as I said to you before, I think she is concerned that this is not the right environment for you.'

Pete looks thoughtful and I can sense he is not at all at ease with me, so I say,

'Pete, is there something wrong, or something else you need to tell me?'

He replies very quickly, 'No, absolutely nothing Lora. I just came to visit and check that you were OK and you seem to me to be fine. I realise you and Isobel will never be best of friends and that is not something that can be forced. You are both strong personalities and have a lot of history of clashes with each other, but that's just the way it is. I just hope that you both can get along well enough now to not cause each other too much hassle.'

'I assure you, Pete, I have no intention of causing problems for Isobel and, as I said before, I am already making some new friends and want to stay here for a while, to see how I get on and whether I can find a job, so please tell her that I am not out to be difficult, or be a nuisance to her in any way.'

'No, I'm sure you're not,' he says, trying to sound more certain. 'So, I'd better get back now and see how they are getting on up at Red House. I believe Isobel is making a special meal for us this evening. We have another couple of friends staying as well.'

'Well, have a lovely evening – and thanks for coming to see me.'

'It has been great to see you – and I really mean it Lora. It is lovely to hear you sounding so positive.' And with that he gives me a big hug and is off back to Red House.

I watch him as he walks off round the corner towards Red House; a rather hunched figure, hands in pockets, and he soon vanishes behind the trees.

I feel rather unsettled after seeing Pete and realise that I have actually missed him quite a lot. He was very much part of my life as a child and part of Ade, which gives him even more of an emotional connection to me. He must have found Ade's death unbearable too. I still feel very puzzled about his sudden disappearance from the island and I am determined, one day, to find out what that was all about and why he was so evasive about it just now.

There is still time to kill before I expect to see Dan, so I put on some warm clothes and go out to face a rather cold north wind and, as it is fine and will be light for a while, it seems a good time to cut down some more overgrown brambles and bushes. This is very different landscape from Morg which was fairly bare and not much work to be done in the way of heavy chopping. We had small patches of ground in which to plant a few vegetables, but it was hard and stony work to get enough depth for things to take root. This is different. The soil here lends itself to an abundance of growth, so I am hoping to be able to try to plant a few things in the Spring. Angela has warned me that it takes a lot of time and hard work to tame a plot like this and suggests I just gradually do what I can. She has mentioned she could ask her gardener, Jock, to go over the ground with a strimmer to get the worst of the weeds under temporary control, but she has warned me that when the spring comes, everything will burst into life again, so we could ask Jock's advice about the best way of managing it all.

I have always had a lot of energy and am very used to hard physical work, so when I was sharing a flat in London, after I had come out of hospital, I found other people of my age had a completely different outlook on life and were more interested in towny things, like shopping, cinema, spending hours on social media. We got on all right, but I know they found me very strange, with my interest in nature and the outdoors, so they weren't a bit surprised when I relished the idea of living in a rather remote cottage in the countryside. I don't expect any of them would want to visit me here and I can't say I miss them at all.

My toes are a bit cold, in spite of finding some extra woolly socks in one of Aunt May's drawers. I am also glad of the woolly jumpers I found. Not fashionable for someone my age – but who cares? I soon get warmer by getting quite a lot more chopping done and building a big pile of rubbish with which I will have fun lighting a bonfire sometime. I carry on until the sun starts to go down and I look over my garden hedge to watch a beautiful sunset above the distant hills. The rooks are coming into roost in the tall trees to my left making such a noise, with their cawing and flapping about, as if each one is trying to find the best place for the night. I enjoy listening to them and I find something very soothing about their harsh argumentative cries.

As I stand contemplating the rooks, a car goes past, towards Red House, but it is not Dan's. Perhaps it is the visitors Pete was expecting and I am beginning to wonder whether Dan has been asked to keep Maisie for the night if there is an adult gathering at Red House. But in a few minutes his car appears and he hoots as he whizzes past with Maisie and I expect to see him coming back soon.

After what seems like an age, he reappears and stops by the cottage and I welcome him indoors. He flops down in a chair by the fire and says, 'Phew, that Maisie isn't half exhausting. She is in and out of the water, jumping and diving, over and under, and an awful lot of "under". She disappears for ages and then pops up somewhere unexpected. Emma feels she can't manage the two of them on her own, so she certainly needs me there as well. There was a swimming instructor there today with a small group of children and she couldn't believe what Maisie was doing at her age.'

'Well, she's just like me then,' I say, feeling excited to know just how she feels in the water. 'I was told I learnt to swim before I could walk, but I have no idea who was the first person to take me into the sea on Morg. It certainly wouldn't have been Isobel. She hates water. Perhaps it was Aunt May as I know she quite liked swimming.'

We make a cup of tea together in the kitchen and I tell him all about Pete's visit this afternoon and how he seems keen for Isobel and me to get on better together.

'I think I persuaded him that I am fully recovered now from my past and that I have no intention of causing any problems, but we'll have to see how things go, as I would love to think Isobel trusts me enough for me to come swimming with you all.'

'That really would be great. I'd love to see you and Maisie in the water together. Oh, by the way, I have just met Pete. He was very friendly and interested in my work. He and Isobel looked quite relaxed together. They have a couple of friends staying, who were praising my *beautiful* kitchen,' he says with a flourish. 'I'll be getting quite big-headed soon.'

'Yes, it'll be, "tuppence to talk to you", as Aunt May used to say.'

We talk again about this morning's event with Maisie and Dan tells me that he and Emma could see no signs of bruising or other marks on Maisie.

'You know, she is quite a headstrong little girl. I could imagine she could take a lot of careful handling and patience. I know I've told you before that I've heard Isobel getting quite angry with her at times.'

'Have you any idea what it is she does that makes Isobel angry?'

'It usually sounds more like what Maisie won't do, rather than something that she is actually doing. For instance, today when I went to pick her up, she didn't want to put her coat on and would not co-operate with Isobel and stubbornly just stood there, then just lay on the floor, while Isobel forced her arms into it. Isobel just looked tight-lipped and said nothing, but I feel things would have been different if I hadn't been there.'

'Isn't that just small-child behaviour?' I suggest.

'Yes, absolutely, but Isobel doesn't seem to be willing, or maybe able, to talk to Maisie in a kind, persuasive way. In fact, she doesn't seem to talk to her at all. She seems to have more conversations with her dog. Of course, I don't see a lot of them together, as when I am working with all my tools, Maisie is kept well out of the way for safety reasons – but then, – come to think of it, I don't know where she is, as I often see Isobel coming in and out of the kitchen, doing odd jobs, on the phone, etc. and she hardly ever has Maisie with her.'

'This sounds typical of Isobel,' I say. 'She has probably shut Maisie in a playroom somewhere, with toys, as that's what she used to do with me. Maybe she has a television or a laptop nowadays. Of course, we never had a telly on Morg.'

This takes me back to childhood and all the times I spent on my own, when there were no other children visiting the island. I became very self-sufficient and learnt to amuse myself, playing imaginary games and reading or drawing, but Aunt May was usually around somewhere, if I felt really lonely. I am deep in thought when Dan says, 'She is a very quiet child when she is with us. She's always very sweet and gentle with Charlie and gives him a cuddle, but she doesn't demand any attention from us and she pulls away if we show any affection to her. It's as if she lives in a world of her own.'

'Well, I'm not surprised,' I say 'and she hasn't got Aunt May to run to. Of course, she is much too young to be left to play on her own all the time. What happens on Yoga days, or when Isobel has other activities on at Red House?'

'Isobel seems to welcome people to bring their children and I heard her tell someone the other day that she is delighted for Maisie to have someone to play with and I know she hires someone to come in to take care of the children and help keep them amused. I think she must use an agency, because I hardly ever see the same person twice. Sometimes an older child goes with them, probably a sibling of one of the young ones.'

'So, it doesn't sound as if Maisie is always on her own and that she does sometimes have other children to play with, which is good – and how's Emma?' I ask.

'She's fine. In fact, she's got a new bloke. I have been suspicious for a few days, as she has been on her phone a lot. Plenty of texts and then smug smiles. Apparently, she met him at the hotel where he is a new assistant chef. I haven't met him yet, but I cross-examined her, like an overprotective parent, which annoyed her at lot, but she reluctantly realised that I am concerned, bearing in mind her usual poor choice of men.'

'So, do you think he sounds OK? I can understand you being protective, as you both obviously care what happens to each other.'

'Yes, difficult to know till I've met him. She says she'll introduce him soon, but she has asked him round for a meal this evening and she doesn't want me there,' he says with a wry smile. 'I expect she knows I would probably ask too many questions and embarrass them both.'

'Yes, I am sure you would, being such a protective brother, so, would you like some supper here then?'

'Yea thanks – I hoped you'd ask – We could go to a pub if you would rather?'

'No, let's stay here. I have plenty of food, as I've just done a shop with Angela today.

We go to the kitchen and decide to make a cauliflower cheese together, as I can't be bothered to go out in the cold to the garage and fetch anything from the freezer. Dan tells me that Emma usually does all the cooking and she really enjoys it, but he can do basic cooking if he needs to. Like the very few men I've met, he seems to find it difficult to cook and talk at the same time, so we quietly get on with it and soon have a delicious cheesy mound of cauliflower and a pile of mashed potato, which we take to eat by the fire. After we have demolished that, we both feel we need something sweet and I produce a couple of crunchie bars. I realise I haven't offered him anything to drink and the only alcohol I have is Aunt May's sherry, but he says he is quite happy with water.

'I have to admit,' he says, 'I don't get on very well with alcohol, as you will remember from the train episode. I try not to have it very often as I have been told by those around me, including Emma, that I "can't hold my drink". More than a couple of pints of beer and I'm not nice to know. I have never been violent, but just rude and unpleasant.' Then after a pause, he says, 'and I'm terrified of being like my father.'

'Well, the fact that you realise that, is surely a very good thing and anyway, I don't like alcohol very much, so I certainly won't force it on you.'

We decide to have a mug of hot chocolate and we giggle, as we settle down on the sofa together, like a couple of sweet old folk.

'This is really great,' he says. 'You are so different from any other girl I've met. I don't think I have ever felt so relaxed in female company (apart from Emma, of course). You don't seem to be interested in the usual girlie things, like loads of makeup and shopping. I can't think of any other girl who'd want to live alone out in the sticks like this.'

'Is that meant as a compliment?' I ask.

'Yes of course it is. But I obviously don't know if you are really craving for a more social kind of life. You don't seem to be missing contact with social media, or even a television. I would be going up the wall with such difficulties with phone calls.'

'You wait till I have my Wi-fi connection. I'll be a different person,' I say jokingly.

'Well, I hope not. You are just p..., pretty good as you are.' He abruptly changes the subject and says, 'have you got any photos from Morg? It sounds an interesting place.'

'I haven't got any of my own, as I didn't have a camera or a phone in those days, but I have found an album with a few which Aunt May, or a visitor, might have taken, if you would like to see them?'

We open up the album and there doesn't seem to be any chronological order to the photos and not all are labelled. There are some of Aunt May, my mother and Isobel, which I presume was when they first went to Morg, as the cottages all look unkempt and unlived in.

'Your mother looks a little bit like you I think,' says Dan, 'but the photos are not very clear and some very out of focus.'

'I don't know who took these. It was obviously early days.' We find the names of the sisters in pencil on the back of one. I see Isobel is in the centre, the tallest and looking as if she is the most important one, with a look on her face as if to say "here I am – just notice me." My mother and Aunt May are standing slightly back, as if they don't really want to be there. There are many photos of the island and Dan notices the sparseness of the growth on the ground and yet how beautiful it looks with vast areas of sky and the various colours reflected in the sea. Although there are only some small rocky hills on Morg, we can see mountains in the distance.'

'What a beautiful place,' says Dan. 'Would you want to go back?'

'Yes, one day I would, but not until I have spent more time away from it and can remember just the good things, like the scenery, the solitude, the sea and the wonderful wild birds.'

'And Ade?' says Dan and then, 'I'm sorry, perhaps I shouldn't have said that.'

'No, that's fine,' I reply hurriedly. 'It is good to hear someone say his name. It reminds me he was real. For so long I had to try to forget him, as I just couldn't cope with the mixed-up memories of my time with him and the horror of what came after.'

I find tears coming to my eyes and my voice faltering and am annoyed with myself, as I thought I had begun to come to terms with it all, but Dan just puts his arm round my shoulder and gives me time to recover.

'I'm so sorry if I've stirred things up for you,' says Dan, 'but I hope you will be able to talk to me about it one day. I know from my own experience when our Mother died, how I had to grieve in my way and in my own time – and then, when I was ready, it was great to be able to talk and share with someone else. Emma was the same, and although we had each other, we were trying to be strong for each other and eventually it was my mother's best friend who we both felt we could talk to.'

'Thank you, Dan, you are very understanding.'

We flick through a few more pages and then come to some of me and some visitors who were staying during one of the summer holidays. In one of them, I am tiny and probably not much more than Maisie's age. I am standing there holding a doll, which looks almost as big as me. Dan exclaims 'Wow, that could be Maisie. You really are so alike.'

'Yes,' and then, with hardly a pause, I get a sudden image of her little foot with the webbed toes and can't help myself from saying, 'I sometimes still believe she could be my daughter'.

I am expecting Dan to react in the way that others have in the past, but he doesn't.

He just says, 'And I can believe it too. Ever since I first met you I have felt this strange feeling that you two are not just Aunt and Niece. Also, the little bits of information you have told me about the past. There are so many things that seem unclear to you.'

I look at him in amazement. Here is someone who maybe is going to believe me. I feel a sudden feeling of panic and take some low, slow breaths. Do I dare allow myself to slip back into that way of thinking? I have spent so long being persuaded by others and persuading myself that it was all imagined. I had got myself into a generally calm and settled frame of mind – and now I feel terrified of falling backwards into those terrible feelings of uncertainty and despair. No... no. I don't want to go back there – I couldn't cope with being like that again. I feel a panic attack coming on and feel breathless and am feeling hot and cold alternately and am starting to shake. I stand up and try to leave the room, but feel glued to the ground.

Dan gets up and puts his arms round me, saying soothing words, while I gradually stop shaking. 'We could explore this together, if you like? I think you need to know the truth one way or the other, or you will never be free of the doubt.'

As I begin to calm down, I say, 'Yes, I really do feel I need to know the answer to this, especially now that I believe Maisie is being neglected by Isobel in the same way I was. I have been thinking the only way to find out for sure is through DNA testing, but I have no idea how to go about this.'

'Have you a theory about what happened?'

'No, not really, just an instinct that I haven't been told the whole truth. You are the first person who has ever suggested that I might be right. I was so brainwashed at the time, that images and memories that came to me were not allowed to even be considered. You see, I was unconscious for the final stages of the birth and I came round very confused. I went in and out of consciousness several times and my memories are very muddled.' Then I add after a pause. 'But then I worry about the baby boy – was he real? Who was he? Was he actually Isobel's, or maybe I had twins? It is very strange – but I never felt I could mourn him. It was as if he never existed – but then, you see, I wasn't even shown his body.'

'Well, you certainly need to know,' says Dan,' and I'd love to help you. Would you agree for me to tell Emma about this? I am pretty sure one of her ex. Uni friends has gone into genetic research of some kind and could probably give advice about DNA testing?'

'Yes,' I say, feeling a slight sense of relief. 'By all means, tell Emma about this conversation, but please wait for me to be ready to take it further. I don't think I can be rushed on this. It is brilliant of you to say you would like to help me and I am really grateful – and now I realise I definitely have to do something sooner or later, I can't always push it to the back of my mind, or the doubt will haunt me for ever.'

He can see I am still very unsettled, so he says, 'Are you OK on your own tonight, or would you like me to stay?'

This is the second time in the past few days, that he has offered to stay the night. I realise that it is such a short time since we first met. Can I possibly know him enough to really trust him? Yet, somehow, I know I can. He really does seem to understand, but as I am feeling so much better now I reply, 'It is very kind of you and thanks for being so very understanding – but no – I will be fine and I think I need time on my own to be able to realign my thoughts.'

We sit for a while on the sofa, with his arm round me and my head on his shoulder, and when it is time for him to go home, I am feeling a huge weight has been lifted from my mind. Here is someone who believes it is possible that I could have been right all along, and is prepared to try to help me find out the truth.

Chapter 14

I spend quite a restless night, mulling over the evening with Dan and the possible consequences of pursuing our suspicions. When I do manage a fitful sleep, my dreams are very disturbed, with images of the final hours on Morg. I see Ade out of reach, way out on a distant shore, sort of floating in the air; Isobel's face looms in and is replaced by Pete's; I see an image of something wrapped in white cloth. I wake with a jolt. I want to see that image again, but sleep will not come to allow me to continue.

At about two a.m. I go downstairs and make myself a hot drink. This is a herbal teabag, with so-called "suitable herbs for sleep inducement", but it doesn't induce me to do anything more than to have a wee and then continue thinking.

By about three thirty a.m. I drift off again and have dreams of lying on a bed, floating above it and hearing muffled voices, which I think are Isobel and Pete discussing something which sounds serious, but I can't make sense of it. I find myself hovering round the island and Ade calling me, but not being able to hear what he is saying. I drift into one of the cottages and hear a baby crying and I go towards its cot, but someone pulls me away and again, I awake very suddenly and find tears on my pillow. I cannot stop crying and continue to sob into my pillow for what seems like hours, but eventually I fall asleep again exhausted and am woken just after nine o'clock by my phone.

I jump out of bed and open the window wide. By sticking my head out I can just make out Angela's voice, but she is breaking up, so I tell her I will ring back. I don't know whether she heard me or not, so I pull on some socks, rush downstairs, find a coat and my wellies and after fumbling with the locks on the door, I go out into the garden at the back. It is a cold frosty morning, but my hands don't have time to get cold before I have contacted Angela and I tell her I have overslept and am now out in the garden in my pyjamas.

'Oh dear, I'm sorry, so I won't keep you long. Are you still able to come to lunch tomorrow? We would love you to come. I am sorry not to have called you yesterday evening, but I forgot till it was very late.'

'Yes, I'd love to,' I reply. 'What time would you like me to arrive? I could come on the bike?'

'No, no, I'll pick you up about twelve thirty if that's OK?'

'Thanks, that's fine and I am really looking forward to it.'

'And, by the way,' says Angela, 'I will be seeing Isobel this afternoon, with the leeks that I promised her. I may see you on my way. So, bye for now. I don't want you to freeze.'

She rings off abruptly and I don't have time to ask her what to wear. I am not used to social occasions with older people, but then I realise I may see her later and can get details then.

I am thoroughly awake now and though the bathroom is quite cold; the shower is electric and beautifully hot. Unfortunately, the towel is cold and rather damp, as I forgot to dry it by the stove yesterday, but I am soon dressed, ready for breakfast and to face the day. The dreams keep coming back to me, but I realise that bringing up the subject of my suspicions about Maisie and the past, like we did last night, is something that I have avoided doing for many months. I will have to decide whether I am mentally strong enough to continue doing this.

I make some lovely hot porridge for breakfast and enjoy it with a cup of coffee. The stove has gone out overnight, as I didn't remember to organise it properly last night, so I put on an electric fan heater, which soon warms up the small sitting room. I am still feeling a bit shaky and realise my eyes are probably very puffy from crying, but hopefully I won't need to see anybody until I have had time to recover. I notice a car going past up towards Red House, but it is not one I recognise, but then I don't know one car from another, except I do know Dan has a blue one and Isobel has a large four-by-four, and it is neither of those.

The postman arrives and delivers some junk mail. As I pick it up off the floor, I realise I can't think of anybody who would write me a letter, or even a postcard, as the few acquaintances I had in London don't know my address and I left a forwarding address with the post office when I moved here. It will be Christmas soon and I can't imagine what Christmas will be like here. Perhaps Isobel will feel she should invite me to Red House? It might look very odd to her friends if she doesn't. I wonder what Dan and Emma do at Christmas? I expect they spend it with relatives or friends.

I am feeling better after breakfast and go and splash my face with cold water to see if this will hide the signs of stress. I look a bit better afterwards and begin to feel much more positive as the morning goes on and, as I potter about doing not very much, I spend time thinking about last night's discussions. The more I think about it, the more I know I simply must find out, one way or the other, whether Maisie is my daughter, or whether it is still a fantasy that I have never managed to come to terms with. I know it will be painful, but I survived a very stressful night and have come out of it alive and, at the moment, I am confident I am feeling fairly rational. I am sure it is essential, but I feel very apprehensive about doing a DNA test and also wondering how this could be arranged with Maisie. I think it is quite an easy procedure of just taking a swab from inside one's cheek. This would be no problem for me, but perhaps Emma or Dan could think of a way of getting one from Maisie.

A car comes down from Red House, followed by Isobel's. I see her glance towards me as she passes and I think I glimpse Maisie in the back. I realise I am looking out for cars and hoping Dan will appear. As it is Saturday, I don't believe he has any extra work today, but he does do small jobs for people at odd times and being self-employed means getting work when you can. I can think of one or two jobs he could do for me. For example, I have a wobbly kitchen unit that needs fixing, and a shelf here and there would be useful. Also, if I decide to get Catty back, I will need a cat flap, which he has said he would do.

I am just thinking about Catty when a police car draws up and Chris climbs out and comes to the door. I feel my heart thumping and I don't know why. What sort of news could she have?

'Hello Lora,' she says, sounding cautiously friendly. 'I am afraid we still haven't got any definite news for you. We have been asking around and have been told about several young lads in the village who have been causing a bit of trouble. Nothing very serious, but just expensive, mindless pranks, like broken wing mirrors on parked cars and bits of broken fence, etc., but we know all the families and their parents and they have all been dealt with in the appropriate way. I don't think there is much more we can do for now, so unless you have any more unpleasant experiences, we will just keep on the look-out.'

She looks at me inquiringly and then says, 'Have things been all right with you since? No more unexpected events? No strange people hanging around, or odd cars coming and going?'

'No, I can't say anything strange has happened. The odd car does go up and down to Red House, but Mrs Gray has quite a lot of visitors at irregular times.'

'Well, I'll just go up and see her and check all's well with her and don't forget, you can phone us if you are worried, or see or hear anything suspicious.'

'Thanks,' I say and she has gone before I remember to mention that Isobel has just gone out.

It is difficult to put my mind to doing anything definite this morning, but having looked at Aunt May's photos last night, gets me thinking about her. In respect to her, I do some cleaning, recognising how I owe it to her to keep the place looking cared for, as her generosity has given me somewhere to live – and more. She must have been very concerned for my future welfare.

I am remembering her warmth and kindness and her patience as she taught me how to read as a small child, as well as other basic education. She did leave the island for short periods, but when she was there, she was busy helping Isobel a lot of the time, especially when we had visitors. When she was around, I always knew she was a person I could turn to if I needed anything. She was not a strong personality, but a gentle person and I never heard her argue with Isobel or anyone else. Looking back, I think Isobel took her for granted and I don't think she was ever aware of just how much work Aunt May did without complaint. It seems so very sad that she should die so young. She was only fifty-six, I believe. I was told she was cremated and her ashes are in the Churchyard of the village where she was born, so sometime I would like to go there.

I don't know when it was that Aunt May left the island, or what prompted the move. As I am very vague about events at the time of the births, I don't remember Aunt May being around at that time, but I can remember there was very bad weather and there being no chance of going to the mainland. The only people I am aware of being with me were Isobel and Pete.

In my resolve to give respect to Aunt May, I find some beeswax furniture polish in one of the kitchen drawers. It is rather dry but I manage to rub some of it onto a cloth and get to work polishing one of May's small tables by the armchair near the fire in the sitting room. It is hard work to rub the polish well in, but I find it quite therapeutic and after a while I am getting rather a good shine on the beautiful old wood. Aunt May has left two or three lovely, old, probably antique, pieces of furniture. She certainly didn't have anything like this on Morg, so I plan to go over each piece gradually, encouraged by the one I have just done. I am just getting started on a larger table near the back window, when there is a loud knock on the door.

Dan is standing there with a multi-pack of crunchy bars. 'Thought you might like these,' he says, handing them to me.

'Thanks,' I say, feeling a bit surprised at the unusual present, but very pleased to see him.

I show him what I have been doing and he seems impressed. 'That's rosewood,' he says, 'just look at the wonderful shapes and range of colours now that you've polished it.'

'The table by the window is proving less obliging,' I tell him.

'Well, that's mahogany and it looks as if it needs a really good clean before you wax it. It has probably been used as a dining table and has had no end of bits of food and grease dropped on it through the years. I can let you have some of my special mixture to use if you like?'

'That would be very helpful,' I say, but feeling a little irritated that, yet again, I am relying on his help, when my nature is to be able to get on and do things myself.

'So, what sort of night did you have?' he asks, anticipating my reply.

'Not so good,' I say, and then tell him about my dreams and how little I slept.

'How are you feeling now?'

'Surprisingly good, considering my lack of sleep. I think I am pleased at how much stronger I feel. I am always so frightened of losing control again, but I actually feel I can cope pretty well at the moment. Are you OK?'

'Yes, I was awake quite a bit myself, thinking of ways to proceed – that is, of course, if you are ready and/or willing.' He seems to notice me hesitating for a moment.

'Have you had a chance to mention anything to Emma? And – oh, how did her date go?'

'Yea, they seemed to have a good evening and are spending the day together today and are taking Charlie with them somewhere, but I don't know what they have decided yet. In answer to your first question – we had time to talk at breakfast and Emma is pretty sure she can get information for you about DNA and how to get tested. She will certainly support you too, if you decide to go ahead. We are both very fond of Maisie and are extremely concerned for her welfare.'

Isobel's car goes back up towards Red House as we are talking and I tell Dan that Angela is planning to visit Isobel this afternoon. A few minutes later Angela appears at my door and presents me with some leeks.

'I see Dan's car outside, so I won't stay, and I've got Geoff in the car,' she says, 'but would you like a few leeks? I am just going to take some up to Isobel.'

'Yes, I love leeks,' I say, not absolutely sure how to cook them, but Aunt May's cookbooks will have instructions. Then I ask her, 'About tomorrow, um, what should I wear?'

'Oh, nothing special. Whatever you feel comfortable in. We don't dress up and it's not a party – just Geoff and me. What you are wearing now, looks fine to me.'

'All right, I might clean myself up a bit,' I reply, as I look at my shabby sweater, with a couple of holes in a sleeve. 'It's really good of you to ask me and I'm really looking forward to meeting Geoff.' This is partly true. I am actually quite nervous at meeting him, as I have no idea what to expect from an important London businessman.

Angela heads off up to Red House and I take the leeks into the kitchen. I am expecting Dan to immediately tell me how to cook them, but he doesn't, so I put them in a bag on a shelf, without saying anything and feeling very relieved that he hasn't jumped to give advice. I realise I am beginning to feel rather too attached to Dan and I do want to hold on to my own sense of independence. I don't quite know why, but I think it is a matter of keeping confidence in my own ability to survive on my own.

'Let's go to the pub for lunch,' Dan suggests.

'That's a good idea,' I say, 'but only if we each pay for our own'

'OK, I know you're wanting to keep your independence, but I could afford to treat you to lunch you know.'

'Yes, I am sure you could, but I should really be treating you, as you are doing so much to help me at the moment.'

'Yes, but you gave me supper last night.'

'Yes, but you and Emma fed me on Thursday night.'

'So perhaps we had better keep a special chart of who buys what and when,' he says with a laugh.

He drives me to "The Fiddler's Arms", a pub in a nearby village. We both decide it is a funny name.

I tell him I have noticed several pubs since I have come down South, called The King's Arms and I have been told that this refers to a King's Coat of Arms, but I can't imagine a fiddler has a Coat of Arms. According to the Inn sign, this fiddler is playing a fiddle and has a determined look on his face, with one hand on the strings and the other holding the bow, so we both agree he needs two arms to play the instrument.

As we are quite early and not many people have arrived yet, and although we have not booked, we are lucky to find ourselves a little table in a corner by a window, which looks out onto a small stream with willow trees along the bank. Dan buys a pint of bitter and I have a coke and we look hungrily at the menu. I am glad to see Dan hasn't chosen anywhere too posh or expensive and we both choose fish and chips, which Dan assures me are usually very good here.

He must notice me looking a little anxious as he puts the glass of beer on the table.

'Don't worry,' he says, 'I am only having one.'

I feel embarrassed and say, 'Oh, I'm sure you're fit to drive on just one pint.'

We have a delicious lunch and the conversation inevitably turns to the "Maisie Quest", as we have started to call it. I tell him I have definitely decided I want to find out the truth. Those strange dreams last night seem to have stirred something in my mind and I find snippets of memory are coming back to me, urging me to find out more.

'Would it be helpful to talk about it now?' he asks. 'I'm not trying to rush you, but I am very willing to listen any time you are ready.'

I feel hesitant and am not sure why. Perhaps it is because I really hardly know him – on the other hand I feel I've known him forever. It would mean trusting him on a huge level. I am going to need emotional support whatever the outcome of the DNA tests and I wonder how my relationship with him will develop.

'I would rather not talk about it here,' I reply, after a pause, 'as I am pretty sure I will get pretty emotional and that would not only be inhibiting, but embarrassing. If you are really willing to see this through with me, I would rather talk about it at home or at your place sometime. If Emma is willing to listen also, I think it could be helpful to me, as she has actual experience of giving birth.'

'That sounds sensible,' says Dan, 'and as I told you, Emma is wanting to help as well. She seems to have taken to you in a big way and, as I said before, we are both very fond of Maisie.'

We agree that we will meet sometime next week to give me time to get used to the idea and to give us all some breathing space. Dan knows I am going to lunch with Angela and Geoff tomorrow and I reassure him that I am certainly not going to mention anything about the "Maisie Quest". Dan knows I have confided in Angela about my past up to a point and that she has been very kind and helpful to me in all sorts of practical ways. But I have never indicated to her that I am still fixed on the idea of Maisie being my daughter and she thinks I have left all those thoughts behind me.

We continue with our lunch and have fun looking at the people around us and making silly comments to each other about the décor of the pub, with its horse brasses which have probably never seen a horse, and adorning fake beams, which, Dan says, he can tell are made of MDF with no traces of wood grain or knots to be seen.

This is obviously a new extension to an old building, with attempts to make it look antique. We are having fun with lots of jokes and anecdotes, when Dan suddenly stops short.

'Have you heard the one about –,' he starts to say, and then 'Oh my God, there's Kate.'

'Who's Kate?' I ask, watching him as he stares through a doorway into another dining area.

'She's my ex.' He says.

'Is she the one you've just broken up with?' I ask, while I wonder what will happen next and feeling disappointed that our enjoyable lunch has been interrupted so abruptly. I can only just see through to the other room from where I am sitting. If I lean forward and peer round I can glimpse a group of young people, who are settling into seats round a table. It looks as though they have only just arrived and would not have come past us on their way in.

'Yes, that's her. Do you mind swapping places with me, as I don't think she would see me from where you are sitting and I really don't feel like talking to her at the moment?' Then he adds, 'Just as I was enjoying a relaxing lunch.'

We discreetly change places, and from where I am now sitting, I can see a girl with wavy blonde hair with her back to us, having an animated conversation with the rest of the group, amidst lots of laughter. I check with Dan that he is sure it is her and at least I am glad to know he had been enjoying his lunch with me. But he looks very unsettled now and I ask him if he would like to leave. We have already ordered rich chocolate brownies and he says he certainly doesn't want to forego those, so we sit rather awkwardly waiting for them to arrive. When we have finished our delicious feast of chocolate and pocketed a free peppermint each, we go to the bar and pay our bills. Luckily there is another door we can leave from, so we don't have to go near Kate and her group.

When we get outside into the fresh air, Dan takes a deep breath and says, 'Phew, that was a close one.'

'And would it have been so awful for her to see you with somebody else?' I say, 'even if we are just good friends,' I add.

'No, of course not,' he replies. 'In fact, if you don't mind, I would like to walk past the window where she is sitting and while not waiting for an answer from me, he puts his arm round me and marches past, pauses for a moment, waves and walks on.

I am a bit annoyed at being used like this, and tell him so.

'Oh, I'm sorry,' he says. 'I know. That was a cheap trick.'

I invite him back to the Cottage for coffee, and he looks very remorseful, so I suggest we talk about it back there. We drive back in silence and I realise I have been so absorbed in my problems since we met, it has been selfish of me not to have explored more about his recent situation. On arriving back at the cottage, we get in some more logs for the stove, which was just still alive, and after gentle persuasion, it perks up. With the help of one of the electric fan heaters, the whole room soon warms up. We each sit either side of the fire in a small armchair each. We are avoiding the sofa for the moment, as it seems we both need to have our own space and Dan continues to look a bit distant and is obviously a bit taken aback at having seen Kate so unexpectedly.

'You see, I deliberately chose that pub, because I didn't think she would be there, as she has always chosen places the other side of Ford, where most of her other friends live, so it was the last thing I expected to happen.'

'Do you want to tell me about any of it? I mean the breakup or… whatever.' I don't quite know how to broach the subject, as although we have both talked a lot about the past, this is much closer to the present and Dan is obviously feeling very raw still.

'Well, yea, I would like to explain a bit and difficult to know where to begin,' he says, 'So the beginning is probably the best place to start,' he adds. 'We have known each other for many years on and off. We were at primary school together and then went on to secondary. She has always been very academic and studied hard, whereas I have always preferred practical subjects and, although I have always loved reading and studying things that interest me, I can't say I worked very hard at subjects on the school curriculum. I scraped through necessary exams, but always knew I wanted to be a carpenter, or work with wood in some way. I look at your lovely beech trees out there and I really appreciate their structure and am aware of the creatures that live on them and in them and the wonderful objects that can be made from the wood. It must be in my blood, or nowadays, one would say my genes, to feel so passionate about the subject.'

'It is great to see someone so sure about what they want from life.' I say, 'So, Kate's very different from you?'

'Yes, as I said, very academic and actually very ambitious to have a well-paid job and make lots of money. We were "an item" at secondary school, for some reason. I know I found her very attractive, but so did most of the other boys, so I was rather envied by my classmates. When she went to university and I went to a local college for a bit and then got the apprenticeship, we broke up and went our separate ways. We both made new friends and had new brief relationships, but about a year ago we met up again at a party and both found the attraction was still there. Unfortunately, or maybe fortunately, we gradually found that we really had drifted into different sorts of interests and lives. We tried to keep the relationship going, but she realised before I did, that really we had very little in common apart from the past. She had made a lot of new friends while being away at uni. and become even more materialistic and ambitious and I can see now that I felt like the country bumpkin and somehow inferior to all her sophisticated friends.

Emma had come back from university unchanged and is still the person she has always been, perhaps with more confidence and obviously with qualifications to make something of herself. She has always told me not to compare myself with others and insists my way of life is just as valuable as all the people who have been to university. I have just as important skills.'

'Yes, you certainly have,' I say. Isobel and Pete were always going on about Ade getting to uni. and saying there was no other way to get on in life.'

'And the government goes on about it too,' says Dan' They keep saying how important it is for everyone to get to university, so you can probably understand how someone like me can have a "chip on my shoulder". Please excuse the pun! – although I must admit,' he continues, 'they are trying to encourage apprenticeships a bit more nowadays.'

'Yes, I can understand, as I am wondering what on earth I would be any good at, with the little education I have had. I have never taken an exam in my life. No, that's not quite true, I did pass a basic course in computers – and I did pass my driving test,' I say with a laugh. 'But, Dan, you have an enviable skill and I would think of you as a far more valuable person than some fat businessman in London.'

As I say this I think of meeting Geoff tomorrow and wondering what he is like and I think of Angela who is a financial expert and she is a lovely person, with obviously huge skills in her field of work.

'No, we can't judge people's value, can we? As long as we try to contribute something positive to life, that's the best any of us can do.' I suggest. 'So, what happened to finally end your relationship with Kate?'

'Well, she decided, quite rightly, that we were going nowhere fast. We went up to the gig together and I found her friends so different, almost as if from a different planet, and I never had anything to contribute to their conversations. I found my mind wandering when I was with them all in a group and she accused me of being rude and distant. I accused her of having pretentious friends. She was furious and the next thing I knew, she was outside with one of her friends and to put it mildly, they were VERY close.'

'Oh, shit,' I say. What else can I say?

'And we don't even like the same music,' says Dan. 'I know that doesn't matter, as a lot of couples don't. There is so much variety to choose from nowadays and you don't even have to share it with anyone, but it does help to have something in common.'

'Yes, I think the kind of life, similar ambitions, places you like to be in are important to share – and certainly a sense of humour,' I add.

I think about how Ade and I seemed to have so many interests in common, but recorded music was something we hardly ever experienced together on Morg, unless someone had a battery-operated CD player. As a family, we were quite musical and made our own music with a selection of musical instruments which we shared around, according to who could play them. I used to play the guitar and was told that I had a good singing voice, but I was a bit too embarrassed to sing in front of any visitors I did not know.

We continue to chat through the afternoon and have tea and some rather stale buns, which we toast in front of the fire on a toasting fork which looks as if it had been well used by Aunt May. The buns are delicious with lots of butter. We then play cards with a couple of packs we find in a drawer and have soup for supper.

What a domesticated evening, I think to myself, as Dan puts his coat on to leave and gives me a quick rather embarrassed kiss on the cheek and we both thank each other for an enjoyable day…

'I hope you enjoy your lunch tomorrow,' he says as he goes out of the door.

'Yes, I'm a bit nervous about meeting Geoff.'

'Let me know how you get on, won't you?'

'Yes, I'll text you from the garden when I get back,' I shout as he gets into the car and drives off.

Chapter 15

I wake early next morning and notice a heavy frost on the lawn, so I shower and get dressed, with an extra sweater and thicker socks. When I go downstairs, I quickly put on the fan heater in the kitchen while I get my breakfast. I am used to keeping warm in changeable weather, so it is not as difficult for me as for someone used to central heating, and I will get the stove going after breakfast.

It is difficult to concentrate on doing anything this morning, as my mind is preoccupied with thoughts about the Maisie Quest, and also wondering what the lunch will be like today. I have no problem worrying about the food, as I like most things, but having no idea what Geoff is like, is making me anxious. I realise I'm hoping he will be as kind and understanding as Angela, and I do hope he doesn't think I have been imposing on her help too much. Anyway, I will have to wait and see and I decide to give the kitchen a bit of a clean, as doing something physical seems to relieve my stress levels.

As I'm cleaning inside the cupboard under the sink, I notice that it is loose at the left side. As I rub cleaner onto the wall it becomes looser and I can see something that looks like a sheet of paper sticking out at the back. There is just a corner and I try to get hold of it but it begins to tear, so I fetch a torch and can see there is some handwriting on it, but not visible enough to read.

This is so frustrating, as I can't see how I can move the cupboard without the whole sink unit moving with it, plumbing and all.

The cupboard next to it seems to be very firmly fixed at both the top and bottom. The gap between them both is too narrow to get my hand through and I would need something long and thin to poke in between the two sides. I search the cottage for something appropriate and can find nothing but a long knitting needle. As I push it into the gap, I can feel it coming up against something fairly soft, but it won't reach in far enough to shift anything. The work surface, which is firmly fixed, stretches right along the top of the cupboards and is certainly not something I could remove, so It is becoming obvious it would mean dismantling the whole thing, which I am definitely not prepared to try and do.

It would seem ridiculous to get someone to pull all this apart, just to find an old shopping list, but who would put a sheet or sheets of paper between the cupboards, and nothing could have slipped in from the top? I have to stop myself getting too excited and my imagination going wild.

I promised I would phone Dan to tell him about my lunch experience and decide I will tell him about my discovery then. Maybe he would be able to saw through one of the side panels, or he might have some bright idea of what to do. Then my curiosity and impatience get the better of me and I decide to phone him now. There is no reply, so I leave a message on voicemail, saying. 'Hi, Dan, I've made a discovery that may be interesting, but I 'll need your help, with possibly a saw. I'll talk to you later after the lunch. Lora.'

All this takes my mind off the lunch and I suddenly realise it will soon be time for Angela to pick me up, so I hurriedly change into something clean and tidy and brush my hair and think I look reasonably presentable, apart from my nails, which are rather ingrained with grime. A quick scrub and they too look presentable and I am ready just in time to put on my coat as Angela drives up.

Angela seems to sense that I am rather nervous and says,' You look very nice and I hope you aren't anxious about meeting Geoff, as I can assure you he is very easy-going. You will find him very – I suppose straightforward, would be a good description. He is used to meeting all kinds of people of all ages.' I am not sure if this sounds reassuring or not. It could mean anything, so I don't reply immediately, but then say, 'thanks I'm looking forward to meeting him.'

. . .

Geoff is there at the door to meet us and I can hear Bess quietly whining behind the kitchen door. He comes straight out and shakes my hand.

'Lovely to meet you Lora, and you are just as pretty as I thought you would be.'

I don't quite know what to say to this. Perhaps this is what older men think girls my age want to hear, so I don't tell him he is just as fat as I thought he might be, but I just smile and tell him I have been looking forward to meeting him.

After commenting on the weather and all that sort of thing, we go into the sitting room and Geoff asks me what I would like to drink. I don't like to say what have you got to offer, but before I can say anything he says, 'We've pretty well all the usual things, sherry, gin and tonic, whisky, beer, glass of wine.'

'Oh, I'd love a glass of wine, please.'

'Red or white – we have both open?'

'White please,' I reply and Angela says she would like the same.

Geoff goes to the corner of the room where there is a drinks cupboard and pours out the drinks. He helps himself to what I think is a whisky and water, as it is a sort of brown colour. No one on Morg ever drank anything but wine, in spite of it being whisky territory. While he is getting the drinks, I look at him more carefully. He is about Angela's height, but certainly quite a lot fatter. I think I would describe him as a large, round person. He has a round bald head and a red face and what little hair he has on the side of his head is quite grey. I would think he is quite a bit older than Angela, but I have no idea what age that would be, as I am no good at judging. He is wearing a long sleeve, dark green check shirt and red/brown corduroy trousers that seem to match his face.

Angela is wearing a pair of beige, tweedy trousers with a paisley shirt and I feel I have chosen the right clothes myself as I'm wearing my smartest, cleanest jeans and a loose cotton, blue and white top. I have brought a thick sweater which I found from Aunt May's collection, but certainly don't need it in the centrally heated room.

I needn't have worried about meeting Geoff. He soon puts me at ease and chats about everyday things. He tells me about his job in London and I listen politely, but not really understanding what he is talking about. He seems to know a bit about me already, as I know Angela has told him about my background, and he appears to be quite impressed as to how I am coping with life at the cottage and the strange events that have been happening.

Angela goes to the kitchen to check on the joint that is due to come out of the oven. I offer to help, but she says, 'No, you keep Geoff company. I won't be long.' Bess comes into the room and seems pleased to see me and comes and lies on my feet.

'She's got you trapped now,' says Geoff. 'She only does that to people she doesn't want to leave.'

'So, I feel honoured,' I say, thinking that my feet will soon go numb with her heavy weight.

Angela has cooked us a delicious lunch of roast lamb, crispy roast potatoes and mixed vegetables. This is followed by apple crumble with cream. We have more wine with the meal and I find my second glass is a bit much, as I am certainly not used to it. I have to make sure I'm not talking rubbish, but the atmosphere is very relaxed and we talk about many things. I hear from Angela and Geoff about their lives and how they have enjoyed their fifteen years at Ridge Farm and how it is so lovely to be able to escape from the hustle and bustle of London into such beautiful unspoilt countryside. As Ridge Farm is fairly high, there are long distance views over the surrounding hills and fields. It is so different from Morg, but just as beautiful in a completely different way.

'Do you miss the wildness and solitude of life on the island?' asks Geoff.

'Yes, in a way I do, but sometimes it could feel really claustrophobic, with a lot of visitors and not much space in the cottages. That is when we liked to escape and disappear to the sea and swim in all weathers, when most of the visitors would find it too cold. In the winter it could feel lonely and deserted, but I loved to walk and watch the birds and enjoy the freedom.'

'We've visited Scotland several times for holidays and it is very beautiful up there, but I would imagine it could feel very lonely and cut off if one lived permanently on a remote island.' Says Geoff.

'Well, I grew up knowing nothing else. I seldom went to the mainland, so you can imagine how I felt when I suddenly found myself deposited in London. It was a real culture shock.'

'So, how do you think you will settle in the cottage then?'

'I've only been here two weeks, but I think I will be OK I like the idea that it's fairly isolated, as that's what I'm used to, I'll be able to get out and about once I have the car on the road. I must admit I am feeling very fond of the cottage already, and in spite of strange happenings, it seems to hold the atmosphere of Aunt May and I think she would like me to stay.'

'Well, it's early days yet,' says Angela, 'and you'll have plenty of chance to change your mind.'

After lunch I go with Angela to the kitchen and help her clear up, while Geoff takes Bess for a walk. He had offered to help clear, but Angela said we'd do it together.

'This is such a good chance for him to get some fresh air and exercise', she says as she loads the dishwasher and I wash some of the bigger pans that won't fit in. 'I am a bit worried about his weight and London lifestyle and he would never consider going to a gym. He has just turned sixty and he really enjoys his work and says he would like to keep on working in London, but I wish he would work from home some of the time, so he could get more fresh air and exercise. He has had a sedentary job ever since university.

'You seem to keep very fit,' I say, 'but then you spend a lot of time down here don't you, and you have Bess to walk.'

'Yes, and I'm fifteen years younger than Geoff and take plenty of exercise as I love walking. In the summer, I do a lot of gardening and help with the animals. Talking of animals, have you been considering what to do about Catty?'

'I want to give it a bit more time to see how things are at the Cottage. I certainly don't want to get her back if I feel there is any danger to her.'

'I saw Isobel yesterday,' says Angela, 'and she told me the police had been to see her and didn't think there would be any more trouble.'

Then I think to myself, that maybe Isobel is still trying to convince Chris about my neurosis, but I don't mention this to Angela. 'Yes, Chris came to see me too,' I reply,' and she told me just to keep a look out and let her know if anything else strange happens, so I'll wait a few days and then phone Maureen at the Animal Centre. How was Isobel?' I ask, changing the subject.

'She seems fine. She has Pete staying with her and I think he is due to go back to The States in a couple of days. The funny thing is that Geoff says he was at uni. with Pete. They weren't doing the same course, as Pete was training in medicine, but they were on some student committee together. Geoff came up to Red House with me yesterday and he and Pete seemed quite surprised to see each other and had quite a lot of catching up to do, while Isobel and I exchanged vegetables.'

'Did he and Pete get on at Uni? I mean were they friends?' I say.

'No, Geoff said they were just acquaintances really and said Pete was always rather quiet and just followed what other people were doing. Yes, they got on well enough, but he found him difficult to get to know. He seemed to be a bit of a loner – kept himself to himself.'

I think of how Pete was with Isobel and seemed to need her to make decisions, so that he could just follow her lead. But then she was such a good organiser of everyone. While I am mulling this over, Angela says,

'By the way, Isobel seemed in a much more positive mood about you and the fact that you might stay on at Blackstone Cottage. She said Pete had been very impressed how you seem to have coped with everything and how you certainly seem to him to have recovered pretty well from the past, so maybe she will be a little more friendly with you now. She did, however, say she was a little concerned that you might be making a rather hurried friendship with Dan, as she has seen his car there quite a lot.'

'What's wrong with that?' I ask, feeling very defensive. 'He has been very helpful and so has Emma.'

'Yes -but you have only known him a couple of weeks, and I think I agree with Isobel that you should be careful and get to know him gradually. Remember he has probably had much more of a social life than you have had and we wouldn't want you to get hurt.'

'Or make a stupid mistake again,' I say rather peevishly.

'No, I am sure you are not going to do anything stupid, but, um, just be careful won't you. He is a bit older than you and you are a very attractive girl. Remember what he was like on the train when he was drunk.'

'No, he explained about that. He'd just bust up with this girlfriend and I am sure he doesn't usually behave like that.'

'Yes, well, you can't be too careful and I am sorry if I sound like an overprotective parent, but I am becoming very fond of you.'

'Ah, but you've only known *me* a couple of weeks and you might well change your mind when you get to know me better.' I reply with a smile.

We both laugh and she gives me a hug.

. . .

Geoff and Angela insist I stay for tea, although I am itching to get back to contact Dan about this morning's discovery. After tea

Geoff drives me home and I invite him into show him around. He seems to like how I have arranged things, but then comments, 'It's a bit cold isn't it?'

The stove was going quite well but I had to admit that the rest of the house was quite chilly.

'Would you consider getting some storage heaters?' he suggests. 'It wouldn't be as expensive as getting central heating installed and nowadays they are much more efficient and economical to run than they used to be. I am sure Angela would know who to contact.' I admit I had never thought of storage heaters, but say I would give it some thought and enquire about cost etc.

As he is about to leave, I say, 'Angela has been so kind to me and done so much to help and she hardly knows me. Do you think she has found me a nuisance, after all she comes down to Ridge Farm for peace and quiet? I do feel guilty, as I am not used to people being so kind and helpful.'

'No, she loves it,' he says emphatically. 'I have been a bit concerned for her being down here by herself so much. I know she prefers country life and, luckily, she can do quite a bit of her work online, but she doesn't have a lot in common with people she has met down here. Most people her age have children and families. I know she goes to Red House for yoga, but I hope you won't mind me saying, Isobel does have some rather strange ideas.'

'Some of her ideas do seem to come from the hippy era?' I suggest. 'I think she picked them up from living in a commune in The States.'

'Yes, that's just it. There is a lot of emphasis on spiritual ideas from ancient eastern philosophies. You see, Angela is a very down to earth, practical person and she does yoga mostly for physical wellbeing and doesn't really get all the spiritual aspect that Isobel teaches. But then, I suppose, that's where yoga comes from – the East, I mean.'

'Well, Isobel has always told me there are many different kinds of yoga teaching – and of course, she also does courses in more modern psychological therapy stuff, like Cognitive Behavioural

Therapy – CBT for short. She has a special "Life skills" programme and she certainly seems to have a following.'

'Yes, she does,' says Geoff, 'and Angela tells me there is quite a range of ages of people who go to yoga with her, both men and women. Do you happen to know how well qualified she is as a therapist?'

'I've no idea. She has always said she trained in The States and I know she has various initials after her name, but I don't know what they stand for. I was never involved in any of her "work", as she called it on the island, although we did some meditations as a group, which I always found helpful and enjoyable.' Then I add, 'She was also interested in the occult and spiritualism, which Ade, having a scientific mind, found very difficult to relate to and called it Isobel's Hocus Pocus. We both kept well out of all that.'

'Well, I could look up her qualifications,' says Geoff, 'but I believe it is still possible to set yourself up as psychotherapist without any officially recognised training.'

Then he adds, 'But of course she is very beautiful and charismatic – but something doesn't quite ring true – to me, who's only just met her. I can't put my finger on it.'

'Too good to be true?' I suggest.

'Yes, that's probably it. Oh dear, I hope I haven't offended you, but Angela has told me a bit about your background and how you find your Aunt Isobel so difficult. Also, how you are concerned about little Maisie's welfare.'

'Thank you, Geoff, for being so understanding. As I said before, Angela has been so helpful. In fact, I don't know how I would have coped without her. I would probably have taken one look at the cottage and run a mile.'

'Well, lovely to meet you Lora. I hope you don't mind my questioning you about Isobel, but I find the whole set- up at Red House quite intriguing.'

'No, I am glad to have had this chat and thank you so much again for the delicious lunch and all the help,' I say, as Geoff gives

me a big hug that nearly breaks my ribs, and then he goes off home
to have some time with Angela before his train back to London.

. . .

And now time to ring Dan, I think, as I search for my phone,
which I eventually find in the kitchen.

It is very dark now, as I take the torch and hurry out into the garden.

Dan answers quite quickly and I am just about to tell him
what I have found, when I hear some rustling in the bushes under
the trees. It is probably a fox or some other wild creature, but I am
so suspicious that I don't say very much, except that I need to see
him, plus some tools, if he can possibly come round. He says he will
be round in half an hour or so. He is helping Emma with Charlie at
the moment who is having a tantrum and doesn't want to get into
the bath. I tell him there is no urgency and to take his time, and
then I run quickly back indoors shutting the door firmly behind me.

. . .

Charlie takes a time to settle and Dan arrives looking a bit
fraught about an hour later.

'Sorry to take so long,' he says. 'Charlie was being particularly
difficult, but he has settled down now. I am glad Emma is firm with
him and won't give in, but of course it takes time and easier with
the two of us.'

'No, I'm sorry to drag you out,' I say, feeling guilty and hoping
this won't be a wild-goose chase. 'I'll show you what I've found,'

'That doesn't look much of a problem,' says Dan. These units
don't look very well put together and a bit of persuasion should
loosen this side,' and he gets out some tools from his bag. In a few
minutes he has managed to open up the gap, without too much
damage and sure enough we see some sheets of paper wedged in.
Dan carefully eases them out, without too much tearing, and hands
them to me.

I hurriedly take them from him and, apart from a short, handwritten bit at the top, they are closely typed on A4 sheets. I find I am standing there shaking, wondering what they are about. I can see "Dear Lora" at the top and then my eyes go bleary and I feel very anxious about what I am about to read.

'Take them into the other room and sit down by the fire,' says Dan, noticing my agitation. 'I'll just knock all this lot back into place and then I'll come in see how you are getting on.'

I sit by the fire feeling a bit numb for a few moments, while I hear him hammering in the kitchen, then with shaky hands, I begin to read silently. There is a wobbly handwritten bit at the top, where she apologises for typing and says her hands can cope better with a keyboard.

"Dear Lora,   *1ˢᵗ Oct. 2017*

By now you should have received my letter to you, which I sent care of Mr Floyd, my solicitor, so there should be no need to explain further about the legacy. I didn't want to write too much personal stuff in that letter, so that is why I told you where to find this more private, detailed, letter. I thought this would be a good place to hide it, so no one tidying or clearing the cottage would think of looking here.

As you know, I went to The States shortly before Isobel wrote to tell me you were both pregnant. I felt sad at having left you, when you both would be needing support and thought of coming back. But then I made the terrible discovery that I had terminal cancer and came back to England anyway for treatment. Isobel sounded so excited about her pregnancy, having reached the age of forty-two and having been trying for years to have a child and the fact that you were both pregnant together, but I concentrated on my own problems and the exhausting and traumatic treatment that I was going through.

I was lucky to find Blackstone Cottage, which suited me perfectly, with a good hospital close enough to travel to and a lovely peaceful location. Then came the terrible news about the death of Ade and your baby and all the dreadful aftermath of those events. Isobel managed to sell the island to someone who had been wanting it for years and, as luck would have it, Red House came up for sale and Isobel moved in with Maisie, who was just a few months old. There was no urgent work to be done on Red House, as the roof was in good repair and Isobel didn't mind living with a bit of peeling paint for a while. It was quite luxurious compared with life on Morg.

I tried to get to see you while you were in hospital, Isobel told me you had been very ill and so confused since the birth and that the Doctors were advising no visitors, even close relatives. At the time, I believed her, as, if I'm honest, I don't think I could have coped with seeing you in such distress. When you eventually came out of hospital and went to the hostel and then the flat, I sent messages via Isobel to say that I would love to see you if you would like to see me and I would wait to hear from you. I never heard a thing, so I presumed you did not feel up to seeing me and Isobel indicated that you were trying to cut yourself off from all memories of the past and start a new life.

If I had been feeling better myself, I am sure I would have persisted, but I admit I was a coward and getting weaker and weaker and I didn't want you to see me like that.

I have now got to the stage when I know I have not got much longer on this Earth as I have been told my condition is terminal and I have decided I don't want to go in for lengthy painful treatments, just to prolong the inevitable. So, as well as regrets about how I feel I have neglected you, I also have such happy memories of my times with you on Morg. You have always been so dear to me and such a sweet, sensible and intelligent girl, that I was determined you should have the cottage to do what you like with. You can sell it and have the money if you wish, but I would love to think of you being there near Maisie for a while, and I will explain why.

Isobel has always been a mystery to me. I don't think I have ever understood how her mind works. People seemed to flock around her, *but she has a way of distancing herself from close relationships. Pete has always been weak, but he adores her, and she treats him with such careless disrespect. Incidentally, I think Pete is basically a good, kind man, but misguided in his devotion to Isobel. She seems to have some almost hypnotic hold over him. She tells me he is supporting her and Maisie financially, so I hope he manages to keep that good job in the hospital in New York.*

I couldn't believe it when Isobel told me she was pregnant. I had always believed she couldn't have any children and I know she and Pete had had all sorts of tests. I think she even tried IVF at one time.

After she became pregnant, she was very amazed and pleased and utterly convinced, and I repeat convinced, that you were both expecting boy babies. She told me she had always wanted a boy and of course, after Ade's death, this could have been some comfort for Pete as well. You may not know this, but she had a friend (can't remember his name), who had put her in touch with her "spirit guide" (called Jonah), who assured her that there would be two little boys who could grow up together.

When I heard your very sad news and that Isobel had had a daughter, I was immediately concerned for the little girl. Isobel was always so strict and cold with you, that I couldn't imagine she would love and care for Maisie. But then I hoped that maternal instinct would be the answer and she would be different towards her own child, even though she is a girl and Isobel had always wanted a boy.

Since living in the cottage, I see a fair amount of Isobel and Maisie and believe my fears are founded. Isobel seems cold and distant from Maisie who is now nearly eighteen months and toddling about precariously. Isobel doesn't seem to have any patience or instinct of how to handle her. I have never seen her violent towards her, but she gets very tetchy with her and doesn't seem to show her much affection. I discretely mentioned to the health visitor that maybe Isobel was suffering from post-natal depression, but of course Isobel convinced her that all was well.

As I said before, Isobel has always been a mystery to me. Us three girls, your mother Rose, myself and Isobel, had a very difficult childhood. I was the oldest and ten years older than your Mother. Then Isobel was born three years later. We were brought up in a household of very rich parents. Our father's family had originally made a great deal of money in the coal and steel business, but our parents were disappointed at having girls and none of us showed any aptitude in following them in their business, which then revolved around oil and other commodities. We were cared for by a rather strict nanny and hardly ever saw our parents, who were only interested in social climbing and making lots of money. Our mother was beautiful and a socialite, but nowadays I think she would be called an "airhead". She certainly wasn't interested in children. I am sure our upbringing influenced the three of us, but in different ways. Your mother and I were very close, in spite of the age difference, and I felt protective towards your mother and Isobel, but Isobel was difficult from the start and was always out for herself, not seeming to care about anyone else. We tried to be "big sisters" to her, but she rejected any closeness. Maybe this was because of our upbringing and having no parental love- or perhaps she inherited an ability to be distant from those around her. Who knows?

Our parents both died in 1993. One of their many extravagancies was a small aeroplane, which they both enjoyed, but unfortunately it crashed into a mountain in bad weather and they were both killed instantly. I was the only one of the three of us to go to the funeral. Your mother didn't want to go and Isobel was in America. It was an occasion of mixed feelings for me. As I felt I never really knew them, I could feel no great sadness – but it was also a knowledge that there would never be a chance of an understanding or reconciliation. This means, of course, that after I have gone, Isobel and Maisie will be your only close relatives, unless you ever want to, or manage to track down your father, which might be possible in the future, with all the new internet technology.

As we three grew up, we went our separate ways. I became a teacher and your mother studied law at university then went to work as a solicitor in London. Isobel decided she didn't want a conventional life and took herself off at the age of eighteen to California, where we had some very distant relatives. While she was there she met a man who was very much older than her and she lived with him in some sort of commune. It sounded like a left-over from the hippy era. We all lost touch with her for a few years, apart from a few hurried letters, from which we gathered she was really enjoying living "an alternative lifestyle". We didn't know what she meant by this, but eventually she came back to London, having broken up with this man and she set herself up as a "Life skills instructor", which included teaching meditation, yoga and aerobics. She seemed to do very well with this and was extremely enthusiastic about her experiences in California. For a while we all shared a flat in London, but we were hardly ever there all at the same time. I was away for a few months and when I returned was very surprised when your mother said she had married Nick Laslo, who I had never met, but then discovered it was because she was pregnant with you and they had married in a hurry – but he then left her in a hurry also, without leaving any contact details. She never heard from him again and had no success in trying to track him down.

When Isobel went to live on Morg and suggested that we all join her there, it seemed such a lovely idea – and a big adventure. I was tired of teaching in the state school and your mother wanted to get away from everything. By then you were about three months old, so we joined Isobel and Pete on Morg.

I am sure I told you, when you were a child, that your mother was a lovely, kind, intelligent person. The only secret we had from each other was about your father and to this day I don't know why she didn't want to talk about him. It must have been her way of putting the past behind her. There has always been a mystery about her death also. It was believed by most people that she had deliberately drowned herself, and that she was suffering from post-natal depression, but I have never believed this. I think it was an accident, as she adored you (her new baby) and it was out of character for her to desert you. I had certainly not thought of her as seriously depressed. However, although she was a very, very good, strong swimmer, she was inclined to be reckless about going out in unsuitable, dangerous weather. She seemed to be drawn to the water and often we were surprised how she seemed unconcerned about the dangers. Her body was washed up on another island several weeks later and she was eventually cremated and we threw her ashes into the sea from the little cove where she had always gone to swim – as we all felt this is what she would have wished.

From the moment you were born, she told me that she would call you Leonora (Lora for short), so this is what you were christened – a week after your mother's body was found.

This is how you came to be brought up on Morg and, just like everything else, Isobel took over, saying she loved little babies and she seemed to care for you. Pete was part of Isobel's life and I knew he was a kind man, so, I trusted they would look after you when I was busy doing part-time teaching back on the mainland. It was only when I came back to live on the Island permanently and was taken on to help with your education and that of any other visiting children, that I got an indication of how emotionally neglected you were and I tried to make up for it. Isobel always wished you were a boy and said she couldn't cope with your pig-headedness and wilful-ways (as she called them). I can't think how she thought a boy would be different.

When Ade came to Morg, I was so delighted to see you having such a wonderful relationship with him. There had been a few other children visiting at various times, but no one with whom you seemed to have much in common. You were about nine when Ade first started coming to Morg during school holidays and he would have been about eleven. You were inseparable and he was the best thing that

*could have happened to you. As you both became older and he was
seriously studying for exams, he got you interested in new books and
a wide interest in the world at large and you were both absorbed in
learning about the wildlife on the island and how we all lived a simple
self-sufficient life. You became alive and full of fun and it was a joy to
see you so happy.*

*I just felt compelled to write all this to make sure you realise that
your mother really did love you and that I have always been sure she
did not mean to leave you. Also, I love you too, and I do have a lot
of guilt about not really giving you the support you needed. That has
been a great regret on my part and I do hope you'll forgive me.*

*Anyway, my dearest Lora, I hope you have a happy life and make
the best of yourself and I don't mean you have to have huge ambitions
of money or fame, but just be your usual kind and thoughtful (and
sometimes wilful) self.*

With all my love – May"

(then written in pencil with shaky writing), *"The ghosts are
friendly – just give them love. Perhaps you could clean up the black
stone and repaint the name of the cottage in white. It has been looking
rather scruffy and uncared for and the ivy seems to love creeping all
over it.*

. . .

Dan comes in just as I am finishing reading it for the second time
and he can see from my face that I am feeling very emotional, with
tears on my cheeks. He says nothing but comes over as I stand up to
pass him the sheets of paper. He holds me close while I try to recover
my voice, but I can't help sobbing and find it impossible to speak.

'It's OK' he says, 'just take your time. Would you like me to read it?'
I nod, then say, 'I just need a little time on my own. Please read it,'
I go out into the garden. I don't notice how cold it is. I have come
out without my coat and the frost crunches under my thin shoes,

as I wander around. There is a very clear sky and bright moon and I find myself drawn round to the black stone and as I reach out to touch it my hand almost sticks to its cold surface. I had previously removed some of the ivy, but I will do as Aunt May asks and as soon as possible, I will give it a clean and repaint the wording. All I can see in the moonlight is a dark cold object, but as I stand there in front of it, I find myself falling to my knees and putting my arms round it. As I do this it seems to get warmer and I whisper – 'I will take care of you and this cottage until you show me it is right to move on.'

I then make my way back into the cottage, feeling a sense of calm resolution.

'Are you OK?' asks Dan, looking anxious. 'It is freezing out there.'

'Yes, I know, and I am fine now. I'll just warm myself by the fire. It is beautiful out there you know. A bright moon and sparkling frost.'

Dan finds one of Aunt May's rugs and wraps it around me. Then he makes some hot drinks and we sit together on the sofa, quietly watching the flames gently flickering in the fire.

Chapter 16

Finding Aunt May's letter has given me a definite sense of purpose and the Maisie Quest seems something I believe Aunt May would like me to pursue as well. If I can find out that Maisie is my daughter, that would be brilliant, but even if I am disappointed and find that is not the case and the confusion of the past is really something inside my own head, then I think the truth is what is important. I could still try to be a good cousin to Maisie and do whatever possible to help her. After reading the letter several times and discussing it with Dan, is does seem that Aunt May did not know what went on at the time of the births and, like all the other people who were not on Morg at that time, she believes my severe reaction was to the death of Ade and then the tragedy of the baby and maybe she was right.

. . .

It is now a couple of days since we found the letter and Dan and Emma have been hugely supportive and are intrigued to find out the truth. We have arranged to meet up this evening at Dan and Emma's house and I have offered to take over pizza for supper. They will have been swimming this afternoon, as Isobel had particular plans and was grateful to have Maisie out of the way. I gather Emma is working every morning except Sundays and starts at 8.30 in the morning and finishes at 12.30. After giving Charlie lunch and a short nap, she is free most afternoons. She says Charlie always sleeps well after swimming and should be no trouble in the evening.

Dan picks me up at seven, although I had given a half-hearted offer to bike or walk down. There are no lights on the bike, and anyway the road could be icy on the way home. Emma greets me warmly and says Charlie has gone to bed exhausted after a busy day and he fell asleep while she was reading him a story.

I hand over the pizzas and we decide to eat them with some peas and the leeks which Angela gave me. Emma knows how to cook them, so that's OK. We chat all together and while preparing the meal, Emma opens a bottle of wine to have with our food.

While we are eating, Emma tells me she has been in touch with the friend about the DNA test.

'It is a bit disappointing,' she says,' as Amy's friend Mark, who works in the lab is going to be away for a couple of weeks. He says he is willing to do it when he gets back and could send us a sterile kit when he returns, but the test will be unofficial and not something he is meant to do. He has told my friend that he would be able to tell us if there is a definite match of mother and daughter, but we could not act on it, as we would have to get parent or guardian's permission to get an official test.'

'Well, at least it would let us know one way or the other,' I say, 'and we could then decide on what action to take next.'

'That's right,' says Dan. 'It's a pity we have to wait though. It must be very frustrating for you, after having found the letter.'

I look at Emma and I say, 'Would you like to read the letter? I've brought it with me.'

'Yes, if you don't mind me reading it, I should be very interested. Dan has told me about it, as I know you said he could.'

I hand it over and suggest that she reads it while Dan and I clear up after we have finished eating. We feel very full after our pizza and chocolate mousse. I am pleased they both seem to like chocolate as much as I do. While Emma is reading and Dan and I are in the kitchen, he asks me if I am still OK after finding the letter and he tells me he is quite surprised how calm I have seemed to be over the past couple of days since discovering it.

'Funnily enough I do feel very calm and it is as if Aunt May is supporting me. I have had some strange, muddled dreams the last couple of nights, but not scary, as Aunt May has always been somewhere in them in a comforting way.'

'So, would you feel like telling us what you remember about those past events?' Dan looks and sounds a bit hesitant, but adds, 'Of course if you're not ready, we'd quite understand. Or, if you would rather just talk to Emma, being a woman, who has experienced giving birth and all that goes with it?'

I am touched by his sensitivity regarding this. 'No, I really feel I am ready to talk about things now, and if you can bear it, I would be grateful for you to hear it as well, after all, the three of us seem to be involved in the Maisie Quest. Unless you and Emma have decided otherwise?' I add.

'No, we have discussed this and both feel we want to be part of this. Today, after swimming, Maisie didn't want to go back to Red House. She said she liked staying here better. I asked her why and she just said, 'Your house is not big.' Emma and I tried to find out what she meant, but she wouldn't say any more.'

'I think that shows she is lonely in that big place, alone with Isobel most of the time,' I say. 'It is obvious to all of us isn't it, that she needs help?'

Dan agrees and we go to see how Emma is getting on with the letter.

'Wow,' she says. 'This is really something. It must have been one hell of a shock to find it – and I am sure now you must be feeling even more determined to help Maisie – I am really keen to support you and I know Dan is too – if you are sure you want us to, that is.'

'Oh, I am so grateful that you are willing to help. There is no one else I can turn to, and I don't believe Angela would really understand, having never had a child of her own. I am sure if I had

DNA evidence, she would give all the help she could, but at the moment, I am not a hundred percent sure that she is not influenced by Isobel's stories about my past mental state.'

'Well, let's go and sit down in a more comfortable chair,' says Emma. I'll just go first to check on Charlie and make sure that the monitor is on, then we could finish the bottle of wine while you decide what you want to tell us.'

Emma comes down quite quickly and says that Charlie is fast asleep. She tells me he doesn't usually wake up much in the evenings, so she settles down with us by the fire.

'Um, it is difficult to know where to begin,' I say, 'but you already know the basic facts about my getting pregnant and Ade leaving to go to Africa, not knowing about my pregnancy. One of my greatest difficulties in telling you about it is that they gave me ECT at the hospital when my depression was so bad and medication was not helping at all.'

'What's ECT' asks Dan

'Electro convulsive therapy,' I say. 'It is not used very often, but in very severe cases of depression, which don't respond to normal medication. They strap electrodes to your head and basically give you electric shocks. I was under an anaesthetic, so was not aware of anything. In the past people used to be conscious when they did it, which must have been horrible. They still aren't sure how it works, but when it does it can be life-saving. Anyway, it did help me which was lucky as I gather I had been extremely ill, and I did feel very much more settled afterwards and more willing to accept what everyone was telling me. They explained that my extreme behaviour had been the result of the shock of Ade's death, then the baby's death and then being around Isobel's baby. All this, plus hormones playing havoc, it was not surprising that I was distressed.

Even after ECT though, I am still not convinced of Isobel and Pete's story of what happened and an unfortunate side-effect of ECT is loss of memory, so it left me with even more questions about what really happened. I have many, jumbled up memories of events concerning the birth, and recently having seen Maisie and Isobel, and especially since reading Aunt May's letter, I am getting more and more glimpses of the events during the birth.'

'So, do you think the ECT could have affected your memory permanently?' asks Emma.

'I don't think anybody really knows and also I suppose it must affect individuals differently, but then, I believe I was drugged during and after the birth, so this has added to my confusion.'

'Why do you think you were drugged?' asks Emma, looking horrified and puzzled, 'and then adds, 'I had a lot of gas and air and pain relief, but I was not heavily drugged and was conscious all the time.'

'I don't remember very much about any of it very clearly, but this of course could have been the ECT after-effects,' I tell her.

'Emma, I suggest we stop interrupting,' says Dan. 'I am sure Lora will tell us what she can remember as she goes along, and perhaps we can ask you questions later?' he asks.

'Yes, I would rather like to try to keep the flow going, as things come to me and later we can all ask questions – including myself.' I add.

Emma looks a bit abashed, but then apologises and says she understands how difficult this must be for me, and we all settle back in our seats.

'I think I would like to start at the time of Christmas at Morg when I had told Isobel and Pete about being pregnant, as it was a particularly strange time. Christmas on Morg was never celebrated in a commercial way. We had a few paper decorations, which had been made by various children through the years. There was no tree because Isobel said it was pagan, but I can't think how that mattered, as many of her believes and actions were pagan. There was no holly, also pagan, on the island and the heather was dead and brown by Christmas time, so no good for decoration.

We always gave each other presents, but these were things we had made ourselves, which I think we all enjoyed. But that particular year, I can't remember what we gave each other. I do remember the meal was a vegetarian dish of some sort. Isobel is a good cook, so it was probably delicious, but I was feeling so low I just remember pushing it around on the plate, with tuts of disapproval from Isobel.

After Christmas, Isobel started to change, very gradually, and there was a lot of whispering and quiet talks between Isobel and Pete. They had been considering me having an abortion. I was never part of these discussions, but I remember now praying that I could keep the baby, as it was such an important part of my connection to Ade, and as they told me he should not be told about the pregnancy, I was wondering if I would ever see him again. If I kept the baby, surely he would have to know about it sooner or later? So, I was in a constant state of anxiety.

Isobel's gradual change of mood became more apparent. The day after Boxing Day Isobel went over to the mainland for a couple of days and left me with Pete on the island. When she came back they told me they had cancelled the New Year guests. It was then that Isobel announced that she also was pregnant and what a thrill it was for both of them, as they had both wanted a child and she had had so many miscarriages over the years, it seemed a miracle. Pete said that we should both take it easy and not have to worry about guests for the moment and all that talk about an abortion for me was never discussed again. She seemed excited about her state and kept comparing symptoms with me and how she had had morning sickness and not realised at first why she had felt unwell. She was actually quite nice to me all of this time.'

As I say this, I am feeling quite tearful and take another sip of wine, while Emma and Dan comfort me and ask me if I want to go on.

'It's fine,' I say. 'If I get a bit emotional, take no notice. I feel this is doing me good to be able to get this out of my system.

So New Year came and went and Isobel continued to be pleasant to me. We talked about baby clothes etc. and she started to knit a little blue jacket. She told me that she had had a scan when she went to the mainland and all was fine, but they could not tell the sex of the baby. Pete said they could take me for a scan if I wanted one, but he said, being a doctor, he felt I should be fine without one and also, he didn't believe in unnecessary scans for healthy young people. Isobel had had one because of all the problems she had experienced in the past and the surprise of being able to conceive at all.

For the next few weeks, things continued in a fairly harmonious way. Isobel and I got gradually larger and one day she told me, quite out of the blue, that her Spirit Guide, Jonah, had told her that we were both expecting little boys and how lovely it would be for them to grow up together.

There was still no more mention of what was going to happen when Ade found out about this, as although I knew he had already gone to Africa, he was bound to be back one day and, surely, he would find out then. I didn't like to ask, in case they told me that I would never be able to see him again. Would he not want to tell him ever, that he had a child? Would he never come to Morg again to see his child? Would I be sent away somewhere? I had so many questions and was frightened of asking any of them, in case I couldn't cope with the answer.

Then the terrible news came to us. We had our crackly radio connection to the mainland and Pete decided to do the daily messaging.

He came in looking as white as a sheet and between shuddering gasps for breath, he told us about Ade's death.

We all fell apart and couldn't speak. I can remember the feeling of utter hopelessness and then disbelief. Even Isobel was crying, she and Pete were holding each other, and he was sobbing. 'Are you sure? Are you sure?' I kept asking, but Pete couldn't answer.'

I now notice that Emma is filling up my glass.

'I think we all need this,' she says, and I notice she is opening another bottle.

'For God's sake – don't give me anymore. I don't want to be drunk, as I certainly won't know what I'm saying and if Dan's going to drive me home, I'm sure he shouldn't have…'

'It's OK' says Dan. 'I won't have any more and we certainly don't need to finish the bottle.'

I look at the glass by my side and decide not to have any more for the moment. I am feeling a bit put out by the assumption from Emma that I need another drink, but then I look at her and I can see she is anxious about the whole situation. It is probably she who wants one, so I ask her if she is OK and is it all right for me to go on.

'I'm so sorry,' she says. 'I just feel so upset for you and how terrible that must have been, but please, please go on.'

So, I continue. 'The next few weeks are rather a blur. Ade's body was flown back and we went to his funeral on the mainland. Isobel made me wear a loose coat to hide my fairly small bump. I met his mother briefly, but can't remember much about her, apart from the fact that she was very distressed and, it is strange what unexpected things can come into the memory. She was wearing a black hat with a small blue flower on the side. I was numb through the service, having been heavily doped with Diazepam and I don't remember any more details, but I know there were the usual sad hymns and one of Ade's school friends gave a eulogy about all his achievements which a teacher added to. I deliberately blocked all of this off, as I knew I couldn't cope if I had listened.

We came straight back to Morg after the funeral. Luckily the sea was calm, so we got a boat straight away.

Over the next weeks, I hardly noticed the spring arriving. Isobel finished knitting the blue baby jacket and started on a blue shawl. She suggested I made something, but I couldn't get started. We ticked along doing our usual chores and there were no visitors. Isobel and I were getting rather tired with our growing babies inside us and I could feel mine kicking around, which gave me encouragement to think that this was part of Ade inside me. Isobel and Pete didn't talk much and we all went quietly about our daily chores. As the weather got warmer, I went for a few walks down by the sea, but didn't feel like swimming on my own. As the spring advanced it just made me feel sadder to think there would be no more times with Ade on the island. I tried to think of my baby and how he would grow up enjoying the island, but then all the practical questions invaded my mind and I found it too stressful to think of the future.

At the end of April there was a sudden violent change in the weather and several storms blew up. The weather did tend to be very changeable in the area, but on the day I went into labour the weather was very wild. I can remember the labour pains getting stronger and more frequent, as the evening got dark, and the wind was howling round the cottages. Isobel looked anxious, as there was no way of getting me to hospital on the mainland if there was a problem, but Pete seemed calm enough and explained to me how to breath properly through the contractions. After a few hours I was in agony and still Pete said everything was going fine. I remember he gave me an injection of something and then my mind became very muddled. I can remember him telling me several times to push and I don't remember much else, until I heard Pete say – "I can see the head," then I was urged to push again... and then I don't remember anything except a gasp from Isobel... and I vaguely remember her rushing from the room with a bundle wrapped in something white and floaty. I definitely heard a baby crying and remember a feeling of relief that it must be all right.

After that I remember nothing until I woke up the next morning. I was on my own when I awoke and was not in my usual bed, or even in the same cottage. I can remember sitting up and saying loudly, "where's my baby?"

Isobel came in quickly from the next room, with a very sad expression, and I don't feel able at this moment to say exactly what she said, but she told me that my baby had died soon after the birth, because he was very deformed and it would have been a terrible life for him if he had lived.'

. . .

At this point I stop, as I feel choked up and can't go on. Dan and Emma come over and they take me to the sofa and sit on each side of me, with their arms round me and they give me time to pull myself together.

'Have you had enough for now?' asks Emma.

I ask for a glass of water, which Dan hurries to the Kitchen and fetches for me. I sit there taking sips of water and after a few minutes I tell them I would like to go on, if it's OK with them, as talking about it is bringing back firmer memories, which are important if we are going to pursue the Maisie Quest. They both agree this is fine and Emma goes and checks Charlie is still sleeping soundly. Then I continue.

'This was the very worst time of all. I don't know how many hours, or even days went by. I felt I had nothing left worth living for, without Ade or his baby. Isobel encouraged me to get out of bed and walk around a bit and to eat and drink but I didn't see Pete at all. She brought me my meals and looked a bit fraught, but each time I asked her where Pete was she said he was busy, either with the boat or some other domestic matter. Then one day when she came in and was annoyed that I hadn't eaten my lunch again, I noticed that her bump had gone. She saw me looking startled and then, looking embarrassed, she told me she had given birth a couple of days ago and had a baby daughter. She said that she and Pete had not told me because they didn't want to upset me.

I didn't really feel anything except confusion. I said that I had been told it was going to be a boy and I think I asked if she and the baby were OK, but I can't be sure. I still don't remember seeing Pete and in my muddled state, I wondered if something had happened to him. Eventually Isobel told me that he had had to leave the island suddenly, as he had been offered a really good job in New York. She promised that he had actually come into say goodbye to me before he left and as I didn't know what day it was, or how long I had been feeling so disembodied, I just took her answer as true. I didn't really care whether I saw her baby or not. Everything had changed since the death of mine and most of the time I wandered aimlessly about, in and around the cottage.

One morning a couple of days later, or I think it was no more than two days, but of course in my confusion and grief, I cannot be sure, I got up and dressed and felt drawn to go down to the little cove where we used to swim. I had no particular plan, but I felt I just wanted to take all my clothes off and go into the water. I had to pass the cottage where Isobel and her baby were and on impulse, I just walked in. There in the corner of the room in a carry-cot was this beautiful baby. The baby was fast asleep and Isobel was not in the room at the time. I just stared at the baby, then I started to cry uncontrollably and I think my tears fell on the baby's cheek and the baby woke up and started to cry – and the cry was exactly like the cry when my baby was born – and from that moment I was utterly convinced this was my baby. Isobel came rushing into the room when she heard me sobbing "that's my baby, that's my baby" I was repeating over and over.

She ushered me out of the room very quickly and left the baby crying. She didn't seem to know what to do or say, but, again, I noticed something very strange. Isobel looked absolutely normal. She was wearing her ordinary clothes and didn't even seem to have the remains of a bump. I could still hear the baby crying in the other room and Isobel hurriedly led me back to my cottage, trying to reassure me. She gave me a tablet and watched me take it and waited for me to drop off to sleep in my bed.

For the next few days or weeks – I can't say how long – Isobel was kind to me. I did sleep a lot and was glad to have pills, as I just wanted to sleep and not wake up. She made sure I didn't have access to the bottle and doled out the pills when she thought necessary.

Anyway, it turned out that Pete had accepted a job in The States and she showed me part of a letter from him, where he asked how I was and sent me his love. Isobel said he had had to go promptly or he would have lost the opportunity. She told me that Pete had previously been over to the mainland to sort out his visa etc. and had registered the death of my baby. She told me that the baby had been cremated and that he had brought the ashes back to the island and that she and I could have a little service of our own on the beach, when I was strong enough. I was told that there was no way that I could have gone with him to register the death, as I was not in my right mind and she assured me that I had signed certain papers and agreed to the baby being called Adrian Paul Wesley. I took this information on board but had absolutely no emotional reaction to it, or any memory of signing anything.

Then, I have a very hazy memory of Isobel and me going down to the beach one beautiful morning, when the air was unusually still and the sun was still low in the sky. I felt I was walking on nothing – as if I was floating above the ground… and now I am remembering Isobel holding my arm so tightly that it hurt.

When we reached the cove, Isobel opened a box or tin, which she said contained my baby's ashes. I can remember I still had this unreal floating feeling, as we took it in turns to sprinkle the ashes into the lapping water at our feet. It made strange grey patterns in the water and one time when there was a sudden breeze, some of the ash blew up over Isobel's long, skirt. She let go of my arm, as she frantically tried to brush it off. I don't remember feeling any emotions during this event. It was as if it was nothing to do with me and I was just an onlooker.

I certainly did not get any better during the days to follow and it was during this time that one day I found Isobel's baby, Maisie, alone and crying in a room, with Isobel doing something, so-called important, elsewhere. I went in and picked her up and she looked at me as if she knew me and I certainly felt I knew her. I had found I was still producing milk occasionally, although I had been told that I should have dried up by now, so I decided to feed her. She seemed very hungry and took to the breast with no trouble and when she fell asleep, having had enough, I winded her and put her back in the cot. I did this several times over a few days, until Isobel found me one day and was furious. She called me a filthy slut and I was never going to be allowed near her baby again. After she had simmered down she actually apologised to me and said that it was natural for me to feel maternal towards Maisie, having just lost my own baby, but explained that I probably had medication in my blood, which could affect the milk and might not be good for Maisie. From then on she made sure I was never near Maisie.

Although I am even more hazy about the sequence of events from then on, I do know that I became more and more confused and Isobel was finding it increasingly difficult to know how to cope with me. Maisie was a very noisy baby and Isobel did not seem able, or willing, to breast feed and bottle feeding seemed a problem. I can remember the stressful atmosphere and feeling helpless to do anything about it. I felt so sure that all I had to do to settle Maisie was to pick her up and comfort her, but this was completely forbidden by Isobel. To give Isobel her due, I am sure I was still claiming Maisie as mine, which must have been impossible for her to deal with.

By sometime in June, I believe, some visitors were expected and it was then that I was dispatched to the mainland and Isobel took me to a private clinic run by someone she knew. It was a lovely peaceful place and everyone was incredibly kind to me. There were a few other "inmates", but I remember so little about them or any of my time there. It must have been extremely expensive. I know I had one-to-one counselling, but couldn't co-operate at all, so of course there were plenty of pills, doled out at regular intervals. All the staff tried very hard to get me to off-load my feelings, but quite honestly, I had buried all emotion deep inside and the depression took over completely.

One day, in spite of their strict security, I managed to steal some tablets and swallowed the lot. Of course, when I was found unconscious I was rushed to hospital and revived. I can remember coming to and being so devastated and angry at still being alive. It was soon after that it was decided ECT should be given – and I think, as controversial as it still is, it saved my life. I started to gradually come back and join in with the rest of humanity. The clinic took full responsibility for me having got hold of the pills and I have been told that they agreed to keep me on for free, until I was better.

I did gradually recover from then on and was told all the reasons for my depression and strange behaviour. I was reassured that I was not a freak and that my reactions had all been a combination of double-bereavement, PTSD and hormonal disruption.

With all this help and reassurance, I did, in time, believe in myself again and could understand the logic of how I had behaved and the sequence of events. I left the clinic and went to live in a hostel for a while and then a shared flat for some time. I went to a college and learnt a bit about computers and modern life. I learnt to drive and passed my driving test. This you already know.'

I stop and look at them both and Emma speaks first.

'That all sounds very, very distressing,' she says. 'I don't think I could have coped with all that without freaking out. In fact, I know I couldn't. I have always thought I would know Charlie's cry from the moment he was born, but I never had to question it or doubt it. He was with me all the time.'

'Sheep know their own lambs too. It's nature,' says Dan and we all laugh.

'Well, now you can understand how important it is for me to know one way or another. There are still so many unanswered questions. For example, how could Pete just vanish to America, leaving Isobel with their new baby? On the other hand, if, it was Isobel's baby that had died, surely they would both have been too upset for Pete to leave? None of it makes sense to me. How was I so unaware of everything that was going on around me?

'I agree,' says Emma. 'Either way, it seems very odd for him to leave. Surely a new job could wait? I'm sorry, Lora, I'm not doubting your conviction – just thinking aloud and trying to make sense of it all.'

'I know,' I reply, 'so, the sooner the DNA test is done, the sooner I will be able to get on with my life, whatever the outcome.'

Emma puts an arm round my shoulder. 'We are so glad to have met you,' she says, 'and I think it was very brave of you to talk about it to us. I think we all need to sleep on it now and have patience. You know we'll support you whatever the outcome.'

'Well you have been very good to listen to me and I think I need to go home and try to get a good night's sleep. Would you be able to take me home now Dan?'

'Of course,' he replies and, whether you like it or not, I am going to get my sleeping bag and spend the night on your sofa.'

Chapter 17

I sleep very well, but with lots of muddled dreams again, some of them involving Aunt May, which feels very comforting. I awake about seven, get up and shower and am surprised to find Dan already in the kitchen eating a huge bowl of my Crunchy Nut Cornflakes.

'I hope this is OK' he says with his mouth full, 'but I suddenly remembered I promised to go to a job in Ford this morning.'

'That's fine,' I reply. 'I'll make you some toast if you like?' and he nods enthusiastically.

We sit munching away together and then, between mouthfuls, we check that we both slept OK. I thank him for staying on the sofa and he assures me it was very comfy and anyway, he can always fall asleep anywhere and not much wakes him. I tell him it was nice for me to know he was there if I was worried, although he acknowledges, I would probably have had to shake him hard to wake him if I had needed anything.

After a hurried coffee, we agree that we will talk this afternoon and possibly all meet up as Emma will be off duty then. He tells me he has a very quick job to do in Ford and an estimate to give for a larger job.

. . .

I tidy up for a while and can't help thinking of my lovely friends while I drift about in the kitchen. Then the phone startles me and I have to go into the cold, frosty garden. It is BT saying they would like to come in and fix my landline this morning. This is great news, so I tell them I will be in and just as I finish that call, Angela phones and suggests a walk with Bess. She has been in London earlier in the week and thinks Bess would like a change of scenery, as although the Grahams walk her every day when she is away, it is usually the same route. I tell her I have someone coming to fix the phone, but I would love to give her a coffee and she can walk Bess when she wants to.

The telephone man arrives quite quickly and is a bit grumpy. I gather my internet connection will not be very good and he tells me the signal will not be strong enough for me to download games. I tell him I don't need it for games but he continues to be negative, telling me how slow it will be. Anyway, I now have a land line and an easy number to remember, so communication should be a bit easier.

After he has gone, Angela arrives with Bess. We have coffee and spend a bit of time organising an email address for me. Then she produces the telephone number of someone she recommends seeing about storage heaters and she urges me to get this organised, as she cannot believe that I can live in such a cold house. I tell her I'm fine and that Aunt May must have been OK for the couple of years she was here. Angela does not realise how tough we became on Morg, but I thank her for her trouble and promise I will contact the person. She then reminds me that I still haven't done anything about getting the car on the road yet and I tell her that I would be phoning the garage for an MOT, as all the other paperwork is through. She seems keen to keep me motivated and before she can remind me of anything else, I tell her I have decided to get Catty back.

'Oh, that's great,' she says, 'so that's an incentive to get the car going and you can go and fetch her. Then she adds rather quickly, 'Oh, I don't want you to think I wouldn't want to take you, but I am sure you want to be more independent, especially as I may soon be in London a bit more, as an extra bit of work has cropped up.'

'You are right, I have been depending on you since I've been here and it will be good for me to get organized. I must say, I feel more encouraged already, having got the landline phone and internet connection this morning.'

'Talking of which,' says Angela, 'Isobel phoned me earlier to confirm that she will give me a yoga session this afternoon. I had asked for one, as it is always very helpful and relaxing after an intense few days in London. She asked me whether you have a landline yet and at that point I didn't know the man was coming this morning, so I said I didn't think you had.'

'I don't want her to know my number,' I say in a firm voice, 'so please don't tell her will you?' I am imagining getting mysterious calls in the middle of the night, just to frighten me.

'I won't mention it to her,' says Angela,' but I thought that this afternoon, I will try and tactfully find out a bit more about her life with Maisie, as it is a private yoga session, I think I am the only other person who will be there this afternoon. I have been wondering a lot about Maisie, since you and I were last together, and Geoff and I were discussing your worries, especially after you told me how unkind Isobel used to be to you.'

'Well, it would be great if you can get some idea of how she copes with Maisie and I know Dan and Emma are rather worried about her. She certainly seems to enjoy their company in a quiet way and gets on well with Charlie, but does not say very much and is never keen to go home after she's been with them. Emma thinks it's strange that Maisie calls her mother "Isbel" and not mum or mummy, as most small children she knows. She told me that yesterday, after swimming, Maisie didn't want to go home and said something about preferring their house, as it is not so big.'

'She sounds like a rather lonely child', says Angela looking thoughtful, and then suddenly – 'Oh, look at the time – I must take Bess for a quick walk, or I'll be late for yoga at this rate. Do you want to come?'

I agree to go and we have a lovely walk through the fields, as the sun has come out and there is only a little frost left in the shade of trees and hedges. We then have a snack lunch together and I offer to look after Bess while Angela goes off up to Red House.

. . .

Dan and Emma arrive about two thirty, with a huge welcome from Bess, who then decides enough is enough and flops down in front of the fire. I explain that Angela has gone up to Red House and they tell me they have left Charlie with Aunt Jane, who sometimes has him for an afternoon, if Emma is busy. They seem pleased to see me and I'm certainly pleased to see them. Dan had done all he had needed to do this morning and the job had gone well. He had delivered the promised estimate to a new customer, who had agreed it on the spot.

'I hope you're OK after last night,' says Emma. 'I certainly felt quite wound up about it all, but I did get to sleep, did you?'

'Yes, I slept very well and I'm sorry if I left you feeling unsettled,' I reply. 'Aunt May seemed to be with me in my dreams, which was very comforting. She seems to accompany me in my dreams more since I read the letter. I don't suppose you've had much time to think about everything I told you, have you?'

'Well, actually, says Dan, 'we did talk about it over lunch today and, if you are up to it, we'd like to comment on a few things and ask a few questions?'

'Yes, that's fine. I was hoping you would, as we certainly have a lot of unanswered questions and I am beginning to feel more strongly that finding the truth is more important than clinging to a possibly false hope. I think I am so much stronger within myself, with all your support and having off-loaded all these feelings. I am just longing for the truth.'

'So, if this is really OK with you, we will go over a few things?' Emma looks at me quizzically.

'Yes, absolutely,' I reply.

Emma seems to be the one who wants to start the conversation off and I feel happy for her to do so., 'As it seems you have been feeling such a strong conviction that Maisie is your child, it would seem that Isobel and Pete took her from you at the birth and it was her baby who died. But why would they take Maisie from you unless their baby boy had been born damaged and died before you gave birth to Maisie?'

'I know, this has been really puzzling me. The logical part of me is saying, that what I have been told all along is true. When I was in labour, Isobel was with me and definitely still very large, as I can remember her leaning over me at one time, with her huge bump nearly in my face and thinking you wait till your turn. I bet you'll scream too.' Then I add: 'unless I was very deluded, she certainly seemed extremely pregnant.'

'You also told us,' says Emma, 'that you remember that Isobel gasped as the baby was born, which would make sense if the baby did not seem well, don't you think?'

'Yes, but it definitely cried very heartily and didn't sound at all weak. I have been thinking that the gasp could have been because she was expecting it to be a boy.'

'That's true,' says Emma thoughtfully. 'You said how you are sure Isobel was still pregnant and hadn't given birth before you went into labour, so she surely would not want to steal your baby at that stage. But as you are not sure about the timing of events later, she might have given birth to a damaged baby boy after you had given birth to Maisie.'

'Just a minute,' says Dan. 'Would Pete have disappeared off the scene so quickly, allegedly to America, and left Isobel with a new baby, after what would have been a great event for them both?'

'Oh, it all seems a terrible mystery to me,' I say 'and I don't feel I can go on making guesses anymore. I am feeling more and more frustrated and I would just like to stop thinking about it for now and wait till we get the chance to do the DNA test.'

'You're absolutely right,' says Dan. 'We are just going round in circles, but there is one more interesting puzzle, if you can bear to hear one more thing?'

'OK' I say with a sigh. 'If it is relevant.'

Dan continues. 'During lunchtime we did a hurried search for registrations of births and deaths online. We found Maisie Wesley's birth on the 1st of May, but nothing for a baby boy with suitable names for that time in the births or deaths files. Mind you, we didn't do a very thorough search and of course we didn't know exactly where to look, but there was nothing in the area where we found Maisie's.'

'Perhaps they didn't register the birth or death,' I suggest, as they certainly didn't want anyone to know about my pregnancy, or presumably the fact I'd given birth. She told me they had registered it, but perhaps they didn't.'

'But wouldn't they have had to have a death certificate for a cremation?' asks Dan.

'I am sure they would,' I reply. 'Surely no reputable crematorium would cremate a body without evidence of who it was?'

We all agreed that this was an important point and then Emma said there were one or two other things puzzling her about the story. 'If Isobel was expecting her baby about the same time as you, I would have thought it might have been possible to be able to tell the sex of the baby when she had the scan – or perhaps it was too early in the pregnancy.' Then she adds, 'Did you see a picture of the scan?'

'I was never shown one, but perhaps she showed it to Pete?'

Emma looks thoughtful again and then asks, 'What is a spirit guide?'

'Isobel has some very esoteric beliefs and she claimed she had a spirit guide called Jonah and when she meditated she would get messages from Jonah, who would give her advice and sometimes predict things that would happen. As children, we used to giggle about this and in tricky situations, we would say, 'I wonder what Jonah would say about this?''

Emma starts to laugh and Dan says, 'I can't believe it. I thought that sort of belief went out with the hippy years, with people high on LSD and other hallucinogens.'

'Well, I think Isobel is still, on something,' I say and then add, 'actually strange things did happen sometimes and Jonah seemed uncannily accurate, but it was probably coincidence. Ade certainly didn't believe in any of her odd beliefs and was impatient with his father for being so happy to tag along with anything Isobel said.'

'So – Jonah wasn't expecting Maisie to be born then,' says Dan with a laugh and Emma and I both look at each other and start laughing too.

After a bit of a pause, Emma says, 'are we agreed that we have reached a dead end for answers at the moment and that poor Lora needs a break from all the questioning from us?'

She looks at me as she says this and I reply, 'Yes, you are right. Everything is so distorted for me about those days and I cannot be sure of when Isobel gave birth. I don't even know what day it was when I gave birth. All I can remember is the terrible storm, so we could have both had our babies very close together and, who knows why, for some reason I was kept well-drugged?'

Dan looks concerned and says 'yes, I'm sure Lora must need a break and the best thing to do is to try to get that DNA test as soon as possible and try to think of other things in the meantime. Did you say you are thinking of getting Catty back?'

'Yes. I would love to get her back but am still a bit concerned for her safety.'

'I would think she would be OK' says Emma, 'with the police being so involved, I doubt whether anyone would try anything again.'

We all agree it is a risk worth taking and when I get my car going, I can go and fetch her, that is if Maureen at the animal centre is still in agreement.

We spend a bit more time talking about practical things like a cat flap, which Dan says he can install. We also talk about the possibility of storage heaters, which they both agree would be a good idea and then, after a quick cup of tea, Dan and Emma go back to pick up Charlie.

. . .

As expected, Angela comes into see me after her visit to Red House, but she is a little later than I expected and declines to stay for supper, as she must get back and give Bess her food. I tell her Bess has been asleep by the fire all afternoon and Angela is not surprised, as she'd had a good, lively walk earlier and obviously feels at home here. She says she had an interesting time with Isobel and after a quite strong session of yoga exercises, then a nice relaxing meditation without too many esoteric references, they had time for a chat.

. . .

She tells me Isobel seemed in a very friendly mood and they talked about gardens and how difficult she was finding it to get staff to help and how lucky it is that this is not a busy time for her and she can cope with keeping things ticking over for the time being, but will have to do some serious searching for staff in the spring. She only has part-time people helping on and off at the moment. Angela asked her how she coped with Maisie being around all the time and was told that she and Maisie are fine. She said she keeps Maisie occupied with plenty of books and drawing materials and told Angela that she is a very easy child – no trouble at all and that she is very bright and is already learning to read. She also said that Dan and Emma were absolute godsends and how useful it was to have them nearby to take Maisie when necessary and how Maisie enjoyed her swimming.

'So where was Maisie while you were doing yoga?' I ask.

'I was told she was up in her room watching a DVD,' says Angela. 'Apparently she has some favourite ones she can watch when Isobel really needs her to be quiet.'

'Did you see Maisie at all when you were there?'

'No, I didn't, and Isobel didn't go and see her or fetch her down when we had finished the session. Isobel offered me a cup of tea and I asked her if she wanted to check on Maisie or bring her down to be with us but she said she wouldn't disturb her, as she knew she would prefer the DVD and she would have to interrupt her soon for her tea and bath time.'

'I bet she's shut in her room,' I say bluntly. 'Just like I was.'

'Well, we can't be sure, can we? And as we've said before, she may be different with her own child, and you've said that Emma has looked for bruises etc. and can't find any marks of physical abuse, so I can't think what else we can do. Before I left I suggested maybe I could look after Maisie for her sometimes, if Emma and Dan are not able to and then I asked her if she thought you, Lora, would like to have a few odd jobs to do, or perhaps babysit for her sometimes. She seemed quite keen on the idea of my helping occasionally, but she looked very defensive when I mentioned you and said she didn't think you would want to, as you hadn't looked interested when she had suggested it to you previously, and anyway she didn't think you would be very reliable.'

'Ooh, the liar,' I say. 'She has never suggested that I go anywhere near Red House, or Maisie. I can assure you; she won't allow that.'

'Well, I thought it would be interesting to see her reaction, especially after Pete had reported how well you appeared to him and how you seemed to have completely recovered from your breakdown and moved on with your life.'

I feel so tempted to tell Angela all about the potential DNA test, but no, I must wait till after the test result and then I know Angela will support me whatever the outcome.

Chapter 18

It is now Friday two weeks later and I have done quite a lot in the last couple of weeks. It seems amazing that I have only been here about a month. During these past two weeks I have cleared up a lot more of Aunt May's things inside the cottage and taken some to charity shops.

I have had three night-storage heaters installed in strategic places, the most useful being on the landing outside my bedroom near the bathroom door, which I can keep open to prevent freezing pipes. I didn't want one in my bedroom. I have always been used to and like a cold bedroom.

Dan has been helping me clear a bit more in the garden and having removed the ivy I enjoyed cleaning the black stone. I think Aunt May would be pleased with the result and we found the name Blackstone Cottage had previously been painted on the side facing the lane, so, today, I repaint the name in white and it looks very smart. Something is a bit strange though. After I finish painting the stone, I can't help noticing that there seems to be a child's face on the side of the stone facing the cottage. It does not look deliberately carved but, appears to be formed from the surface of the stone itself. I can see it very clearly, but Dan finds it more difficult to make out. Sometimes when I look at It, it seems to be sad, but other times, I believe I see a slight smile.

We are waiting for the DNA testing kits to arrive, as Emma's contact is now back from holiday and has promised to send them as soon as possible. Each day I have been looking out for the postman in anticipation and he has noticed me hovering at the door when he comes. He has promised to put any package in a box behind the garage if I am not there when he calls.

Although Dan has been fairly busy with work of his own, he has spent a lot of his spare time helping me and has put a cat flap in the back door, as I have arranged to pick up Catty on Monday. He has also done some odd jobs in the kitchen, like mending the cupboard and putting up some extra shelves. I have absolutely insisted on paying for this and, as he was reluctant to tell me the cost, I tackled Emma on the subject and then they both understood how important it is to me to feel independent and not indebted to Dan more than I am already for his time and patience.

He and I seem to get on so well together. He is quite different from Ade, who was highly energetic, quite talkative, with lots of exciting topics, whilst Dan is calmer and seems to be a deep-thinking person. He doesn't talk much, but has a good sense of humour and is sensitive to the moods of people around him. He is very good with Charlie and it is obvious that Charlie loves being with him too. Emma and her new man, as Dan calls him are spending a great deal of their spare time together, so I think Dan is quite enjoying my company, or I hope so. We have been going for some lovely walks together around the fields and hills and I have been so interested in learning about the countryside round here, as it is like a different planet from Morg. He explains that this is mainly an area based on chalk and the hills are called downs and have many ancient burial sites and encampments. There are some beautiful views for many miles from some of these sites and it does give me a wonderful feeling of space and freedom, as I enjoyed so much on Morg. But I do miss the sea and I believe it is about forty miles to the nearest coast. It is not a very wooded area and most of the trees are beech, as are the ones around the cottage, together with a few yews. Dan is looking forward to the spring, when he can show me all the changing colours and different shades of green – and go down to the sea.

The car has passed its MOT, with a few minor hitches and I have taken it out a couple of times, once just to get the feel of it and explore the local area a bit, and once to Wasbury to do some food shopping and I am looking forward to going to fetch Catty on Monday.

I have asked Angela and Geoff to lunch on Sunday. I can't think what I will give them that will live up to Angela's expert cooking, but Dan says he'll help and says he is sure they won't expect anything too grand. So, we've decided on a casserole, with lots of vegetables and baked potatoes, and we can pick up some sort of delicious looking pudding from a supermarket tomorrow. Angela has been spending more time in London these past two weeks but is expecting to be down at Ridge Farm for most of next week.

Angela suggested that I asked Isobel and Maisie to lunch too, as she said it would be good for me to be friendly towards Isobel, even if she did not want to make the first move and it might break the ice and give me a better chance of seeing more of Maisie. We decided it would be worth a try, which I did, but to no avail. Isobel seemed rather taken off-balance when I asked her and made an excuse of having something else already planned. Oh well, I tried.

. . .

The lunch goes well, and Dan and I feel quite pleased with our culinary efforts. Without spending too much money, we seem to have given our guests a good meal. Anyway, they both have second helpings and I don't think it was just to be polite.

It has been raining most of the morning, but it clears after lunch and as Angela and Geoff have brought Bess with them and as she has been lazily sleeping by the fire all through lunch, we all decide to take her for a walk. We put on our wellies and Angela and Geoff come and inspect my newly-painted wording on the black stone.

'That looks really good, but I must admit I can't see any discernible shape of a face on the back,' says Angela, peering at it from different directions.

'Well, it must be my imagination,' I say,' but look more closely. I can see eyes, nose and mouth, smiling today. Oh yes – and there is some hair. Can't you see?' And I try pointing out the features to them.

'No, sorry,' say Angela and Geoff together.

'But I can sometimes see it,' says Dan coming to my rescue.

'OK,' says Geoff, 'then, maybe it depends on the light and the different ways we all perceive things. The light falls on it at varying angles at different times, so sometimes you can see it and sometimes you can't. We are all individuals and how we interpret things must vary enormously.'

'Well, you are both young with better eyesight than us and neither of us is wearing our glasses,' says Angela.

While we are thinking about this, we all walk on towards the little gate from the garden to the field beyond and then Angela says, 'Have you been to the little Church down in Wasbury? I think, according to my map, this footpath is a short cut to the village and I believe the little girl, Alice Perkins, from Blackstone Cottage is buried in the Churchyard. You might like to go and look for the gravestone sometime.'

'I'd like to go now,' I say, 'but you all go on for your walk if you like, as I'm sure Bess would not be interested.'

Dan decides to come with me and the others agree that Bess needs a long run and they both need some exercise after London life and a big lunch, so we arrange to meet back at the cottage at four o'clock.

After a while we come into the village. It is a shorter route than going by road and round the first corner we find the little Church. It has a square tower and a Norman arched porch leads down some stone steps into the main part of the Church, which Dan tells me is 12th century. I think it is beautiful. It is so simple, with plain leaded glass windows, through which you can see the bare winter trees swaying in the breeze. There is an altar with a plain blue cloth and a few candlesticks here and there, and Dan tells me the pews are very old and made of oak. I suddenly feel very overwhelmed by the silence and simplicity of the place and sit myself down in one of the pews. Dan wanders round for a minute of two, then comes and joins me. We sit in silence for a while and then find we are holding hands. We look at each other and smile and then I say, quietly, 'Let's go and find Alice Perkins'.

There are many gravestones in the churchyard, some very old and hardly readable, others with more legible wording and some much more recent ones are easy to read. We walk round for what seems like a very long time, each of us looking in different areas, when suddenly, I come across a little grey stone with faint, but readable wording. It says:

"In loving memory of Alice Perkins, 1st May 1883 – 6th November 1886".

'Look – she has the same birthday as Maisie,' I exclaim.

We both feel moved looking at this stone and feeling a connection with the cottage and now with Maisie as well. We take time to absorb the meaning of all this. I tell Dan, I can sense Aunt May with us at the moment and, as usual, this makes me feel very warm and comforted. We slowly leave the churchyard and as we get to the gate, I look at my watch and see it is twenty-five to four. We'll have to hurry to get back to the cottage, not to keep the others waiting as they haven't got a key.

When we get back the others are already there, but they tell us they have only just arrived, so we all go inside and have tea and biscuits while I tell them about our visit to the church and finding the gravestone.

'I believe your Aunt May used to put flowers on the grave occasionally,' says Angela. 'I had forgotten, but now I remember Isobel telling me that the little girl's birthday was the same as Maisie's.'

'Do you know if there is anyone in the village who would have been related to the girl's family?' I ask. 'That part of the churchyard seems fairly neglected and although it looks as if the grass is cut occasionally, most of the graves have weeds growing round them.'

'I've lived in the village all my life,' says Dan 'and I haven't come across a family called Perkins, but that should be quite easy to find out. I can ask around if you like.'

We all agree that would be good and I vow to myself, that as long as I am living in the cottage, I will try to put flowers on her grave on her birthday. I am hoping more and more that I'll be staying in the Cottage for quite a while, as I'm beginning to love the place and the people I've met. Of course, I'm not sure how I am going to feel after the DNA result, but I think I will still want to stay, even if the result is not in my favour, as I will want to honour Aunt May's wish to look out for Maisie's welfare. I feel such a strong connection to her whatever the result and wonder what I will do if I find out that she is my daughter. How would I go about challenging Isobel? Anyway, it's no good worrying about details, as we haven't even received the testing kits yet.

Angela sees me looking thoughtful and presumes I am thinking about picking up Catty. 'I'm sorry I can't be with you tomorrow, but I have to be in London for a few days this week, but I hope all goes well and she settles in quickly. I am sure she will, as she seemed perfectly at home before.'

'I think she'll settle OK' I reply, 'but I just hope I'm doing the right thing and that she will be safe here, with no more mysterious events.'

They all tell me they think it will be fine and I shouldn't worry and it is worth taking the risk, especially as the police have been involved and word soon gets around in a small neighbourhood. But I do worry. The others, except Dan, don't know my suspicions about Isobel.

. . .

I have changed my mind! I wake early next morning and decide I can't bring Catty back here to the possibility of anything happening to her. I think how awful it would be if Isobel thought of anything more to do to harm her. What about poison? It would be quite easy for Isobel to put something into some tasty food and leave it nearby. Not where her dog could get it – but she would find a way.

Having made that decision, I will still go and see Maureen and explain more fully the reason for my worries. I have found a small, faded photo of Isobel from Aunt May's album, which I am taking along in case it jogs Karen's memory. As the image is unclear, I have found a little magnifying glass, which I've put in my bag also. All Maureen knows at the moment, is that the police have been fairly reassuring, but I think if I am brave enough to tell her the whole story, she would be reluctant to take the risk.

Having put the carrying box back in the garage, I set off in my little car, leaving about the right time to reach the Centre by ten o'clock, as arranged with Maureen. I arrive at the Centre and Maureen is there to meet me in her office. She asks me to sit down on a rather rickety wooden chair and tells me that Karen and some volunteers are doing chores, so she has the morning set aside for paperwork, of which she says there is always a great deal.

I start off straight away telling her my doubts, 'I am sorry but I still feel I cannot take Catty at the moment and I really do need to explain the background. You must think me a terrible time-waster, but that I am sure you wouldn't want Catty to come to any more…'

Then she interrupts me… 'Wait – just a minute – before you go on, I have literally only just put the phone down. The police phoned to tell me that they have found the culprits.'

'What, who?' I am feeling very confused.

'The louts who were causing so much trouble. They were caught red-handed last evening putting a cat in a plastic bag, which they then threw in the river – just the other side of Wasbury. Very luckily somebody saw the whole thing and filmed it on their phone and to cut a long story short, they were arrested. The cat was OK and is safely back with its distraught owners. Apparently, they have been causing a lot of other trouble recently, but I don't know any more details. The police wanted to know whether I'd heard of any other cats going missing.' She looks at me, as if that is the answer to my problem.

I feel very much off balance, having been building myself up to tell her all about my suspicions of Isobel and I can't think of anything to say but, 'Oh good, that's great.' Thoughts are whirring through my mind. So, have I been wrong all along? If it wasn't her, then – my mind is going numb. The effigy – who did that?

Maureen is saying things that I am not taking in and then she looks at me and says, 'Aren't you pleased? I thought you'd be delighted to know that Catty should be safe with you now that we know there won't be any more trouble from that lot.

'Yes, yes, of course I'm pleased.' I say pulling myself together, 'it's just that I wasn't expecting this news and of course I am very pleased, but I was preparing myself to tell you that I didn't think it would be safe to take her back. But, of course, now that's changed everything. – Hasn't it?' I realise I am questioning myself here.

'So, are you trying to tell me you don't want her after all?'

'Oh, no, I definitely want her. I was just taken by surprise.'

'Well, I suggest, that if you were not ready to take her back today, as I presume you haven't brought a carrier with you, I could bring her over to you tomorrow and I could see your cottage and surroundings and help you settle her in.'

She looks a little put out that I am not jumping for joy, but agrees I am absolutely right in putting the welfare of Catty first, before my own needs. As her phone has been ringing on and off since I arrived, which has been another distraction, she switches it off.

'They'll have to wait,' she says. 'Is there anything else you want to ask me? You are still looking worried and uncertain.'

'Well, I wondered whether you had found out yet anything about the strange person who collected Catty from you, as you see, I have a photo here,' – and I take it out of my bag and show it to her.

'So, this is obviously somebody you know.'

'Yes, she lives close by and is actually my aunt.

'Well, why on earth would you suspect her of stealing a cat?'

'Oh – I don't know really. She is a bit strange.' I don't want to go into all the details of my relationship with Isobel, so I say, 'Maybe she was doing it as a surprise for me. I know she wouldn't have got a cat for herself, as she doesn't like cats, but adores her little dog.'

Maureen frowns, 'Can't you ask her?'

'Well, you see, we don't get on, but do you think I should do that?'

Maureen sighs and sits back in her chair and is obviously puzzled by the whole situation. Then she says, 'I think the best thing to do first is to find Karen, who is working here today, and ask her to look at the photo and see if she recognises the person. Whoever it was, managed to keep her car away from cameras, so we don't have a reg number and she managed to keep her face well hidden. If Karen recognises her, then we can decide what to do next. We haven't rehomed a black cat to anywhere near Wasbury for well over a couple of years, so you can see it is still a mystery.'

We find Karen cleaning out a kennel. She looks quite young and very shy and certainly doesn't strike me as a person who could stand up to Isobel.

'Have you come to fetch Catty?' she asks.

'Not just yet,' says Maureen, but we would like you to look at a photo that Lora has brought, to see if it can jog your memory about the woman who took Catty from here. You see, Lora thinks she might know the woman.'

'Yes, I, I will er, have a look, but it all seemed to happen so quickly – and I am so sorry…'

'Yes, I know you are sorry, and you've been forgiven and I know you wouldn't do it again,' says Maureen with a smile,' but if this does jog your memory, it could be useful, in solving the mystery.'

I take out the photo and hand it to her. She says it is difficult to see and she can't really say she would recognise her, so I hand her the small magnifying glass and she looks at it very carefully and shakes her head. 'I'm sorry, I really couldn't say if that is her. She was wearing dark glasses and faces look so different then – and she only took them off – actually put them on her head – when she was looking at and talking to Catty. Then she had her back to me. I'm so sorry I can't be more help.'

'Is there anything more you can remember about her?' Maureen asks her.

Karen looks very thoughtful and then says, 'She was tall, about your height,' she says, looking at me, 'and as I said before, she was smartly dressed and a fairly posh voice, but she sounded very kind and told me about her daughter missing her old cat. How she lived a long way away and couldn't come back another time. As I've said before, she seemed so genuine and persuasive – but I promise I won't make the same mistake again.' Poor Karen looks very upset and near to tears, and Maureen and I try to reassure her that she is not in trouble, but we just needed to know whether the person in the photo might be the right one.

When Maureen and I get back to her office, she says, 'I'm sorry, but I don't think that proves anything, do you?'

'No, it doesn't, but I just thought the photo might be helpful.' I reply. 'Maybe I should ask her sometime.' I add, thinking to myself – no way. I could imagine her biting, sarcastic reply.

'Anyway', says Maureen, 'Catty has come to no lasting harm and she really needs a loving home now and I can see that you would give her that, so, if you like, I could bring her over to you tomorrow, check things over and help you settle her in?'

'That would be great,' I say, 'I have been so looking forward to having her back, and now I hear that she should be safe, I can feel more relaxed.'

'That's good then, I'll just get your details, so I'll know how to find you. I expect you'll find you have a message from the police, if you look on your phone now.'

Sure enough, there was a text from Chris, saying she would be contacting me. I say my goodbyes and thanks to Karen and set off for home.

Chapter 19

I drive home with feelings alternating between the excitement of getting Catty back and the guilt that I might have believed Isobel could do such a diabolical thing as putting a cat in a plastic bag. I had never known her to be cruel to an animal. Mind you, we did not have pets on the island, but I am told she certainly loves her little dog, Whisky. This gets my imagination going and makes me wonder about my sanity again. Perhaps I am maligning her, by believing Maisie is not her daughter. Supposing I am the bad person for thinking these seriously awful things about her. I don't really like myself very much at the moment. Even more reason for the DNA tests, I think.

Arriving back at the cottage everything looks peaceful and I immediately go to check whether the postman has been and left anything in the box. I hardly dare look as I start to open the lid and find a brown package inside. There is nothing on the outside to identify what it is, but I am not expecting any other mail, so impatiently I unlock the front door and rush inside, eager to open it. First, I lock the door behind me and take the package upstairs. I have such a feeling of subterfuge and guilt at what we are planning to do. I open the package and sure enough, there are two identical kits, with instructions as to how to use them.

I know Dan has a busy day with work, so I leave a text message saying the parcel has arrived and I know he will contact me as soon as he can. I really should get myself something to eat, but am feeling too wound up, so I nibble on some dry biscuits and read the instructions on the kits. It sounds quite straightforward, as long as one is careful to keep everything clean and not contaminated with anything else. I can't see a problem with doing mine, as it is just a matter of taking swabs from inside my mouth, but wonder how Dan and Emma would manage with Maisie. How would they persuade a small child to co-operate – and in a way that would not get her running to Isobel and telling her all about it afterwards? I decide I will do mine as soon as I can but, then realise that my mouth must be clean and I need to clean my teeth, rinse my mouth and not eat or drink anything but water for about an hour before taking a sample. This is frustrating, but I do the cleaning process, then fill a glass of water to drink when thirsty.

I eventually get a message from Dan, apologising for not replying earlier, but he has only just looked at his messages. He says he will call in about three, as Isobel has unexpectedly asked him to look after Maisie this afternoon. He has agreed to pick her up and take her to Emma, as he has to go back to work.

. . .

Now It is nearly three o'clock and I have managed to do my swabbing and left them to dry, standing upright in a clean glass, as suggested. Dan arrives and I am glad he calls in before picking up Maisie.

'Sorry, I've had a rushed day,' he says, 'and I won't be able to stop long now. As you know, Isobel likes punctuality. It is great to hear you've got the kits, so do you want me to take Maisie's now and Emma could have a look and possibly do Maisie's test today?'

I sound a bit hesitant when I reply. 'I am a bit worried to know how she is going to do it, especially if she is there alone with the children… How will she manage to get Maisie to co-operate and keep Charlie from climbing all over her and contaminating things…?'

'Don't worry,' he says hurriedly. 'She's done it before. She had to do it for Charlie, as there was a paternity objection from her ex. And anyway, I'll finish work about five and we can do it together then – or another day soon. Emma has huge imagination and I am sure she'll think up some sort of game. She's brilliant like that.'

'OK,' I say, but I know I look and sound concerned, as I hand the package over. 'There are instructions with the kit and I've done mine.' I show him the glass with them standing to dry. Are you sure you and Emma are happy to do this?'

'Yea, absolutely fine. I must rush. Emma's car's being serviced, so she couldn't pick up Maisie. See you later, when I bring Maisie back. Probably about six thirty. Is that OK?'

'That's fine,' I say and as he hurries out I just wish I could have told him about all my anxiety and doubts, but he is obviously in a huge hurry.

. . .

After Dan leaves to go to fetch Maisie, I find I am feeling quite faint and feel a panic attack coming on. My limbs feel numb so I try to concentrate on my breathing and giving myself positive reassurances. I am finding it is taking me a long time to calm down, so I decide to walk round outside for a few minutes in the cold air. The sky is overcast, but it is not raining and I happen to glance at the black stone and for a few seconds, I could swear I could see the smiling face of the child. This brings me up with a start. Maisie is the important person here and whatever my doubts and fears, I must be strong enough to get the DNA tests done, so I take myself back inside and suddenly realise I am quite hungry.

I go to the kitchen to make myself a cheese sandwich and notice the cat flap and realise I had temporarily forgotten about Catty arriving tomorrow. The thought of Catty's presence gives me a feeling of comfort and with the sandwich and a glass of water inside me, I feel strong enough to concentrate on the idea of the test. I put my DNA swabs away in the special envelopes provided and hide them away in a drawer in my bedroom. In spite of having had the locks changed, I still find myself a bit uncertain about security. The strange events of the past few weeks are so difficult to put aside.

I now try to concentrate on Catty, to take my mind off the DNA test. Last week, before my doubts about getting Catty back, I had washed and dried the rugs that were in Aunt May's cat basket and bought new feed and water bowls, as the others looked stained and cracked. I put everything in the right place to be ready for her arrival. There is plenty of cat food in a kitchen cupboard and I had also bought new cat litter, so that I can try to keep Catty in at night, as Maureen suggested. I am wondering whether Catty is used to a cat flap and am hoping that she used one when she lived in a family previously. Anyway, I expect Maureen will help me with this.

I get a message from Dan at twenty past five, saying, 'All OK We've done it – tell you all about it later.'

I am very impatient and feeling rather sick, waiting for him to arrive.

Dan doesn't manage to get to me till about seven thirty. He had had a message from Isobel asking him to keep Maisie a bit later and so they gave her supper with Charlie. Poor Dan looks exhausted and is very thankful when I ask him to supper, as Emma's friend is joining her for a meal and he doesn't want them to feel awkward if he is there too. I can't wait to hear the details of how the testing went, so I give him a glass of Aunt May's sherry, as I still haven't remembered to buy any beer. I am so relieved to see him and thankful that he wants to stay, as I really need his company.

'It went very well,' he says, as he sinks down into an armchair. 'I couldn't believe how easy it was. I got home about five and Emma had already managed to get Maisie's mouth clean and ready in plenty of time and taken the swabs which were high on a shelf in a glass, drying. I asked her how on earth she had managed it and she just shrugged and told me she had played a game with them of teeth cleaning and had got some cotton buds for Charlie to play around with too. The children seemed to have forgotten about it by the time I arrived, so we deliberately didn't mention the game and talked to them about other things while they ate their supper.'

'Wow – that's great,' I exclaim. 'Clever Emma. So, what do we do next?'

'If you can let me have your samples this evening, Emma is seeing her friend, Amy, tomorrow and Amy can give them to Mark, the bloke from the lab, as she is seeing him in the evening. Does that sound OK?'

'Yes. That sounds perfect, but I am amazed that it could all happen so quickly – and do you realise we are nearly at the point of no return? Sounds quite scary.'

'You've still got time to change your mind.' He says, giving me time to reply, and when I just nod and tell him I realise that, he says, 'But, I hear that Mark is having to be very cagey about the whole thing, as it is all unofficial and he won't want to put anything in writing, so if you are happy for him to have your phone number, he can contact you direct, as soon as he manages to do the tests. Can we give him your number?'

'Yes, sure, but have you any idea how long it would be? Days, weeks, months?'

'No, I got the impression it would probably be days, but we can ask Amy to check that.'

I am not sure how I feel at this moment. I know I am impatient to know the outcome as soon as possible but, is the uncertainty worse than if I get a negative answer? At least, at the moment I have hope, so I will have to do my best to be patient and try and concentrate on other things, such as tomorrow, when Catty is due to arrive.

Dan sees me looking thoughtful and says; 'Bit of a waiting game isn't it? I can assure you Emma and I realise this is very difficult for you, so we can only hope results come through quickly.' Then he notices my expression and adds: 'You must be feeling very anxious about it, but as we don't know when he will phone, Emma and I can't be sure we will be around when you hear from him.'

'Yes, I must admit, I really don't know how I will react when I hear the result. I keep trying to prepare myself and it would be great to have your support whatever the outcome, but that is probably not possible.'

'I will ask Emma to see if she can find out when it's likely to be, so that we can be with you – if that is what you would like?'

'That would be really good, as I don't know if I could handle it on my own and I can't ask Angela, as she knows nothing about this.'

'Of course, Emma and I will support you. This is a real big issue – your whole future depends on this.'

Then my voice becomes shaky and I blurt out – 'Yes, that's what's so terrifying. I know I want a positive answer, but then – could I look after a child? I've never known any small children very well and at the moment I don't feel very grown up myself.'

Dan looks very concerned and as he comes over and puts his arms round me, he says, 'I'm so sorry. I have been just taking it for granted that you would cope. I just feel so sure you would be great with Maisie. You seem so much more grown up than your age. You've had a tough life and had to be your own strength virtually always, but all this must seem a very big responsibility.'

'God, you don't say. The whole thing is freaking me out. Oh, and I haven't told you about Catty yet and it turns out Isobel may not be the monster I made her out to be.'

We agree to go to the kitchen to get something ready for supper, where I can tell him all about it. Earlier I had taken a casserole from the freezer and there is plenty for two, so we are deciding whether we can be bothered to prepare any extra veg.

'So, what's this about Isobel, then?'

'No, Well, it's a bit of a story. Do you want some more of Aunt May's sherry while I tell you about it?'

'No, I'm fine, just itching to know what has happened.'

I tell him how, when I woke this morning, I decided I was still not feeling safe enough to have Catty back. Then I tell him about the morning's visit to Maureen; the louts having been arrested; Karen not recognising the photo, and my guilt about suspecting Isobel.

'What happened next?' Dan asks,

'Maureen thinks that Catty should be safe now they have caught the people responsible for several evil deeds and she is bringing Catty over tomorrow morning.'

'You agreed to this, I presume?'

'Yes – I did and still feel very confused and guilty at believing Isobel could be quite that evil. I feel really bad about that.'

'Well, I think anyone who can take a cigarette to a child's arm is capable of almost anything,' says Dan, as he puts some carrots in a saucepan on the cooker.

. . .

It is a cold evening and, in spite of the new storage heaters taking the chill off the house, after supper, we both go and sit on the sofa in front of the fire. I get my laptop and try to find something interesting to watch. Dan is used to finding all kinds of films, but we end up looking at funny things on You Tube and also Dan introduces me to some of the bands that he likes and we listen to a variety of music. I feel so relaxed with him and we both have the same sense of humour and we tease each other a lot. Every now and again, I call him "Odd Socks", which he pretends to be annoyed about and he then calls me "Spider", which really does annoy me.

After a while though, I start to feel uneasy again and I find myself wondering where this relationship is going. At the moment we are just very good friends and I have no idea whether he feels anything more than this, or whether he is mainly interested in the Maisie Quest and getting that sorted. I admit to myself that I am getting more and more fond of him and am finding him very attractive in his quiet way.

We are listening to some music when I start to think of Ade and immediately feel a pang of guilt that I could find anyone else of interest and then, comparing him with Dan again. They are very different. Ade will always be such an important part of me and I can't imagine there will ever be a time when I don't think of him at least once a day, but would I feel the same if Maisie is not his child? We had such a carefree time together. Life with him was always exciting and very eventful. He went about things as if there was no tomorrow, and of course, there never would be a tomorrow for him, but neither of us could have guessed that then. He had no patience with Isobel's "fancy" ideas and couldn't understand why Pete stayed with her. He told me he only came to the island to see me and for the freedom of being able to swim and go fishing, but I knew he soon got bored and was glad to get back to the mainland and his many friends and activities. He said he couldn't wait for me to be old enough for him to take me and show me the world beyond Morg.

It is so difficult to imagine what would have happened if he hadn't died. Would he have found out about my pregnancy and everything that followed? Possibly not. He would have probably still been in Africa all the time I was in hospital. I wonder whether he would have believed me, or whether Isobel and Pete would have convinced him, as they managed to convince everyone else. Perhaps I wouldn't have been so hysterical about the baby, if I hadn't been so distressed by his death. Oh, it is no good wondering – everything would have been different.

'What are you thinking about?' asks Dan. 'You look rather sad.'

'Oh, just wondering,' I say.

'Do you still miss Ade a lot?'

'Yea, and particularly now, with all this uncertainty in the air. I can't help wondering how he would have tackled a problem like this.'

Dan looks a bit uncomfortable and I feel I need to explain to him, so I say: 'One thing I am thinking is that Ade would have gone about things in a very dramatic way, if he had heard about me being ill and in hospital and believing they had my (our) baby. He had no respect nor fear of Isobel, nor of his dad Pete, for that matter, and would have probably come home and demanded a DNA test immediately. He could be rather hot-headed at times and might have even made the whole situation worse – if that's possible.'

'We will never know,' says Dan, thoughtfully, 'so let's find a really good film to watch and try not to think of what is to come, or what might have been.'

'That's a very good idea,' I say, while trying to sound more positive, as we settle down again for the rest of evening.

Chapter 20

Dan left rather late last night but said he didn't have to be up very early this morning. He took my precious sealed DNA package and put it in his pocket. We joked that he must not forget it and take it to work with his sandwiches in the morning. I know that there will definitely not be any news from the lab today, so I can concentrate on Catty's arrival and hope that Maureen will approve of Catty's new home. I am so glad to have this distraction, as I know I am going to find it difficult not to feel worried and tense awaiting the results. I force myself to eat some cereal, although I feel rather sick from apprehension and from having eaten rather too much chocolate with Dan last night.

At eight thirty the landline phone rings and makes me jump, as I am not used to hearing it yet. It is Maureen saying she hopes it is not too early and she is about to leave with Catty, already in a box in the car. I assure her that is fine, even though I am not dressed yet (I don't tell her that, of course). I realise she starts her days much earlier than I need to and as it will take her about half an hour to get here, I have plenty of time to get ready.

Maureen arrives in a rattly old van at exactly the same time that Isobel is making her way down the lane. Luckily there is room to pass, as Maureen draws in rather close to the black stone.

'That's very smart,' she says, as she climbs out of the van and I explain to her the history of the stone.

. . .

'Oh, Catty will like sitting on that I expect' she says, as she looks around. 'This looks like cat heaven. Plenty of hunting areas. I would suggest, though, as I have said before, keep a cat indoors at night if you can, then nesting and baby birds have a better chance of survival in the spring.'

'I'll show you around indoors, then,' I suggest and Maureen follows me as I show her Catty's bed, new bowls and the smart cat flap. 'Do you know if she has been used to a cat flap in the past?'

'Oh yes, the family she was with definitely had one. Yes, this all looks absolutely fine. I know she will be very happy here. So, are you feeling more confident now and have you heard from the police yet?'

'No, I haven't – only a message to say they would be in touch.'

'Well, they contacted me again last night, as we had a question regarding one of our kittens which we had recently re-homed and had gone missing, but luckily it turned up unharmed at its new home. I was reassured that the people involved with the cruelty were being "processed", as they called it, and not to worry any more. I know the police are particularly busy at the moment, with a spate of drugs and burglaries, so I don't expect animal welfare is top of their list.' Maureen hesitates for a moment, then she asks, 'so do you feel confident enough to have her now?'

'Oh, absolutely,' I enthusiastically reply, then I hesitate and add, 'but of course we do have occasional traffic going up to Red House and several visitors come and go...'

'There's always a risk giving a home to a cat and complete safety is something we can't guarantee, as they are a law unto themselves, but I think this home is as good a risk as anywhere, so I'll go and take out the box. Keep her indoors with her litter tray for a couple of days, just to settle her. She already knows her way around here'.

Maureen is right. Catty goes straight in, and after checking each room, goes and sits in an armchair by the fire. I give Maureen a cup of tea and she gives me a few more tips about cat care. After refusing to accept more than ten pounds from me, as "Mrs. Brown" gave ample, she drives off to get on with her work at the Centre.

After Maureen has left, the first thing I do is text Dan to tell him that Catty is back. Then I wonder what on earth to do next. I must keep the doors and windows shut, which is not much of a problem, as there is a biting east wind attacking the front of the house, and I don't feel like doing much outside. Catty is looking very settled and gives me a look as if to say, 'this is my chair. You can have the other one.'

How am I going to bear the waiting? I am going to have to find a lot of jobs to do to keep my mind occupied. Then I realise there are only just under four weeks to Christmas and I have no idea what I will be doing during that time. I had noticed the shops had been building up the pressure for several weeks but had not given it much thought. With so much else going on I really don't know how normal families behave, although I know a lot of presents are involved, with Christmas tree and holly etc. I suppose I could write a Christmas card list and I would certainly like to find some presents for my new friends and Maisie, of course, but all this sets me off thinking of Maisie again and I really must find a way of coping with all this uncertainty. Cooking is a good idea, I decide, so I go to the kitchen and look out Aunt May's recipe books and thumb through until I find a page with the ingredients I already have. I don't want to have to go shopping today, as I want to stay with Catty to make sure she feels at home. I am just getting started on an apple crumble when there is a loud knock on the door which makes me jump.

It is Isobel, looking incredibly glamorous, in a long swirling, woollen coat, in very subtle greys and browns. She has a long green/grey scarf, skilfully draped over one shoulder. She always manages to look amazing, although takes no notice of current fashions. Her high-heeled black boots make her look even taller and I am glad I am now tall enough myself, not to feel intimidated by her height.

I hurriedly ask her in and shut the door promptly, in case Catty escapes, but Catty is still sitting in 'her' chair and only lifts her head momentarily as I take Isobel into the sitting room.

'So, I see you've got the cat back,' she says and Catty gives her a withering stare and stalks off upstairs.

'Yes, she's called Catty,' I reply.

'Not very original. The name I mean,' she says, and immediately changes the subject. 'The reason I came to see you is to tell you that Maisie and I are going to New York for Christmas.'

'Oh,' I say, trying not to sound too shocked. 'That sounds, um, fun.'

'Yes, Pete and some friends have invited us over and they live in this lovely apartment...'

She goes on describing in great detail where they will be staying and who will be there and what they will be doing, but I am feeling in such a daze, I can't take any of it in and can't think how to respond, so just make the odd polite comment. I do eventually pull myself together to ask her when they are going and when will they be back.

'We are booked to fly out on the 14th December and plan to come back sometime early January, but I am not sure of the date yet. Anyway,' she continues, as she makes her way back to the door, 'I thought I had better let you know, as the house will be empty while we are away,' and then as an afterthought, 'I expect you will probably be spending Christmas with your new friends.'

'I haven't given much thought to Christmas yet,' I say. 'I have only been here a few weeks, and just beginning to feel settled, so I may stay here. What are you doing about your dog?'

'Whisky's going into kennels. He knows the people and has been there several times, so he'll be OK.' She looks at her watch, 'I must hurry off, as I have Christmas shopping to do and it's getting late and I think it might snow later.' Off she goes, with her coat, scarf and hair all dancing around in the wind.

I am left rather speechless at the door and then remember I must not let Catty out. As I glance at Isobel's car I can't see Maisie in it. She is quite small, so I can't be sure if she is there or not.

I go inside and sit down in the first seat I come to which is a hard, wooden chair in the small hallway. I feel too stunned to know what to think or do next, but eventually manage to make my way into the kitchen to try to concentrate on my cooking. While I'm mixing the crumble for the pie with my fingers I realise that if the answer to the DNA test is negative, then it might be easier for me if Maisie is away in New York for Christmas. Yet, on the other hand, if it is positive and she is my daughter, can I challenge Isobel before they go, or would that make the situation dangerous? I would still have no solid proof and she might even decide to leave Maisie in America with Pete, who is officially her father, after all. I will need a lawyer – that's definite – if the test is in my favour. I try to concentrate on making the crumble and then realise the mixture I have made is far too much for the apple I have prepared, so I put some in a bag in the freezer and find myself a frozen vegetable pie to thaw out for supper. I don't know what Dan's plans will be for this evening, but both pies will be big enough for two if he comes for supper.

Having finished cooking, I decide to go for a bit of a walk, in spite of the cold wind, to try to calm myself down and clear my head a bit. I put on extra layers of clothes and set off down the lane. I think Isobel may be right and snow could be in the air, so I must remember to check the weather forecast when I get in. I am still finding it difficult to remember that I can connect to the internet now, although it can be rather slow. I walk down the lane towards the village. It is a bit more sheltered down there and I find a footpath that takes me down to the Church, so I decide to do a circuit round and come back up the field and into the garden. I walk very fast, as it is bitterly cold, but welcome the fresh bracing air. Soon I reach the Church and find the little gate to the footpath and I climb up the path through the field till I reach my garden gate. From this position, I can see Red House very clearly through the bare trees and, as I look up, I can see a child's pale face at one of the top windows. I wave and the little figure waves back and then jumps up and down, as if on a springy chair. Luckily the window looks firmly shut and although I only get a brief glimpse, I am sure it is Maisie and wonder who she has with her.

When I get back to the cottage, it feels so cosy and it is a relief to get indoors, so I temporarily forget what I have just seen, but then the image starts to trouble me and I wonder. Surely Isobel wouldn't leave Maisie on her own when she goes shopping? I try to distract myself by making a cup of tea, but it is no good, so I put on my coat again and sneak round the lane to Red House. Isobel's car is certainly not there and she has left the garage door open. I decide to go and ring the doorbell and if someone answers I can make the excuse that I am expecting a parcel that hasn't arrived and wonder if it has been left there. I ring the bell a couple of times but no one comes to the door. Of course, I can't be sure that the bell can be heard right up on the top floor and there could well be a babysitter up there. I try the door handle and it is definitely locked, so I creep round to the back door and find it is locked too. Then I hear a car coming up the lane, so I quickly dash behind the shrubbery, from where I catch a glimpse of Isobel's car. I then struggle through the trees, with difficulty, tackling the undergrowth, and reach my cottage, rather out of breath.

It is twenty-five past twelve and although I didn't notice what time Isobel came into see me, she must have been out at least a couple of hours. I get myself a snack lunch of salad and cheese and sit in the sitting room to see whether Isobel goes out again to take a babysitter back, but I see no sign of any car going in either direction. Catty is being very friendly and wants to sit on my lap, but I tell her she has to wait until I have finished eating and she seems to understand and looks longingly at my food. I am determined not to give her anything to eat until her supper time, as Maureen has told me she had a big breakfast and it is important to keep to a routine, as this will make her feel more secure.

After I have eaten I welcome the warmth of her on my lap while I try to concentrate on reading a magazine for a while, but find it difficult and I can't help wondering whether Dan has had time to check his messages. I know that when he gets into a job he gets really absorbed and doesn't answer his phone. I find myself dozing off by the fire, with Catty purring on my lap, when the phone rings. It is Dan, who is having a quick lunch break, so, trying to be brief, I tell him about this morning's events. He is shocked to hear about the New York visit and also about my suspicions about Maisie being left on her own this morning. He tells me that sometimes a girl called Linda does some baby-sitting for Isobel and she probably would not hear anyone at the door if she were up in Maisie's room, but we agree we must keep an eye on the situation, as leaving a child of that age on her own could be a criminal offence. I hear from Dan that the DNA samples have been duly passed on and that Mark will try to phone me on Friday evening, when he should have had time to do the tests. Before I have time to ask Dan if he wants to come to supper tonight, he tells me he has to be out visiting an elderly relative in hospital this evening, so I wish him all the best and we agree to contact each other tomorrow, when he doesn't expect to be quite so busy. I feel disappointed after having prepared a meal for us both, but I can keep the apple crumble to share with him another time. This evening is going to be a real drag – thank God I've got Catty.

. . .

The next three days are an agony of waiting. I keep myself as busy as possible doing repetitive chores, as I can't concentrate on anything that takes much thought. Catty is a huge comfort. She has settled in so well and it is as if she has never left. Maureen phones me on Wednesday morning to check that all is OK and suggests letting Catty out on Thursday morning after breakfast, which I do, after showing her that the cat flap is open.

It is now Friday morning and Dan and I have been in contact on the phone a lot over the past couple of days, but I am not expecting to see him till this evening, when he is coming to supper and to be with me for THE phone call.

After a restless morning, doing mindless jobs and talking to Catty, before she sets off through the cat flap to explore whatever cats explore, I eventually manage to do some cooking in preparation for supper this evening. I really do feel as if my mind is going to explode and don't feel like eating anything for lunch, so I am very glad when Angela, who is back from London today, phones me to catch up on the week's news. She has had a busy but interesting time at work, but is glad now to be able to spend some time at Ridge Farm and has brought work home which will occupy her for the next week. I tell her about my news from Isobel and her Christmas plans, which she is surprised to hear. Then says she is really needing a break and would I like to go for a walk with her and Bess this afternoon? I jump at this suggestion, as it will be lovely to see her and help to pass the time before this evening's phone call.

It is not quite so cold this morning as it has been over the past few days and there is a hazy sun trying to show its face. In spite of a few snow flurries on Tuesday night nothing has settled and Catty has been coming in and out of her cat flap quite frequently. It is early days, but I managed to keep her in last night, and apart from some rather angry scratching in her litter tray, she seems to be accepting this idea, especially as she insists on sleeping on my bed at night. Angela brings Bess over to my place, as there are still plenty of tracks and footpaths around here that are new to Bess. We decide not to bring Bess indoors, as I don't want to disturb Catty or introduce her to Bess until she is properly settled in. We start off down the garden and when we get to the gate Angela notices me peering up through the trees.

'What are you looking at? She asks, 'Is there an interesting bird in the trees?'

'No,' I say,' I can sometimes see Maisie looking out of her bedroom window and then a few days ago I believe Isobel might have gone out in her car, leaving Maisie on her own.' I hastily add, 'I can't be sure about this and she may well have had a baby-sitter,' and then I go on to tell her what I had done.

'She certainly should not leave a child her age alone in the house. That could be very dangerous. She does sometimes ask Linda, a girl from the village, to baby-sit, but I believe she is away on holiday with her family at the moment. Are you sure Dan and Emma weren't in charge?'

'No, they were both working that morning.'

Angela is quiet for a while and I notice she is getting a little out of breath as we climb up a long sloping track, which is deeply rutted here and there from heavy tractor wheels. The ground is chalky and rough with flint stones and is quite hard going and Angela has put Bess on the lead, as there are sheep in a field to the left. There is a strong wire fence along the track, but Angela knows Bess would find a way over, as she is so tall and agile. We eventually reach the top of the hill, as the sun is trying to peep through the hazy clouds and although there is still a chill wind, we are warm enough after our climb to stand and appreciate our surroundings and misty views.

'Phew, I'm not as fit as I'd like to be,' says Angela and then, after a pause while she gets her breath 'So, what do you think we should do about Maisie? If we are thinking she is left alone in the house sometimes, I think we would probably need to challenge Isobel – or get in touch with social services.'

I am feeling so tempted to tell Angela about the Maisie Quest, but I would rather wait till I have the phone call and know what I am dealing with.

'Yes, I certainly think something should be done… but, um, I am expecting a phone call this evening, which could affect everything – and I'm sorry, but I don't want to talk about it yet, but I promise I plan to tell you all about it directly I hear from this person. I know I sound very…?'

'Mysterious' says Angela, looking at me intently. 'Yes, OK, but of course I'm intrigued to know what's going on.'

We walk on over the top of the hill and join a track going down to the right. There is a sheep-free area where Bess can have a free run, but she seems satisfied to stroll along with us, stopping for a sniff now and again.

'I'm afraid she's getting old,' says Angela, but I think she is pretty good for her age. These big dogs don't live very long unfortunately.' As we reach the bottom of the hill, Angela tells me she thinks we can reach the village if we keep on to the right and I tell her that we can, as I have walked this way with Dan.

'And how is Dan?' she asks.

'He's fine. Very busy at the moment, which is good, because being self-employed is so worrying if there is not a queue of jobs waiting.'

'Yes, it can be difficult and he obviously has to take every job he can. So, you see him quite often then?'

'Yes, he's a good friend and so is Emma,' I add, so she doesn't think there is more than friendship going on. 'He's coming round this evening actually.' And I go on to explain about Emma's new man and how Dan is being tactful by keeping out of their way some evenings.

Angela looks thoughtful for a bit and we walk on until we join up with another path towards the village. 'I am wondering what you are planning to do for Christmas and whether you are seeing Dan and Emma over the holiday. If not, Geoff and I are wondering whether you would like to spend it with us at Ridge Farm. We are not planning to do anything special this year and various family members are otherwise engaged, so it might not be very interesting for you…'

'Oh, I'd love to,' I say enthusiastically, before she has time to finish. 'I have not made any plans and I believe Emma and Dan have a large number of relatives who I am sure they will want to be with. Are you sure you would want me, though? I can help you with cooking and that sort of thing.'

'That would be wonderful,' she says, and gives me a hug as we make our way home.

It is getting quite dark, by the time we get back, so Angela decides not to stay for tea, as she needs to get things ready for Geoff, who will be arriving later. She wishes me good luck with the mysterious phone call and as she leaves, says 'Don't forget to tell me all about it.' And I assure her I will let her know.

Chapter 21

It is now five thirty and I am waiting for Dan to arrive. I've done all the cooking and am leaving it to keep warm. He said he couldn't get to me before six, but we are not expecting the phone call till later this evening. I am feeling all my old anxiety symptoms welling up inside and I have to call up all my strategies for coping. So, I am sitting comfortably and breathing low and slow, when the loud ring of the landline phone brings me up with a start.

I hope this is not Dan saying he is going to be late, so I hurry into the hallway, where the phone is, and pick up the handset.

'Hello,' says a strange man's voice, 'Mark here. Is that Lora Laslo?'

'Yes, yes, it's me, Lora' – and I hesitate, completely taken by surprise. 'I wasn't expecting you to phone till later.' I can feel my heart thumping.

'I'm sorry to phone so early, but it is the only chance I have this evening to talk privately and I am sure you are anxious for the news. Is it OK to talk to you now?'

'Yes, – and you can probably hear by my voice, I am certainly very anxious.'

'Well, I'll come straight to the point and tell you that you will be pleased to hear that the result I found is a perfect mother daughter match – well, as perfect as one is capable of saying.' There is silence from me for a few moments, so he adds, 'I think that is the news that you wanted?'

'Why yes,' I exclaim and can't think of what to say next.

'Now, you must remember that this is a completely unofficial result and in no way can you use it legally. As you know, you should have got the child's guardian to give permission, so how you go about things from now on, will have to be given a lot of thought. I suggest you find a good lawyer to help you obtain a legal test.'

'That's amazing news,' I say, as I gradually gain my senses. 'Are you sure, absolutely sure? '

'Yes, I'm sure – but as I said...'

And I interrupt him 'It's not official. Yes – I understand. But it is a huge relief to know.'

'I'm so glad it is helpful, but I must still emphasise, I don't want to be a part of any of this and as far as I'm concerned, we have never had this conversation, OK?'

'Absolutely.' I say emphatically. 'Emma, Dan and Amy are the only other people who know about this and I'll make sure that you are kept out of any further consequences. Thank you so much, Mark. I really can't thank you enough.'

'Well, I wish you the very best of luck. I have a child myself and can only begin to imagine what you have been going through. So, bye for now – and I am sure I will hear of the outcome in a roundabout way.'

After I've thanked Mark a million times more and put the phone down, I feel I want to go outside and dance around, shouting to the world, 'I was right all along; I have a daughter,' but of course, I don't do this. I go and sit down quietly and wonder, what on earth do I do next? How would I ever get Isobel to agree to a DNA test? I am not mad – I'm not mad – I keep repeating to myself.

Catty is sensing the atmosphere and has even left her supper uneaten and is fussing around my chair. 'It's all right,' I tell her, giving her a stroke. 'Let's go and find your food.' I stand by her while she eats slowly and she keeps looking up at me, just to be sure everything is really all right. I nearly forget to shut the cat flap but manage to do so before she finishes eating. Then, I see Dan's car lights approaching, so I switch on the outside light and go out to meet him. It is very cold, but I certainly don't feel it.

I shout 'He's already phoned and it's wonderful news,' Dan stands for a moment, as if he can't believe what he's heard.'

'Shh,' I whisper. 'just a moment, let's go inside. I don't want any risk of being overheard.'

'You mean it is positive and it's what you wanted to hear?' he whispers back.

'Yes,' I say, as he grabs me round the waist, swings me around and when he puts me down we have the best kiss I could ever imagine.'

We go into the cottage and Dan shuts the door firmly. He already knows the Catty routine. We just stand in the hallway, holding each other close, then we start to laugh and dance about, before Dan says, 'Sorry, I've forgotten something. I'll be back, before you know I've gone.' And he runs out to the car and returns with some bags, but the light is not bright enough to see what he has brought, until he gets inside the door.

'I've brought you some flowers,' he says, looking a bit embarrassed and handing me a bunch of red and pink rosebuds.'

'Oh, they're lovely,' I say, giving him a hug.

'And' he adds, opening a bag, 'I brought some wine for you and some beer for me, as I didn't know whether we would be celebrating or drowning our sorrows and they would do for either event.'

'I never thought of that,' I say, but I have cooked a rather nice meal – unless I've burnt it,' I say, as I rush to look in the oven. 'Phew – it looks OK.'

We decide it is a little bit early to eat, but a packet of crisps would go down well with our drinks, so we go and sit on the sofa, me with a glass of wine and Dan with some beer. We both give a big sigh of relief as we sit down and look at each other and smile. Catty, who had been wondering what all the fuss was about had rushed upstairs, but she now appears again, walks stealthily over to her chair and settles herself down, with an expression of 'what the heck's going on?' We talk to her quietly and she soon looks happy and starts to doze off.

We take quite a long time over our supper, as we have so much to talk about and I phone Emma to tell her the good news and of course she is delighted. I have to tell her all about the secrecy and how we are going to have to think carefully of how to proceed and she says she will be very discreet and certainly won't mention anything to anyone, even her friend, Paul.

'How do you think we go about finding a suitable lawyer?' asks Dan. 'After all, you can't just trust finding someone online.' 'Or the yellow pages,' I say and we both laugh. 'The solicitors who dealt with Aunt May's probate might be suitable, but they may not specialise in this sort of thing.'

After some more thoughtful silence, I say to Dan, 'I realise how I haven't dared to think deeply about any of this before getting the result, as it felt like tempting fate, but now that I feel confident in myself and my own sanity, I would rather face Isobel and demand the truth, before even mentioning I want official DNA testing for Maisie.'

'How do you think you would be able to do that?' Asks Dan. 'Don't forget you have only four days at the most before they are off to New York on Wednesday and it would be awful if Isobel and Pete decided to get American lawyers involved and Maisie stayed out there.'

The thought of this is just too much for me. 'That had crossed my mind,' I say, and as I look at Dan with tears in my eyes, he holds me close and says, 'Look, the first battle is won and we don't have to rush anything. I just have a feeling this will turn out all right in the end, if you can have a bit more patience. It would be a pity to spoil your chances by being too hasty now.'

'Yea, I know. It has been a slow three and a half years of uncertainty for me and I definitely don't want to do anything hasty to muck things up now.'

'Well, I want to support you all the way with this, whatever happens. I'm not giving up on you now. Unless you want me to. Perhaps you've had enough of me? I have been like your shadow over the past few weeks.'

'Dan, I don't know what I would have done without you. You have been amazing.'

I look at him earnestly and then say, 'Do you want to stay the night – not on the sofa – but with me?' After that kiss, I know that is what we both want, so I add 'and I am on the pill'.

This needs no answer, so we make our way upstairs, closing the bedroom door after us. Catty will have to have her own bed tonight.

. . .

We are late down to breakfast, but it is Saturday and Dan doesn't need to go to work, although he had planned to possibly finish off a job this morning, if nothing more important turned up. 'It's much more important to be with you,' he says. 'Shall we spend the rest of the weekend together?' 'Yes, let's do that,' I reply and we give each other a kiss.

I have fed Catty and opened the cat flap, but she doesn't seem in much of a hurry to go out, as it is pouring with rain. She decides to go up to her bed in the spare room, where she can get some peace and quiet, away from us chattering. Dan rings Emma and she is not surprised at what we have arranged. She already has plans to meet up with Paul and, again, she promises, hand on heart, that she never talks to Paul about the Maisie Quest.

While we are clearing up breakfast, I say, 'Dan, I don't want to keep going on about the Maisie Quest, as I think we both need a break and not talk about it all the time, but I must just mention that I had an odd dream last night. I woke up with memories briefly flashing through my mind of the time of the birth. In this dream I am coming in and out of consciousness and I see this baby. It has just been born and is crying loudly and it looks perfect. Doesn't look deformed. Then I feel something over my face and I very faintly hear a gasp from Isobel and mutterings about a girl. So, when I wake this morning and find the duvet is over my face, it takes me a few moments, to realise it was a dream, but it did seem more like a memory than a dream.'

'You were a bit restless as you were waking up this morning and I did wonder if you were all right and I was about to ask you if you were OK, when you suddenly sat up and smiled.'

'Yes, I sat up and smiled with enormous relief, that my memories are real and I was never out of my mind and this has given me a huge feeling of empowerment. I can start really believing in myself, with no more nagging doubts.'

'That's great,' says Dan 'and what would you like to do today? It's pouring with rain and I think there is a bit of sleet in it too, so I don't fancy a walk, do you?'

'No, certainly not. Perhaps we could go to the cinema if we can find anything good on.' I suggest. 'Oh, I have just remembered I said I would phone Angela this morning. When we were out for a walk yesterday, she was suggesting talking to Isobel, or getting in touch with social services about Isobel neglecting Maisie and I mentioned that I was expecting a phone call last night that could be relevant, but I said I did not want to tell her about it until I had received the call.

'No, we don't want her stirring things up at the moment,' says Dan.

'But what do you think I should say to her? How much should I tell her?'

'Do you trust her completely? I mean, she wouldn't break your confidentiality would she?'

'No, I am sure she wouldn't. I know she is absolutely on my side – and she is just the sort of person who might suggest a good lawyer. By the way, did I mention to you that she has asked me to spend Christmas with them at Ridge Farm?'

'Um, no, you didn't. What did you say?'

'I said yes, as I was sure you and Emma would be involved with all your various friends and relations.'

'Oh dear, I was just thinking this morning, how I would like us to spend Christmas together, but you are right. Emma and I have already committed ourselves to various family dos. We have agreed to stay with Jane, our aunt, and her family and there wouldn't be room for anyone else. If you were going to be on your own, I had planned to opt out of staying with them and asking if I could spend it with you.'

'Ah, that's lovely,' I say, 'but this is obviously a good solution. I'll miss you though.'

'Yea, I'll certainly miss you too.'

After clearing up breakfast, we look online to see if there is anything worth seeing at the cinema anywhere near. We can't find anything we like the sound of. I have only been to the cinema a couple of times in my life and that was when I was in London, so my repertoire is very small, but Dan has much more up to date knowledge and has already seen one of the films mentioned. We both agree that the others don't sound particularly interesting either, so we decide we'll go out for a celebration lunch and see if Emma is free to join us, plus Charlie, of course. Dan phones Emma, who jumps at the idea, as Paul has other plans today.

Then I phone Angela, but Geoff answers the phone and sounds pleased to hear me and says, 'Yes, Angela is expecting a call from you. I'll just go and fetch her. She is just taking her boots off, as she has been out inspecting the animals. 'Angela;' I can hear him call. 'Lora on the phone.'

While we are waiting, we catch up with our general news and Geoff tells me he understands we still have worries about Maisie and I say that is what I need to talk to Angela about, as there has been a slight development.

'Well, here she is, so I'll hand you over. Good to hear from you Lora. We'll speak soon, bye.'

Angela sounds very anxious to hear what's going on.

'This is a bit difficult, um,' I pause and then 'You see I couldn't talk to you yesterday, but there has been a development in the Maisie situation. Um, you know how I've been wondering about my past and being ill when my baby was born. Um, and you know how Isobel has been accusing me of trying to take her baby – and saying I was deranged in my mind and that was why I went to hospital?'

'Yes,' says Angela, patiently waiting.

'Well, the truth is,' and I pause while I get my breath, 'I have proved Maisie is my daughter.'

'How? – Have you done a DNA test?' asks Angela, sounding shocked.

'Yes,' I quickly reply and before I have time to continue, Angela interrupts.

'You'd have to have Isobel's permission. How did you manage that?'

'Well – I didn't, so the test cannot be considered official, but it has clarified things for me, so at least now I know that I am in the right if I pursue things further. Look, this has to be very private for the moment, as the person who did the test for us does not want to be implicated in anything further. He works for a laboratory, but he might get into trouble, as he did it unofficially.'

'Are you sure he knows what he is doing? I mean is he qualified – trustworthy…?'

'Yes, I'm sure he is – but this is something he was not meant to do. I promised I would not go into details about him or where he works, but I feel confident about what he told me and he strongly advised me to get official, legal testing done and, if necessary, get a lawyer if Isobel or Pete were not agreeable.'

'Gosh,' says Angela. 'This is a turn up for the books. I must admit I don't really know what to say next. There are so many questions to be answered.'

'Yes,' I say, 'such as the dead baby boy... Look, can I come and see you and Geoff quickly? I mean, are you busy this morning, or could I just pop up in the car, for a few minutes and talk about it a bit more?'

'Yes, you do that. We've nothing special on this morning, so come as soon as you can.'

. . .

I tell Dan what has happened and he reluctantly agrees that I really have to see Angela immediately. It is now ten past eleven. Dan has booked a table at the Angel Inn in Wasbury for one o'clock, so if I'm not back before that Dan can lock up (very carefully, I remind him) and we will meet there.

Both Angela and Geoff are waiting anxiously to see me and they take me into the sitting room. They both look very shocked, and immediately Angela says,

'If the DNA test is true, this means they stole your baby. – I can't believe it – and surely this will be a matter for the police, especially if Isobel is about to take Maisie to the States.'

'Yes, I say hurriedly, 'but I don't want to rush anything and we have to be careful how we handle it all, as Isobel is so unpredictable.'

They both agree with me and I take my time explaining to them what has happened over the past few days. After lots of cross-examining from Geoff, which I feel I deal with pretty calmly, they seem very much on my side and agree that a lawyer will be essential and promise to give a lot of thought to finding someone suitable.

Angela tells me that she has had a phone call from Isobel early this morning, cancelling a yoga meeting on Monday, as Isobel told her that she and Maisie are going to London on Monday evening and staying there until their flight from Heathrow on Wednesday.

We all agree that we must not give Isobel any reason to be suspicious before she goes, in case she decides to delay coming back or leaves Maisie with Pete.

'We will have to be very patient,' says Angela, 'and in the meantime, over Christmas, we have time to think and plan a strategy. I know this will be particularly difficult for you and we'll do our best to keep you occupied over Christmas, if you still want to stay with us.'

'Oh, yes, I am so, so, grateful to you both. I know I am going to find it hard waiting for Maisie to come back, but I know I have to be sensible and not rock the boat.'

I then tell them about my developing relationship with Dan and neither of them sound at all surprised. Of course, I get another cautionary reminder of how quickly this has all happened and I must be very careful not to get hurt. I realise they do really care what happens to me, which is something I am not used to since my early life when Aunt May was around.

. . .

Lunch at The Angel is great fun and of course we have to be very careful what we talk about, in case of eavesdroppers, but I find it light relief to hear about other things in Dan and Emma's lives. We don't stay long after our delicious lunch, as Charlie, who has actually been very good and occupied with some paper and crayons, is getting rather tired and wanting to use the crayons on inappropriate things other than the paper. We go back to Lime Tree Cottage, Emma and Dan's place, for coffee, where we spend a quiet afternoon chatting, while Charlie has a sleep.

Dan stays with me overnight again and the weather is much better on Sunday. Although still cold, we force ourselves out of the cosy cottage in the afternoon and go for a long walk, which we both find very therapeutic and it allows us to let go of some of the urgent, impatient feelings we have about Maisie. By the evening, Dan is showing no signs of going home, so we relax by the fire together, with Catty, who leaves her chair and spreads herself over both our laps on the sofa.

'I think this is all going to turn out all right,' says Dan, 'and anyway, there is nothing we can do about it for the moment.'

'Yes, I feel it's going to be OK too, eventually,' I say, then I add. 'I know, it will be impossible to feel really settled until all the loose ends are resolved, including the official test. And how about the dead baby boy? That is a terribly sad thought. He must have been Isobel's, so no wonder she wants to keep Maisie.'

'That's no excuse though, for putting you through all that pain and anguish and still living the lie, after all this time. And Pete too. He's just as much to blame.'

'Yes, I know. Let's hope someday soon we'll get an answer to it all.' Then I pause and relax against him. 'This feels all right – you and me, I mean – us?' I ask tentatively.

'Perfect,' he says. 'But, I wish I didn't have to go to work tomorrow.'

'We can make sandwiches for you here, if you want to stay,' I suggest.

'I was hoping you'd suggest that' he laughs, so we get some packs of cards out of Aunt May's little drawer and decide on a competitive evening of card playing, which Catty doesn't enjoy at all, especially the noise of the cards slapping down on the table when we play Racing Demon and she sulks in her own chair.

Chapter 22

Dan goes off to work at eight o'clock this morning, with sandwiches made from our weekend left-overs. It is still fairly dark and the bitterly cold east wind has returned, so I don't envy him. He hopes to be finished with this particular job by mid-afternoon and I plan to go into Ford to do some Christmas shopping this morning and get something little for Maisie and give it to Isobel to take with them when they go to London. I gathered from Angela yesterday that Isobel has a dental appointment this afternoon and is going to London later this evening.

After I've fed Catty and let her out and then tidied up a little, I set off in my little car to Ford. It is quite busy in town and although there are still a couple of weeks till Christmas and it is a Monday morning, there seem to be masses of people about doing Christmas shopping and I find parking quite difficult. The noise of the hustle and bustle of town and Christmas Carols everywhere, makes it difficult for me to concentrate, after the quiet of the cottage, but I manage to find a charity shop selling cards and I buy some for my friends and a couple of acquaintances from London days. I have completely lost touch with any of the visitors from Morg, so I buy a mixed pack of ten, which should be plenty. I find a bookshop and get a cookery book for Emma and spend a long time trying to find something for Dan, but eventually find a very interesting book on country things relating to this area. Maisie and Charlie are fairly easy to find books for, as there are plenty for their age group and I make sure they are recently published for Christmas, so they won't have them already. Angela and Geoff are not so easy, so the shopkeeper suggests I buy book tokens for both of them, as I know they love reading. I feel quite pleased with my presents and after having bought some wrapping paper, I go to the supermarket to top up with food items and then make my way home.

It is half past one, so I have a pasty which I'd bought and is still hot and very delicious and then I wrap up Maisie's present, so I can take it round to Isobel before she goes out. I hope I haven't missed her already, but I can leave it in her porch if I have. I have nearly finished wrapping it when I see her car go past. She is driving slowly and glancing my way as she goes past, but I can't see Maisie. I don't suppose she would take Maisie with her to the dentist, as I never had my teeth checked as a child. In fact, none of us on the island ever went to a dentist. We seldom had sweets or fizzy drinks and I don't remember any of us ever having toothache. I wonder what's prompted Isobel to go to a dentist. She was always very particular about us all cleaning our teeth regularly. Anyway, there's no point in thinking about that and I will finish wrapping Maisie's present and write a Christmas card for Isobel and Pete. I might as well try to be pleasant before we have to start difficult proceedings.

I put on a warm coat and then something prompts me to take my phone. I really don't know why I feel I need it, but it turns out that it is a very lucky that I do. I also lock up the cottage, although I am only going around the corner to drop these things off. I suppose, in the back of my mind, I am wondering whether I will see Maisie and/or a babysitter and I will ring the doorbell to see if anyone is there.

I ring the doorbell and knock loudly, but no one comes. I go around the back and down the garden to see if Jock the gardener is about, but he is nowhere to be seen. As I walk back to where I can see Maisie's window, I hear some loud thumps coming from the direction of her room and as look up the noise stops and I can see a small hand tapping on the window, but I cannot see a face. My heart misses a beat and I feel I cannot leave and go home without checking the doors and finding out if anyone is there. All the doors are locked, so I try and guess where Isobel would put a spare key. As it is not under any of the flowerpots or a doormat, I suddenly think she might keep one in the summer house. I find that door is unlocked and as I feel around on the shelves and look in corners, I come across something cold. Sure enough it is a large key. I am beginning to feel a bit shaky, but am compelled to go and try it in one of the doors.

It fits the back door perfectly, and with my heart beating loudly, I don't allow myself to hesitate but go inside and call out – 'Hello, is anyone at home?' There is no response, so I wander around downstairs and finding no one there, not even the dog, I make my way up the stairs to the first landing. There are several shut doors and I call out again, but no reply from any of the rooms. I know Maisie's room must be up on the next floor, so I go up another, rather narrow, flight of stairs and knock on the door which I think should be the one leading to Maisie's room. I hear a whimper from inside and try the handle, but it won't open and there is no key, so I feel around for a light switch, as it is rather dark up here with only one small window. When I switch on the light, I see the door is firmly shut with a large bolt.

I hurriedly undo the bolt and go inside and what I am faced with fills me with utmost horror.

Maisie has been tied by a rope attached to a toddler's harness and the other end of the rope is tied to a large wooden chair. She has managed to drag the chair, which has fallen over, and has climbed onto an armchair by the window, but obviously could only just reach the window to tap on it, as the wooden chair had wedged itself behind a table several feet away.

'Oh Maisie,' I exclaim and am rushing to untie her, when I suddenly have the presence of mind to get out my phone and take a photo, before I take off her harness. Having taken the photo, I struggle to undo the buckles on the harness as she won't keep still and keeps trying to push me away. She looks very pale and frightened. I eventually manage to untie her but, as she shrinks away from me she is saying, 'Isbel cross.' And she bursts into tears. She won't let me give her a cuddle and continues to push me away, apparently extremely scared.

'It's all right Maisie. You are safe now,' and I try and console her, but she continues to shrink from me, repeating 'Isbel very cross,' over and over again.

I am just getting out my phone again to dial 999, when I hear a door slam loudly. My heart doesn't seem to know how to behave and almost stops beating. I feel paralysed, but know I have got to do something. Then footsteps start to come upstairs. I tell Maisie to stay where she is and say I am going to talk to Isobel, and gathering myself together, I rush out of the door and down the first flight of stairs, as I don't want to confront Isobel in front of Maisie and frighten her even more. Just before Isobel reaches me, I quickly hide my phone deep in my coat pocket. I feel annoyed with myself that I haven't managed to dial 999, but think it is probably too late now, as she would grab the phone from me before I could get through to anyone and it is safer for me to keep my phone with me.

'What the heck are you doing here?' she shouts at me.

I try to stay calm and say, 'Look, let's go downstairs and I will explain. Maisie is OK, but she is very upset and I am sure you wouldn't want to make things worse.' I can't believe how calmly I have said this. It is my anger that is giving me strength.

'Come on then, explain yourself,' says Isobel glowering at me, as we arrive down in the kitchen.

'Well, I came round to leave a Christmas present for Maisie, as I have heard you are going to London this evening. I walked round the house to see if anyone was around and looked up and saw Maisie's hand tapping on her window.'

'That's a lie,' says Isobel furiously. 'She couldn't possibly have reached it.'

'Well she did and anyway, what on earth were you thinking of tying her to that chair? She had managed to drag it across the floor and heaven only knows how she didn't come to hurt herself – and to leave her on her own, locked in her bedroom in an empty house.' I realise I am saying all this very forcefully, without feeling any fear of Isobel. At this moment I feel stronger than Isobel. My maternal instinct and absolute fury is what is spurring me on.

Isobel looks at me with utter disdain. 'You think you've won, don't you?'

'What do you mean?' I say. 'This isn't a matter of winning anything. This is a matter of child abuse'.

'Ah, you think I don't know about your little plot,' she smirks.

'What do you mean?' I say again.

'I know you've been testing Maisie's DNA, but you've done it without my approval and it means nothing. I hope you realise; it means nothing.'

I know I must look dumbfounded and take a few seconds to ask, 'What on earth do you mean?'

'Maisie tells me everything. Everything she has been doing when she is out with Emma and Dan. She told me in great detail about the tooth-cleaning game and the mouth swabs etc. She thought it was great fun. She even told me about the swabs drying in a glass, 'like little soldiers that must not be touched.' Isobel looks triumphant and then continues, while I frantically try to gather my thoughts. 'So, I am taking Maisie to New York, where you would have one hell of a battle to get her back. I know you haven't got the sort of money you would need to fight a legal battle and we certainly wouldn't give consent for an official DNA test without a fight.'

I look at Isobel with many questions racing through my mind. Her baby boy's death must have affected her so badly that she felt had to take my baby? And Pete must have agreed, and that's difficult to understand? But there must be much more to it than that, I feel sure. So, I say as calmly as I can, 'why do you need all this power over me? What have I ever done to deserve it – and surely you can't really care that much about Maisie if you treat her like you do?'

'Do you really want to know?' she replies, staring at me with her weird, hypnotic eyes. 'You won't like what you hear.'

'Of course I want to know.' I say indignantly.

'I hate you – you little bitch. There I've said it. I always have – and before you ask me why, I will explain.

You are exactly like your mother. You are too bloody clever. She always did everything better than me. She always got her own way. She was poisonous to me. She stole the love of my life, Nick Laslo, and then, to make matters even worse, she got pregnant by him and produced you. You looked like her from the moment you were born. You might as well have been a clone. I pretended that I didn't care – and anyway Nick left her pretty quickly – which pleased me no end.'

'So, why did you agree to look after me then, if you hated me and the whole situation so much? Could you not find my father and get him involved?'

'No – he disappeared without trace and anyway, after your mother died, May was the one who persuaded me we ought to keep you – and I must admit, as a tiny baby you were very sweet and I was pretty sure I couldn't have children. It was only when you got older and looked and behaved more and more like your mother, that I found it difficult to be around you.' She says this with such venom, that I cannot believe she is a normal human being.

I want to know why she ever wanted to keep Maisie in the first place. I can't believe she would just keep her out of spite, but it does sound as if this is indeed the reason.

'Why did you ever want to keep Maisie?,' I ask' and what about the baby boy?'

She looks at me with an even wilder look and then screams. 'I wanted a boy. I didn't want a bloody girl, so go upstairs and find your horrible little daughter. She was a good baby – but not a boy – and as soon as she started to disobey me and act like a little demon, as girls do, I regretted everything I had done for you and your offspring.' She stamps her foot and shouts again – 'so, what are you waiting for – you can have her, but you'll regret it.'

She storms out of the house, leaving me feeling dumbfounded and for a few seconds I am rooted to the spot. I have seen Isobel angry in the past, but this is a side of her that she never shows to outsiders and I have never seen her so vitriolic as these past few minutes. She sounds obsessive – as if this is something she has been holding inside herself for years.

The sound of Isobel slamming the door brings me to my senses and rush up the stairs to find Maisie. On the way up I am thinking how stupid and thoughtless of me to ask about the dead baby. It was my mentioning the baby boy that naturally set her off into even more of a delirium.

I find Maisie still sitting on the chair where I had left her and she is shivering. It is quite warm in the room, but she is obviously very frightened, so I approach her in as calm a way as I can and try to reassure her that Isobel has gone out and that she has asked me to look after her.

'I'll find you a nice cosy blanket to wrap you in, as you look a bit cold' and she nods and looks at me wide-eyed. I put a blanket round her and she snuggles up to me, while I sit wondering what to do next. Of course, I must ring the police and fumble for my phone in my pocket.

I have just started to dial the first 9 when there is a huge explosion from somewhere downstairs and the whole house shakes. I instinctively pick up Maisie and hurry down the stairs and as I reach the next landing, I find thick black smoke billowing up from the floor below. We both start to cough and it is obvious we cannot go down any further, so I carry Maisie into the first room I come to and slam the door behind me.

With trembling fingers, at last I manage to dial 999. It seems to take ages for any answer, but it was probably only a few seconds, and I shout – 'please send police and fire brigade urgently to Red House near Wasbury' and I frantically try to remember the post code, which comes to me after a few attempts to get it right. 'There's been an explosion and the house is on fire and I have a small child with me on the first floor. Hurry please hurry.'

A calm voice on the other end of the phone, asks me a few more questions then tells me on no account to leave the room and to keep the door shut and wait for the fire brigade.

I look around me and see this is probably Isobel's room. The smell of smoke seems to get stronger and I am desperate to get Maisie out and wonder whether I can tie sheets or clothes together to lower her out of the window. I go to the bedroom window to see if I can open it, but it is a heavy sash window and I can't budge it. I look outside and pray someone will come soon and then, to my horror, I see Isobel running down the lane completely enveloped in flames. She starts to scream and I hammer on the window and shout…

'Roll on the ground, Isobel', but she cannot hear me and disappears behind the trees down the lane. Again, I'm rigid with shock, but very relieved to see Maisie had not been looking out of the window, so she wouldn't have seen Isobel.

I am frantically trying to remember the fire drill we had when I was in the hostel in London, as the smell of smoke seems to be getting even stronger and I think it is mainly leaking through a rather large gap under the door. I need to find something damp like a towel and luckily the shower room adjoining the bedroom has some nice thick towels. I put them all together under the shower at full power and rapidly soak them in water. I don't bother to wring them out but rush them to the bedroom door and lay them along the crack on the floor and over the door handle. I can hear a roaring noise throughout the house and realise the flames are probably already coming up the stairs. I notice there is a window in the shower room, which is big enough to fit Maisie through, so I drag a sheet off the bed and take off the duvet cover and tie them together, but they are still nothing like long enough.

As I go to the wardrobe to look for some other suitable articles, Maisie, who has been standing quietly watching me, suddenly says, 'No, no – Isbel's baby,' and she frantically tries to pull me away.

'What do you mean, Maisie? Where is there a baby?' She points to something hanging on the back of the door. I look at it and all I see is some straps with something padded hanging from them. I haven't time to think about it but grab at it, as the straps could be useful.

'Don't touch,' cries Maisie, looking really scared. 'Isbel cross.'

'It's OK Maisie. It is not a baby,' I say as, at the back of my mind, I realise what it is. It is a kind of corset that women sometimes use when they are heavily pregnant. I can remember Isobel saying she was getting one, as her back was giving her trouble. But, what I realise now, as I frantically search through the cupboard for more long items to tie together, that this one is stuffed full of removable padding, and for a moment there is a flash of realisation – there possibly never was a baby!

I haven't time to think about it now and realise I have nothing like enough material to make anything long enough to lower Maisie to the ground. There is absolutely nothing I can do but wait. I take Maisie into the shower room, where the smell of smoke has not yet reached, and put my arms round her and decide I will try to tell her a story. Of course, I am far too distracted to think of anything, so I take her to the window, where I can see if anyone comes and I try singing nursery rhymes and Maisie starts joining in, but the smoke has affected our voices. It feels so right to have her close to me and even if we don't come out of this alive, at least we are together at last. Thoughts flash through my mind – I should have done things differently – if only I'd… said something different – not mentioned the baby. If only – if only. It's no good. I just have to pray that whatever happens to me, please, please keep Maisie safe. She feels so trusting, as she cuddles up to me.

Just as I am beginning to think this must be the end of everything and no one is coming to our rescue, I hear sirens in the distance and the sound gradually gets closer. Together, we wait impatiently and watch the blue lights appearing as the fire engine and two police cars come up the lane behind the trees. Maisie puts her hands over her ears, as the sound of the sirens gets louder and I tell her, in my croaky voice, that they are coming to help us and it will be all right. They rush to the house and stop. I shout through the little shower room window as loud as I can – 'We are up here.'

After what seems like an eternity, a fireman comes up on a ladder and, with shaking arms, I pass Maisie to him and he carries her, protesting, down the ladder, while I call to her to hold on and that it will be all right. Having opened this window, although the door to the bedroom is shut, I can hear the main bedroom door burst open and the smoke starts to seep through into the shower room. I stick my head out of the window to try to get some air, while another fireman comes to the top of the ladder. I don't know how he does it, but I soon find myself being carried down the ladder, still gasping for breath. As we reach the bottom, I see the bedroom alight with flames and smoke.

. . .

The relief is enormous. Maisie and I are both OK and are soon inside an ambulance, where we cling to each other. We have both inhaled some rather toxic smoke. Maisie seems dazed and tries to pull off her oxygen mask. I hold her hand and try to reassure her that the masks we are wearing are to make us feel better. I keep seeing horrible visions of Isobel in flames – and as Maisie and I are rushed to hospital, I try to discreetly ask what has happened to Isobel. I don't want Maisie to hear, but I am quietly told, that although this particular ambulance crew don't seem to know details, they do know she was found lying in the lane on the way down to Wasbury and is already on her way to hospital. It is a relief to know she has been found and at least she should be in capable hands.

Maisie and I are checked over very carefully at the hospital and they decide to keep us both in overnight to make sure we are OK. I am feeling very shocked and Maisie is extremely confused and keeps saying, 'is Isbel cross?' and I have to keep reassuring her that she is not and that she has gone away for a while and that she has asked me to look after her. I insist on staying with Maisie all night, as we have both gone through a terrible ordeal and I know I need the security of her by my side, as much as she needs me.

The police come to ask interminable questions and I tell them precisely what happened, as well as I can with a croaky, trembling voice. I show them the photo of Maisie on my phone and they insist on keeping my phone as evidence. At this stage they can't tell me what caused the explosion and the fire experts are studying the site, but I do gather that Maisie and I are very lucky to be alive, as the whole of the centre of the house, including the roof above Maisie's room, has been completely destroyed. I feel particularly vulnerable without my phone, but luckily, I have already let Dan and Angela know where we are and I can't wait to see them, as I am feeling very emotional and don't want to break down in front of Maisie.

All the staff in the hospital, either don't know where Isobel has been taken, or are reluctant to say, but I eventually find out she has been taken by air ambulance to a special burns unit, as she has very extensive burns and she may not survive. I am told she is unconscious at the moment and can't tell anyone what happened. In spite of everything she has said and done, I can't help feeling incredibly upset. She must have been in absolute agony.

Dan and Angela arrive within a few minutes of each other and are so very relieved to see us both looking pretty normal, although very untidy and obviously shocked and incredibly tired and plugged into various bits of equipment. Angela is very business-like and says she has had a long talk with the police and explained the complicated situation with Isobel. She has managed to get agreement that she will take care of Maisie and myself when we come out of hospital and will try to help them to track down Pete in New York, as he will be expecting Isobel and Maisie in a couple of days. She asks me whether I have any idea of Pete's address, as Red House is so fire-damaged and still not safe enough to enter at the moment, to look for any information. I tell her I have never been told where he is, or even which hospital he works in, but I suddenly remember that Geoff had said that Pete had talked to him about his work and Geoff might remember the name of the hospital, so Angela says she will phone Geoff to find out what he knows.

Dan comes in and gives us long hugs, finding his way through masks and various tubes, hanging from us both. 'Thank God you're both all right. I can't imagine what you've been through.'

. . .

Maisie and I are kept in hospital for three nights and treated for shock and smoke inhalation.

Maisie is moved up to a paediatric ward and I insist on going with her, as I am her mother (I keep telling them). I recover quite quickly, but special care needs to be taken of Maisie's delicate young lungs. We have a lot of visits from the police and I have to answer the same questions over and over again, which I understand is essential, but it does keep up the feeling of tension and it is difficult to concentrate on anything else.

The time seems to drag by, and I keep being haunted by the dramatic events and have feelings of panic. I have to try to stay calm, as I don't want Maisie to pick up on my mood, as she seems surprisingly unfazed. She doesn't mention Isobel once while we are in hospital, but she asks for Dan and Emma and is very pleased to see them when they visit, and she tells them all about her adventure of being carried down by the fireman. It is apparent she is too young to realise the danger she has been in and I am glad I have managed to keep myself together enough for her not to sense the extent of my fear. She also says she wants to see Pete and I tell her she will see him soon, but she doesn't ask about going to New York for Christmas and I wonder if Isobel told her that had been her plan.

I find it very difficult to sleep at night in a small fold up bed supplied by the hospital and lie restlessly by Maisie, who sleeps soundly. I am particularly bothered by remembering Isobel shouting at me in such a deranged way and by the terrible image of her running down the lane in flames.

And then – what about the maternity corset, with its bulky padding? Was she ever pregnant? Perhaps she lost the baby early on and wanted to keep up the pretence of being pregnant? But surely Pete would have known? The more I dwell on the whole situation, the more I realise how extremely mentally unbalanced Isobel has been and it all seems so very puzzling and sad. It also appears that Pete must have been involved in all the subterfuge – and why? I am particularly sad about this, as I had always thought, in the past, that Pete had my welfare at heart – but obviously not. I wonder if they have managed to contact him yet and how will I feel when I see him?

Chapter 23

It is now Thursday and Maisie and I are discharged from hospital, but we shall still have to go for regular check-ups. The Doctors are impressed at how well we have both survived the smoke and they say it was probably due to my diligence that we weren't worse affected.

Geoff and Angela have managed to find Pete. Geoff remembered Pete saying that he worked at the Maryday Clinic. Needless to say, Pete was devastated at the news and I am told he arrived yesterday and has gone straight to Isobel, who is in a hospital some distance from here.

The only news we have of Isobel is that she is still unconscious but is doing as well as can be expected, which sounds to me that no one is prepared to make any predictions. Dear Angela and Geoff are being so very helpful and supportive and are letting Maisie and I stay at Ridge Farm for as long as we like, so we can await news about Isobel from Pete.

I am so relieved that Maisie appears to accept our arrival at Ridge Farm, and is pleased to have left the hospital with all its contraptions and noise, and she doesn't seem to be picking up on the tension that the rest of us are feeling. I am so overwhelmed at having her with me and find myself reluctant to let her out of my sight and keep touching her to make sure she is real. She seems to like being with me and enjoys having a cuddle – and holds my hand when we go out to see the farm animals with Angela. She is a bit wary of the large cattle, but is fascinated by them and laughs at their huge pink tongues and the way they munch at their food.

Surprisingly, she seems completely unalarmed by the size of Bess, who must look enormous to her, but Bess is very gentle with her and behaves as if she has known her forever.

Angela has put a small fold-up bed next to mine in my bedroom and Maisie has already tried it out for size and is so glad we have a room together. She obviously doesn't understand at all what's going on, but has accepted that I am looking after her. When Dan and Emma come to see us, as they did a lot, when we were in hospital, seeing us all together seems to give her reassurance. She is gradually accepting Angela and Geoff as well, and Bess of course.

Dan and Emma are being wonderful, giving us love and encouragement, while we wait for news. Dan is sleeping at my cottage for the time being, so he can feed Catty and go straight to and from work from there. We talk on our phones a lot and he says there is not much to be seen of Red House from the cottage, because of the trees, but from the cottage garden he could just see the shower room window, from which we were rescued, and Isobel's bedroom window which is just a large black hole. However, when he went up the lane and looked at the front of the house, he could see it was completely gutted in the middle and the whole centre of the roof was missing, with a few charred beams here and there. I hope that when I eventually get back to the cottage the view of Red House from my home won't be too visible. Luckily, I have no windows facing that way. It is going to be hard enough to cope with the memories of the traumatic events, without seeing the devastation of the building as well. It is sure to take a long time for rebuilding or repairs to be done. Red House is under police guard and no one is allowed access except the forensics team.

Dan tells me that there have been a lot of sight-seers from the village and other areas and the press have been trying to find out information, so he is glad to be staying at the cottage, to keep an eye on the place and send people away. He tells me that one of the firemen had told him that, before Isobel lost consciousness, she had been shouting, 'I killed them, I killed them, and she confessed the whole event to them.'

We haven't yet been told the cause of the explosion, but we have been told that a burnt, almost melted, petrol can was found in the hallway and we can only assume Isobel set fire to the petrol and got caught up in the blast. Hopefully, this will all be made clear after forensic reports. It is so horrific to think of the pain she must have been in. I am just so relieved she is unconscious now.

After a tense and restless day, Angela and I spend an unsettled evening, anxiously waiting for news from Pete. Geoff has been at work this week and taken his car up, so that he can bring Pete down here if he wants to come. We have a light supper of omelette and salad, which Maisie picks at without much enthusiasm, so Angela makes her some little sandwiches with her delicious jam and Maisie enjoys these. After supper and giving her a comforting bath with bubbles, I manage to get Maisie into her bed, in pyjamas borrowed from Charlie. But she is too wide awake to go to sleep and keeps asking me lots of questions, which I do my best to answer without committing myself to too many certainties. She wants to know where "Muffy" is and I gather that Muffy is a soft toy which she usually sleeps with. I find it difficult to answer this sort of question. The best I can do is to say that Muffy is at Red House, and that Charlie has given her a friend, who needs a nice cosy bed. This is a soft rabbit toy that Emma says Charlie won't miss as he has so many, and Maisie can give it a name. I have no idea if it is anything like Muffy, but she takes to it immediately, and snuggles down with it, but then seems too sleepy to think of a name.

I stay with her until she seems fast asleep, with her thumb in her mouth, then I creep downstairs to find out if there has been any news.

Angela tells me that Pete phoned and is going to stay up there with Isobel, as she is not doing too well. She is unconscious, is covered in sterile dressings from head to toe and there are tubes attached to her from every direction. They are not too optimistic about her recovery. In fact, they indicated that it may be only a matter of hours before her whole body gives up the struggle. She is heavily sedated to keep her out of pain. Angela tells me that Pete sounded very emotional as he can't even hold her hand. This must be simply terrible for him and no matter what he has done to deceive me, he doesn't deserve a punishment like this.

I sit down with Angela for a while and we both find it difficult to know what to talk about, so we watch a bit of television, but don't take it in. In fact, if you asked me what we had been watching, I don't think I could tell you. Eventually, we decide enough is enough and have an early night.

. . .

I have hardly slept at all, going over and over all the recent events in my mind. I wonder how I am going to face Pete when we eventually meet up. Of course, it will all depend on Isobel. Whether she lives or dies; if she lives, how damaged will she be? None of this can be known at the moment and my mind is in a turmoil.

Angela sees me looking drawn and exhausted and encourages me to sit down and have some breakfast, but I don't feel hungry.

Maisie, on the other hand seems quite hungry and tucks into a bowl of nut cornflakes and then a boiled egg, with brown toast soldiers to dip in the yolk. This is an egg she had collected with Angela yesterday from one of the resident hens that run around the yard.

'You certainly seem to like your food,' suggests Angela to Maisie.

'I like nice food,' she says, as she sits swinging her legs under the table. 'I won't eat horrid food. I spit it out and Isbel...' 'then she promptly asks, 'Where's Isbel?'

'Isobel's gone away for a while,' says Angela.

'Yes – gone away,' Maisie repeats, as if she is just confirming what she has been told already.

After breakfast, Maisie is very pleased to go with Angela and Bess to see the animals, and collect more eggs from the henhouse, while I talk to Dan on the phone.

He sounds so concerned for me and it is lovely to know he really does seem to care, but I insist that he must continue his life as usual, as I am being well supported by Angela. He will finish work early this afternoon and suggests that Maisie might like to go for a swim with them and maybe I might like to go too. This sounds such a lovely idea, but I tell him, that I will have to wait and see how things are this afternoon, as we haven't heard from Pete yet this morning. I discuss this with Angela and she agrees with me that if Maisie would like to go, then it would be a good idea to give her a change and take her away from the anxious atmosphere here.

'I think you should go too,' says Angela, 'but I quite understand if you want to wait and hear if Pete has any news.' We ask Maisie and she jumps up and down with delight, so we arrange for Dan to pick her up about half past two – and me as well, if I am free to go.

. . .

But no, my swim with Maisie will have to be postponed yet again. We get a phone call from Geoff at twenty past one to say that Isobel has gone. She has passed away peacefully just after one o'clock and Pete is very upset, so Geoff says he will wait up there with him while he finds out what needs to be done next, and then, he will bring him down here. Geoff managed to get himself a bite to eat in the hospital canteen earlier on, but Pete is not wanting anything at the moment. Angela tells me there is probably not much more they can do up there, as it is the weekend, so it will be a good thing for Pete to have a couple of days to gather his thoughts and prepare himself for all the arrangements that will be needed to be done.

I feel very tearful myself, with so many mixed feelings: The main one is relief, and then I feel guilty about feeling relieved and also guilty about being the catalyst for all this to have happened. Then there are mixed memories of the past – some of the times were good and some not too bad – but then there were the terrible times as well. All these things swim into my mind and I am so pleased when Dan arrives. After an emotional welcome, he takes Maisie off swimming, so I can let my feelings go without troubling her.

Angela is wonderful and allows me to let rip. I realise how much emotion I have been holding in for so long – and then the drama of the past few days, where I have had to keep myself together for Maisie's sake – all this comes out in a flood. Angela has to keep insisting that none of this is my fault. Who knows what would have happened if I hadn't found Maisie tied to that chair? Isobel was obviously in a very unstable state of mind and a completely unsuitable person to be in charge of Maisie. So, after a lot of "what ifs", "yes buts", etc. from me, Angela helps me start to come to terms with events.

By the time Dan gets back with Maisie, I am feeling more settled and in control. Maisie is full of excitement about the swim and has to tell me all about it, then Angela takes her off for her tea, leaving Dan and me together.

'I'm so sorry,' he says and he holds me for quite a while as I let a few more tears flow.

'I am so glad you could take Maisie this afternoon,' I say through my tears,' as it has given me time to off-load to dear Angela. My feelings are so mixed up and I'm not looking forward to seeing Pete. I feel so angry at him – yet I know he will be an emotional wreck. I can't imagine how we will be with each other.'

'I know you'll manage,' says Dan. 'You'll both be emotional and that will be a good thing and hopefully open up ways of talking about it all.'

Then Dan tells me that Maisie was very quiet in the car but fine once they got to the pool and met up with Emma and Charlie, in familiar territory, where she is always happy and relaxed.

After Angela has given Maisie her tea, she comes out to us and asks Dan if he would like to stay for supper, but he says he had better get back to the cottage to feed Catty and he has some paperwork to do before the weekend, but then perhaps we can get together over the weekend, so we agree to talk on the phone tomorrow morning.

. . .

Geoff and Pete don't arrive home until after ten and I'm glad Maisie's gone to bed and fallen asleep very quickly. She was very tired after her swim and being with Dan, Emma and Charlie has relaxed her, as it was a normal event in her life to be with them.

I feel awkward when they come in, but Pete just holds out his arms to me and immediately my anger melts and I feel such sadness and compassion for him. We hold each other for a while and then Pete says,' I'm so very sorry for everything I've done. I don't expect you to ever forgive me.'

'No – I don't know that I will, 'I reply bitterly. 'You have a hell of a lot of explaining to do.'

I push myself away and Angela comes to our rescue by saying, 'we must all have a good night's rest and leave conversations for the morning. Everyone's too stressed and tired for recriminations tonight. Come on, we've got to eat something then all go to bed.

Geoff has a whisky, having offered one to Pete, but Pete just has a glass of water, while Angela has wine. I don't feel like a drink and I start helping to put things on the table for supper. Pete looks devastated and Angela insists that we all sit down quietly round the kitchen table and have lovely soothing fish pie that she and I made this morning. Pete says he couldn't eat anything, but Angela says, 'Pete, if I have to spoon-feed you myself, you are going to have at least a few mouthfuls.' And we all laugh, as he picks up his knife and fork and starts eating slowly.

After he has finished eating, Pete says, 'That was delicious, but look, I am really exhausted and I think my bed is the best answer. Thank you all for everything.' Then he adds, 'Lora – can we have a good talk tomorrow?'

'Yep,' I reply abruptly. 'We must.'

While Angela is showing Pete his bedroom, Geoff and I have a quick chat and I ask him how Pete was coming down in the car.

'He seemed absolutely consumed with grief and we hardly talked on the journey, and I certainly didn't challenge him on any past events, if that is worrying you.'

'No – Angela said she was sure you wouldn't. Pete told me he would like to have a talk with me tomorrow, so I must brace myself for that.'

Then, when Angela comes down, we decide it is time for a good night's rest, so we put the dishwasher on and leave the rest of the clearing up till tomorrow. I go up to the bedroom and see Maisie lying so peacefully in the little bed. I had left my bedside light on with its dim bulb and she doesn't stir when I stand quietly looking down at her. She is lying on her right side, holding the unnamed toy rabbit close to her chest. I feel such love and am very tempted touch her and give her a kiss, but she looks so deeply asleep I don't want to wake her.

I get undressed and ready for bed as silently as I can. As I climb into bed and switch out the light I find I am shivering. Memories and images of the fire and Isobel in flames, are so difficult to ignore and I wonder if I will ever be able to stop them invading my mind. It is very dark in the room with the thick heavy curtains and in the blackness I see Isobel's face sneering at me. It is no good. I'll never get to sleep in this dark room, so I get up and put the light on in the shower room and leave the door slightly ajar to see if this helps.

This does help a bit – but then the worry of facing Pete tomorrow, makes me toss and turn in my bed. I can't imagine what he is going to tell me or how I am going to react. I get out of bed and wander around a bit and eventually climb into bed again and have a disturbed sleep, with conflicting dreams – and through all of this Maisie sleeps on without stirring.

Chapter 24

It is now Saturday morning and once again Maisie and I come down to have breakfast with Angela. We manage to get down early enough to help Angela with the clearing up from last night and to get some breakfast things ready. Maisie is quite helpful at carrying small things that won't break but we discourage her from helping us empty the dishwasher, as although she insists she always helps Isobel with this, Angela doesn't want to risk her good china and glasses.

While we are clearing up the postman arrives with a huge pile of letters. The whole house seems to be littered with Christmas cards, either ones already strung up round the sitting room, or ones waiting to be written or sent, so this must be such an especially inconvenient time for Angela and Geoff to have to be dealing with us. I am not used to seeing such a display and it reminds me that I will have to re-think my Christmas ideas and also buy another present for Maisie. I mention to Angela about my concerns of how disruptive we are being to their lives, but she just shrugs it all off, as if there is nothing more important than our welfare at the moment.

We haven't told Maisie yet that Pete has arrived, as we want her to eat her breakfast first without the additional excitement, so before Angela and I sit down, Angela takes me aside and says quietly, 'I hope Pete's all right. His light was on late and I think I heard him tapping away on his laptop when I crept out at one thirty to go to the loo.'

'I expect there are a lot of formalities to go through,' I reply. 'I didn't sleep too well myself, wondering how we are going to face each other today.'

We are having a simple breakfast of cereals and toast. Angela says Geoff often likes a cooked breakfast at weekends, so she is keeping everything that might need cooking in the fridge. It is difficult to know what they both might feel like eating, after such an exhausting few days.

Maisie seems to have quite a good appetite again this morning and is enjoying another boiled egg, with toasted soldiers, after some cereal. She seems quiet and thoughtful and after finishing her egg, she suddenly says, 'Isbel's not coming back.' She looks at me as if to say this is a fact. Then, with a quick change of subject, she turns to Angela and says, 'Please may I have bread?'

'Yes, of course you can,' Angela replies and cuts her a slice of bread and spreads it with butter and then asks, 'Would you like jam?'

'Marmite, please.'

'I'm sorry I haven't got any Marmite,' says Angela apologetically.

'I 'spect Isbel's got Marmite. Butter, please?'

At least Isobel has taught Maisie good manners, I think. This was something she was always very hot on with any children around and I can remember many times being told off if I forgot my p's and q's as well as a good slap if no one else was looking. I don't question her remark about Isobel not coming back. I am expecting the meaning of this to become clear later and am glad Angela does not remark on it, but we look at each other with raised eyebrows.

It is lovely for me to see how well Angela and Maisie are getting on. They seem to have really taken to each other and after breakfast they are ready to go out to feed the chickens and collect the eggs. It is quite a cold morning, with a slight frost, but the sun is trying to come through and there is a pink glow in the sky, which can mean rain later. The weather is always so changeable. Maisie has got some warm clothes borrowed from Charlie, who seems to have an abundance of clothing, given to him by various relatives. Although Maisie is a few months older than Charlie, the clothes seem to fit her well enough and I realise I am going to have to take her shopping soon, but there is no urgency for this.

It is now nearly ten a.m. and Geoff and Pete still haven't surfaced, so, before she and Maisie go out to feed the animals, Angela asks me to let her know when they come down as she would like to see how they both are.

They both appear about fifteen minutes later and neither of them want more than toast and marmalade. Geoff seems fine, after a good sleep, but Pete looks very thin and drawn and when I ask him how he slept, he says he found it difficult to settle, but has had a very good rest, in a very comfortable bed.

I call Angela and Maisie rushes in and straight up to Pete, without taking off her boots or outdoor clothes. Pete picks her up and she flings her arms round his neck and they give each other lots of kisses. It is obvious that they really love each other and that she has missed him. Maisie shows no hesitation in settling herself on his lap, after he helps her take off her muddy boots and thick coat.

Pete eventually manages to eat a little cereal with encouragement from Maisie and then she suddenly announces, 'Isbel gone.' She looks intently at Pete and then continues, 'Isbel gone away.'

'That's right,' says Pete, looking taken aback – and he looks enquiringly at us and we shake our heads as if to say we've said nothing to Maisie.

'Who will look after me?'

Pete looks at me and says, 'Lora will – and Dan and Emma – and I expect Angela and Geoff sometimes.' He looks at Angela questioningly – and she smiles and nods – and I will too, as much as I can.' This seems to satisfy Maisie for now and when Angela suggests that she and Maisie take Bess for a walk, as Pete will be busy with lots to do, Maisie goes off with Angela, very excited at the idea of a walk with Bess.

As they go out, Pete and I are left with a rather awkward silence, then he says, 'Lora, we must have a talk. Is there anywhere we can be on our own without interruption?'

'I am about to ring Dan, so I will see if he can take Maisie again and we could go to the cottage and leave Angela and Geoff for a bit of a break.'

'Sounds a good idea, but first I would like to print something off, so while you talk to Dan, I will try to find Geoff, who I think is in his study. Do you happen to know whether they have a printer?'

'Yes, I'm sure they have. They work a lot from home.'

While Pete goes in search of Geoff, I phone Dan, who is very happy to look after Maisie for a while. I tell him how I am not looking forward to talking to Pete, as I have such mixed feelings and I know I shall really feel like having a go at him, which may not be fair, as he is in such shock after Isobel's death.

'Oh come on,' says Dan 'you are in shock too and fucking hell they did steal your baby – and anyway you need to know what really happened and I think you need to get the truth out of him and tell him how it has affected you.'

'Yes – you're right. I have a right to feel more than angry.'

We chat away for a bit until Pete comes in with some sheets of paper, which he has obviously managed to print. Dan says he will come up right away, wait for Maisie to get back from her walk and then take her down to Lime Tree Cottage.

This plan seems to suit everybody, including Maisie, who wants to know where everyone is going to be, before she goes off with Dan to find Charlie's toys. Emma is working this morning and Charlie is with her and Dan says they will all be together at lunchtime and will be happy to keep Maisie for as long as we wish.

. . .

I drive Pete down in my car in silence and when we get to Blackstone Cottage I can't face going to look at Red House, but

Pete walks on up the lane and has a look. I realise I will have to see it sooner or later, but one thing at a time. I take myself into the cottage and look for Catty, who doesn't seem to be at home, so no soothing cuddles from her. Pete comes back and reports that it still has tape and no entry signs around, which we suppose is for public safety and maybe the forensic people have not finished yet. He says the centre is a charred shell and can't believe there is anything of value left inside. Presumably, all Isobel's documents and papers will have been destroyed.

Pete and I settle down in the sitting room, after I have lit the stove. Dan must have been warm enough with the storage heaters, but I am feeling cold, which is probably from nerves. I sit in Catty's chair and Pete sits the other side of the fire and takes the printed sheets of paper out of his pocket.

'I have printed this off for you to have as proof or evidence, if ever you need it. I have confessed everything about what happened on Morg and I hope you will have the patience now to listen to my story and learn how incredibly sorry and ashamed I am for everything that happened to you. This has all been a huge burden of guilt for me to carry and I have no excuse, except to admit to being a very weak person, who should have had the guts to do things in a very different way.' He sits in front of me, looking a very tired and broken man, clutching several sheets of closely typed paper. I find myself already feeling sorry for him, but am also very impatient to get some explanations.

He offers the sheets of paper to me, but I tell him I would rather have them later and to put them away for the moment, so he folds them carefully and puts them back in his pocket. Neither of us feels like a coffee or hot drink and agree we feel a bit over-coffeed after breakfast.

Pete looks very tense, with his hands gripped together, as he takes a deep breath and says, 'I'd like to start by telling you how I met Isobel and the circumstances surrounding me at that time – if that's OK with you?' he asks.

'Well, if it is relevant to why you stole my baby, then fire ahead,' I say impatiently. 'And why were you so controlled by Isobel? It is as if you don't have a mind of your own.'

'Yes, my story is extremely relevant and yes – I admit – I was controlled by Isobel.'

'OK then, I'm waiting.' I fidget in my chair and hope his story really does throw some light on things.

'Well, I met Isobel about twenty-three years ago. It was before you were born and before your Mother Rose, and May and Isobel went to the island. I was going through a very tough time. My wife, Jenny, Ade's mother had gone off with another man and taken Ade, who was a tiny baby, with her. I was a young Doctor, working very long hours and I was drinking too much. When Jenny left, I started drinking really heavily and the small, country GP practice where I was working, as good as gave me the sack and told me not to come back till I'd sorted myself out.

I never did go back, because one morning, when I was drinking coffee in a café, nursing a sore head after a heavy drinking bout the night before and realising I was fast running out of money, Isobel appeared in the doorway. She looked long and hard at me in that funny way she has, I mean had – when she seems to look all round you, taking in everything about you and making you feel "all enclosed" – do you know what I mean? – almost like being under a spell. All one's troubles would disappear.'

I know just what you mean,' I reply emphatically. 'A lot of people felt like that.'

'Well, she went and got herself a large coffee and a very large pastry and came straight over to my table and sat down. After a moment or two she cut the pastry in half and offered half to me, saying 'you look as though you need this.' In fact, it was just what I needed, as it was fairly plain and I still remember now, how it tasted of cinnamon and had crunchy sugar on the top. It is funny how we remember these odd things.' He pauses for a few moments and then continues, 'that was how it all started. She literally took me over and it seemed to me, in my impoverished state of mind and body, that she was my guardian angel.

She shared a flat in Putney, with her two sisters, May and your Mother, but they were both away at the time. She looked after me and fed me and stopped me drinking. I am not sure how long we were there, but it must have been a few months. During that time, I told her all my woes and she told me all about the fact that she had had a long affair with your father, Nick Laslo. She told me the affair had come to a 'natural end'. That was the way she put it and then she discovered that after she had finished the affair, Nick and your mother had got together secretly and that your mother then became pregnant with you. What she didn't tell me at the time was that she, Isobel, had had two late mis-carriages while she had been with Nick – both – boys. When I discovered this more recently, it made a lot more sense of her later behaviour.'

'Oh my God yes, that answers a lot,' I say.

'Anyway, to continue the saga. I became absolutely besotted with Isobel. It seemed she had rescued me from myself, and when she and her sisters decided to go and live on Morg, I was delighted to be invited to join them. Isobel had made a kind of name for herself amongst a needy group of people, rather like a kind of guru. She took many people under her wing and she seemed to be able to tune into what people needed, emotionally and spiritually. We were all in awe of her, except your mother and May. They were not influenced by her so-called powers. They knew her too well as a sister, with normal human frailties, but they liked the solitary way of life and were happy with the yoga and meditation groups which Isobel ran. Neither of them intended to stay there very long, but it seemed a wonderfully peaceful place for a baby, especially with that beautiful summer weather we had that year.'

'Was I born on Morg?' I ask, as I had never been clear about this.

'No, you were about three months old.'

'Isobel used to tell me I was born there, but Aunt May told me I was born in England.'

'Well, Aunt May was right. In fact, your mother was living with her in the Putney flat and you were born in a hospital in Wimbledon; St. Mary's, I think it was. Isobel and I had already come over to Morg and got things organised, then May and your mother and you followed.'

Pete goes on to tell me about life generally on Morg, as he experienced it, and how Isobel had convinced him that she was a caring and loving person, with very special abilities for healing and helping others. He is horrified when I show him the burn marks on my arms and says he had realised that she was very strict with me, but she never let him see the nasty side to her nature. He had become completely dependent on her emotionally and financially and it was only when I became pregnant that the shock of it seemed to throw them both into a turmoil of uncertainty.

'When Ade died, I really fell apart. He had meant so much to me and I was so proud of his academic achievements at school; taking A levels early and his ambition to do such interesting and useful research work. I felt he would succeed where I had failed in life – and the shock of his death was unbearable.

When you got pregnant, to begin with, Isobel was adamant that we should keep the baby – Ade's baby, as she kept reminding me – and was convinced it would be a boy. She kept going on about us keeping Ade's baby, 'This will be your grandchild', she said to me 'and we can't have a sixteen-year-old being in charge of Ade's baby. She will want to leave the island and we will lose all control of what happens to the boy.' Also, she went on about Ade being seventeen, and nearly an adult, and could be accused of being a child abuser, as you were underage and only fifteen when you became pregnant. She persuaded me that Ade should not know about the pregnancy, as he was due to go off to Africa and he might change his mind and not go which would be very detrimental to his future. I admit, I did agree with this.'

'So, how did she think I would react?' I say angrily. 'Nobody seemed to have taken any notice of my feelings,'

'Well, she said you had as good as confessed to her that you did not want a baby and that you wanted to leave the island and start a life of your own, as a normal teenager.'

'Well – that's absolute shit,' I exclaim. 'Why did you not question me about it yourself?'

'Well – I don't know. We were all in such turmoil and arguing in circles. Anyway, I was hoping when your baby was born you might want to keep it and stay on the island, and then it would be up to you what happened. Then, when she announced she was pregnant too and was excited about bringing the babies up together, I thought this would be the answer. As you probably know, we had been hoping for a baby for ages. We had had various tests and nothing came to light as to what the problem was, and we were told that it may just happen one day, so when she did become pregnant Isobel was convinced it was a turn of fate. Jonah, her spirit guide told her it was meant to be.'

'Oh – stupid Jonah again. Did you go along with all that crap? Ade thought it was all rubbish and called it "Isobel's Hocus Pocus".'

'No, not really – but she did seem to find him convincing. And he did sometimes come up with accurate predictions. Of course, after Ade was killed, her pregnancy seemed even more of a lucky turn of fate.'

Pete looks thoughtful. Then I say, 'Ade used to say to me that he couldn't understand why a person like you with a scientific mind, seemed to go along with all of that. He couldn't understand either, why you were so controlled by her. He always felt there must be some reason for her having such a hold over you and wondered whether she was blackmailing you for some reason.'

Pete looks very uncomfortable and shifts about in his chair and then takes a deep breath and says, 'Yes, she had a very strong hold over me. In fact, there is something very important which I need to tell you, which happened while I was still working as a GP. I confessed what happened to Isobel when I first met her and we were both telling each other about past secrets. She held this over me like the "Sword of Damocles" and she used the information many times to undermine me and threatened to pass it on to the police if I didn't follow her every whim. I have written about it on the paper I have printed out for you, but I will tell you now, as it relates so much to future events.'

'So, she was blackmailing you?' I feel flabbergasted at the thought and very anxious, but curious about what he is about to tell me, and then he begins.

'While I had been working as a doctor, one of my patients was a young girl of twelve, who confided in me that her father had been sexually abusing her. She was terrified of him and although she had tried to tell her schoolteacher, she was not believed, as her father happened to be a very well-respected policeman. She felt unable to tell her mother, who was devoted to him and she was sure would never believe her. At the time, it was before all the scandals about celebrity paedophiles, and abuse was often denied or not believed in most cases, especially as he was a policeman, known and liked in the community. I tried to raise the alarm with social workers but was told she was a child known to fantasise and, of course, it was all nonsense.

I knew he used to frequent a certain pub and that he was a heavy drinker. No one seemed to question his drinking and driving, not even the publican. So, one evening I waited in my car outside the pub to challenge him about the abuse. Remember, I was a drinker myself at the time. When he came out later that night and was on his own, I went and gave him a piece of my mind, at which he swore at me and drove off at great speed. I knew the road he went down was quite deserted, with no houses and with woods on either side, so I followed him in my car- also very drunk, don't forget-. He knew I was following him, so he speeded up and went much too fast round a left-hand bend and crashed straight into a tree on the right. I staggered out of my car and could see that his car was a crumpled mess and he was trapped inside and was certainly unconscious, if not dead.

I hadn't got my phone with me, so I turned around and drove as carefully as I could back home. I didn't stop on the way to make a call, even though I did go back past the pub and then various other houses. In fact, I got home, went inside and went straight to bed. I never reported the accident. I heard later that he had eventually been found dead and it was claimed that if he had been found earlier, he could possibly have been saved.'

'Oh my God – Pete what a terrible thing – you must have felt dreadfully guilty.'

'Well, no. I didn't at the time. I felt he had got what he deserved, but when I told Isobel about it, in the early days when we were getting to know each other and she was starting to try to help me with my drink problem, she was very shocked and told me that I should have helped and that it was not up to me to judge this man. What about my Hippocratic oath? She was right, of course'. Then Pete pauses and looks very contrite. 'She never let me forget this and held it over me like a moral blackmail. Also, later on, she told me she had recorded evidence of my confession. Of course, I don't know whether this was actually true, but then anything seemed possible with Isobel.'

We both pause for a moment and look at each other and then I ask, 'Do you know what happened to the girl?'

'Yes, I have kept in touch with her on and off ever since, and although she went through much emotional turmoil during the rest of her teenage years and needed a lot of therapy, which I helped organise for her, I am so relieved to have found she has got on very well in recent years. She has been to university and is now working as a psychiatric nurse in a hospital, up in the north of England. She got married not long ago and is expecting her first baby. I have never told her what happened regarding her father's death.'

'So how do you feel about all this now?'

'Oh, I do feel very guilty. Every day I think about it. It was a huge deception on my part. It was not up to me to judge him, and who knows how things would have turned out for the girl, if he hadn't been killed. The "what ifs" of life can never be known.'

'If Isobel was so judgemental of you over this, didn't she think what she was planning to do with my baby was morally wrong?' I ask feeling very indignant.

'No, she could always argue her way around everything and I was always too weak to go against her. Anyway, I will explain what actually happened over the time of Maisie's birth, then you might begin to understand.'

'Yes – tell me. That's what I really need to know.' I have been finding myself feeling a bit of sympathy for Pete, but then I am reminded of everything and my hurt and anger comes to the surface again. How could he have been so weak? and I shout, with utter fury and emotion.

'No – I can't understand it. You drugged me and took my baby away. That's evil and unforgiveable.'

'Wait a minute,' says Pete, interrupting me, 'I didn't drug you. I gave you a pethidine injection while you were in labour, but I never gave you anything after that.'

I am now crying with tears of fury and Pete looks distraught with guilt and contrition. 'Well, why was I so out of it after the birth – and sleeping so much – and in such a daze? Then I am taken to hospital and even given ECT. That could have had a lasting effect on my memory. How could you possibly believe that was the right thing to do?' I blurt all this out with such anger.

'I never drugged you. And what's this about ECT? I swear I never knew anything about that.'

We both pause and look at each other, and then Pete says, 'she must have been drugging you. After the birth she must have been drugging you.' He puts his head in his hands and then says, 'I don't suppose you know what happened after the birth.'

'No, I was not aware of anything after the birth, except feeling completely out of it and sleeping a hell of a lot.'

'OK. – Well, I'll tell you now what happened.' He pauses and takes a deep breath. 'As Maisie was born, Isobel gasped when she realised it was a girl and rushed out of the room with the baby who was crying. I stayed with you and made sure you were OK and that the placenta had come away and you were not haemorrhaging. You were still very drowsy from the Pethidine. Some people do react to it more strongly than others.

Then I went out to find Isobel and the baby, meaning to bring her into you. Isobel stood in front of me and refused to hand the baby over, and said, 'It's a girl! A bloody girl!' And she screamed at me, 'this spoils all my plans,' and at that she put the baby down on a table behind her, ripped off her maternity dress and tore off a corset and flung padding all over the floor. 'There,' she said defiantly, 'now you know. There is not going to be another baby and we are going to keep this one.' She then turned round and picked up Maisie who, by now, was crying loudly. – She wouldn't let me near her.

Pete goes on. 'I was so shocked I couldn't speak. I rushed to the kitchen and found a bottle of something strongly alcoholic and drank it all. This was the first alcohol I had had in years, and I then collapsed unconscious on the floor.

I don't know how long I was there for and when I came to, I found myself fully clothed, but lying on my own bed with Isobel standing over me holding Maisie and looking very happy. 'It's OK' she said. 'Lora's fine and this dear little baby is going to be fine too. You and I will give her a lovely life.'

Then things gradually started to fall into place. When she was first pregnant she was very happy and excited about it. She showed me the scan, after she had been to see her doctor on the mainland and all was fine for a while. She was knitting baby clothes and comparing notes with you, but after a while she said she had a lot of back pain and said she had great trouble sleeping and she insisted on sleeping in one of the other cottages away from me. I never saw her naked after this. She said she felt squeamish about the baby moving and wouldn't let me near her.'

'Yes, but it was your baby too. You should have insisted.'

'Yes, I know. Yet another thing I should have done. But I did manage to persuade her to go back to see the Doctor to make sure everything was OK, which she did, and when she returned to Morg she reassured me that all was well but she seemed in a funny mood. She said she had had another scan, but had forgotten to bring a print back with her. I should have smelt a rat then, but I realise now she must have had a miscarriage some time previously and probably not even been back to see the Doctor at all.'

'So, what happened after you collapsed drunk on the floor?' I ask impatiently.

'She was all sweetness and light. She said the baby was absolutely lovely and she adored her already. She said you were fine. She went over all the reasons why we should keep the baby and said you had rejected the baby and wanted us to look after her.'

At this, I feel outraged and shout, 'Pete, this is incredible, lies, lies, lies. I know I would never have said that, even in a drugged state. How could you possibly have believed her? Did you know she had told me my baby was badly deformed and had died soon after it was born?'

Pete looks shattered and starts to shake with emotion. 'I'd no idea she had told you that. I know this is no excuse, but I was drinking so heavily, I really did not know what was going on. I wasn't allowed anywhere near you and Isobel was getting more and more disgusted with me, but she let me drink and didn't hide the bottles.' He pauses for a moment and sits in a crumpled heap, as if he is trying to disappear, and while I am dumbly trying to gather myself together, he suddenly blurts out, 'A day or two later Isobel suddenly confronted me and told me that she had packed up all my things, including my passport and that I must leave straight away and she had arranged for a boat to pick me up. She said she couldn't stand having a drunken slob in her house any more as this was not the right environment to bring up a child.'

My God, and you just left, without even checking on me?' I say incredulously.

'Yes, to my shame.' He says, 'I was just allowed to look round your door to say goodbye, but you were sleeping at the time.'

'Yes, I remember that from somewhere in my drugged mind.' I say coldly.

'I don't expect you to ever forgive me,' he says with emotion. 'I know I will never forgive myself. Now I realise everything I did was to satisfy mine and Isobel's needs, as I felt so dependent on her, and now – she has gone… 'he wipes tears from his face. 'I don't know how I feel. There is a huge relief, but a guilt at not feeling sad enough. It must have been a dreadful death.' He takes a few moments to gather his thoughts together and then continues, 'All the money I have been earning in New York has been going towards her and Maisie's welfare at Red House. However much I sent, Isobel seemed to need more. I certainly don't begrudge supporting Maisie and hope to go on doing so.'

Pete somehow manages to look even smaller. I can't believe he's a grown man. He must have been surviving on Isobel's hypnotic powers ever since he met her. Then I realise he must have been a very damaged soul before he met her and she had been acting like a life-support system for him ever since that chance meeting in the café.

I am now swaying between compassion and anger towards him. Then, as he looks so pathetic, I want to get up and go and comfort him, but then my anger gets the better of me and I stop myself. As he dries his tears with a bit of kitchen roll, which I hand to him, he sits there like a small child and I feel so much more mature than him.

He recovers his composure after a few minutes and I can't help confronting him with anger and passion. 'Didn't you feel even a teeny bit guilty when you went, leaving me and Maisie in Isobel's hands?'

'Yes, terribly' he replied, beginning to break down again,' yes terribly guilty, when I eventually sobered up – but then in my drunken state I really didn't know what I was doing or thinking. She kept repeating that you had said you didn't want the baby and she really did seem to have taken to Maisie, giving her lots of attention and bottle feeding her successfully. Before I left Morg, she gave me a copy of a letter which she said you had written, in which you said you didn't want the baby and wanted us to look after it. I was told that you wrote it when you were pregnant, but there is no date on it.'

'My, God, I don't remember ever writing that.' I exclaim. 'I do remember from time to time, talking about my doubts of being able to look after a child in the future, but I certainly have no recollection of writing a letter like that. Have you got the letter with you?'

'No, it's with my belongings at Ridge Farm and I'll show it to you when we get back.'

I am sitting feeling stunned and let Pete ramble on a bit, while I try and take it in.

'Isobel was fiercely protective of this beautiful, tiny baby.' He pauses to mop tears again, and then goes on.

'I was extremely lucky to have the job in New York to go to. All organised by Isobel or course. It was Bob Saunders, who stayed with us several times on Morg, who said he could give me a job any time and that is where I ended up and have been pretty well all the time since. Isobel has been over with Maisie to visit me several times and I had glowing reports about you and all seemed fine. Maisie seemed in good spirits and always pleased to see me.'

'So, did you really not know about me spending time in the clinic and having ECT for serious depression, or that Isobel had invented the myth about my dead baby?'

'No, I had no idea. I had regular reports from Isobel, saying how she was loving looking after Maisie and how you were doing extremely well having left Morg and had a very good life of your own with good friends – but I swear to you – I never knew about the clinic or the ECT or how bad things were for you. Isobel was in charge of your welfare and all the reports I got from her were so positive.

It was only when I came over to visit Isobel recently, that she told me that you seemed fine now, but had actually been through a bit of a hard time and had spent a short time in a clinic, but had recovered well and you were now leading a happy independent life. She didn't tell me the extent of your problem and never mentioned ECT. When I came to see you recently, without telling Isobel, you seemed fine and you didn't mention anything about the clinic. I did wonder why Isobel was very agitated when I told her I had been down to see you, but she looked relieved when it was obvious that you had said nothing incriminating against her or about how very unwell you had been.'

'So, what about the dead baby?' I ask. 'Isobel took me to sprinkle the ashes of the dead baby in the sea off Morg?' So, as there was no dead baby – they must have been ashes – from the grate.'

Pete leans forward with his elbows on his knees and covers his face with his hands, as I tell him the details.

'How grotesque', he exclaims. 'I swear I was completely unaware of any of that.'

'Yes – How grotesque,' I agree – and have to leave the room.

I go out and slam the door. I am feeling so angry with Isobel and confused about Pete. I walk round the garden, in the very cold wind, without a coat. I know I had been suspicious that there was no dead baby, ever since I saw Isobel's perfect figure after she was said to have given birth. And this was confirmed when I saw the padded corset hanging in Isobel's cupboard. But remembering that we had a mock funeral on Morg is just the last straw.

I am standing looking at the black stone but I can't see the image of the child's face at the moment. I am beginning to realise how cold it is outside when Catty appears and comes up to me purring and doing her usual slalom round my legs. It is as if she is telling me I must go back in and finish this process.

When I go back indoors, Pete is not sitting in his chair. For a moment I panic and fear he is not coming back, but then I hear the loo flushing and realise he has been in the bathroom. He comes back into the room, looking a wreck, with his hair dishevelled and his face blotched with tears.

'I wanted to splash my face with cold water,' he says, 'but didn't know whether I could use the hand towel.'

'Of course you could,' I reply, 'but I could get you a clean one if you like.' I realise he sounds like a child asking for permission.

'No, that'll be fine,' he says, and trudges off up the stairs again. Perhaps he felt he had to ask Isobel for guidance on every little action.

When he eventually sits down again, Catty jumps up onto his lap and he strokes her as she settles down in a comfy position. It is a lovely excuse for him not to have to look me in the eye, as he helps her settle.

I have calmed myself down quite a lot since my escape to the garden. Now I realise that, although Pete had blindly gone along with Isobel's decisions, there seems to be a huge amount he had not known about. That is, if he is telling the truth now.

'So, you really didn't know how ill I was when I was in the clinic, or the fact she had invented my dead baby?' I repeat again.

'No, I swear to you, I didn't. Isobel only sent me positive messages. I wrote to you several times, but never got a reply, so I don't imagine you ever got my letters. Isobel said you wanted a new life with complete independence from us.'

'So, Isobel must have organised the whole thing and sanctioned the ECT, without consulting you?'

'Yes, she had always been your official guardian since your mother's death.'

'Did you and Isobel ever get married?' I ask, 'I believe Maisie's birth is registered with you both as parents?'

'No, we weren't married, but yes, Isobel registered us both as Maisie's parents.' Then he hurriedly goes on to say, 'But I am going to put all that right. I plan to get everything straight and out in the open. I don't want any more deception or lies. That is the reason I have written all this out for you, so you can be sure I will keep my word.' He takes the papers out of his pocket again and hands them to me. 'Please read them, when you feel like it, and let me know if there is anything else you are not clear about.'

I take them from him and put them on the table beside me and as neither of us feels like going out to the pub, I find some bread and make a couple of cheese and tomato sandwiches, but they just sit on the plate, as we are not hungry. I pick up the notes and start to read them, while Pete stays in his chair stroking Catty.

He has written about everything he has told me this morning, including the part about the dead policeman and I suddenly feel uneasy and ask, 'Did Geoff see these notes when they were being printed off this morning.'

'No, he left me to do them and I deleted everything afterwards. Why do you ask?'

'Well, it is evidence, isn't it? Couldn't you be sent to prison for this, or at least be struck off from practising medicine again?'

'Well, it is what I deserve and I don't want to hide anything anymore. I want to confess everything.'

'Why?' I ask. 'What good would it do?'

'I can't bear having all this on my conscience anymore.'

'Pete – just think about it. What you do, won't just affect you. There's Maisie to think about. You are her grandfather and she loves and needs you. Anybody can see that. There's your valuable work as a doctor and people who depend on you at the hospital. I know you can survive without Isobel's power to hold you up – you have just got to recognise your own value.' I hear myself saying this with Aunt May's voice in my head.

Pete doesn't answer but looks thoughtful and near to tears again.

I am still thinking of Aunt May, when I take the sheaf of papers, open the front of the stove and throw them in. They catch fire immediately and, in a few seconds, have gone.

Pete looks at me open-mouthed. 'Why on earth did you do that?'

'Well, you must do what you think is right and as far as I'm concerned, I am going to ignore the fact that you have ever told me about that policeman. What you do about that, if anything, is your business. But Pete, I trust you to do the right thing regarding Maisie. You must make sure she is made legally my daughter. I am quite prepared to tell the authorities that I was too young, suffering a bereavement and very ill at the time of her birth and in no fit state to look after a baby and that is why you and Isobel took her over. I don't need to tell them anything else.' I find myself saying all this with an inner conviction. 'What else you do, no one else can advise you, but I am sure you can find your own inner strength – and not let Isobel's negative power influence you anymore.'

Pete looks utterly amazed and says, I'm sure you could never forgive me – and I wouldn't expect you to.'

'Well, I don't know whether I will ever forgive you Pete, but I feel we have both been victims of Isobel in one way or another and I really don't know what to think. She was a very charming person to so many people, with a hugely powerful personality and I would hate to think of her winning the final battle over us. I hope you don't go to the police and confess about the past, but I do hope you will think of Maisie's happiness and future and let me get an official DNA test done, and convince the authorities that I am now fully capable of looking after my own child.'

Pete continues to sit in his chair, looking rather bewildered, and Catty jumps down from his lap, as if to say, 'Well, think about that then'. She strolls off to find the cat flap and takes herself out into the garden.

It is now mid-afternoon and it will be getting dark soon, so I suggest we go for a quick walk to clear the air, before we go back to Ridge Farm. Pete has come unprepared with no outdoor clothing but a warm coat. We find a pair of Dan's wellies by the kitchen door, which are a little big for him, but will serve the purpose.

A brisk walk round the garden and field does us both good and before we get into the car to go back to Ridge Farm, I say, 'All I ask, Pete, is that you accept that Maisie is my daughter and do whatever is necessary to make that official.' And I feel like saying – for heaven's sake grow up and stand on your own two feet. That's what I've had to do.

As if reading my mind, Pete looks thoughtful and says,' Now I know I can't rely on Isobel anymore, or worry about recriminations from her, it does feel like a kind of freedom and I'll be entitled to do things my way. It will take a bit of getting used to, but I promise you, I will make things right for you and Maisie.' Then he hesitates for a moment before continuing, 'There is one other thing which I must tell you, as I think it is of utmost importance.' He takes a deep breath and then the words rush out, 'I told you about my drink problem and how Isobel had originally helped me overcome it.'

'Yes,' I reply, wondering where this conversation is going.

'Well, I am an alcoholic and realise now that she didn't really help me – she just held me up and prevented me from really tackling the problem myself. All the time I was with her I was relying on her strength and not facing the music myself. When I arrived in New York, I was in a bad way and having bouts of heavy drinking again and I put it down to the shock of everything that had happened recently on Morg. My friend Bob was very helpful and I decided I really wanted to accept my problem, so to cut a long story short, I got professional help and joined Alcoholics Anonymous and I haven't touched a drop of alcohol for two years and one month, to be exact. It has been a struggle and I have found it incredibly difficult up to now, but the strange thing is that since Isobel's death, only a few days ago, it is as if I can now really make it my own decision about not drinking. Do you understand what I mean?

'Yes, I think I do.'

'Now, I really know this is something I have to do for myself. Not for Isobel or Maisie, or you, or anyone else. The other night when I arrived at Ridge Farm and Geoff had a whisky and offered me one, it was the first time that I really felt I did not want one and that it was my choice not to have one. This is in spite of the shock of everything that has been going on in the last few days.

'This sounds like a new beginning for us all,' I suggest, as we get into the car to go back to Ridge Farm and I feel impatient to see the mystery letter.

Chapter 25

When we arrive back at Ridge Farm Pete goes straight away to find the letter for me and I simply can't wait to see what it says, but my patience has to be tested again. Dan has already brought Maisie back and Angela has persuaded him to stay for tea and when Maisie rushes up to me and looks anxious, I put the letter out of my mind and straight into my pocket and give her a nice long cuddle.

'I want you to stay at Widge Farm,' she says, and then, 'I want Pete too,' and she runs over to Pete, who picks her up and holds her close. Then she turns to me and says, 'Pete looks sad. Why?'

'He was sad', I say, 'but he is better now. Aren't you Pete?'

'Yes, yes, I'm fine now.' Maisie seems to accept this without further question and then goes on with great excitement to tell us all the interesting things she has been doing with Dan, Emma and Charlie today. They were going to go swimming, but the pool was closed for some reason. However, Dan and Emma seem to have kept them well occupied – drawing, making things and watching a film on television, plus eating a large lunch.

While Maisie decides to sit on Pete's lap and ask him where he has been and what he's been doing, Dan and I manage to slip away into the kitchen where we are alone for a few moments. We hold each other close and I tell him how glad I am to see him and I agree to tell him later what went on between Pete and me.

'It was so worthwhile,' I say, 'so many things came to light and my head is in a whirl and I feel utterly exhausted. Before I tell you about it all I simply must look at a letter that Pete has given me. I haven't had a chance to read it yet. With trepidation, I pull it out of my pocket and look at it. It is in a plain white unsealed envelope. As I hesitate to open it, I say to Dan, 'Pete told me that Isobel claimed that I had written this during my pregnancy – so here goes.' I take a deep breath as I open it and I can see it is in my handwriting and has my signature. I quickly read it in silence and this is what it says:

Dear Isobel and Pete

As you know, I am expecting a baby and I just want to tell you that I don't want to have the responsibility of looking after a child, as I am much too young and will want to have a normal teenage life and then get some training and have a job, before being a mother, with the responsibility of a child. I am hoping that you will both take care of my baby and give it a good life, which is what Ade would wish.

Love from Lora

I burst into tears and Dan has to stop me tearing the letter up. I thrust it at him and tell him to read it.

'Wait, wait,' he says soothingly, as he reads it through. 'Give yourself time to think.'

'That's rubbish,' I say, as I pace the floor, 'I never, ever would write something like that, and seeing Maisie just now – looking so happy – I can't imagine not wanting her. I feel such love.'

'So, are you sure it is your handwriting?' asks Dan, as he hands it back to me.

'Yes… yes, it is,' I say as I hold it with shaking hands and try to scrutinise it.

'I think it sounds as if it was dictated to you,' says Dan. It doesn't sound like it would have come from you. It is completely without feeling – unnatural. Do you think you were drugged?'

'I have absolutely no idea. I am certainly completely unaware of ever writing it.' I start sobbing, with uncontrollable tears and Dan holds me close while I take time to calm down and try to collect my thoughts. After a while, I say, 'I do remember being with Isobel, in heated moments, during pregnancy when I was feeling ill with morning sickness and if we had a row, I would stomp off and say I didn't want the bloody baby… but that was before Ade died… when I was sometimes feeling angry at him for getting us in this mess. And now I can't imagine…' I trail off and Dan quietly asks,

'Can I have another look at it please?' and I hand it over and go and stare at one of the shiny, stainless-steel lids on the cooker. I can see the distorted shape of my face in the curving surface of the lid. This is just how I feel – distorted, I say to myself.

Dan comes and stands by me and puts his arm round my waist. 'Looking at the wording, it says "what Ade would wish" not, "what Ade would have wished", so I think it was written before…'

'… before Ade died?' I suggest. 'but I still have no memory of having written it' and then I suddenly say 'ECT – could it be something erased from my memory?'

'Possibly, but it still doesn't sound like a natural way of writing something so personal and so important.'

We are still mulling it over, when Angela comes into put the kettle on for tea and, somehow, she has managed to magically produce a few small cakes and biscuits.

She seems to notice our strained expressions and says, 'I expect you two would like a chance to catch up with each other's news, so I suggest, after we have all had tea together, you two could go into Geoff's study while Geoff and I and Pete look after Maisie for a bit.

'Oh, thank you Angela,' I say and give her a hug and a kiss. 'You are great.'

I feel thankful to have time to think of something else for a while as we have our tea. I am not at all surprised to find I am not hungry, even for a mouthful of one of Angela's cakes.

. . .

When Dan and I have the chance, as Angela promised, to have some time to ourselves, we put the letter aside for the time being and I tell him all about my time with Pete, except for the story about the policeman. I am determined to keep my promise to Pete and ignore what he has told me about that event. I do say to Dan that some of what Pete has told me I have promised to keep to myself but it makes a lot of sense in explaining Pete's behaviour. Of course, Dan is curious to know what this is about, but he understands that I am adamant that some things are told in confidence and have to remain that way.

When I tell Dan about burning the papers, Dan looks at me in horror and says,

'Why on earth did you do that? You have nothing now to ensure that he keeps to his word.'

'Oh, he will. I know he will. We have come to an agreement, which suits us both.' I then tell Dan about the fact that I am willing to say, to whoever needs to know, that he and Isobel had taken charge of Maisie, because I was not well and, at that time, not fit to look after a child.'

'Well, that's going to look odd. I mean the fact that they actually registered her as their baby.'

'Yes, he is going to confess to all that.' Then I suddenly realise, and add, 'The letter, which was written by me, did actually give them permission to take her over.'

'So, how do you know Pete won't want to claim her and take her back to America with him? After all, he is her grandfather and she is the only connection he has with his son.'

'No, I know he won't. He wants me to have her, now that I am fit and well and wanting to take care of her. I know he is sincere over that.'

I can see I haven't convinced Dan, who asks, 'What happens if Pete, for some reason, is taken ill, or something unexpectedly happens to him before everything is sorted?'

'Well, I would be next of kin for Maisie, wouldn't I? And another, official, DNA test could prove I am her mother.'

'I suppose so,' he says, reluctantly, 'but, I still think you have probably destroyed some good evidence which could have helped ease the process along.'

'But you weren't there this morning, and I can assure you Pete will do the right thing. In fact, I am now seeing Pete in quite a different light. There was so much he didn't know about.'

'Don't you think this might be a good time for you to talk things through with Angela and Geoff. They are quite a bit older than both of us and have had more experience of life. I think you told me Angela was a Magistrate at one time, so she would probably have some good advice. Also, after this weekend, there will be all sorts of people, including the police, asking hundreds more questions. Social Services will be involved to make sure of Maisie's welfare if she stays with you.'

'Yes, you're right. I know Angela has been trusted to be in charge of Maisie for the weekend, but of course there will be a lot more formalities to go through, and Pete is saying he is not sure if he is allowed to leave the country yet.'

. . .

When Dan and I join the others in the sitting room, Pete and Maisie are busy playing snakes and ladders. I look at them and think, this is what I would like the future to be and that we can make something positive come from the dreadful past. I hope this relationship between them can continue through the years, wherever we all happen to be.

That evening, after I have put Maisie to bed and read her a story, and she has fallen asleep, hugging Charlie's spare rabbit (still with no name), I sit beside her for quite a while, just looking at her and stroking her hair. I just feel so amazed at the wonder of her being my darling daughter and how lucky I am and how nothing must come in the way of my resolve to be a really loving mother to her.

After a while, I drag myself away and join the others downstairs. I tell everyone I would like to move Maisie down to the cottage as soon as possible, but I suppose I will have to be considered to be a fit person to look after her first. Dan says the press and other snoopers seem to have lost interest in the sight of the burnt-out house for the moment, having written up many conflicting stories in the papers. I suggest, if Dan and I take Maisie down there tomorrow and show her around and spend the day down there, possibly with Pete as well, this would be a start in getting her used to being there.

As I am thinking about this, Angela comes up to me and says anxiously, 'Can we both have a quiet word together?'

'Yes, of course,' I reply, while she leads me into the study and shuts the door.

'I know it is really none of our business, but Geoff and I are very concerned about what happens next regarding Pete. I mean, did you have a good talk this morning – and what conclusions have you come to regarding the way forward with Maisie?'

'Yes, I'm so sorry Angela, I haven't up-dated you on everything yet. Pete and I had a very good talk; very emotional but we have resolved many things, and I realise this is just the start of getting everything sorted.'

Angela continues, 'We realise that the police still have more questioning to do with all concerned and Social Services are coming on Monday morning, but we all need to be clear in our minds as to what you are wanting to happen next.'

'Oh, I'm so sorry Angela. I've been so wrapped up with the whirlwind of events, that I've talked to Dan, but left you both in the dark. We would really like a chat with you and Geoff and get some advice. Of course, I intend to tell you about my talk with Pete, so if you and Geoff could spare some time, I would love to have your views on how to go on from here.'

. . .

I imagine this is what it feels like to have a family get-together, with a civilised discussion, as we sit round the big kitchen table that evening. Pete joins us too, as I am sure they will want explanations from him. I am a bit worried that Pete will tell them about the policeman, but he doesn't, but he does explain how he is an alcoholic, how Isobel had taken him in and stopped him drinking and how he had felt completely dependent on her. He explained about the phantom baby, his complete drunken breakdown and his being banished by Isobel. He told them how Isobel had deceived him into thinking I was fine after the birth, about his complete ignorance of my mental state after the birth, and all that followed.

There is a lot of cross-examining from Geoff and Angela, but Pete seems much stronger and able to talk about it all, after having got it off his chest talking with me this morning.

They are both amazed by the strength of Isobel's negative power and Pete's powerlessness. Geoff, being the more pragmatic of the two, finds it more difficult than Angela to understand how things came about and how they could behave as they did.

'Well,' says Geoff, when Pete has finished. Then he takes a deep breath and continues, 'I can imagine there must be more to it than you have told us, but I insist,' and he looks at Angela for agreement, 'you must, simply must, put in writing, before you leave here, confirmation that Lora is Maisie's mother and explaining the circumstances in which you became custodians of Maisie while Lora was ill.' Angela and I nod in agreement, 'and how, now, you are happy for Lora to take Maisie back.'

'Yes, I know,' says Pete, 'and I'll do it right away.'

'And we won't let you leave until you do.' Says Geoff.

Later that evening Pete gets down to the serious task of writing the letter and after some rewriting of the details, we all read it. When we are fully satisfied, Geoff and Angela and I, all witness his signature.

· · ·

Sunday morning starts off bright and clear, with a slight ground frost. Pete seems pleased to come down to the cottage with us and we set off about ten. Maisie is excited at the thought of seeing inside the cottage. She jumps out of the car quickly when we get there and goes immediately to look at the black stone.

'The little girl looks happy,' she says, as she stares at the back of the stone. I go round and have a look and she certainly does seem to have a smile today.

Dan agrees with me and then says, 'It is funny how some people cannot see her at all, yet we seem to see her quite often.'

'I suppose, as Geoff said recently, it is according to the light sometimes – but also what we want to see and what shapes we make from the rough, cut stone.' As we are looking at it, I think to myself that this is how we see people. We don't always see them in the same way and sometimes it takes a different light to see another aspect of them.

'Have you seen the little girl before?' I ask Maisie.

'Oh yes. Lots of times. I walk with Isbel... but Isbel says no when... 'She trails off and then says, 'Let's go in the house.'

We go into the cottage and we go and explore each room. I tell her not to frighten Catty if she is in at the moment. Then, I show her the spare bedroom. I don't ask her if she would like to have it as her bedroom yet, as I am not sure how long we will need to be under Angela's supervision at Ridge Farm. She seems to like it and I explain to her that this is where Aunt May used to do her sewing and she is intrigued by the tailor's dummy.

'She'd like some clothes,' she says. And I realise I still have a few of Aunt May's clothes in the cupboard, so I tell her I am sure we could find something suitable for her when we have finished looking around.

Meanwhile Dan and Pete have gone off to look at Red House and they come back and tell me that, although it is a Sunday, there is a surveyor up there looking at the ruin. He was pleased to see Pete, as he wasn't sure who to contact about the house. He told Pete that what is left of the outer walls seem pretty solid, but there is nothing worth keeping from the inside structure. It is all charred beams and scattered bits of burnt furniture. He thinks the best thing to do would be to knock it down and build again. They agreed that probably there will be difficulties regarding insurance, as it has been suggested it was a deliberate fire and Pete told him that he is thinking he would probably like to sell the site to a developer. He had joint ownership with Isobel, and has no wish to rebuild or live there himself. They exchanged details and Pete said he will be in London for a few days and then may come back down here for a day or two, before going back to New York.

I am glad to hear what Pete has to say about the house, as I was wondering what would happen to it. I like the idea of a completely new house there, as it wouldn't be a constant reminder of Isobel and the fire and all the stressful past few weeks. Dan tells us a developer would probably want to build several houses up there, if they could get planning permission, as it is a large plot. I am pleased to remember that the deeds of my cottage show the copse of trees belongs to me, as they were all part of the original farmland and Blackstone Cottage was also part of that farm. The trees would still be a good barrier against any building going on up there.

'So, are you planning to go on living here?' Pete asks me.

'Certainly, for the time being. I haven't had time to gather my senses yet. It has all happened so very quickly. It is only just over six weeks since I arrived here. My head is still in a whirl, but one thing I am really sure of is that I really want to take my daughter back and this is the most important thing that has ever happened to me.'

I say this loudly and firmly, while looking straight at Pete and Pete replies emphatically, 'Yes, this is certainly going to happen.'

We have some coffee and talk about possible plans for the next few days. We have the shadow of the meeting with a social worker hanging over us tomorrow and we still don't know when Pete will be allowed to go back home. Pete will have a lot to do in the next few days and I am relieved to notice a much more adult look to him today. I am sure, if his nerve holds, he will find very practical ways of dealing with everything. I cannot bear the thought of Isobel having a hold over him even after her death, but he did say a heavy cloud was lifting and he certainly has a more positive look about him. He is also standing up straighter, which seems to give him extra height and an air of confidence.

Then Maisie comes into the room, carrying Aunt May's blue blouse. My heart skips a beat when I see it, and she says, 'Aunt May wants to wear this… and she wants more clothes.'

I am finding it difficult to respond immediately and Dan whispers to Pete that the blouse was one of the mysterious happenings. Then Dan says to Maisie, 'Would you like Lora and me to come up and see what we can find? There may be something better.'

I hesitate, but he takes my hand as we follow Maisie up the stairs. I notice she is an agile child. She must have had plenty of practise stair climbing at Red House and we are soon in the bedroom. Maisie had managed to open a drawer in which I had put a few of Aunt May's clothes which I had wanted to keep. I had forgotten that I had stuffed the blue blouse into it in a hurry after the strange event.

'Perhaps we could find something nicer than this,' I suggest, as Maisie pulls out the blue one. 'This one is very creased. What about this flowery one – and the pale blue skirt would go well with it?'

'No, she likes this one,' Maisie says firmly. 'Don't you think she would like the flowery one just as well?' asks Dan, holding it up and showing it to Maisie. 'It's got beautiful colours.'

'No, she wants this one.'

'How do you know that?' I ask, suddenly realising that Maisie is right.

'Cos, she tells me. She likes it best.'

An odd feeling creeps over me and I know that this is true. It is as if Aunt May is agreeing and by putting on the blue blouse, we will be exorcising some of Isobel's control.

'Yes, I think she would look best in this blue one and I take it and put it on the dummy and firmly button it up. Dan looks a bit amazed by my reaction but I smile at him to show I am quite OK 'It is very crumpled,' I say,' but I can iron it tomorrow. Now, let's find a skirt. There are two here. Which one would you suggest?'

There are only two to choose from – a white one with red spots and a plain blue one. Maisie chooses the spotted one. It has an elastic waist and a full skirt and is easy to slip it on. I am immediately transported back to memories of Aunt May wearing these and feel very sad and nostalgic and Dan puts his arm round me, while I fight back the tears.

Maisie seems delighted and rushes down to find Pete and to show him what we have done.

Dan looks at me doubtfully and says, 'Are you OK with this?'

'Yes, I am actually. Surprisingly, I feel it is absolutely right and I know Aunt May would be so pleased.' I give him a big kiss and say 'Thanks for bringing me up here. I wasn't sure I could face it, but am so glad I did.'

Pete comes up and makes appreciative comments to Maisie, then he turns to me and says, 'Dan tells me this is the blue blouse that…?' and I nod, and then he says, 'May used to wear this quite often. I remember it was one of the first things she made on her sewing machine after she brought it to the island, and she was so proud of it and we all told her how it matched her eyes. I don't remember the skirt, but she had several colourful outfits, and I must admit, I don't usually notice what people are wearing.'

As we go back downstairs, I hear the cat flap moving and Catty arrives to meet us. She looks a bit puzzled by the invasion of people and turns straight round and goes outside again. We are chatting in the sitting room about plans for the next few days, when I look out of the window and see Catty sitting on the black stone. She is facing the lane and then she stands up, stretches and turns to face the cottage. Maisie asks if she can go outside and talk to her, so I say I will come with her and we can see Catty together. I don't want her rushing up to Catty and scaring her off.

As we get close to Catty, Maisie says, 'Oh look, the girl is smiling and she likes Catty to sit on her head.'

'Yes, she looks quite happy, doesn't she? Just go slowly up to Catty and let her sniff your hand before you try to stroke her.'

Maisie does as I suggest and Catty jumps straight down and starts rubbing her face against Maisie's legs, which makes Maisie giggle. They both seem to be perfectly relaxed with each other and I am so relieved to see this. It is obvious Catty is used to children from her previous home. I tell Maisie that I must go back indoors and see what plans the others have for the rest of the day, so she and Catty follow me back indoors. As there is not much food in the fridge, we decide to go into Wasbury and buy a few things for a picnic lunch. Angela has promised to give us supper before Geoff goes off back to London for the week.

We are all waiting by Dan's car, as that is the one with a child seat in it, and we are discussing where to go to get some food. There is a small supermarket in Wasbury, which is open on a Sunday and also a farm shop a few miles on. We are finding it difficult to decide exactly what we need, when suddenly I look round and Maisie is nowhere to be seen.

She can't be far away, I think, so I call her, but there is no reply. 'Where can she have gone?' I say to the others.

'Oh, no,' says Dan, looking worried and starting to run up to Red House. I run after him and Pete stays to see if she appears from somewhere else.

Sure enough, we find her at what is left of the front door. She has gone under the tapes, but luckily not gone any further than the front steps and she is staring at the gaping hole of what is left of the centre of the house. As we get near to her and are calling to her and telling her not to go any further, she turns round and says, 'Are you cross? Lora cross? And rushes up and puts her arms round my legs and I can feel she is shivering.

'No, I'm not cross,' I try to reassure her several times, while Dan calls out to Pete to say we have found her.

'The house is broken,' she says. 'The stairs all gone and where's my bedroom?' and she bursts into tears. I pick her up and carry her back to where the others are waiting. I suggest they go on and do the shopping and I'll take her indoors. We wave to the car as it drives off and I start to take Maisie to the cottage. As I start to go towards the front door and put Maisie down on the ground, while I get out my key, she says, 'I want to see Red House.'

'What, now?' I ask and wondering what to say next, and then I think it might be a good idea to go back there and we can talk about it quietly.

'Now, please,' she says, looking at me with a determined look. I take her by the hand and we make our way back round the corner of the lane. I tell her that we are not meant to go under the tape, because it is not safe to walk on all the bricks and bits of wood lying around, but we can look at it all and talk about it.

It is quite cold standing there, but we both have our warm coats on.

'Red house is broken,' she repeats.

'Yes, it is very broken,' I say 'and nobody can live in there anymore. That's why the firemen came to rescue us out of the window,' I say and I take her over to see the side of the house where the remains of the window stares at us.

'Was It burning?' she asks, 'like logs in a fire?'

'Yes, it was burning.'

'Why?'

Oh my God, how do I get round this one, I think? We had certainly no intention of Maisie seeing all this – and I, myself, hadn't felt ready to face it, but here we are and an answer is needed.

'Well, we think a big log fell out of the fireplace downstairs and Isobel hadn't made it safe before she went out, so the fire spread right through the house.'

'So, Isbel's naughty. Lora cross with Isbel?'

'No, I am not cross with Isobel now, as I know she is very sorry, but I was cross when I had to get the fireman to rescue us and with all that horrible smoke. That smoke was nasty wasn't it?'

'Yes, black smoke and… and we go to hospital.' She seems satisfied with this for the moment and I only hope I have said the right things. She starts to lead me to the cottage and as we get round the corner, Maisie suddenly says, 'Isbel's gone away. She not coming back – ever.'

'Yes, you are right and you told me so before. How do you know this?'

'She tells me. She says she goes a very, very, long way.'

'When did she tell you this?'

'In my sleep she tells me. I'm not scared Isbel cross now. I'm hungry. Do we have food soon?'

'Yes, when the others come back from the shop.'

We go into the sitting room and I'm glad to notice the stove doors are firmly shut. I feel utterly exhausted and really worried whether I handled the situation in the right way. After all, I am not at all used to dealing with a child and I really hope I am going to be able to look after my daughter. It certainly seems a difficult task, however much I love her.

. . .

Later that afternoon, at Ridge Farm, Pete and I decide we should discuss what needs to be done about Isobel's little dog Whisky. Dan goes back to have supper with Emma, and we have a quick supper before Angela takes Geoff to the station. When she gets back, she takes Maisie upstairs for her bath so that Pete and I can talk about Whisky while Maisie is out of earshot. It is so lucky he was not in the fire, as Isobel had put him into kennels for the Christmas period when she was due to be away. I tell Pete that I know Whisky and Catty would not get on, so I am certainly not wanting to take him in. Anyway, he is a grumpy little creature and Pete says he knows Maisie does not get on with him either. Maisie hasn't even asked about him since the fire. Pete tells me he thinks Whisky and Isobel had a love-hate relationship and he probably needs an understanding person to give him a home. I suggest I talk to Maureen in the morning, as I feel sure she would take him into the Animal Centre, assess his behaviour and advise us what to do.

Suddenly Pete says, 'Good God, I'd forgotten. Isobel's car is registered in both our names and if I can find a key, I could bring it back here and make use of it.'

'Yea, I noticed it today. It is sitting outside, well away from the house and outside the police tape and never got near the fire, but I don't believe she would have left the keys in the car, would she?'

'It is unlikely, and if she had, I am sure somebody would have driven off in it by now.'

'When I went to Red House, looking for Maisie on the day of the fire, I found the spare back door key in the summer house in the garden, but didn't see any other keys. Mind you, there was a lot of mess in there and it was obviously used for storing junk and I didn't look any further after I had found the key I needed.'

We decide we can't ask Maisie if she knows where spare keys are kept, as this could be confusing and unsettling for her, so we will go along in my car, take a torch, and see what we can find.

After Pete and I have both read Maisie a bedtime story and we've settled her down, we tell Angela our plan and set off for Red House. It is a bright moonlit night and the house looks so sinister as we shine our torch up into the dark hollow of the ruin. There is still a strong smell of charred remains in the damp night air, so we don't linger. After checking the keys are not in the car and the doors are locked, we make our way to the back garden and to the summerhouse. We should have brought two torches, as the ground is very uneven, but Angela could only find one and I don't particularly feel like going to the cottage to find mine.

There is certainly a lot of junk, boxes, flowerpots, broken garden tools, plastic tubs and other stuff that Isobel hasn't got around to sorting to take to the dump. We carefully check the shelves where I had found the back door key, but there are no other keys. We are just wondering whether it is worth going through all the other junk in the dark, when Pete shines the torch underneath an old chair and sees a corner of a plastic bag, sticking out. He hands the torch to me, as he gets down on his knees to reach it and pull it out. It rattles with a metallic sound as we take it outside to open it up. Sure enough, there is a bundle of assorted bunches of keys. There are two sets of car keys and Pete sounds hopeful that one of the sets looks to be a likely match and starts to hurry back to the car.

'Wait,' I say. I can't keep up. The moon has gone behind a cloud and the torch is getting rather dim. 'I think I have found something else rather interesting.'

Pete reluctantly waits for me, as I shine the torch into the bag again. My hand is shaking as I pull out a pair of keys with a white label, and in the fading torchlight, I can just see "BC" written on it.

'Look, these are the old keys to my cottage, which Isobel denied having.'

'Wow,' says Pete. 'Are you sure?'

'Yes, I recognise the shape. The larger one is a bit unusual.'

I am feeling a bit disembodied and for a few moments forget what we originally came for, as we reach the car and Pete fumbles with the car keys in the torchlight.

'Eureka,' he exclaims, as one of the sets turns out to be the right one. He switches on the ignition and, in spite of the cold, the engine starts first time. We both hug each other and decide to get back to the warmth of Ridge Farm as soon as we can.

. . .

We have a quiet evening, while we wonder what tomorrow will bring. Pete doesn't know when he will be able to leave, as he wants to get up to the hospital again and see what plans he can make for Isobel's funeral. Angela says that the social worker who is coming tomorrow morning at nine, will certainly want to see Pete as well. It may be some time before he is allowed to leave the country, but he hopes to have some news from the police tomorrow.

That night, I don't sleep very well, as I am worrying about tomorrow and all the questions I will be asked. I will have to appear to be a responsible adult and hope my time of mental illness won't affect my ability to take charge of Maisie. When I eventually do get to sleep, my dreams are very muddled and stressful and by the morning, I am feeling pretty frazzled.

Chapter 26

It is raining when I get up in the morning. The sleety rain is battering against the bedroom window while I dress, which doesn't help my feeling of apprehension. Having had several nights of disturbed sleep, I am wondering how I am going to cope with yet another stressful day and I start to shiver as I look at the weather outside. Although the bedroom is as warm as usual, it feels as if the outside world is cold and hostile.

I dressed Maisie earlier and I wonder if I will ever get used to the joy of helping her into her little clothes – If I am allowed to take care of her. The alternative doesn't bear thinking about. She is still wearing some of Charlie's clothes and doesn't seem to mind that they are not hers. Perhaps she remembers Charlie wearing them and they are familiar to her. Anyway, she is happy to put them on and Angela takes her down for breakfast while I try to make myself look like a grown up, responsible mother in clean jeans and one of Aunt May's cosy, but unfashionable jumpers.

Pete seems a bit tense as well, but Angela is her usual calm and cheerful self and she makes sure we all eat something, although my lovely toast and jam does taste a bit like sweetened cardboard this morning.

At nine o'clock promptly, there is a rap on the door and Angela greets someone who she obviously knows.

'Oh, hello Clare,' she says, sounding surprised. 'I didn't realise it would be you coming to see us. That's lovely. I'll take you into meet the others.'

Angela introduces a young woman, probably in her thirties. She has very short blonde hair and is smartly dressed in a dark suit, with high- heeled shoes, and carries a big file of papers. 'This is Clare Williams from social services' she says as she turns to me with a smile. 'I have known Clare for years and there is no need to be nervous, Lora'. Angela introduces us all, including Maisie, who just looks at Clare suspiciously.

Soon we are sitting round the kitchen table with cups of tea and coffee, and a soft drink for Maisie. I take to Clare quite quickly, while feeling cautious, but she soon puts us all at ease. She listens to my story attentively and seems very sympathetic to what I have been through. While I am telling her about my relationship with Isobel and then the horrible details of the fire, Angela takes Maisie to play with some toys.

Pete and I are feeling comfortable talking to Clare, when, there is suddenly another rap on the door and Angela opens it and comes in with two policemen. It turns out that they want Pete and me to go to the police station in Ford and make official statements. My heart sinks at the thought of going through it all again, but we gather ourselves together and after leaving Maisie with Angela, Pete and I set off in the police car. Clare says she will come back and see us later.

Visiting the police station and all the further questioning seems like another nightmare.

I don't know how I can get through it – but I do – in a daze – I am feeling numb and now can't remember much about it all, except Chris was there with two other men, who all try to be friendly, but I can't remember their names.

I suppose I answer all the questions satisfactorily, although I feel disembodied like some sort of machine on automatic mode, because they eventually take me to another room with a cup of coffee, while I sit on my own, waiting for Pete to go through the inquisition too.

. . .

After what seems like a week, but is actually an hour, Pete appears with the police and they all look quite relaxed. They reassure me that I should be able to look after Maisie under Angela's supervision for the time being, until everything is legally sorted.

'Thank you, thank you, '

I say and give a huge sigh of relief, as I feel myself coming back into reality.

Then Chris continues. 'You realise there will have to be an inquest regarding Isobel's death and you will have to give evidence, Lora. Nothing will happen before Christmas. Also, we will have to contact the Clinic and your previous, and current, Doctors, to hear their sides of your story. This is because the circumstances of Mrs Gray's death are very unusual. Meanwhile, we have told Doctor Wesley that he can go home when he wishes, as he wasn't involved or a witness to the fire, but he will be coming back in the New Year for the funeral arrangements, when the body has been released by the Coroner.'

This all sounds very daunting, but for the time being things look much rosier.

. . .

When we get back to Ridge Farm Angela suggests we both try and relax for a while, before she phones Clare to say we are back. We both feel completely drained, but understand that Clare has been delayed by another case and won't be with us for an hour or two. This gives Pete and me time to be distracted by playing games, such as snakes and ladders, with Maisie and we both gradually calm down.

Pete and I have both managed to relax a bit and have had an early snack lunch by the time Clare returns. She explains she just has a few more loose ends to sort out.

She turns to Pete and says, 'So, you are Maisie's grandfather. Is that right?'

'Yes, I am, and Isobel and I have had charge of Maisie since Lora's illness, but she is absolutely fine now and I am very happy for her to have her daughter back, as I know she will be a really good mother to her.'

This seems to satisfy Clare, who says, 'After I have contacted your doctor, Lora, and made sure you are fit and well, I see no reason why you cannot be in charge of Maisie. It will be a good idea for you still to be under Angela's supervision for a while and I will need to see your cottage and make sure it is all suitable for a child.' This sounds like Maureen and Catty; I think to myself. My home has to be OK for a child as well as a cat.

After a few more details are sorted out in her paperwork, Clare has to rush off to see someone else and she wishes me all the best and says she hopes to get down to see the cottage soon.

. . .

That afternoon Pete is busy with emails and other important issues, before he packs to drive to London tomorrow to sort out matters concerning Isobel. To give us a welcome change of scenery, Angela and I take Maisie to buy a few essential clothes and then, as it is getting rather late and I feel exhausted, we briefly look in at the bed shop, and find a suitable little bed for Maisie when she eventually comes to Blackstone Cottage.

The staff at 'Softly Sleep' where I got my bed from, are very helpful and we soon choose a small bed for Maisie, and they promise to deliver it before Christmas.

As we arrive back at Ridge Farm Angela suggests that we stay with her till after Christmas, as I had already agreed to spend Christmas with her and Geoff and this would be less disruptive for everyone, Maisie in particular. She suggests Dan can spend as much time with us as we like, and as he has arranged to be with his relatives over Christmas already, this could be the easiest all-round arrangement. I tell her I think this would be lovely, but I would need to spend some time each day at the cottage because of Catty, and I could take Maisie with me, as that would gradually get her used to being there.

The next urgent thing to do, concerns the little dog Whisky. Pete and I are worried about what will happen to him, as he is an innocent victim of all that has happened. I contact Maureen, who sounds very sympathetic, in her brusque way, and insists that she will go and see the dog at the boarding kennels this afternoon. Pete has given me all the information, as Isobel had asked him to settle the bill with them when she left Whisky there. I am realising that in the latter days of Isobel's life, Pete was paying for more and more. Maureen says she will let me know how she gets on. I tell Angela that I will keep my fingers crossed and hope with all my heart that Maureen will have a solution, as I am feeling rather guilty that I don't want the dog, but I do still want him to have a happy future – none of this is his fault.

I spend the early evening feeling a bit apprehensive about Whisky, but Maisie is a great tonic for my mood and I soon get my energy and enthusiasm back, so while Angela takes Maisie out to shut up the chickens for the night, I phone Dan. He is on a job in Ford, but is very glad of the interruption and keen to hear what has been going on. I wearily give him the gist of our meetings this morning and how relieved I am that things seem to be turning out all right. He acknowledges that I will be nervous about the inquest, but I will have time before that to concentrate on Maisie. I tell him about Pete and I finding the cottage key.

'Well, you have more good proof of Isobel's wily ways, now you've found that key,' he says.

'Yes, it is another boost to my confidence to know I was right about her all along – and that you and Emma trusted me, Dan, when others didn't. By the way, did you have a good evening with Emma last night? There was no light on in Blackstone Cottage when we went last night.'

'Well, actually, it was a very good thing I was there. Poor Em, she seems to have had another lucky escape. She and Paul have broken up. She had heard rumours that he might be playing around.

They had a big row and she challenged him and he admitted he didn't want to be tied into a relationship at the moment.'

'Oh, poor Emma. Please give her my love.'

'Well, she's coping very well and I believe she saw it coming. I must admit, I'm not sorry. You know how protective I am over her. I thought he was a big-headed, pompous prat. Anyway, Christmas is coming up and she will be spending it with all our family.'

'Including you,' I say rather sadly.

'Yes, including me – but perhaps next… 'and he stops for a moment, 'no, that's perhaps too far ahead. You'll probably be sick of me by then. Anyway, how do I know you will want to be with me at all now the Maisie Quest is over?'

'Of course I will want to be with you – and Maisie will want you too, but the last thing I want, is for you to feel tied to us and, as I keep being reminded, we have known each other for such a short time and in such strange circumstances, you might feel you want a bit of a break from us at least?' Then I pause a moment and ask, 'What about your feelings for Kate? It's not long since you broke up with her and perhaps you are just on the rebound from her?'

'Well, of course I have thought about that a lot and it might look like that to someone else, but I can assure you that the way I feel about you is much more real and meaningful and I probably need time to prove this to you. I would really like to have time with you in more normal circumstances, so we can relax and explore a more everyday kind of life,' then he hesitates, 'but I have been wondering whether you would want to get right away from all this and maybe visit Pete with Maisie in New York? After all, you have a whole new way of life to consider and this may have stirred up a lot of past feelings…'

'…You mean, concerning Ade?' I interrupt.

'Well, yes, I would think that in all that has happened recently, Ade must have featured so much in your thoughts.'

'Yes, he has been on my mind a lot and always will be, as he is part of Maisie, but now I have got her, I feel I can relax in the knowledge that I am absolutely certain he would be relieved to know how this is turning out. I know it is going to take time for me to get over all that has happened in the past and since I came here, and to get used to the fact that my whole perspective on life has been shaken up and put into new places with new people. Something came into my mind yesterday, which has given me new food for thought.'

'And, what's that?' he asks.

'Well, when I've finally got the Maisie Quest legally put right, I would like to contact Ade's mother. I mean, she has absolutely no idea about all this and she is Maisie's grandmother, after all.'

'Yea, I had wondered about that. Sounds a good idea to me – but one thing at a time. There are still a few obstacles to get over yet.'

There is silence for a moment and then I say, 'Look, this is a rather serious conversation to be having over the phone, especially as you are meant to be at work. Would there be any chance of you coming over this evening? Angela is determined that Maisie and I stay here till after Christmas and I would like to be able to help her in every way I can, so I could go and get some fish and chips for us all this evening, as I know she hasn't cooked anything yet. Geoff went back to London yesterday and I'm not sure of Pete's plans, as he's been busy this afternoon on the phone and sorting things out. I think he plans to leave tomorrow. If we get something early enough, Emma might like to come and bring Charlie. Angela's out with Maisie and Bess shutting up the chicken house at the moment, but I could put it to her when she gets in? What do you think?'

'That sounds a lovely idea, but haven't you all done enough for one day?'

'Well, I've got my second wind now and am feeling so relieved that this morning's events are over. I am sure Pete would want to see you before he goes off tomorrow, so I'll check it out with Angela and Pete and let you know.'

'I could pick up some fish and chips on the way. Save you going out. But please be absolutely sure it is OK with Angela. She doesn't know me or Emma very well.

'No, she's only known you for...' and before I have time to say it...

'... seven weeks,' he says.

. . .

This all goes according to plan and halfway through the meal, Angela says,

'You, know, I am really enjoying this. I feel I have gained a whole new set of friends and, in fact, it really feels like I have a family at last. Geoff and I have been feeling quite lonely recently. We have lots of London friends, but they all seem to have children and extended families and we have been- yes – lonely is the word. You lot have come into our lives and given us a breath of fresh air and new interests, so I do hope we will go on being friends now, whatever the future brings.'

Then we all spontaneously stand up with our glasses and Dan says 'Here's to Angela and Geoff – our very special new friends.'

'Here, here' Emma and I say together and the two children join in, though they don't know what it is all about, except that it is good news.

As we are all settling down again, my phone rings and I see it is Maureen calling. I had nearly forgotten about her. I tell the others who it is and take the phone into another room.

'How did you get on?' I ask holding my breath.

'Oh, he's a dear little dog. A Norwich terrier, I would think. About four or five years old I would guess. He is very cautious and a bit snappy, but I think that is only fear. He must be very confused. But I don't think I would have much of a problem finding him a suitable home – without children, of course. He is a grown-up person's sort of dog.'

'That's great news,' I say. 'What do you think is the next move?'

'The kennels would need permission for me to take him. I told them the sad story of what had happened and, of course, they had heard about the fire. The whole of the area, and probably the country, has heard about it.'

'Just a moment, I'll pass you over to Pete and he can sort it out with you.'

After they have finished talking, he hands the phone back to me and I thank her for all her help and assure her that we'll pay for his keep and expenses.

'Pete and I have already sorted that,' she says, 'and how's Catty?'

'She's very well and settled in as if she's never left. She gets on extremely well with my daughter, Maisie, and – you are right – she likes sitting on the black stone.'

'I knew she'd like that. So, we'll keep in touch, OK Bye for now.' And she puts the phone down abruptly.

The others are delighted to hear this news about Whisky. I knew that Maureen would find he had some redeeming features.

Pete looks very relieved. 'That's one thing off my list.' Then he looks at Angela and says, 'I'm so very grateful to you and Geoff for helping me and Lora in such a big way. I can't think how I could ever repay you for your kindness and understanding through all this chaos, so I think it is about time I got out of your hair and make my way to London tomorrow, where I still have a lot to sort out.'

'Well, Lora and Maisie have certainly added something very positive to our lives and you will always be welcome here,' says Angela, 'as long as you keep your word where Maisie is concerned – and keep off the drink, of course.' She adds.

'I can assure you. I am totally committed to both.

After supper, Dan leaves with Emma and Charlie, as it is bedtime for Charlie and Maisie. Pete helps me get Maisie to bed and he reads her a story, but it takes quite a while for her to settle, with all the excitement. We eventually manage to get back downstairs, where we find Angela asleep in a chair by the fire.

She looks rather embarrassed when she wakes up and we all realise we are exhausted after a non-stop day of activity and agree that an early night is needed.

. . .

At last I have a really good night's sleep, but wake in the morning feeling sad and wondering why, then realise that Pete will be leaving. While Maisie is still asleep, I lie awake thinking about Pete and remembering our time on Morg before Ade's death. I am remembering Pete with affection and how gentle and kind he was to me, always explaining things that Isobel was too impatient to bother with. He was quiet, thoughtful, and just got on with every day, mundane jobs and one would hardly have known he was there. In fact, it was as if he was invisible. We all took him for granted.

When Maisie wakes, she climbs into my bed and we lie together in a cosy cuddle, until we hear Bess barking, and realise it is time to get up.

Breakfast is rather silent as if no one knows quite what to say, but I am pleased to see Pete is tucking into scrambled eggs on toast and although Maisie says she doesn't want more than bread and jam, she is quite willing to steal the odd mouthful of food from Pete's plate. I wonder how she has developed such a rapport with him, then I realise she and Isobel did visit him from time to time and, also, they Skyped each other regularly. Anyway, he is an easy person to feel comfortable with and now I know all his background story, I am at last getting to know the real Pete.

After breakfast Pete goes to pack up his last bits and pieces and Maisie goes with him to help.

When they come down, Maisie says, 'Pete's going on a big aeroplane.' Then she adds, 'Pete comes back soon with Muffy.'

I give him a surprised look and he says quietly, 'Yes, I have a spare Muffy in my apartment for when they came to stay.'

We stand by the car to say goodbye and wish him good journeys. Angela reminds him to drive on the left and he assures her that that is his 'default mode', as he doesn't drive in New York and used to drive a lot in Britain before going to Morg. He looks confident as he gets into the car and I feel tears in my eyes, as he winds the window up and drives off.

'Pete's got Isbel's car,' says Maisie, as he gradually disappears down the drive.

'Yes, Isobel's given it to Pete, as a present, so now it is Pete's car.' I explain. What else could I have said?

Chapter 27

In spite of the Christmas rush, we hear that Pete has managed to get a flight back to New York and we have arranged with him to communicate regularly by video calls.

I manage to get out, face the crowds, and do some more shopping before Christmas and replace the book I got for Maisie originally, before the fire. Maisie loves the Christmas tree and all the excitement. Geoff and Angela have got time off work over the holiday period and Maisie helps Geoff with all the decorations, while Angela and I prepare the food. Dan spends time with us before he goes to join his family and then we talk to him and Emma by video call on Facebook regularly.

Maisie and I have a wonderful Christmas at Ridge Farm, with an abundance of presents and food. We give Maisie a Christmas stocking and Father Christmas, Geoff, creeps in when she is asleep and puts all sorts of little presents in it. Her delight at finding it in the morning is wonderful to see. This is all new to me, as we had nothing like this on Morg and Geoff and Angela, who can remember Christmases from their own childhoods, really enjoy the whole experience. We have a video call from Pete on Christmas Day and from Dan, Emma and Charlie as well. It is such a joyous occasion that I temporarily forget all the horror of the past few weeks.

During the few days between Christmas and the New Year, Dan and I spend more days at Blackstone Cottage with Maisie. It is such a lovely surprise, when I discover that Dan has made me a small chicken house as a Christmas present and I am so looking forward to getting some "rescued hens", when Maisie and I are settled in permanently in the Cottage. Dan is due to start some new jobs locally in the New Year, so in the meantime, we have a relaxing time together, getting to know each other as a threesome, plus Catty. Some days Emma comes in with Charlie and sometimes Angela and Geoff come down with Bess. We are still waiting to hear from Clare to get the go-ahead to move Maisie in, but she has phoned to say she hopes to come to see us as soon as she hears from the clinic and my London GP, once she is back in her office after the holiday. I feel a bit apprehensive waiting for this, but I know my nice Doctor Fanshaw in London signed me off as fit several months ago and I can't see there will be a problem there. He also knows I have signed on with a surgery in Wasbury. As for the clinic, who knows what they'll say, especially when they are told about Isobel's lies and how she deceived them. As I haven't been in touch with them for quite a while, I am intrigued to know how they will react.

On the first Wednesday in January, after what seems like months, but in fact is just a few days, Clare comes to see us at Blackstone Cottage and thoroughly approves of my little home. She told me that Doctor Fanshaw had given her a good report on my progress and was astounded to hear about all that had gone on since my move to the cottage. But, surprise, surprise – when she tried to contact the clinic, she found that the whole place had closed down. It turned out that the psychiatrist, who had been running it, had been struck off for malpractice concerning another patient and is now living abroad somewhere – so we'll never know whether or not he was in league with Isobel over my illness. Clare says he must have known there was something fishy going on, as he could never have had a previous doctor's report about me before he took me in. It must have been based just on Isobel's persuasion and money, presumably. After I left the clinic and signed up with Doctor Fanshaw, he told me the clinic had a very good reputation and he trusted their clinical judgements and treatments, but he had seemed surprised that there were no previous notes about my health before the clinic, who said they had been lost and had some round about excuses.

So now I have the all-clear to look after Maisie and I am sure there will be no problem over the official DNA test which we are now proceeding with.

Maisie's bed is ready in the spare room, so she can get used to seeing it there. She seems very pleased with it and bounces around on it. She loves the new duvet and pillow covers, which Angela and Geoff gave her for Christmas. I am feeling a bit nervous about my new responsibility but I realise that the daily visits to the cottage have been beneficial to me as well as Maisie.

. . .

It is now the second week in January and we are all well and truly at home in the cottage. It is so wonderful having Maisie with me and she is settling in well and loves her new bed with the newly named 'Wabbit.' Occasionally she comes into my room at night, as if she is checking I am really there and, after a cuddle in my bed, I, reluctantly on my part, take her back to her own bed, where she settles quite quickly. Dan spends some nights with us and some at his cottage with Emma, as Charlie has been rather difficult to manage since the excitement of Christmas. This afternoon, Dan has just taken Maisie to visit Emma and Charlie, so I have a couple of hours on my own to get on with some chores and be alone with my thoughts.

Since all the excitement of the past couple of months, life seems to have whizzed by in a kind of haze. Apart from occasional times when I remember all the stress and anxiety, I seem to be gradually finding myself in a state of calmness and I could even call it happiness. Dan is very patient with me and says it will take me time to believe that those dramatic events are over. I sometimes wake suddenly in the night, with my heart beating fast, until I realise that Maisie and I are safe. Maisie appears to be less moved by it all than me, but how do I know what goes on in her little mind? She doesn't seem to miss Isobel, which makes me wonder whether there was ever much of a bond between them. On the other hand, she doesn't seem a nervous child affected by a traumatic upbringing. Perhaps Isobel didn't treat her too badly on the whole. She still reminds me from time to time, in her very definite voice, that 'Isbel gone.' I tell her that Isobel is happy in a new home. One day, she will need to know the truth.

She sometimes tests me to see if I get "cross" and I tell her that I can be cross, but not like Isobel and I will never hurt her if she is naughty and that I will always love her. She is beginning to see that this is true and she already knows Dan would never hurt her either.

We have heard that the Coroner has released Isobel's body, so Pete will be able to plan for her funeral and he hopes to come over soon. Pete has told us she always said, when the time came, she would want to be buried in the village where she was born. I don't know whether I would want to go to her funeral, but Angela says it could be a final closure for me. We still don't know when the inquest will be, and that is a shadow on my mind, but Angela tells me it will be fine and she'll support me. She knows about that sort of thing after her experience as a Magistrate.

Yesterday, I had a very good bit of news. Maureen has taken Whisky to the Animal Centre and one of her helpers seems to have fallen for him and is keen to give him a home. This seems very fortuitous, as she must be used to dealing with all sorts of difficult animals and will be taking him on – "with her eyes open" – as Aunt May would say.

I am just sitting here by my lovely stove and thinking of all the good things that have happened, when I see Angela's car draw up. My first reaction is – oh dear, what's happened now? – but as I open the door to her, she calls out, 'Happy New Year again'.

'And Happy New Year again to you too,' I reply as we hug each other. 'Do come in and have a cup of tea.'

'I was hoping you'd say that', she says with a smile. 'I've just been walking Bess, and have been thinking over all that has happened and thought it might be a chance to say a few things to you that have come to my mind. I don't want to keep stirring things up for you, but I would really like to have chat with you, if that's OK. By the way, I believe Dan is with Emma this afternoon. Is that right?'

'Yes, and they have Maisie with them too. I'm not expecting them back just yet, so it would be nice to have a chat' I say, wondering what is on Angela's mind as I go to put the kettle on and search in the cupboard for some biscuits.

'Yea,' I've been sitting here thinking about things,' I say, as I come back into the sitting room carrying tea. 'We have all been so busy. It has been nice to have a pause to sort through my thoughts.'

We take our tea and sit by the fire. Catty's out hunting somewhere, so I can take her chair. I am wondering what Angela is going to say.

'Yes, it has all happened so quickly,' says Angela. 'The tragedy of Isobel's death has affected me too. You see, I know what it is like to want a child and not to be able to have one. When we got married Geoff and I were so keen to have a family, both being only children, but I had several miscarriages and we tried IVF to no avail.'

'Oh Angela, I'm so sorry. This whole situation must have been so painful for you.'

'Well yes and no. I felt such compassion for you and your loss when you arrived here all on your own. Then when you told me about the successful DNA test, I was so delighted for you, but also great sorrow for Isobel, especially now I have learnt all about the background to her behaviour. She was obviously a very bitter and unhappy person and although I would never condone the underhand and deranged way that she behaved, I am so aware of how emotionally difficult it is to accept that one can never have a child and she was apparently extremely badly affected mentally by her situation.'

'Yes, I can understand that now,' I say, 'especially now I have learnt about her long affair with my father and the two miscarriages during her time with him. How awful it must have been for her when my mother became pregnant and then gave birth to me.'

'Well I'm glad you understand. I am not in any way trying to negate what she has done, but I am pleased that you can accept that her disturbed mental state, must have been, in the main part, the result of her struggle to come to terms with her life's events.'

'Yes, it has all, gradually, been falling into place for me and I do feel desperately sorry for Isobel. And she certainly paid a huge price for her deception. I'll never, ever forget the sight of her running down the lane engulfed in fla...' I can't finish the sentence and Angela comes over and puts her arm round me, as I start shaking.

'It's OK' she says soothingly. 'You will always remember it, but you will come to understand it eventually and see it for what it was. A very sad event, which was never your fault.' Then she adds, 'Don't forget to contact your ex-counsellor, Maggie. She may be able to recommend you to someone in this area, if you need help with coming to terms with the traumatic times.'

I think about this and realise, I could never afford to pay a private counsellor and help on the National Health would take weeks or months to happen, so I hope I will be able to cope on my own with the help of my friends.

I don't say this to Angela, as I know she would offer to pay, so I just reply, 'You are wonderful to me, Angela. I can't believe how lucky I was to meet you in the car park that night, although I know now that Dan would never had harmed me.'

'No, not deliberately. But you might have both ended up in the ditch.'

We both laugh and then I say impulsively, 'Would you consider being my – er – new mother? Unofficial, of course. I am not asking you to adopt me.'

'What – Stepmother – do you mean? Yes, of course I would. I'd be delighted, but perhaps "Newmother" is a more apt name don't you think?'

'That sounds perfect and could Geoff be my "Newfather"? Do you think he would agree to that?'

'I think he would be delighted. I'll ask him this evening if you like, or maybe you'd like to ask him yourself.'

'No, I'd rather you did. I would feel embarrassed – especially if he didn't like the idea.'

We continue to sit by the warm fire and chat about life in general. I tell her how Dan and I are planning to take things slowly in our relationship, but we certainly want to try a life together now, with Maisie, of course, and see how we all get on, in a settled domestic atmosphere. I don't know whether Dan will be living here all the time, as I explain to Angela about Emma being on her own with Charlie and neither Dan or I want her to feel neglected or lonely. Gaining care of Maisie so suddenly is not something I expected to happen so soon and if Isobel had still been alive, I think it would probably have taken at least a few months, if not years, to get things sorted out, and I think Isobel would have made negotiations as difficult as she possibly could.

Angela tells me she is wanting to spend even more time now down at Ridge Farm and to become more involved in the smallholding and animals, as well as develop her garden a bit. Geoff still has a few more years before he wants to retire and he enjoys his job in London and the travelling he does relating to work, so she feels she herself would like to concentrate more on Ridge Farm, still doing some office work from home as well, but perhaps taking it as less of a priority.

'Does that mean we will still be able to see each other quite often?' I ask hopefully.

'Oh, I do hope so,' she says emphatically, 'but, and this is a big but, I don't want to interfere in your life. I want to see you settling in, making new friends, and getting to know your daughter. This is going to be a very new way of life for you.'

'Oh, yes, I realise that, but I hope you won't mind me asking for your help occasionally. I will try not to be a nuisance and call on you too much.'

'Well, you can call on me as much as you like and as well as being officially looking out for you and Maisie at the moment, I am going to be your "Newmother".

As Angela says this, we see Dan's car arrive and Angela gets up to leave. I tell her not to rush off, as I am sure Maisie and Dan will want to see her. But she insists that she must get back, as she needs to feed Bess and see to the other animals, as the Grahams have been having a break over the New Year. They greet each other in the doorway, with plenty of hugs and kisses to and from Maisie and, after we have all waved goodbye to Angela as she drives off, Dan and Maisie come in by the fire to tell me all their news.

Maisie is very excited after her afternoon playing with Charlie and after she has told me all the details of what they did, she decides to go up to her room and play with the doll that Angela gave her for Christmas, so Dan and I have time to ourselves. I ask him how Emma is after her break-up with Paul.

'She seems fine,' says Dan thoughtfully. 'In fact, I think she is getting more and more convinced that he wasn't right for her, or for Charlie. He was trying to take over from her where Charlie was concerned and I certainly didn't like his heavy-handed approach with him. Anyway, another bit of news is that she has applied for and been accepted for a new job in a hotel up near where Jane, our aunt, lives. She will live with Jane and Jane will help look after Charlie. It is promotion and better money, so she's off there in about six weeks.'

'Wow, so what do you think of that then?'

'Mixed feelings, of course and I'll certainly miss her and Charlie, but I think it will be a very good thing for her. They won't be too far away to visit quite often.'

'So, what about you and Lime Tree Cottage?'

'Well, we'll let that. That is, if you'll let me come and live with you?' he asks, looking a bit awkward. 'We did talk about seeing how we would get on living together for a while.'

'Yes, I think that's a great idea – and you'll always have your cottage to take back, if we can't stand each other.'

We are just having a long kiss together on the sofa, when Maisie appears in the doorway, and says, 'Come – see.' She looks a bit worried and starts to walk slowly towards the stairs.

We extricate ourselves from our embrace and follow her upstairs. She takes us into her room and says, 'look,' as she points to the tailors' dummy.

'Look at what?' we both say in unison.

'The pretty thing,' she says, pointing at the blouse.

For a moment I don't know what she means, as it all looks the same as usual. The crinkly blouse that still needs ironing. I must do that tomorrow, I think to myself, – then I notice something different about it. There is something dangling from the bottom of the blouse.

'Dan, look at this!' I exclaim. 'Did you put this on here?'

'No, of course not. What is it?'

'It's Aunt May's brooch that she lost many years ago. We spent hours searching for it when she lost it on Morg, as it was very special to her. We never found it.'

'So how on earth did it get here?'

We look more carefully and see the clip is not fastened and the brooch is precariously dangling from the blouse. It is a tiny little gold brooch, consisting of a single bar, with one small pearl in the middle. I am sure it is the same one that we searched for all those years ago.

'Where did you find it Maisie?' I ask, as calmly and gently as I can.

She shrinks away and then says, 'Are you cross?'

'No, no – we are very, pleased. We are certainly not cross. Where did you find it?'

Maisie points to the cupboard floor where the blouse had been hanging when I first came to the cottage. 'There.' She says.

'This is wonderful, Maisie. You are a clever girl to find it. We lost it a long time ago. I think it will look really good, pinned to the collar of the blouse, don't you?' Maisie nods and smiles, while I attach it to the collar, and fasten the stiff clasp.' Then I add, 'when you are a big girl and can fasten the clip yourself, you can wear it on your own clothes.'

I look at Dan in astonishment. 'I can't believe it,' I eventually manage to say, and then I laugh and add, 'I wonder what Jonah would say about this?'

'Hocus Pocus' we say together and then all three of us join hands and sing 'Hocus Pocus' and laugh as we dance round the bedroom floor.

The strange events of Blackstone Cottage seem to have taken a happier direction, but as Aunt May used to say, 'There is no such thing as happy ever after.' We have no idea what the future will bring, but for now, Maisie, Dan and I and – Catty, of course, are all feeling very much like a happy family.

The End

About The Author

Alix Robinson was born and brought up in Mere, south west Wiltshire. She lived in London and worked in an Advertising Agency for a few years. Then she married and she and her husband moved to Kent where they lived with their three children for many years. During this time Alix trained and worked as a psychotherapist. When the time came for retirement she and her husband moved back west and are now living in south Wiltshire again.

BV - #0014 - 271022 - C0 - 198/129/19 - PB - 9781913012540 - Matt Lamination